CHANGING OF THE GUARD

George Bush was leaving the CIA. He'd cleared his desk of personal mementos, leaving only a pale blue blotter. The rugs from Tientsin and Peking had been rolled for storage. Bush stood looking out the large plate-glass wall at the bare trees and gray skies over the Potomac.

"They weren't interested, Eleanor."

"Not at all?"

Bush shook his head. "I told the President"—Bush corrected himself—"the President-elect . . . I told him and his people when I went down to Plains that we'd brief them on Korea. They said thank you and that's the last I heard of it."

Bush turned and took Eleanor's hand. "Eleanor, thanks. You helped make this the best job I ever had. Thanks and best wishes."

She smiled. "I remember the mood of this place after they named you to replace Bill Colby. They expected you to stumble. I think a lot of them wanted just that. But you were good. Better than any of us had hoped. You kept your door open and you listened. We'll miss you." Pausing in the door, she smiled. "To borrow one of your phrases, Mr. Director, you did a darn neat job."

CENTER GAME

Robert Andrews

BANTAM BOOKS
NEW YORK · TORONTO · LONDON · SYDNEY · AUCKLAND

CENTER GAME

A Bantam Book / September 1989

ISBN 0-553-28141-0

Published simultaneously in the United States and Canada

Bantam Books are published by Bantam Books, a division of Bantam
Doubleday Dell Publishing Group, Inc. Its trademark, consisting of
the words "Bantam Books" and the portrayal of a rooster, is
Registered in U.S. Patent and Trademark Office and in other
countries. Marca Registrada. Bantam Books, 666 Fifth Avenue, New
York, New York 10103.

Aside from well-known historical figures who travel herein without aliases, the characters in this book are entirely fictitious. Many of the events actually took place as described, and certain intelligence organizations and operations are portrayed as accurately as possible.

CENTER
GAME

Chapter 1

Panmunjom, Korea

Swinging axes and pikes, thirty North Korean soldiers were suddenly on them. Art Bonifaces, who seconds earlier had been thinking about home leave, broke a stranglehold of one North Korean, then drove a stiffened hand deep into the stomach of another. Turning, he saw a burly Korean, huge even by American standards, raising a double-edged ax over a figure crumpled on the ground, which Bonifaces recognized as Mark Barrett. Bonifaces saw, too, that the ax was already covered with blood.

Captain Arthur G. Bonifaces was killed before he got to the big Korean. Both he and Lieutenant Mark Barrett died in the Demilitarized Zone—the DMZ—between North and South Korea on an August morning in 1976.

Those DMZ killings that summer set in motion a chain of events in which CIA and KGB, each for very different reasons, rebelled against President Jimmy Carter and General Secretary Leonid Brezhnev, and in so doing, prevented a nuclear war.

History is not tidy. The end of one story becomes the beginning of another. And so, it is unsurprising that this story begins two years before the DMZ killings.

Moscow—April, 1974

Remarkably, Directorate I—Planning and Analysis—
made a number of significant contributions to the Asian
study. Remarkable, because Directorate I was the slag heap
of the Komitet Gosudarstvennoy Bezopasnosti. But then,
every intelligence agency needed a safe place to dump the
burnt out, the incompetent, and the aged. The KGB was no
exception.

Few requests for information that came from outside
the KGB received such high priority. But this had been
called for by the General Secretary, Leonid Brezhnev
himself, and that alone demanded instant attention. And
so, Vasili Petrovich Kiktev had clipped a "flash" routing slip
on the document, thus requiring evaluations by Directorate
I as well as the First and Sixth departments—the offices
responsible for KGB operations in the United States and
East Asia.

Spirits were running high at 2 Dzerzhinsky Square.
Yuri Andropov had just become the first KGB chief to be
chosen a full member of the Politburo since Stalin's
Lavrenti Beria. And, in what would later prove to be a
crucial move, three of Andropov's trusted subordinates had
gained seats on the Central Committee. Internationally,
the fortunes of the United States continued to decline—
thanks to Viet Nam and Watergate—while those of the
Soviet Union were on the rise. Bright prospects indeed for
the Committee on State Security.

On June 20, 1974, Yuri Vladimirovich Andropov had
just turned fifty-nine. Officially he was sixty, and had
received the usual birthday accolades the party awards its
senior officials. As a boy he'd advanced his age a year to get
into technical school. The Soviet bureaucracy had proved
impervious to his later attempts to set the record straight.
The affair amused Andropov. There had to be a moral

somewhere in that. How a lie told to further a forgotten ambition survived and achieved a life of its own.

Andropov made it a point to arrive early—but not noticeably so—at the regular Thursday afternoon meetings of the Politburo. He thus had time to catch up on the Kremlin gossip and rumors that provided tantalizing hints of who was currently in or out of favor.

The KGB chairman had noticed that no matter how early he came, one or perhaps more of Leonid Brezhnev's toadies had preceded him. Today was true to form: Kunayev, the former head of the Kazakh Communist Party, was slouched in his chair, talking in whispers with Andrei Kirilenko, who had been Brezhnev's assistant in Dnepropetrovsk, an industrial city near Brezhnev's birthplace in the Ukraine.

More members of the "Dnepropetrovsk Mafia" took their seats. The room was filling up with others as well. Among the last to arrive was Suslov, said by many to be Brezhnev's éminence grise; Suslov, the unyielding Stalinist who had passed up the opportunity himself to become General Secretary in favor of Brezhnev; Suslov, who had guided Brezhnev in the dismantling of the "liberal" reforms of Nikita Khrushchev.

Finally, when all had been seated, Leonid Brezhnev entered. Thickset, with huge black eyebrows, Brezhnev was a bearlike man. Heads turned toward him, following his wobbly progress as he shambled toward his chair at the head of the table. He gave no nod or other sign of acknowledgment, even to Suslov. He might as well be in an empty room, Andropov thought.

Because Yuri Andropov knew that Brezhnev's physician had made a fortune from illicit drugs, Yuri Andropov also knew that Leonid Brezhnev had recently suffered a series of light strokes and that the future held the prospect of increasingly severe health problems.

But if the General Secretary's health was failing, his gluttony was not. Leonid Brezhnev was as grasping as ever, and, if possible, had become even more proficient in amassing luxuries only dreamed of by the Soviet proletariat. At times his greed had been almost infantile: the old man actually cried in disappointment when West Germany's visiting Chancellor, Helmut Schmidt, gave him an antique shotgun. At least Schmidt's predecessor, Willy Brandt, for all his naiveté, had had the wit to present the General Secretary with a steel-blue Mercedes.

Brezhnev took his chair and, without looking back, thrust his hand over his shoulder, wriggling his fingers impatiently. An aide who'd followed the General Secretary into the room quickly put a folded handkerchief into the outstretched hand. Suspiciously, Brezhnev inspected the handkerchief. Then slowly, deliberately, he began cleaning his glasses. The process took at least two, perhaps three minutes, Andropov estimated, as the man carefully breathed on and polished each lens. No one spoke; all eyes were fixed attentively on the General Secretary.

There Brezhnev sits, Andropov thought, decomposing along with Russia's future.

Finally Brezhnev put on the glasses. For the first time he seemed to notice the meeting agenda before him. He frowned and pushed it roughly away with the back of his hand, causing the red-bordered paper to spin slowly on the polished mahogany table. His aide set an open file before him. Making a final small adjustment to the glasses, Brezhnev scanned the papers for a moment.

"We will dispense with our routine business," he announced, looking first to his left, then to the right, glancing at each member. "Instead we will take up a matter of much greater significance," he paused for effect, "a matter of new directions for the *Rodina*"—the Motherland.

In this same room Stalin had begun the Great Terror; it was here that Beria had been shot; and later, where Khrushchev had been deposed. It was a room in which men kept special watch. A room in which the unexpected kindled sudden fear.

Andropov suspected what Brezhnev was about. The others, tense in their ignorance, sat stock-still. Even Suslov was frozen: a wax-museum effigy, unblinking, waiting. The ticking of the Fabergé clock on the mantel filled the room.

Leonid Brezhnev pushed a button on the panel set into the table before him. A map of Asia flashed on the screen.

The relief was palpable around the table. Momentary closing of eyes, breaths exhaled, color again in faces.

Brezhnev hesitated. Eyes again focused on the map. "I wish to talk today about establishing our rightful presence in the Pacific Ocean."

Brezhnev consulted his notes, wiped his lips with the handkerchief, then began in a coarse baritone. "We face three obstacles. First, there are our good friends, the Americans, who have bases in the Philippines, Viet Nam, Taiwan, Korea, and Japan." As the General Secretary named off each country, a light arrow from the projection booth flew around the Pacific basin.

"Then, of course, we have the revisionists in Peking, who mistake Mao Tse-tung's senility for wisdom." At this, there was much nodding and chuckling at the General Secretary's wit. As might be expected, Andropov noted, the Dnepropetrovsk Mafia led the chorus.

"And in the more distant future, we have to watch Japan. Thus far, progressive forces have kept Tokyo from rebuilding its military establishment, but who knows what might happen should the relationship between Japan and the United States continue? Sooner or later Washington might prevail, and we would have to contend with a reborn Imperial Navy. The yellows would then realize the goals for which they fought World War Two, the establishment of an economic web ensnaring the lesser Pacific nations."

There were the beginnings of boredom: the faint rustling of papers and a wave of coughing and throat clearing. Brezhnev paused and looked severely around the table. The room fell instantly quiet.

"Our most immediate problem—the Americans—seems on the way toward turning in our favor. It is only a matter of time before Hanoi crushes the puppet armies of Saigon. When this happens, the loss of American prestige, credibility, and power will be enormous." There was a muttering of exclamations, more smiles.

Leonid Brezhnev arched his thick eyebrows. "But will this loss be sufficient to drive the Americans from Asia? If they manage to hang on, our support of our Vietnamese friends will have been in vain." Catching himself, Brezhnev added, "Except, of course, to unite that nation under the banner of socialist solidarity.

"But the Americans . . . What would happen if they suffer another calamitous loss in Asia on the heels of Viet Nam? Their Congress has had enough of Asian wars and support of petty fascist dictators such as Park Chung Hee and Ferdinand Marcos. Might not a second defeat drive the Americans back to Hawaii?" Brezhnev paused. Nodding agreement around the table, the members of the Politburo leaned forward to hear the rest. "Might not a second defeat in Asia prove to be the unmaking of the NATO alliance, as the Europeans lose faith in the Yankees' ability and willingness to fight?" The excitement was now palpable. Eyes glinted with feral fierceness.

Leonid Brezhnev smiled benevolently. "I suppose just such a defeat for the Americans. While we have opportunities in a number of areas, I have a very specific target in mind."

Brezhnev's blotched hand poised briefly over the control panel as he peered through his bifocals to find the right button. He jabbed once and the map of Asia disappeared. He jabbed again and was rewarded with a map of Korea.

Much later, in a room in which the very air seemed exhausted by smoke and anxiety, Leonid Brezhnev summed up. "It is decided, then, that we begin work at once on the Korea proposal."

Kirilenko raised his hand. "I gather, Comrade Brezhnev, that the Committee on State Security will be the leading element in our plan?"

Yuri Andropov caught his breath. That fool Kirilenko would not have dared to ask such a question without Brezhnev's approval. More likely he'd been put up to it by the General Secretary.

"Moscow Center," began Brezhnev, using the favorite party sobriquet for the KGB, "will certainly make a major contribution."

Brezhnev looked down the table to Yuri Andropov.

Andropov has played his hand well, Brezhnev admitted. His ingenuity at stealing the secrets of Western military technology gained him the backing of the generals. That alone would not have been enough to allow him to force his way on to the Politburo had it not been for the attention Andropov paid to gathering evidence of indiscretions of high party officials. Brezhnev himself had cold thoughts about the files Moscow Center undoubtedly maintained on him and his family.

Adopting what he intended to be a soothing voice, he gestured with his open hand to Andropov. "And we will certainly make use of the considerable talents of Yuri Vladimirovich." He dropped his hand to the table. "But since this is an endeavor that so greatly calls upon our armed forces, I believe you will agree with me that the bulk of the planning and execution of special tasks will fall upon the GRU."

The Glavnoye Razvedyvatelnoye Upravleniye—the chief intelligence directorate of the Soviet General Staff—is an arm of the Ministry of Defense, and has a much larger budget and manpower allocation for espionage than does the KGB. Nonetheless, Moscow Center looks on the GRU with contempt; for it is only the KGB that has been entrusted with the special responsibility of preserving the Communist Party itself, the very political heart of the world socialist revolutionary movement. It is the KGB alone that claims the title of "Sword and Shield" of the party, the guardian of Lenin's legacy. A KGB officer never accords his or her GRU counterpart the grudging respect paid to rivals, such as CIA or the British Secret Intelligence Service. Rather, KGB officers consider it a grave affront to be mentioned in the same breath as the GRU, a motley collection of hooligans and hoodlums whose political illegitimacy and lack of professional finesse are an embarrassment to the Revolution.

Leaving the Kremlin, Yuri Andropov seethed. He had barely managed to conceal his surprise, to remain expressionless, as if he'd been a partner to the decision that would give the lion's share of the intelligence work on the Korea operation to the GRU. But he could keep up the pretense only so long. He hurried to his car. He was still distraught. At the office he'd have to pay attention to a dozen other matters. So instead of returning to Dzerzhinsky Square, he had his aide drive him out the Prospekt Kalinina.

Andropov sat in the back of the car deep in thought. He realized that Brezhnev intended to chart the course of Russia from beyond the grave. A victory over the Americans in Korea, he reflected, would put the General Secretary in an unassailable position to name his successor from among his cronies. The only organ of the State that the Dnepropetrovsk crowd didn't control absolutely was the KGB, and Brezhnev was smart enough to know that Moscow Center could stop him. The Korea plan therefore was designed to destroy Moscow Center as well as the Americans: Brezhnev would no doubt dump the dirty work of the plan on the KGB and fix things so that the inevitable failures of the GRU also ended up on Moscow Center's doorstep. And Brezhnev knew he could count on the GRU's longstanding jealousy of the KGB to help him.

The KGB chairman peered through the tinted window at a large ornate building on his left. "Slow down, Sasha."

His long-time driver turned to ask, "That place, Comrade Andropov. I do not recognize it."

Taken aback by the unexpected question, Andropov hesitated, then smiled. "It's the theatre, Sasha. The Central Puppet Theatre."

The American defeat in Viet Nam came as Leonid Brezhnev had anticipated. The routine afternoon meeting of the KGB Collegium that day was particularly distasteful and especially unproductive. Belenkov, chief of the First Directorate, was roaring drunk, celebrating the liberation of South Viet Nam as if he had been the architect of the North Vietnamese victory. Laughing, he waved a photo enlargement of the helicopters taking the last Americans off the roof of their embassy in Saigon. Andropov, unsmiling, cut the meeting short and asked Kiktev to remain behind.

Motioning Kiktev to sit, Andropov moved his own chair so that their knees nearly touched.

"Who would have thought, Vasili Petrovich, that it would have come so easily at the end? The Americans defeated themselves, of course. They never were certain as to what they wanted. They were unwilling to do what they had to do to win. But they were also afraid to call it quits."

Andropov leaned back. "They will agonize over this for years to come." He waved his hand in languid dismissal. "Whatever. The important thing is that the world has watched the Americans abandon allies they had sworn to stick by. The world has also seen them lose their first war, and perhaps their courage as well."

He put his hand on Kiktev's shoulder. "I think it is time for Comrade Kiktev to see our friends in *dezinformatsia* to move our General Secretary's modest plan forward another notch or two."

Langley, Virginia

He was led into a small well-lighted but windowless room with pale cream walls. To his left was a desk and a stenographer's chair. On the desk was the lie-detector—a large attaché case lying opened and flat, exposing its wire guts and a rolling scroll of paper. On his right, a brown lounge chair. Without being told, he sat down.

"Lean forward." The examiner strapped what looked like a black coiled telephone cord around John Freeman's chest. A blood-pressure cuff was then wrapped around his left arm and a small electrode fitted over the left ring finger.

Freeman faced a blank well. The machine and the examiner were behind him, out of sight. The polygraph had so drawn his attention that he couldn't recall even the basics of the examiner's appearance. He felt the cool draft from the air-conditioner vent and a betraying bead of perspiration forming between his shoulder blades.

Two days before, a gangly gray-haired woman from the Office of Security had explained the procedure.

"There are standard questions we ask—to make certain there's nothing in your past that could be used to blackmail you once you're in." She pushed a strand of hair back into place and paused, miming that she wanted an answer. He said nothing. She frowned and continued, her voice sharper, more shrewish. "The other questions corroborate the information you gave us on your personal-history statement." She pointed to a sheaf of papers.

Freeman felt his pulse race.

Gray Hair's pitch rose. She glared at him over her horn-rimmed glasses. Her voice probed. "You do know, don't you, about the Agency's responsibilities regarding the polygraph exam?"

Freeman started. "What responsibilities?"

Now smug, pleased with Freeman's reaction, she purred, "In most instances we evaluate applicants who are not federal employees. Should they fail the polygraph, we simply don't hire them."

Gray Hair leaned forward. Her face seemed to stretch out of shape, to distort itself into a leer. "In your case, however, Colonel Freeman, such a failure would be reported to your parent service." She looked at the personal-history statement. "Yes. Reported to the Army. All adverse information we discover could be used in administrative or disciplinary actions against you."

He choked back a surge of anger. For an instant he wanted to wrap his hands around her scrawny throat. This bitch was threatening him with a court-martial. Dismissal from the service. Even prison. "I understand."

Gray Hair smiled again. "You can choose to withdraw your application," she offered. "It would be without prejudice."

"I'm not worried about the test," he lied.

"No, Colonel, I'm certain you're not."

He heard the slight rustle of paper behind him, then the disembodied voice of the examiner. "I'm going to go over each question without the machine on. If you can't answer yes or no, we'll make the question more specific so that you can give a yes-no answer. Then we'll turn the machine on and use the modified questions."

Another rustle of paper. Freeman strained to listen, to

find out if the machine, indeed, was turned off. Was there any reason to keep the machine on secretly? The breath-monitor cord was tight across his chest.

"Have you ever disclosed classified information to someone not authorized to receive such information?"

"I've been handling classified information for almost twenty years," he replied. "I can't say that somewhere, somehow, I didn't say something to somebody. I rather imagine now that it's likely that I did."

"But can you think of any specific instance when you gave classified information to someone you knew who wasn't supposed to have it?"

"Not that I can recall."

"Yes or no, please."

"No," Freeman replied.

Then he remembered the night, just before returning to Viet Nam, when he'd been unable to sleep. Helen had awoken. They'd smoked cigarettes and then he'd told her about the assassinations.

The singsong voice had come from down the trail to his left. It was a popular Vietnamese love ballad. Nguyen Van Hai, enforcer of party discipline in Dinh Tuoung province, was stumbling drunkenly. Freeman had waited until Hai passed by, then stepped onto the trail and with a smooth swinging motion looped the piano wire garrote around Hai's neck and jerked the handles together. Hai gasped, brought his hands up to his neck and began great heaving convulsions. Freeman pulled the wire tighter.

"There . . . I . . . told a friend about something in Viet Nam. At the time it was classified. It involved . . . I couldn't sleep afterward. Later, in the States, I couldn't sleep. I told her what was bothering me."

"Why did you tell her?"

"So I could sleep."

The examiner was writing something. Did he know what it was like when you couldn't escape endlessly turning over the fragments of memories of people and events you'd tried to forget forever? Did he care?

"How long ago was this?"

John Freeman blinked in confusion and attempted to focus on the half-heard question. "The thing in Viet Nam?"

"No, Colonel Freeman. How long ago did you tell your friend?"

"About five years ago."

More writing. How will they check that out? Haul in Helen? What would she remember? What would she say?

"Can we use the question: 'Aside from certain information you divulged about operations in Viet Nam, have you ever discussed classified information with anyone you knew was not authorized to receive such information?'"

He could almost hear his heartbeat; there just had to be other times over the years when something had slipped out. But to someone he "knew was not authorized"?

There. That was the key—he might have said something. Something might have slipped. But was it intentional? Was it in front of someone who he *knew* didn't have a security clearance?

My God, was there no end to it? How far could they make him go with this?

"I guess we can use it."

"Have you ever misappropriated government property?"

There was the Browning nine-millimeter automatic they'd given him in Viet Nam. The one with the bogus serial numbers that made it impossible to trace, and for which they hadn't made him sign a receipt. He still had it. How could he return something that didn't officially exist, yet obviously belonged to the government?

"Have you ever taken part in any conspiracy to overthrow an established government?"

Overthrow a government? How about his years in MACV's Studies and Observations Group, the cover for the Pentagon's covert operations in Southeast Asia? Hadn't he worked with others to overthrow the North Vietnamese government? Couldn't that be called a conspiracy?

"Have you ever made a false official statement while working for the U.S. government?"

He remembered the flight plans he'd been told to

fabricate. Plans that showed operations in South Viet Nam, when in reality they'd flown at night in black airplanes to parachute men and supplies into Cambodia, Laos, or North Viet Nam.

They worked through six more questions, adding qualifications and modifications. Freeman was drained. The very things for which he'd been given medals in Southeast Asia now threatened to betray him. The cover stories become false official statements. The missions against Communist terrorists become assassinations. Honor becomes dishonor, and a grateful nation becomes the inquisitor.

He could hear the examiner flipping switches. The questions came quickly.

Finally it was over. "Mr. Freeman, did you have any problems with any questions?"

What the hell did he mean by that? Did he see something on that paper scroll?

"No, how did I do?"

Pause. "How do you think you did?"

More writing. Then the tearing of paper.

"Mr. Freeman, stay where you are. I've got to show these results to my superior. I'll be back in a moment."

Freeman saw the examiner as he left. A small soft, doughy man: bald, wearing a synthetic short-sleeve shirt and a stained brown tie. He breathed deeply, then inwardly slumped into the chair. What now? He was still hooked to the box. The pens were still recording. Loosed from the questioning, Freeman examined the room. Straight ahead, just at eye level, he saw the small hole in the wall. A fiber-optics spyhole? They could be watching him while he's gone. Why?

In less than an hour he had been forced to relive a lifetime of the tormenting inner debates in which the only choices had been lesser evils; to tell the smaller lie, to cause the least pain, to kill the fewer innocents. Corrosive waves of long-buried Calvinist self-recrimination again washed over him, punishment for failing to meet his own impossible standards. The polygraph had put him at war with himself. He felt beaten and angry.

The examiner came back without the paper. "We're finished. We'll be in touch."

"Did you . . . did you see any problems? Any rough spots?"

The short bald man looked at him, smiling slyly. "How about you, Colonel Freeman, did you see any problems? Any rough spots?"

John Freeman straightened his tie as he crossed the huge white and gray marble foyer. His eye was caught by a glass case projecting from the wall on his left. The case held a book, opened, in which CIA officers killed in the line of duty were honored. He recognized none of the names. Many—most—entries consisted only of a simple black star beside a blank line, marking those whose names could not be divulged—men and women whom secrecy had followed into death.

Above the book stars were chiseled into the wall, along with the promise from the Gospel of John: "And ye shall know the truth and the truth shall make you free."

He stood for a moment, looking at the inscription, oblivious of those passing by, then muttered softly to himself, "I suppose so." Turning, he walked past the security guards and out the doors to his car.

Eleanor Trowbridge scratched behind her ear with the eraser end of a stubby number-two Dixon pencil. Confronted with large bones and a height just under five feet, she had years ago given up attempts to mask her stocky body. She paid little attention to makeup. Her short, curly gray-streaked hair framed a round wrinkled face. Large dark brown eyes looked on the world with frank curiosity and good humor.

She was a woman without frills. Her clothing, like her writing, was simple and declarative. In her suite of offices she generally padded about in stockinged feet, having kicked her shoes off somewhere under her desk early in the workday. This morning a man's cable-knit burgundy cardigan with two missing buttons and holes worn in the elbows partially covered a bright floral-print dress.

The office itself was carpeted in gray, the walls a bone white. Three floor-to-ceiling windows gave light to ferns and African violets. Her battered rolltop desk with a brass lamp was deep in books and papers. Seated on a chair that barely let her toes touch the floor, she wrestled with the draft intelligence estimate before her.

The Pentagon analysts always took the long way around everything. Why is it, she wondered, that military people will charge up any hill you put in front of them, but when faced with a piece of paper, they always diddled about, never quite getting to what they really wanted to say?

"Maritime activities focused on techniques devoted to harvesting of sea life for massive human consumption . . ." Eleanor clucked. The number-two slashed. "Fishing . . ." inserted the number-two Dixon.

She had gotten into the intelligence business straight out of Barnard. World War II had just begun, and a call for Asian scholars had come from Harvard's Langer, who was setting up shop in Washington for Bill Donovan. The Office of Strategic Services. She learned to write estimates of Japanese strengths and weaknesses from garbled scraps of prisoner interrogations, secret-agent reports, and incomplete radio intercepts. They were trying years in which she bent a spirit of free-ranging academic inquiry to meet the demands of those who sent men to fight and, necessarily, to die.

With the disbanding of OSS after the war, she transferred to the State Department's East Asia Bureau. Later, there was Harry and the necessary resignation: no married women were allowed in the Foreign Service of the world's greatest democracy. Then came the tragic irony of Harry's death just a few years later. It was Averell Harriman, over pepper vodka at the Serbian Crown, who persuaded her to come back into the government, this time into Harry Truman's creation: the Central Intelligence Agency.

John Freeman rapped softly on the open door. "Mrs. Trowbridge?"

She saw a tall, slender man who held himself erect

without the exaggerated ramrod effect sought by so many professional military officers. Before she could respond, he entered the office. He walked easily, but with the slightest trace of a limp. He carried himself with an assurance that told of a man unintimidated by new surroundings, an assurance that was kept from arrogance by a diffident smile. The files said he was forty, though he could have passed for a year or two either side.

His clothes reflected a certain reserve, a guarded fastidiousness: olive poplin two-button suit, polished loafers, white Oxford cloth-shirt collar buttoned over a subdued-green foulard tie. He wore no jewelry except for an expensive but plain gold watch with a leather strap.

His face was long and deeply tanned, faintly marked by a faded scar extending from just below his left eye almost to the corner of his mouth. The files had mentioned other wounds as well, Eleanor remembered. As he came close to her, she saw his eyes were a deep green and his brown hair was neatly trimmed, but longer than prescribed by Army regulations. His hand was hard and muscular.

"You're Colonel Freeman." She motioned to a pair of chairs near a low table. "Coffee?"

Freeman hadn't finished nodding before Eleanor was on her feet and headed toward the door. "Cream? Sugar?"

"Cream."

Freeman scanned the office. Two bright Indonesian batiks on one wall. None of the ego pictures, though she could probably fill a wall or two; he'd heard she had known just about every leader and intelligence chief in Asia.

Eleanor returned and set the coffee down. "I'm better at getting coffee than my secretary, and she's better at editing my scratchings and putting together cables. We agreed long ago that she wouldn't get the coffee and I wouldn't interfere with running the office."

He took up the coffee cup and raised it with a slight gesture, nearly a toast. "Thanks."

"Getting to the point, Colonel Freeman—"

"John."

"John." She thought for a moment, then explained, "As the National Intelligence Officer for East Asia, I've got to publish estimates on every aspect of the area. I know the politics of the region." A mischievous smile quickly came and went. "And our economic analysts are so divided in their field that no two of them can agree long enough to put anything over on me. But the military issues are on the increase. I need help with those.

"But first, satisfy my curiosity. Why did you come out to Langley? I would have thought you'd be better off pursuing your career at the Pentagon."

Freeman stirred his coffee, then carefully laid the spoon on the saucer. "I never was attracted to the conventional Army. I got into Special Forces early and stayed there. Repeated tours in Laos and Viet Nam. Worked with the hill people doing scouting missions along the Ho Chi Minh Trail. Then MACV-SOG for some hit-and-run stuff in North Viet Nam. 'Not career enhancing assignments,' the flesh peddlers in personnel told me.

"Then I got wounded. They told me I wouldn't be jumping out of airplanes anymore. So the Special Forces couldn't use me and the conventional folks didn't want me. I'd worked with tactical intelligence enough to find it intriguing. It's about what the other guy can do and why he might do it."

"Almost as interesting as jumping out of airplanes?"

John Freeman didn't smile. "Almost."

"You know there's a file on you downstairs, don't you? You were in the early days of the Phoenix Program."

Freeman stirred his coffee again. Phoenix had been put together to compete with the ruthless but effective Viet Cong political cadre that waged the war of the villages, that indoctrinated and organized the peasants into a rural resistance movement. Phoenix called for a varying mixture of propaganda, politics, and if needed, violence. The killing was to be selective—a last resort. But Phoenix soon became a convenient hysteria-inducing code word for the anti-war critics who immediately tarred the United States for running a murder-for-hire operation.

"Yes." He looked steadily at her, his mouth set.

Eleanor waited for more, then got up and walked to the desk. "You don't want to talk about it."

Freeman didn't hesitate, but the softness of his voice kept him from being curt. "That's right."

Aviation Week and Space Technology—June 7, 1976

The White House yesterday received classified briefings regarding assessments of Soviet ICBM developments contained in CIA's most recent National Intelligence Estimate. According to informed sources, the NIE claims that the Soviet Union is unlikely to achieve an ICBM reentry vehicle accuracy better than a 300-meter CEP before the mid-1980s.

The implications of this estimate are far-reaching. If correct, this means that the U.S. Minuteman missiles are safe in their underground silos and remain invulnerable to a Soviet surprise attack. . . .

Langley, Virginia

The East Asia watch officer in the Operations Center called Eleanor just after lunch.

"Mrs. Trowbridge, we've got a Flash-precedent from U.S. Forces Korea. There's been an incident of some kind in the Demilitarized Zone. Apparently, Americans are involved."

By the time Eleanor arrived, the Operations Center had increased to alert status, filling in previously empty desks with Korea specialists. The Senior Watch officer waved a paper at her.

"Eleanor, what we seem to have is," he consulted the paper, "two American Army officers were with a work party near the Panmunjom area. They were in there to supervise the clearing away of undergrowth and trees. It's been a routine kind of thing. But this time they were jumped by North Korean troops."

"And . . ."

"Both officers dead. Beaten to death with axes."

"Is there anything else?"

The Senior Watch officer shook his head. "Not now. Not right now."

"What's our status?"

"DIA and NSA have increased their watch on North Korean radio comms. We're working with the Pentagon to get some satellite photography of assembly sites the North Koreans would have to use if they're going to try anything big."

Eleanor squinted again at the center's wall-size crisis map and status board showing the whereabouts of key U.S. government leaders as well as those of other nations. "Tell the Director I'm going over to pick up somebody from DDO. We'd like to see him in about twenty minutes. Oh, and find John Freeman. He's down at the Farm. Have him get back here and start setting up the task force operation."

A few minutes later, in a far corner of the huge CIA headquarters building, Eleanor pressed the button beside the door. From a small loudspeaker to her left a metallic voice demanded her badge number and the name of the person she wanted to see. She answered, then waited. When the lock gave a loud click, she pulled the door open and entered a small anteroom in which a receptionist sat. "I'll take you in to see him, Mrs. Trowbridge."

DDO, or the Directorate of Operations, regards itself, not without good reason, as the elite action arm of CIA. Responsible for mankind's oldest and most complex espionage—spying by human agents—the DDO also inherited from the Office of Strategic Services that World War II organization's charter for special operations. "Special Ops," an infinitely elastic term, includes among other things, planning and running small wars, formation of foreign political parties, operation of businesses such as airlines and shipping companies, and establishment of newspapers and radio stations to support—very discreetly—the foreign policies of the United States.

The DDO was falling on hard times. Spies and CIA officers who recruited and ran them had always been anathema to the professional diplomats at the State Department, who, at best, considered human agents unreliable, high-risk ventures. At worst, they were potential embarrassments—messes left on the drawing-room floor, which had to be cleaned up by the Foreign Service.

The view from Langley, on the other hand, was that the State Department felt far more threatened by DDO than by the KGB. But until the mid-seventies State had few alternatives to DDO if it wanted to know what was going on in areas of the world denied to polite diplomacy.

With the coming of age of satellite technology, however, State had begun to breath easier. The high-flying satellites were far less intrusive than some CIA officer operating from the American embassy in Moscow who doubly sinned—first, by suborning "honest" Soviet citizens to spy on their own government, and worse, by doing so while posing as a Foreign Service officer. And after all, argued the Foreign Service, who could doubt the veracity of photographs that could tell you with an accuracy of millimeters the sometimes astounding bust measurements of the women at the Sevastopol nudist beach?

Eleanor followed the receptionist to an unmarked door. The woman punched a code into an electronic cipher lock and stepped aside to let her pass.

"Hello, Lew. I suppose you've gotten word about the DMZ thing."

Lewis Parsons was spare and balding, permanently tanned by years of windburn at the helm of *The Slithy Tove*, which now was berthed in nearby Annapolis. For over twenty years he had been a field man, running agents into China, North Korea, and North Viet Nam, sometimes using *The Tove*, sailing out of CIA stations and bases from Djakarta to Inchon. He'd moved with zest and enthusiasm through Asia's upheavals and crises, unscarred except for a growing conviction that the total worth of mankind was considerably less than the sum of its individual parts.

In Kuala Lumpur there'd been the affair with the Australian woman who'd turned out to be an officer in Canberra's intelligence service. There were the requisite nasty scenes, and then an even nastier divorce. And so they'd brought him back to Langley.

Lew Parsons now watched over the agent nets that had once been his, offering—with decreasing frequency—suggestions that were routinely routed, filed, and later—in accordance with the appropriate Agency directives—routinely destroyed.

Parsons nodded. "I just talked to our Chief of Station in Seoul. The South Koreans are upset as hell. The Blue House is getting some kind of demand together for an operation against the North."

"You're not surprised?"

"No, if I were Park Chung Hee, sitting in the Blue House, I'd insist that the U.S. do something, if only to show that we're not about to cut and run the way we did in Viet Nam."

"I remember something years ago at Barnard. A lecturer told us that great powers set the international agenda. Now our clients dictate the terms."

"What's next?"

She motioned to the door. "The Director. Bad news doesn't improve with age."

Five minutes later Eleanor and Lewis Parsons were in the Director's office. George Bush was angry.

"You sit there and tell me those bastards beat two of our guys to death some four *hours* ago and we *still* don't know the details? What the hell kind of operation do we have here?"

Parsons flushed. "Sir, I understand how you feel. But dammit, we concentrate on the denied areas. For what's happening to American troops, we have to depend on the Pentagon."

The flash light blinked on Bush's desk. He picked up the scrambler telephone, made a note, and hung up.

"Kissinger's called a Washington Special Action Group meeting for seven this evening. Eleanor, I want you with me. I'll have to give some kind of intelligence briefing. Keep it limited to five minutes. No charts. On your way out, tell Mathias; he'll make the access arrangements for the White House."

* * *

Back in her office, Eleanor carefully misted the ferns. The WSAG meeting hadn't gone well at all. Ford and Rockefeller had been in Kansas City at the Republican Convention, as had Rumsfeld, the Secretary of Defense. The Chairman of the Joint Chiefs had been represented by a junior sit-in. With so many of the principals absent, Kissinger had had to finesse the problem and set up a follow-up meeting for seven-thirty the next morning. This would give CIA the rest of the night to come up with a clearer picture of Korean motives. The Pentagon and State would have time to develop a list of responses for the President. Having tended to the ferns, Eleanor Trowbridge poured a cup of coffee and sat down at the telephone.

Unlike the CIA Operations Center, another vital control room exists in which the desks are usually empty, the telephones and datafax machines silent. The Task Force Complex is kept in waiting to handle crises that would divert the center from its continual monitoring of worldwide events.

By eight P.M. the underground facility was filled with those who soon would become members of the Korea Task Force. One portion of the area was given over to the specialists in collection. Another section was taken up by the analysts, who gleaned the collectors' "take" to draft assessments for customers in the White House, Pentagon, and State Department. To the side was a small kitchen, dominated by a bank of microwave ovens and a huge coffee urn. There was the usual milling of people thrown together who were normally unaccustomed to working as a team. Maps were being pinned to display boards, communications systems undergoing checks, and latecomers searching for desks.

Eleanor dragged a straight wooden chair to the center of the room. She climbed onto it and beat on a metal wastebasket with a yardstick. A crowd assembled around her and conversations tapered off.

"Let's get started. We can finish the administrative arrangements in a moment. At seven-thirty tomorrow morning the Director has to brief the Washington Special Action Group on the DMZ incident. The WSAG will then propose American responses. Kissinger will carry these options to the President in Kansas City.

"I have to be at the Director's home by five-thirty A.M. to brief him. We should have our first draft of the Director's briefing, along with backup charts, by four A.M. We have about eight hours.

"I think we have to address three questions in the briefing." She turned and waved the yardstick at the blackboard behind her. "First, what is the current state of play on the Korean peninsula? What are the reactions of the various parties—the ROK's, the North Koreans, the Chinese, the Soviets? Don't forget the other players, such as the Japanese.

"Second, the President wants our appraisal of the extent to which this was a deliberate incident. Can we make a case that Kim Il-Sung ordered it? Or was it a foul-up by a local junior officer—did some low-ranking officer or sergeant start something he couldn't control? Or was it something in between?

"Lastly, we ought to come up with a list of North Korean targets that the Pentagon might wish to consider hitting in retaliation. DOD will of course have a lot to say about this, but it seems to me we could find some appropriate North Korean military targets that we can hit with low risk. I can't imagine that the President wants this thing to end up with a batch of American POW's on Pyongyang television.

"John Freeman will coordinate the drafting of the briefing. If you need to get more information from DDO, NSA, or photography, see Lew Parsons."

By two A.M. Eleanor had in hand a nine-page background narrative for Bush, from which he would develop his own informal presentation. There were also three photographs of the DMZ area, taken by a high-flying SR-71

Blackbird out of Okinawa's Kadena Air Force Base that had been scrambled by the Strategic Air Command's intelligence center in Nebraska. Blown up to four-by-five-foot posters, they showed the nearest North Korean troop-assembly areas. All activity levels appeared normal.

Eleanor was making notes from the narrative when Lew Parsons came over with a woman in tow. She was pretty, brown-haired, in her thirties, and dressed in penny loafers, khaki slacks, and a pale blue Oxford shirt.

"Eleanor Trowbridge, this is Susan Forbes. She does North Korea command-and-control analysis for DIA."

Eleanor vaguely placed her. She had a reputation in the Defense Intelligence Agency as one of the few experts on the structure and location of North Korea's military headquarters and their relationships with each other.

"Ms. Trowbridge—"

"Mrs."

Forbes hesitated.

"Eleanor, Susan has—"

With a flash of exasperation, Eleanor cut him off. "Lew, I'm a tired old woman. I've had a long night. How about letting her talk for herself." Turning to Susan Forbes, Eleanor smiled, pointed to the chair. "Let's make it just Eleanor. I'm sorry I was cranky."

"Eleanor." Susan Forbes nodded, the elder woman's assertiveness having briefly taken her aback. "While the SR-71 was taking pictures of the DMZ area, it also took some peripheral photography of the headquarters cantonment of the 280th Commando Brigade near Yongyon-ni. It's one of North Korea's special-forces-type units. We've seen subordinate elements at various places along the DMZ, but the headquarters has been in the same place for the past ten years. This latest photography shows changes in the truck park."

Eleanor blinked. Intelligence specialization has come of age, she thought. We now have experts in truck parking. She sighed. "What do truck parks have to do with the thing in the DMZ?"

"I don't know. Maybe nothing. But the change is significant in itself. I've seen the same kind of precise groupings of vehicles in the Soviet Union. At the *spetznaz* camps."

"Are you saying that the Russians have come to Korea?"

Forbes took a breath and framed her reply carefully. "I'm saying that we have one bit of evidence that an elite North Korean unit has changed a pattern of behavior in such a way that indicates some sort of Soviet influence. It probably has little to do with the killings. But it's something that ought to be looked into."

Impatiently, Eleanor turned back to the drafts on the table in front of her. "Thanks, I'll give you a call when we get all this out of the way."

Moscow

Kiktev had been waiting for nearly an hour. He forced himself to sit on the hard chair and maintain a semblance of calm. Inside, his guts were churning. It would not be pleasant. Those yellow bastards. He'd probably have his ass roasted for this.

A young lieutenant came to attention before him. "Comrade Andropov will see you now, Colonel." Andropov, unlike his contemporaries, didn't allow female secretaries in his personal offices. More secrets are lost through a stiff penis, he'd say, than through a loose mouth.

Andropov was standing, looking out onto Dzerzhinsky Square. Surprisingly, he wasn't angry, but spoke in a calm, measured voice. "Well, Comrade Kiktev, our Korean friends have given in to one of their periodic blood lusts. What now? What effects will this have in the near term? What does it tell us about our ability to control the Koreans?"

Kiktev remained silent until Andropov turned to face him. "I'm not certain. We don't know what the Americans will do. But they haven't the stomach for starting something in Korea so soon after Viet Nam. And then, too, Comrade Andropov, there are the American elections in less than three months.

"We have been particularly fortunate," Kiktev continued. "This farmer—this man Carter—has already proposed withdrawing the American army from the southern part of Korea. Who knows? Perhaps the killings might even make him more determined to do so. Should this man be elected President and carry out his scheme, the door will be completely open. Kim Il-Sung's tanks could be in Seoul within hours.

"As for your question about the reliability of our friends, they know that they must go along with us if they ever want to reunify their country. And they know, also, that keeping the Americans in the South could mean the end to that dream.

"We both have much to win. They get to reunify that barbaric country of theirs, and we get the—"

Andropov, having heard enough, slumped into his chair. "Yes, yes, Vasili Petrovich. I know the line. I know it well. 'We both have much to win.' I believe our General Secretary used words to that effect." He removed his gold wire glasses and put them carefully on the desk blotter, then wearily rubbed his eyes. "And I remember wondering whom he was talking about. Who would be the real winners?" Like one who suddenly realized he'd been talking to himself in the presence of others, Andropov stopped abruptly.

Sensing it would be imprudent if not dangerous to pursue Andropov's remark, Kiktev sought safer ground, choosing a topic bound to elicit an enthusiastic response at any level in the KGB—criticism of the GRU. "I cannot understand why we are in a supporting role to those fools at the Aquarium," he groused, using the KGB pejorative of choice for the glass-walled GRU headquarters.

Grateful for the diversion, Andropov flashed a quick smile. "Ah, Vasili Petrovich. You are too eager. Let the Ministry of Defense see to equipping and training our little yellow friends. We don't need that headache. And let Comrade Brezhnev pursue his plan for the Americans. We shall do what we do best." He wagged a cautionary finger at Kiktev. "But never underestimate our part in this. If there is some foul-up, I want no one to point to us, or you and I will learn firsthand of the efficiency with which we operate the State's northernmost labor camps." Andropov rubbed his hands together as if warming them. "I'm not anxious to have some bastard write a book about one day in the life of Yuri Vladimirovich."

McLean, Virginia

In the Northern Virginia telephone book, it was listed as O'Toole's. But the sign outside, facing McLean's Old Dominion Drive, said Bill's Seafood. The ambivalence discouraged new trade, which was fine with John J. O'Toole, the proprietor and manager. For reasons never quite clear, O'Toole's had years before become a preserve of the DDO.

O'Toole's was decorated in what one critic identified as "authentic Irish dirty." Faded crepe-paper shamrocks, John Wayne posters, and Culinary Institute of America T-shirts hung on the walls. The booths were cracked Naugahyde originally of a green color, and the sex of the toilet was undetermined. But the hamburgers were unarguably the world's best, and when topped with a half-inch slice of nose-clearing onion, set the diner up for O'Toole's ice-cold draft beer. Abuse was O'Toole's stock-in-trade, and it was rumored that he'd been out in East Africa with the Agency years back.

Freeman's eyes adjusted slowly to the dark. He saw Parsons had taken the booth most distant from the john and had gotten well into a pitcher of beer.

"Buy a feller a drink?"

Parsons motioned to the opposite bench and waved for another glass. O'Toole, as usual, ignored anything short of a slur of the IRA, and so Parsons went behind the bar, selected a chipped mug from the shelf, wiped it with a dirty towel, and set it down in front of Freeman.

"Come here often?"

"Hell, John, you effete elite in the upper echelons are too used to Rive Gauche or La Bagatelle. You get out of shape. Your stomach can't take real food. I eat here to keep in shape for Asia."

"No sacrifice too great."

The only waitress took their order, bringing unasked another pitcher.

"Jesus, Lew, I can't work this afternoon if I help you with that one."

"Not a helluva lot of work to do. Pick up the pieces after the DMZ thing."

John Freeman made rings on the tabletop with his mug. "We've become a pathetic sight—Uncle Sam with a kick-me sign on his butt. They do something outrageous, we posture a lot. The White House makes all sorts of strong noises. The usual loonies in Congress say we ought to put our faith in the United Nations. In the end, it's all the same. We fold like a cheap suitcase."

O'Toole himself brought over the hamburgers, a plate in each hand, his thumbs over the top buns to keep the thick sandwiches from spilling over.

"Mr. O'Toole, sir, I just hope to hell you washed your hands after you went wee-wee."

"Fuck you, Lew. Saves on salt."

Freeman continued, "Lew, can you imagine how we look to the rest of the world? We put the entire U.S. Second Division on DEFCON One alert, sent two aircraft carriers into the Sea of Japan, and orbited B-52's just south of the DMZ, and after all that, we go in and chop down a tree."

Parson wiped a fleck of mustard from the corner of his mouth, leaned back in the booth and eyed the woman with the tight skirt who'd taken a stool at the bar.

"Nice ass." He poured more beer. He took on a tone of harsh irony. "It's what the pussies at State call 'a proportionate response.' One of them said that, he really did. Said it on CBS. And, of course, CBS approves of proportionate responses too." He paused. "Two of our guys for one of their goddamn trees."

They finished eating in silence.

Parsons pushed his plate away and drained the last of

his beer. "There was that interesting thing, though. The truck park."

"What do you mean?"

"Didn't Eleanor tell you?" Parsons inspected Freeman's plate and found a lone potato chip, which he appropriated and ate. "I suppose she didn't think it was much. It was the night we worked on Bush's WSAG briefing. I got approached by one of the DIA analysts about some photography. Showed changes in one of their special-forces training camps. Motor-pool layout changed over to the same kind the *speznaz* uses. The analyst thought it was something. Eleanor wasn't impressed."

"Who was this?"

"DIA analyst. Forbes. Nice ass."

The afternoon autumn sun splashed the ferns. Eleanor had just put on a new tape, Fasch's Concerto in F Major, and was looking forward to spending an hour or two writing an article on the defeat of China's T'ang Dynasty armies at the hands of the barbaric Thai of Yunan. And now here were Parsons and Freeman, reeking of beer and wanting to talk about Korea. She looked at the manuscript and sighed.

"What kind of estimate on Korea?"

Parsons, leaning forward, elbows on knees, opened his hands. "The military balance between North and South Korea. No allies. Just the two."

"Lew, you know what something like that could take. If we really wanted to start from scratch, we'd have a lot of digging to do."

"Eleanor," interjected Freeman, "you know better than I do that we really haven't taken a good look at Korea in years. Viet Nam was the high-priority item. We've ignored the peninsula for a long time."

"We've ignored a lot of places for a long time. We've got an entire continent south of us that we haven't paid attention to in decades."

John persisted. "Eleanor, I haven't been around this place as long as you and Lew, but as we sit here, the Democratic nominee for President of the United States is calling for withdrawing our troops from Korea. The DMZ killings apparently only reinforced his convictions. We admit we haven't done a bottoms-up look at the situation. If we don't, then the people at State and the Pentagon will get used to running the world without us."

She looked at the ferns and the sun. She wondered if the T'ang had realized that the defeat by the Thai was the turning point for their dynasty. Just after they had lost in Yunan, they suffered a second defeat at the hands of the Arabs at Talas, thus ending one of China's most brilliant and influential periods and beginning five hundred years of military and foreign-policy decline.

Eleanor pushed the T'ang away. "Set up a meeting and put together an agenda. The sooner the better. I suppose we might as well try to figure out where we're going."

Freeman met Susan Forbes three days later. He'd had to call ahead before he drove into the nearer Virginia suburbs to Arlington Hall Station, where the scattered Defense Intelligence Agency maintained the bulk of its analysts on Korea.

He was getting restless sitting on a metal folding chair when the door to his right opened.

"John Freeman?"

"Yes. Ms. Forbes?"

"Susan."

About five feet seven inches, Freeman estimated. Slender, brown hair, green eyes, and a good smile. Distinctive hints of a nice body, even under the loose sweater. The strength of her handshake surprised him, and he was momentarily transfixed by her direct manner. Then, in confusion, he realized he still held her hand. He dropped it abruptly, making matters all the worse. "The *spetznaz* business. Korea," he blurted in confusion and embarrassment.

Still smiling, she cocked her head. "This way. Come on back."

She led him through the crammed work area to a cubicle that was surprisingly neat, with two framed Ansel

Adams prints on the dividers and a small arrangement of dried flowers in a cobalt-blue vase on the desk. She reached around the cubicle divider and pulled back a folding chair. With one hand, she flipped the chair open and positioned it facing hers, then sat down at the desk.

"Eleanor told me about the truck-park changes. Have you had a chance to do any more work?"

She shook her head. "Not really. I've gone back over the SR-71 photography, but the angles are all wrong. I'd rather have a shot or two from straight overhead. And there's the problem, too, of time. Now that the task force is disbanded, I've got other things to do. The hired hands on the DIA plantation do as we're told, and right now those commando camps are about last priority."

"What would you do if you had the priorities and the resources?"

"First, I'd make a hypothesis that, for whatever the reason, the Soviets have increased their presence in North Korea. Then I'd work out some sort of survey, cull through the files of existing signal intercepts, photography, and human agent reports for any kind of supporting evidence." She thought for a while and then continued. "If we came up with anything there, we'd probably have to call for some specific collection missions. But as I said, somebody's got to lay out the priorities."

"Eleanor's given the go-ahead on an estimate."

"That'll do." Susan Forbes looked at her watch, then stood to end the conversation. She cocked her head at Freeman. "Eleanor Trowbridge. What's she like? How is it, working for her?"

Freeman realized he wanted to see the Forbes woman again, for reasons that had nothing to do with Korea or working for Eleanor Trowbridge. "Questions that deserve a better answer than I have time for here. Lunch tomorrow?"

"Thanks, but I've got to get ready for our monthly update briefing." She folded the chair he'd used and put it back behind the divider, then gave him a tentative smile. "Some other time? Give me a call."

She walked him to where he turned in his badge to the

old woman behind the glass. When she shook his hand, he was surprised again at her strength.

Langley, Virginia

Eleanor counted noses. Around the table were representatives from Washington's intelligence community who, back in their home organizations, were responsible for intelligence on Korea. Evans from DIA, Hirsch from the National Security Agency, some uniformed people of the military services, and Portale from State Intelligence and Research.

INR contributed little to the intelligence community. But that had never been the intention. Rather, the State Department created INR to be a trip wire; to warn of potential mischief by the Neanderthaler American intelligence professionals who had the horrid proclivity of incessantly questioning the motives of Soviet leaders. As years passed, State also learned to use INR in Washington's bureaucratic wars to cripple, delay, or kill outright those intelligence appraisals that might run counter to policies in vogue at Foggy Bottom. INR helped the State Department enforce the Foreign Service's prime directive: Facts musn't get in the way of the diplomatic process.

"I think we're all here. John Freeman will pass out the proposed terms of reference for the estimate. I suggest we take some time to look them over, then discuss whether or not we want to make any changes. The next issue will be to appoint one of you as the principal drafter and then set a deadline for the first draft."

It was Freeman's introduction to the art form of the intelligence estimate. At Eleanor's suggestion, he'd gone the week before to the Historical Intelligence Collection, where a gnomelike man, one Ibrahim Bazdarkian, rumored to be the illegitimate son of Basil Zaharoff, the legendary arms merchant, gave him a quick but thorough course in intelligence tradecraft.

"An intelligence estimate is an oxymoron," Bazdarkian had whispered to Freeman. "They think that because we have sources and methods cloaked from their view that we can also divine the future. Every time there's a coup d'etat in some back-of-beyond principality and an unknown corporal becomes ultimate leader for the day, they all look accusingly at us for not giving them the exact hour that the troops would leave their flea-ridden barracks. That a coup succeeds is proof that its makers kept their hands hidden. If the coup makers can hide from their own government's spies, how can we expect to find out?"

Bazdarkian had sipped coffee, coughed, and lit another cigarette. "And if prediction is so simple, why aren't our critics rich? After all, they have access to mountains of data on the American economy. They speak the language—though lamentably so—and they understand the culture. Why can't they make a fortune in the stock market? These," he pursed his lips to spit the word, "'experts' can't predict the outcome of elections or even football games. And they would tell us how to run our business."

Freeman had watched Bazdarkian pull for air. "Then why do we insist on acting as if we can predict the future?" he asked.

"There are a number of reasons, young man. You Americans are a people who have been traumatized by surprises, Pearl Harbor being one of the more famous. You are also a people who want to push back the unknown. This drove you west and then to the moon. To you the future is something to be grasped, controlled, tamed. You believe if you spend enough treasure and perhaps enough lives, you will succeed. None of you ever stop, of course, to ask whether the effort will be worthwhile.

"And there is another reason, an affliction of modern bureaucrats regardless of nationality. American intelligence is deathly afraid of having to say 'I don't know,' for it *does* know, as any government agency knows, that saying those three words too often will result in a thinner budget next year."

"And so we shouldn't attempt estimates?"

"We shouldn't attempt predictions, young man." Bazdarkian sat, staring into the smoke. "If an estimate cuts through the political self-absorption at the White House and alerts those fools to the possibility of a problem, then you've succeeded. And if the estimate is exceedingly well done, and you're also very lucky, you might help those fools to think about the problem in some sort of disciplined way. That would be a bonus. A very rare bonus. But don't expect any more."

"The Korea thing. How should we go about it?"

Bazdarkian took another drag from his cigarette. "It must be kept simple. This will be difficult since it is now fashionable to adorn the estimate with stacks of computer printouts they call analyses. Find out the basic military capabilities of the North and South Koreans and compare them in the simplest, most graphic manner. Depth of analysis is important, but the presentation is most important of all."

"The professional war-gaming and systems analysts will call that a bean count and dismiss it."

"Young man," Bazdarkian had rasped with a trace of exasperation, "there are dilettantes who game wars. There are professionals who fight them. The former bend numbers to support their prejudices. The latter know that 'bean counts' do count."

One hundred seventy miles above the southeast quadrant of North Korea, the fifteen-ton KH-11 satellite came to life, turning its attention to the headquarters of the 280th Commando Brigade near the small town of Yongyon-ni.

Instead of using film, the KH-11 took television pictures. It then beamed the video in the form of coded binary signal groups to a receiver at a well-guarded site near Washington, D.C.

At the ground station, computers decoded the signals and reassembled the numbers into the original pictures. The process gave the United States a near "real time" espionage capability that could reach deep into the most denied areas. Since its launch, KH-11 had aroused great enthusiasm in the American government. Its quick response, coupled with the confident reporting of the intelligence community's best photoanalysts, rapidly created the mystique of a risk-free omnipresent spy.

Unseen by American sensors, a silent, dark dwarf satellite hugged the radar "shadow" of the massive KH-11. LIMPET broadcast no signals to betray its presence. But it listened tirelessly to the electronic activity of the KH-11, storing its eavesdropping on magnetic tape cartridges. Then, as it passed over the Tyuratam missile test center in the Kazakh SSR, LIMPET ejected the tapes in a nonmetallic reentry vehicle.

Langley, Virginia

Just as Freeman was clearing his desk, his secretary buzzed. "John, Peter Smith on Red."

He punched the flashing red button that put him on the guarded telephone network that connected Washington's intelligence agencies. "Freeman."

"John, we got something down here you might want to see."

"Now? Christ, Peter, it's Friday afternoon."

"And Pearl Harbor was on a Sunday morning. I just thought—"

"Korea?"

"Yeah."

Freeman carefully finished the daily checkout procedure, making certain that even his appointment calendar and phone book were locked in the safe. He wheeled out of the parking lot, crossed the Potomac and headed toward the Navy Yard. Freeman approached the single door of Building 312, opened it and stepped in. It closed behind him and locked itself automatically. Through an armored drawer he surrendered his CIA badge to a Marine guard behind a bullet-proof window who then let him in.

Peter Smith was a wiry ex–West Pointer who had left the Army to become a specialist for the Defense Intelligence Agency. An infantry-company commander with the Ninth Division in Viet Nam, he'd won the Distinguished Service Cross—one notch down from the Medal of Honor.

But he was proudest of the time when, alone and carrying only a straightened coat hanger, he'd put down a race riot in a mess hall at Fort Benning.

"John, we got some numbers that don't come out right."

"How do you mean?"

"Saddle up, I'll show you."

Freeman straddled a cushioned stool as if it were a western saddle. He put his face forward into the stereoptic mask. Behind him, Smith flipped switches. Suddenly, Freeman was suspended above North Korea at what looked like an altitude of three thousand feet.

Eagle-Eye was the latest device for analyzing satellite photography. The "photographs" were actually sets of numbers in the computer memory. By moving a joystick, the operator called up from the memory the number sets for specific latitudes and longitudes, and the digitized information instantly formed a three-dimensional picture using two high-resolution television screens. The three-D effect, coupled with the joystick, enabled the analyst to "fly" over suspicious areas, swooping and soaring, instead of hunching over photographs with magnifying lenses. More than one "pilot" had to be reminded that his job was analysis, not touring; some, on the other hand, complained of vertigo. Smith prudently kept a supply of airsickness bags handy.

"We started counting North Korean tanks from the satellite photography. In this area south of Pyongyang," Smith operated a cursor, and a green-light arrow suddenly appeared, hovering beneath Freeman, "we found about two hundred more T-54/55's than we ever spotted before."

With the arrow's help, Freeman found the tanks, clustered in groups of threes and fours. Intermingled were support trucks for ammunition, fuel, and spare parts. The visual effects were so real he half expected some corporal to run out from under the trees and point up to him.

"Well, doesn't that just mean we up the total tank holdings in the North?" He pulled away from the mask and North Korea, feeling a sudden dizziness.

"That's not all you have to do," Smith answered.

"Those tanks are there to support infantry. And where you have infantry, you also have to have artillery."

Smith switched off the Eagle-Eye. He crossed his arms and momentarily studied his shoes. Looking up at Freeman, his face was somber, worried. "What we have here could be a helluva lot of troops we didn't know about."

"Couldn't they have just moved there from somewhere else?"

"Maybe. Except we didn't get anything from NSA. To move that much stuff from somewhere else, they'd have to come up on their radios. They'd just have to. And the guys at Fort Meade would've picked up something."

"And they didn't."

"Not a goddamn thing."

"There's more to it?"

"Well . . ." Smith crossed his arms and leaned back across an old-fashioned glass-topped table where strips of satellite photography were being examined. "If there's been a similar proportionate growth in other traditional troop-concentration areas, we could be looking at an army of forty or so divisions."

Freeman stared at the light table. The American army had sixteen divisions. If Smith were right, North Korea, literally a beggar nation, had put together one of the largest armies in the world.

Langley, Virginia

George Bush was leaving CIA. He'd cleared his desk of personal mementoes, leaving only a pale blue blotter. The rugs from Tientsin and Peking had been rolled for storage. Bush stood looking out the large plate-glass wall at the bare trees and gray skies over the Potomac.

"They weren't interested, Eleanor."

"Not at all?"

Bush shook his head. "I told the President"—Bush corrected himself— "the President-elect . . . I told him and his people when I went down to Plains that we'd brief them on Korea. They said thank you and that's the last I heard of it."

"They didn't want the briefing."

He shook his head. "They didn't want the briefing."

She'd seen it before. Transition. The changing of the government. The newcomers, impatient, wanting to get on with charting their courses for the nation. All so confident that campaign slogans could be translated into sound government programs. And then there were those leaving, weary from the constant ambushes of the opposition. Worn by the unremitting carping and second-guessing of a Greek chorus of media commentators. They knew from their own humbling experience that grand strategies quickly fell apart, degenerated into desperate battles, then into the bloody tactical skirmishes and trench warfare of a daily struggle to stave off imminent disaster.

"We've started an estimate. It ought to be ready when the Carter people get settled."

Bush stared for a long time at a hawk circling in the leaden sky. "I hear they're going to nominate Sorensen."

"I've heard that too. One hears so much these days. I had thought it was going to be an administration of new faces. One of them—that fellow Jordan, I think—said we wouldn't be seeing any of the old names around."

The hawk had plunged from view, probably toward some unseen prey on the riverbank. Bush turned and took Eleanor's hand. "Eleanor, thanks. You helped make this the best job I ever had. Thanks and best wishes."

She smiled. "I remember the mood of this place after they named you to replace Bill Colby. They expected you to stumble. I think a lot of them wanted just that. But you were good. Better than any of us had hoped. You kept your door open and you listened. We'll miss you." She turned to leave. Pausing in the door, she smiled. "To borrow one of your phrases, Mr. Director, you did a darn neat job."

A grin crossed Bush's thin face, making him years younger. He waved, a slight flick of the hand. "Merry Christmas, Eleanor."

Freeman had to quicken his pace to stay up with Eleanor. How could anyone so goddamn short walk so goddamn fast? Just off the seventh-floor hallway, next to the suite of offices for the Director of Central Intelligence, was the conference room.

Eleanor sat down at the middle of the long table. The other National Intelligence Officers, some sitting, others standing, clustered in around her and on the other side of the table. Freeman chose a chair against the wall along with the other deputies and lesser staff. Shop-talk conversations abruptly cut off when the door at the end was flung open.

"Good morning, gentlemen." The new Director of Central Intelligence didn't hesitate in the doorway but fairly shoved his way to the chair opposite Eleanor. On seeing her, Roswell Franks's eyes widened momentarily in surprise and he amended his greeting with "and lady."

Franks was Jimmy Carter's third choice to head CIA. Theodore Sorensen had withdrawn his name partway through the gauntlet of Senate confirmation hearings. Then Admiral Stansfield Turner had begged off, apparently preferring to face the Russians in the Mediterranean. The Air Force pressed, however, and sent Franks as a replacement.

"I don't expect to get to substantive issues this morning. I just want to connect names with faces, since we're all new to each other." Freeman noted that Franks sat well back in the armchair and had a habit of thrusting his chin outward and upward, as if bothered by a tight collar. He was tall—well over six feet, Freeman estimated—with thick black hair and brown eyes. His right hand crept to the pencils on the pad in front of him.

"It's good to be here. As I told the President yesterday, just yesterday, the third time's the charm." Chin thrust. Grin. Tentative smiles around the table.

"I know you've heard a lot about the President's concern with the Agency, and I want you to know that his concerns are definitely, I repeat, definitely my concerns. There's been altogether too much talk about CIA being out of control—unconstrained by any sense of decency. Talk about assassinations, plots, coups . . ." He looked balefully around the table. "Where there's smoke . . ." Another chin thrust.

Franks put on a flat smile, then just as quickly dropped it. "So, in spite of all the advice about new commanders not upsetting the troops in opening speeches, I'm here to tell you that there're going to be changes in how this place does business. I'm the boss. I'm in charge here. And I'm only answerable to the President of the United States." Franks again looked around the table, searching for a sign of mutiny. "The first thing you people are going to learn is that the talented and loyal will stay. The others will not." Franks was now rolling the pencils across the pad with his fingertips.

The room was still except for the sounds of chair squirming. Freeman saw that Eleanor had her hands clasped in front of her on the table and was apparently looking straight into Franks's eyes.

Franks glanced at an index card. "You must be the 'E. Trowbridge' they list here. I didn't realize Langley had ladies in these positions."

A silence of perhaps three seconds followed.

Eleanor leaned forward. "If you don't call me lady, I won't call you flyboy."

Franks recoiled, and for the first time his eyes swept the entire room. He sniggered—an unexpectedly high-pitched nervous giggle. Given the opportunity for a face-saving release, the table broke into laughter, followed by the back-benchers.

Later, headed back to the fifth floor, Eleanor walked more slowly. Alone in the elevator, she looked up at Freeman. "Well, what about that?"

"Lady, that flyboy doesn't like you."

Chapter 2

Longitude 127°41'E
Latitude 39°11'N
(The Sea of Japan)

North Korean radar operators along the Sea of Japan were used to the American overflights. At least once a day a Boeing RC-135U, a four-engined jet transport crammed with electronic listening gear, took off from Japan. Code named Bright Wing, these missions usually flew to the north-northwest, nearly to the border of North Korea and the Soviet Union. Bright Wing would then begin a series of interlooping circular orbits, each moving progressively toward the southwest, until reaching the coast of South Korea at the thirty-eighth parallel.

On board the aircraft, specialists sat at consoles, probing and poking at the web of radar, microwave transmitters, and other communications that made up an electronic fingerprint that was uniquely North Korean. Frequencies and times were recorded, as was the traffic—the sheer volume of broadcast information from various military and civilian radios. All this was grist for the analysts at the National Security Agency's headquarters at Fort Meade, Maryland.

The Americans hoped to avoid surprise by detecting any changes in North Korea's electronic landscape. Over the years, electronic intelligence—ELINT in the jargon of the trade—had put together the bits and pieces from Bright Wing and other operations. The pulse repetition frequencies of X- and S-band radars as they tried to detect aircraft. How the North Korean Army relied on clumsy telephone lines to avoid enemy interception of their radio messages and the direction finders that could bring in hostile artillery in time of war.

On April 15, 1969, North Korean MiG's downed a slower EC-121, killing all hands. Since that time, the Americans provided escorts for Bright Wing, usually F-4's from Japan or South Korea. The North Korean Air Force prudently remained on the ground.

Had the North Korean interceptors scrambled this particular night, they would have found that the familiar flight path was being flown by a Lockheed C-141 Starlifter, a jet transport whose radar image is identical to that of the RC-135. But unlike the RC-135, the Lockheed airplane has a huge clamshell door at the tail, a door large enough for trucks to be driven into the cargo bay.

The last orbit of the Starlifter took it to within four nautical miles of the North Korean coast. As the big plane approached the turn point, the crew pulled on individual oxygen masks and began to depressurize.

Slowing to near stalling speed coming into the turn, the C-141 entered North Korean airspace. The clamshell door was now fully open. At the edge of the ramp two helmeted figures in electrically heated pressure suits hooked themselves to a common harness that linked them one behind the other. Loaded with equipment bags, they clumsily stepped off into the night sky, 39,000 feet above the Sea of Japan.

Frank Kim immediately pulled the ripcord that began deploying an oversized ram-air canopy. A cross between a glider and a parachute, the ram-air was a large black nylon rectangle of more than three hundred square feet, with vents, flaps, and open gores that gave it great maneuverability and a forward speed of about twenty-three knots. He checked his instrument panel: altimeter and stopwatch were winding down normally. The compass, however, showed a course of forty-nine degrees—out into the sea. He pulled at the left steering toggle and the parachute turned toward a heading of 267 degrees magnetic. From jump

altitude with predicted tailwinds, the ram-air glide ratio of
three to one would land them at least twenty miles inland.
Almost a one-hour descent. He slowed the flow rate of his
oxygen and settled back to enjoy the ride down into Korea.

"That's deep enough. Let's cover this shit up and get
out of here."

Kim and Joseph Chun had landed without mishap,
lugged the equipment from the drop zone, and buried the
parachute in a ravine. It might later be found; the important thing was that it not be found soon.

The two scrambled out of the ravine, checked compass
bearings, and, shouldering bulky rucksacks, struck out to
the southwest. Although the Manchurian wind was at their
backs, the bitter cold cut through them. The weight of their
packs and the uncertain footing as they stumbled to stay off
the skyline put them behind schedule.

"Frank. I make it about five, maybe six more clicks."

Kim sipped from his canteen. Joe was right. Best case,
they couldn't get to the target before 0300. That left about
two hours until dawn. Impossible to put on the tap, then
make it to the pickup point in time to beat the sun.

Kim shrugged. "We'll have to stay over. Use the
alternative. Let's go."

At 0347 they lay on a bare hill overlooking a road
winding through the valley below. Each took turns with the
night glasses, studying a small building, a stone structure
with slate roof, which had a single window through which a
dim light spilled.

Kim passed the glasses to Chun. "No guards outside.
Probably too cold. See the antennas?"

"That's gotta be the place. There's a shed off to the
side."

"Could it be in there?"

"Maybe."

Leaving the bulky backpacks, they started toward the
building. First at a crouch, then crawling, they took
advantage of the sparse shadows, grateful for the first time
for the howling wind that kept the guards inside and
covered the small sounds of their movement. Immediately
to their front was the building. Between them and the door

was a boxy military truck, its canvas side curtains and tarpaulin snapping in the wind. They could smell the odor of wood smoke and kerosene. From inside came the sounds of radio music and the laughing talk of men grateful for warm shelter. To the left was the shed. They were perhaps seven feet from the building when the door suddenly jerked open.

Kim and Chun rolled under the truck, Kim barely getting under the running board before a pair of boots stopped inches from his face. He fought to control his breathing. He was certain his heart could be heard.

The boots shuffled and there was a rustle of clothing. Steaming urine streamed onto the clay inches from Kim, spattering on his face. Kim held his breath. Would the bastard ever quit? What if others decided to join him? What if this guy was going to get in the goddamn truck?

The stream stopped, then sputtered several more times. The boots shuffled again, turned and went back inside the building.

They waited several minutes. Kim nudged Chun and the two crab-crawled from under the truck. Reaching the shed, they found what they'd been looking for—a series of thick cables going in one side of the shed and coming out the other. Chun opened the massive old padlock in seconds.

Inside, Chun located the power cable, and, at a spot where it snaked under some shelving, placed the first coil. This would draw the few necessary volts required to operate the second coil, which he saddled over the thick cables back in the dark rear of the shed. Then he connected a gossamer-thin wire from the second coil to the cabling for the transmitting antenna used by the radio operator in the building. From the cushioned leg pocket on his white and gray jumpsuit, he pulled out a small test set and checked the induction. Getting three small green lights, he grunted softly, then carefully wiped away all traces of his work. Crawling to the doorway, he peered outside, shutting and locking the door.

He nudged Kim. They set out toward the hill.

Vicinity of Kosan
Democratic Peoples Republic of Korea

They had spent the day taking turns napping in a shallow cave along a dry stream bed. There had been no signs of human activity.

At dark they moved to the edge of the windswept plateau. Kim took from his pack a small ultra-high-frequency transmitter and screwed in its needle antenna. He then extended the telescoping legs, leveled the radio, and oriented the antenna toward the horizon. Checking his watch, he consulted a small, luminous plastic chart, then elevated the antenna eleven degrees. He pushed the transmit button and a prerecorded message he'd prepared that day was beamed to the satellite in a quick squirt of less than two seconds. He repeated the procedure twice more, using different frequencies, then disassembled the equipment.

Chun, who'd tuned a receiver to a longer-wave frequency, looked up. "Acknowledge. They'll be here at 2315."

"We don't have to start setup until 2250." He yawned, then taking on an Irish brogue, whispered, "Joseph, me bucko, we need a productive hobby with which to while away the empty hours and keep us out of trouble."

They found a cluster of boulders that broke the knifing wind and afforded them good observation of the plateau. The sky was overcast with clouds that threatened more snow. They took up watch positions with a practiced ease, huddling under camouflaged ponchos that added a degree of warmth while making them difficult to see.

They had spent years in the craft of surreptitious entry into denied areas. Sons of Korean immigrants, Chun had grown up in Detroit, Frank Kim in Los Angeles. Meeting first in the Navy's Underwater Swimmers School at Key West, Florida, they'd stayed together in the service— demolitions at Coronado, parachute qualifications at Fort Benning, then to SEAL Team Two in Viet Nam. From

South Viet Nam they'd parachuted, walked, helicoptered, and swum into Communist redoubts in Cambodia, Laos, and North Viet Nam.

Chun nudged Kim. "Time."

They were stiff from exertion and the cold, and muttered curses as they swung the large rucksacks to their backs. Picking their way across the boulder-strewn plateau, they worked downwind. Kim looked at his compass.

"This'll do. We got twelve minutes."

From one rucksack Kim laid out a large balloon and a pressurized gas container. He snapped a heavy nylon line to the balloon harness. Then he and Chun climbed into flight suits, each of which had a heavy forged-steel D ring in the back, between the shoulder blades. To the D rings he clipped the nylon line. Then he opened the gas valve.

"Six minutes."

The balloon was filling too slowly. Kim held the container under his parka, hoping to increase the pressure by warming the gas.

"Five minutes."

The balloon was now taking form. Chun was tightening the various equipment bags to their flight-straps and rings.

"Four minutes."

Finally the balloon was tugging at the line. Kim checked the meter on the gas container. A little more. The balloon had to have the lift necessary to rise to at least four hundred feet.

"Three minutes, Frank."

"Roger." Kim let the balloon go, and felt the nylon line pay out increasingly faster. He could hear the sound of engines in the distance. As the infrared signal lights hit his hands, he turned them on. The line was suddenly taut. Both men felt a bobbing tug at the back of their suits.

"Thirty seconds, Frank."

Kim nodded in the dark. "Never have gotten used to this fucker. It leaves my balls on the ground every time."

Suddenly, the MC-130E Combat Talon popped up over the plateau, rising to about three hundred feet. A V probe on the nose of the four-engined plane snagged the nylon line between the two signal lights, simultaneously cutting loose the balloon. Kim and Chun were snapped up from the ground and in less than five seconds were being towed behind the airplane at 125 miles per hour. In another few seconds the nylon line had been snared by a winch at the aft of the MC-130E. It took less than a minute to pull Kim and Chun aboard over the rear cargo ramp.

The Combat Talon dropped back to an escape altitude of less than two hundred feet. In the cargo bay, lit only by dim red lamps, four U.S. Air Force crewmen trained shotguns on Kim and Chun until Chun waved a recognition signal by forming a T with his hands.

"Shit, fellas, it's just us. Is this any way to treat a couple of hitchhikers?"

Gifan, Iran

Mohammed Riza Pahlavi, Shah of Iran, owed his seat on the Peacock Throne to the Central Intelligence Agency. It had been CIA in 1953 that pulled off the coup d'etat against the increasingly left-leaning Premier Mosaddegh, who threatened to deliver Iran into the hands of the Tudeh, Iran's Moscow-dominated Communist Party.

Because of his gratitude, the Shah permitted the Americans to build electronic listening stations in the wild and remote mountains of northeastern Iran. There, huge parabolic antennas easily captured every detail of Soviet ICBM flights launched from the vast Tyuratam test center, seven hundred miles away. In addition to monitoring the early portions of missile flight trajectories, the American technicians at the sites put airborne and ground sensors and radars on the alert in Alaska and the northern Pacific, so that the splashdown of the Soviet-test warheads could be observed as they landed just off the Kamchatka Peninsula.

As James Earl Carter was being sworn in as the thirty-ninth President of the United States, the Soviet Union launched an experimental modification of the giant ninety-three-foot missile the Americans called the SS-18. Mod-4, as it was to become known, astounded the intelligence community. When the Americans analyzed the data from the Gifan station, they found that the Mod-4 had carried ten warheads. Minute Man III, the most modern American ICBM, carried only three.

Even more chilling were the results from the impact area: each warhead landed less than a hundred meters from its intended target. Had the targets been American missile silos, the missiles within would have been destroyed.

In that instant the balance of terror changed between the superpowers. Before Mod-4, Soviet missiles were only accurate enough to hit large targets, such as America's sprawling cities. But the Kremlin threat to incinerate American cities was not credible. The Soviets knew—as, obviously, did the Americans—that the Minute Man missiles could ride out any Soviet attack. This deadly force, sheltered in invulnerable silos in the American midwest, could vaporize Russia if the Soviets were ever so foolish as to launch first.

The Mod-4 changed all this. Mod-4 meant that Americans no longer could absorb a Russian surprise attack and still have the means to destroy the Soviet Union. Now, a surprise attack was credible. Now, the leading edge of a Soviet missile attack could obliterate the Minuteman force. Then, with their remaining missiles, the Soviets could threaten destruction of America's cities without fear of reprisal.

Washington, D.C.

While Joseph Chun and Frank Kim were busy in North Korea, David Cummings slouched in the tattered overstuffed chair that had been his nest for the past ten years. Around him were cardboard boxes stuffed with clippings, books, and memoranda. In retrospect it seemed truly remarkable to him just how many hours he'd spent in that chair, talking with visitors, scribbling onto a yellow legal pad into the night, sometimes seeing the sun come up over the crenellated towers of the Smithsonian castle.

Cummings was tall and slender, with thick brown hair, blue eyes, and a pale complexion. There was an intellectual arrogance about him, inherited from his father, a professor of philosophy at Notre Dame, and his mother, an accomplished Swedish pianist who'd given up the concert stage for marriage. He'd done well at Harvard. In spite of an aversion to sports and a 4.0 average, he'd been editor of the *Crimson* and he was not unpopular with his classmates, something that always seemed remarkable to Cummings.

That morning he'd realized that it was thirteen years to the day since he'd arrived in Saigon to be the special assistant to Maxwell Taylor, the American ambassador.

"You Americans want to save us from Marxism," Pham Ngoc Thao had argued on the terrace bar at the Continental Palace, "but we can't afford your democracy. You have people you call poor who make political statements not by sacrificing themselves, but by blocking highways with their cars. Even your progressive newspapers don't recognize the irony! A nation whose poor own automobiles! Yet you claim to know what is best for a society whose wealth has been ravaged by Western imperialism for centuries. You, who stood by when we were overrun by the Japanese and who helped the French return to empire—you now want to 'save' us from Ho Chi Minh, who is first a Vietnamese nationalist, and only incidentally a Marxist."

Cummings continued meeting with Thao, who introduced him to others. And so, when his tour in Viet Nam was finished, he resigned from the State Department and accepted a fellowship offered by the Foundation for International Relations. There, he contributed to the debate in opposition to the American war in Southeast Asia. He forged intellectual links with progressive factions in Hanoi and Moscow—people of compassion who shared with him his opposition to the "might is right" elements that plagued the governments of Viet Nam, Russia, and America.

He wrote about America and Asia. At the World Peace Council's Vienna conference to assess the effects of the recent end to the Viet Nam War, old friends encouraged him to explore the parallels between South Viet Nam and South Korea. This led him to publish in the summer of 1975 an article in which he outlined the merits of withdrawing American forces from Korea.

The response was heartening. Senator George McGovern called South Korea's President Park Chung Hee a "disreputable tyrant," warning that American troops in Korea "could trip this generation into another wrong war in another wrong place at another wrong time." Congressman Stephen Solarz, Democrat of Brooklyn, joined in: "We ought not to be involved in a situation where we are likely to get involved in military conflict on behalf of repressive regimes such as we did in Viet Nam."

But the most gratifying response had come from Plains, Georgia. Cummings had gone there little over a year ago to become an advisor to the Carter campaign, and tomorrow he would be sworn in as the Assistant Secretary of State for East Asia.

Sakata, Japan

"Gotcha, you bastard." Specialist Seventh Class Kenneth Watanabe had been searching the side-lobe frequencies of the North Korean transmitter at Kosan for thirteen hours straight and had nearly given into the urge to start smoking again. He had reprogrammed the automatic scanner for the twenty-third time, then, on the first stop, he'd made the hit.

Major Gradison Finch rolled a chair up beside Watanabe and put on a spare headset. "Tape on?"

Watanabe nodded.

In the shed outside the Kosan radio station, Chun's induction tap was working flawlessly. Picking up the uncoded messages and conversations on the cable, it then fed them out the antenna whenever the shortwave radio transmitted its messages. The pirated information rode a wavelength slightly different from that broadcast by the transmitter. Watanabe had found the proverbial needle in an electronic haystack.

Finch listened intently for several minutes. Then, thumbing through a code-word list prepared by NSA, he officially christened the new source "Algernon."

All of this was as yet unknown by the North Koreans

manning the Kosan radio site and by the commander of the 280th Commando Brigade and his Soviet advisors.

Alexandria, Virginia

Susan Forbes put down her chopsticks and watched John Freeman refill his glass. "If East Wind is the best Vietnamese restaurant in the world, why do they have a bartender named Riley?"

Freeman laughed. "It has to do with Khai's view of Americans. He thinks that even Americans who like Vietnamese food want an Irishman pouring the whiskey."

To Freeman, East Wind was a crystalline echo of Viet Nam; not his recollections of the war, but the warm memories of a people and a countryside that could match any in the world for variety and beauty. At East Wind he saw others he knew but had never met. He recognized them because they came to the restaurant for the same reason he returned again and again: to touch that which had been somehow important in his life. It'd been much the same in France, where he'd seen veterans, particularly the *paras*, revisiting their memories of Indochina, sitting at Vietnamese restaurants in Paris and Marseilles, eating *chai giao* and bowls of *pho*, the soup of Hanoi. And, as usual, the French had given the wistful but powerful attachment to Viet Nam a proper and descriptive name. *Le mal jaune*: the yellow fever.

"How long were you there?" Susan Forbes asked, breaking into his revery.

"Just over six years. Spent some time in Laos with the White Star training teams. Special forces. Then to Viet Nam just before the coup against Diem. Left in 'sixty-five. Came to the States, to Fort Bragg. Then back for two more years—this time to SOG. They called it 'Studies and Observations Group,' but that was just a cover. We had the charter for covert operations into North Viet Nam, Laos, and Cambodia."

Susan Forbes looked at him for a time. "You invested

a lot of yourself there. It must have been hard to watch it—the end of it."

John Freeman pushed his rice bowl toward the center of the table. For a moment he stared at the Citadel mural on the wall behind her, then focused on her. "Some of us had hopes for South Viet Nam. For its people. It was their war. We didn't want to fight it for them. We only wanted to help them win. We—some of us—believed the American Revolution was a helluva better model for the Vietnamese than the Russian one. If our ideas—our ideals—could have gotten through to the Vietnamese people, we thought they'd have something worth fighting for; that they could hold off the North Vietnamese without us. But it turned out wrong, and the country became a playground for the American generals."

He took a swallow of beer. "I never cared for the generals. Most of them only wanted to get their tickets punched so they could move up the ladder. But our troops and junior officers were magnificent. I saw the Marines at Khe Sanh and the 101st at Hamburger Hill. We had the best soldiers in the world.

"The fighting was only a small part of the war, though. I don't think we ever understood that. The rest was politics. Politics in the villages, politics in Saigon. The bitter thing is that we were winning the political wars in the villages, and even in Saigon, but we ended up losing in Washington. Even after the American troops left, Congress wanted the war over. They didn't care who won. We were never able to convince the American people that the South could survive, or that its survival even mattered. We pulled the plug on South Viet Nam, and now we're out to do the same in Korea."

Susan Forbes pretended a sudden interest in dessert. They looked at the menu and ordered. She leaned forward across the table. "You promised something about Eleanor Trowbridge."

John Freeman smiled, grateful for the change in subject. "She's a real piece of work. Early in the Second World War she joined the OSS, and stayed until it was disbanded in 1945. The entire time was spent working on

East Asia. After the war she married a Foreign Service officer who got called to active duty—Marines, I think it was—to serve in Korea. He was killed. About the same time, she was offered a job in the Agency, and she's been there ever since."

"How is it, working for her?"

"She doesn't hover over me. She trusts me to know what I don't know."

"Don't know?"

John Freeman leaned forward, taken with her eyes. "The most dangerous thing is not to know your own ignorance. Knowing what you don't know is more important than knowing what you do know. We'd have fewer wars and other assorted miseries if we knew more about our ignorance. I believe Eleanor thinks I have a pretty good understanding of what I don't know."

John Freeman paused to adjust his beer glass more precisely on some invisible line on the table, then laughed. "She's got her faults. Gets wrapped up in something and she loses track of what's going on around her. She has absolutely no sense of direction. Can't even drive a car. She's always thinking about something other than how to get to someplace. Hell, she got lost in the cafeteria once. Kept wandering around the damn tables, going on about New Zealand's energy problems. When she snapped out of it, she'd forgotten she'd eaten once, went through the line and then wondered why she didn't have any appetite. I thought she'd just gone back for seconds."

"Absentminded?"

"No, just very intense. Tenacious. She's the kind who'll gut it out, stick to something even when there aren't going to be any medals. I've seen some pretty damn good combat leaders, guys you want to have with you in hard times. She could match any of them.

"How about you? How'd you end up as the Free World's expert on the North Korean military?"

"Oh, I don't know—it certainly wasn't planned. Like most people, I suppose, I got here—wherever that is—by a series of flukes."

John Freeman listened as she told him of a childhood

in Maine, college at Mount Holyoke, and the Ph.D. in Asian studies at the University of Kansas. "I fell in love with one of my professors. An enthusiast for women's liberation. After we got married, I found he wasn't so taken with the idea in his own home. We didn't fight very well. Instead of clearing the air between us, each argument only made things worse. We—" She shook herself out of the memory of the self-destructive spiral into the days and weeks of ever-growing anger, of each lying in wait for the opportunity to hurt the other. "We got a divorce. I didn't want to stay in Kansas. I'd kept the telephone number of a DIA recruiter who'd visited the campus, and so I called him."

"Where is he now—your former husband?"

"Probably screwing gullible coeds in Lawrence and collecting rejection slips from *The Nation*." She looked at her watch. "Could you walk me to my car? I've got an early morning tomorrow."

John Freeman paid up and said good-bye to Khai and Riley. As he helped Susan into her coat, the smell of perfume in her hair stirred him.

Outside, the sidewalks were still slushy from the last snow of February. He took her arm and she leaned into him.

"You feel good," he whispered.

She gave him a disarming laugh and took a small step away. "Um, and you were there drinking an hour before I came. Here's my car."

She bent forward and kissed him, a quick, light brush of lips. "Good night, John. I had a great time. I'd like to see you again. I'll call."

Moscow

"They spend the first few minutes getting acquainted," Kiktev explained. "They discuss cooperation between Cummings's office and CIA elements responsible for Asian intelligence. There is some talk about American prisoners still remaining in Viet Nam and—"

Yuri Andropov interrupted. "Where were they meeting?"

"In Cummings's home. In the library after dinner. We have distributed complete transcripts to the First and Sixth Departments."

"And Service A?"

"Especially our friends in *dezinformatsia*, Comrade Andropov."

"What do we have here?" Andropov pointed to the small tape recorder Kiktev put on the desk.

"A segment of their conversation in which Cummings tells Franks of the objectives regarding Korea. The first voice is Cummings's." Kiktev punched a button on the machine.

CUMMINGS: Our withdrawal from South Korea is the centerpiece of the President's new policy in the Third World. We've tried too long now to hold back the tide—the course of history in the Third World. We act as if the world's a stage for our own little morality play—the East-West confrontation. Us verses the Russians. We ignore the struggle for basic human needs, for marginal increases in the standard of living. We don't really appreciate how expensive our kind of government is and how few nations can pay that kind of price when they have people starving in the streets. If they have to turn to a Marxist form of government in order to ease hunger and wipe out illiteracy, it isn't the end for us.

Andropov sighed in exasperation. "My ass, how much more of this drivel—"

"It's coming up now."

FRANKS: There're a helluva lot of people out there who don't like the withdrawal business at all. Nobody on the Joint Chiefs . . .
CUMMINGS: No slight intended, Ros, but no one in this administration gives a shit about the JCS or

any of those boobs at the Pentagon. They got their asses kicked out of Viet Nam by a ragtag army of peasants because they insisted on backing every comic-opera general who came out on top of the weekly coups in Saigon. Who's going to listen to the Westmorelands and that bunch now? Carter can handle them. More than anything else, they worry about their perks and promotions. If Carter says "shit," they'll ask, "how high."

FRANKS: There's the media . . .

CUMMINGS: Ros, Ros. You spent too much time flying planes. Around here and New York, most of the media people see Korea as another Viet Nam. Do you really think Cronkite is going to climb into his pulpit to sell the great unwashed the notion that good old Korea is worth fighting for?

FRANKS: But there're still concerns . . .

CUMMINGS: If we do it right, those concerns will go away. The President will have a free hand to implement a truly enlightened and progressive foreign policy for this country for the first time since World War Two.

Seeing a frown beginning on Andropov's face, Kiktev waved a cautionary hand. "And listen to this, Comrade Andropov."

CUMMINGS: . . . thing we have to do is show that the government in Seoul isn't worth the blood of the American boys. The Koreans have a lousy record in human rights, and we're going to make sure the people in this country are aware of it. Some of the dissidents talk about—there's something about secret work on nuclear weapons. That's one your people could check into, instead of worrying about the great Commie threat.

Kiktev switched off the machine. "There's more, but nothing new."

"A splendid start, Comrade Kiktev. And be certain to pass my appreciation to Service A. They're doing very well with our man Cummings."

"He's not 'our man,' Comrade Andropov."

"Close enough, Vasili Petrovich. Close enough."

Langley, Virginia

Roswell Franks was furious. When he'd first read the minutes, he couldn't believe his eyes. Reading them again didn't help matters. He'd suspected he was getting into a real rats' nest. But he never thought it was this bad.

His intercom chimed. "General, Mr. Cabot's here."

Andrew Putnam Cabot was Roswell Franks's number two—Deputy Director of CIA. Franks was fuming. Goddamn Andrew Cabot. Bastard was always so superior. That New England crap about speaking only to God. Or was that the goddamn Lodges? It irked Franks, and secretly intimidated him, to learn that Cabot had been highly decorated in World War II. But Cabot was still a damn civilian—true military accomplishment was more than winning medals. The St. Grotelsex crowd—the Ivy League dabblers and pipe-smoking hobbyists—the Donovan and Dulles recruits, had virtually owned the Agency since it was formed. And look at the mess they'd made of it.

Andrew Cabot never had been a candidate for an Exeter recruiting poster. Short and badly coordinated, athletic competence embarrassingly eluded him. He'd barely gotten through infantry officer training at Fort Benning. That he'd led a platoon, then later a company, virtually intact through the savage fighting near Bastogne, remained a source of secret pride. That he had been singled out as heroic, he found absolutely astonishing, so he chalked off that part of the whole affair as the need for the Army to burnish its image.

Franks pretended to study a memo, letting Cabot stand in front of his desk. Then, looking up, he was momentarily disconcerted by the off angle of Cabot's line of sight.

With all the money he must have, Franks thought, you think he'd get something better than a government-issue glass eye. "Sit down, Cabot. I'll get right to the point. I was reading the minutes of the December NFIB meeting. I'd like an explanation of Pergola."

The little man thought, his forehead wrinkled. "That was the meeting I chaired in Bush's absence." He pursed his lips, hesitated, then went on. "Operation Pergola gave us a source we call Algernon," he explained with slow care. "We'd been working on the details of Pergola for several months after getting conceptual approval. As the minutes indicate, it was a joint operation run by NSA, DOD, and us. We furnished the in-and-out team, DOD provided the transportation, and NSA took over the operations once our people did the job."

"The job. What was the job, specifically?"

"To tap the central trunk lines of North Korean forces along the Demilitarized Zone. From satellite photography and a defector report we identified a good place to plant the tap. Near Kosan. We—DOD, that is—parachuted two of our people into North Korea. They tapped the cables and the Air Force got them out."

"Just like that?"

Cabot gave a small, proud smile. A smile a watchmaker might give to a marveling customer. "Just like that. Of course, the operation took all kinds of planning, and obviously something could have gone—"

"No, goddamnit." Franks was leaning forward over his desk. His face flushed with rage, he began the chin thrusts. "I mean you *approved* a hare-brained stunt. Just like that. What did you people expect to gain from this—this stupidity?"

Cabot recoiled in shock. "We gained what we expected to gain, Mr. Director. And more." Cabot uncrossed his legs. He sat bolt upright, tense in the chair, fists poised on his thighs. "We now have a source that is giving us insights into the day-to-day operations of the North Korean Army. Information that is an order of magnitude improvement over anything we've ever had before in terms of timeliness, pertinence, and reliability. It is pure gold."

"Why do we have to have that kind of information? Why run the risk?"

"First, there's the problem that North Korea is so tightly sealed that China and the Soviet Union look like open societies. From what we can tell, we don't think that either the Chinese or the Russians know much about what's happening outside their missions in Pyongyang and some of their scattered military advisory teams that're billeted with the North Korean military. Add to this that Kim Il-Sung has never given up hope of unifying the country under his rule. Then look at the geography: all Kim has to do is grab Seoul and the South would probably crumble—and Seoul's only thirty miles from the DMZ, a short run down the Chorwon corridor."

Cabot saw Franks tilt his head in impatience, eyes darting, hands restless. He hurried on. "If we have warning of a North Korean attack, we have a chance—a slim one—of holding on. No warning, it's all over. And that's where Algernon comes in. It's a prime source for our indications-and-warning analysts. Any North Korean attack would include the 280th, and if that unit sneezes, we know about it."

Cabot knew now that Franks wasn't listening. "There's something else. Perhaps even more serious than the warning problem. We're concerned that there may be a major realignment going on in the North. In the past, Pyongyang has been careful to balance off the Chinese against the Soviets. But now some of us think that the Soviets may—"

Franks suddenly stood up behind the desk, looking down at Cabot. "Don't give me that 'Russians are coming' crap. I know the problem here. You people just can't stand the idea that secrets might exist somewhere that you don't know about. It's the getting to those secrets that turns you people on. It's all a magnificent game for you people, and the Agency's your playground."

Cabot was now standing, angry, demanding. "Who are 'you people,' Mr. Director?"

"You northeastern establishment types, that's who. You're like Dean Acheson—you believe God should have had your advice when he created the universe. Well, that's over. It's over at DOD and State, and it's certainly over here."

Cabot found himself taking refuge in the inconsequential. Acheson hadn't said that. It was Acheson quoting Alfonso the Wise. God protect the Republic from generals who read voraciously but poorly. Annoyed at himself, he raised his voice to Franks. "I suppose, then, you want my resignation."

"When I want your resignation," Franks snapped, "I'll damn well ask for it. As my deputy you're to see to the internal workings around here, and I'm going to make certain you do just that."

"I can't believe it, Lew, the whole thing caught me flat-footed."

Getting back to his office, Cabot called Parsons, who suggested meeting downstairs in his office, rather than in Cabot's, which shared the same seventh-floor suite with Franks. When Cabot had been Director of Operations, he'd seen to Parsons's safe transfer from Kuala Lumpur after the fuss with the Australian Intelligence Service. In spite of the "Malaysian mess," as wags in DDO referred to it, Cabot valued Parsons for his experience and forthrightness.

"Coffee?" Parsons refilled his mug from the Silex.

"Thanks." Cabot, eyes closed, kneaded the back of his neck. "I don't think it was Pergola so much—the specific operation. Though he's not going to be a Director who's much for that kind of thing. It was that something was done without him controlling it."

"Shit, Froggy, he hadn't gotten through the Senate confirmation when those guys went in. You were still the acting Director."

"It wasn't that. It wasn't a matter of protocol. It's theology." Noticing Parsons's lifted eyebrow, Cabot explained. "We aren't dealing with facts. Realpolitik is out the window. Government now trades in emotion, passion, and articles of faith.

"You offered to resign."

Cabot said nothing, but looked at the floor, embarrassed. Then he looked up. "Yes. But to tell you the truth, Lew, I don't feel all that noble. I found myself worried that he'd accept. I don't know what in hell I would have done. Two of the kids are still in school. My mother's living with Sally and me. We don't have any money. The Agency retirement is all I have, and that wouldn't stretch very far. Not much of a market out there for old spies."

"Why does he want you to stay on?"

"Don't know exactly. I suspect, though, he's got some dirty business in mind and he wants to have an insider front for him."

"Would you stay, then?"

Cabot rubbed the scar tissue that surrounded the socket where his right eye had been. "I don't know, Lew. It bothers me that I worry so about the money. Whatever happened to the principled resignation in American government? Instead, we've developed the convenient rationale that one can be more effective staying on to work from the inside. God, Lew, what happens to courage? Do you just get so much given to you? I think, sometimes, I've used my share up. Used it all up just in getting here."

TOP SECRET
PREDIS/WHITE

Copy 1 of 2
copies

CENTRAL INTELLIGENCE AGENCY
Office of the Director
Washington, D.C. 20505

17 March 1977

The President
The White House
Washington, D.C. 20500

Dear Mr. President:

Shortly after I was sworn in as Director, you urged that I be bold in my plans to restructure the

Intelligence Community. This personal note to you outlines my first steps in that planning process and the reasons for those steps.

From my perspective, I cannot but help agree with Senator Church and others who have characterized the Agency as a "rogue elephant." Without a firm hand at the tiller, CIA could well thwart the foreign policy goals of your administration.

My initial actions will gain control of the "elephant." Specifically, this means reining in the Directorate of Operations. It was the DDO that led John Kennedy down the primrose path that ended at the Bay of Pigs. Of all the organizations within what we call the Intelligence Community, the DDO is potentially the most dangerous. It is the DDO that recruits, trains, and directs human agents—spies. It is the DDO that embarks on "special operations" such as the well-publicized fiasco wherein they wanted to make Castro's beard fall out by use of a doctored footpowder.

We can establish order within the DDO by reducing the size of the organization. I have consulted with personnel experts I have brought in from outside the Agency, and I am confident that we can safely eliminate as many as 800 people. Included, of course, will be those who have caused the great bulk of the problems the Agency has encountered in the past.

I shall keep you informed on a daily basis as to the details of this operation.

Very respectfully,
Roswell Franks
General, United States Air Force
Director of Central Intelligence

Moscow

Yuri Andropov read the letter again and swiveled around. "Well?"

Kiktev pointed to the letter in Andropov's hand. "I first thought it was a Service A practical joke, a forgery. But it's real."

"This . . . this Franks person . . . He's serious about getting rid of almost a thousand of their operations people?"

"The White House believes that CIA is contrary to what it defines as 'American values.'" Kiktev smiled slyly, putting irony into the phrase. "The new President, Carter, appears to be in search of some kind of international morality. At any rate, the practical consequences of this letter could be profound."

"Are you certain of its authenticity?"

Kiktev nodded emphatically. "General Franks already has enemies in the White House who find it satisfying to embarrass him whenever possible."

"And so they give us things like this?" Yuri Andropov waved the letter in his hand.

"And so they give things like that to friends of ours," amended Kiktev.

Seoul, Republic of Korea

The only Caucasian, John Freeman arrived from Tokyo on a Korean Air Lines 747 packed with Japanese men in shiny polyester suits, most of them clutching cardboard carryons. "Cognac," the Korean steward had told him. "They come to Seoul for the weekend. For the whores. The cheap bastards don't buy much else Korean—they even bring their own liquor."

Waving his burgundy official passport, he passed unhindered through customs at Kimpo, where most of his Japanese fellow passengers had been herded together, destined to be very thoroughly gone over by the grim Koreans on duty. Seoul Station had sent a driver, and after a knuckle-whitening ride through horrendous traffic, Freeman checked in at his hotel and slept the rest of the day.

Mark Douglas had been Chief of Station in Seoul for three years. For twenty-three years he'd worked up the Directorate of Operations ladder, successfully avoiding more than a year or two at Langley, spending the rest in Northeast Asia. Slightly over six feet, he stood ramrod straight, his thin, silver hair topping a long face whose fair skin was slightly mottled with a reddish undertone.

"Headquarters said you were here for an orientation. We have a few changes to the itinerary we sent back. Nothing major. Marty—our ops officer—will explain them to you. I'll show you around the station."

CIA's Seoul Station took up two floors of the American embassy, a sealed-off suite that contained its own cryptographic and communications facility, offices, and a special supply room. Douglas led him down a short windowless corridor whose doors were closed, each requiring punching up a cipher lock to enter.

Douglas stopped by one door, manipulated the buttons on the lock, and entered. A tall woman, a Nordic-featured blonde, was standing by a filing cabinet.

"Marty, this is Colonel Freeman. Marty Horton's our operations specialist. She's got responsibility for your itinerary."

Marty Horton fished out a single sheet of paper, acknowledging Freeman with a slight nod. "No changes since yesterday, Mark. He's still on for the DMZ tour in an hour and General Bronowski tomorrow."

Douglas handed Freeman the revised itinerary, which was brief to the point of cryptic. Three days. All times used the military twenty-four-hour clock. Each day began and ended at Seoul Station.

"Evening events aren't on there," Douglas said. "Dinner at my house tonight. Some of the KCIA analysts.

You don't have plans?" Without waiting for a reply, he turned and went out into the corridor.

Freeman had to rush to catch up. He followed Douglas to the end of the corridor and down a metal spiral staircase. At the foot of the staircase Douglas worked another cipher lock. They passed through the door into a small anteroom. Douglas shut and locked the door they'd come through, then turned, and taking a card from his billfold, inserted it in a slot near a door covered with copper sheeting. After four or five seconds relays clicked and Douglas pulled the door open.

"Step up." The room was small and designed to provide a haven for the most sensitive conversations. A room within a room, its walls, ceiling, and floor were separated from the original structure of the building. Douglas turned switches on a panel set into the table and waited for the amber lights to signal that the monitoring devices that would pick up any attempt at electronic snooping were working.

"Sit down, Colonel. Take off your jacket. This place gets warm."

The furniture consisted of a large wooden conference table and seven unupholstered chairs. Douglas took one and waved Freeman to the adjoining chair. "Lew Parsons sent a personal message. Said you were all right."

Freeman stiffened. "That was good of him. I'm glad I've passed muster."

For the first time, Douglas smiled. "Lew also said you could be prickly. I guess we are a closed fraternity in DDO. Some of it's intentional. Most of it just goes with the job. There're the purge rumors—makes us even more paranoid."

Freeman, now relaxed, nodded in agreement. "There's more and more talk of it at Headquarters. Everyone's looking over their shoulders. It's as if the DCI has declared war on his own people—that the Soviets don't exist." Freeman changed the subject and asked about the South Korean reaction to the American retaliation for the DMZ killings.

Douglas frowned. "Well, it didn't exactly stand out as

big-stick diplomacy. You'll get a chance to talk to some Korean analysts tonight at dinner, but my counterpart at KCIA was angry. He told me that the North Koreans had killed two American officers in the same way the peasants butcher dogs before cooking them. They beat them to death. Makes them more tender. 'They kill your officers like dogs,' he said, 'and you Americans cut down a tree.'"

"And the withdrawal . . ."

"They see it as part of the same piece. American loss of will. The South Koreans were our only friends who sent sizable numbers of troops to help us in Viet Nam. Divisions. They fought well. A lot of them died. They were willing partners in the fighting—and the dying—but they feel that we trapped them into being a party to the sellout there. And now we're getting ready to do it to them here. The White House and State are trying to cloak the withdrawal in all kinds of diplomatic fluff, but in the end, it's cut and run. The ROK's know it. The Japanese know it. And you better believe Kim Il-Sung knows it."

"And the Russians."

"The Russians. Yes. Always the Russians. Parsons said you were looking into that."

"You know about the commando training camps. We got the tip-off from the photography of the truck parks. Algernon is telling us a lot about that—the relationship between the Soviet *spetznaz* and the North Korean commandos. But we're also coming on to some significant changes in their other military units. We're seeking tank battalions we never knew existed—new stuff. All that'll be in the estimate. We're also doing retrospective analysis. It's slow work, going back through the old photography and sigint tapes, but we think we can find out just when the military buildup began. And there had to be a reason for it. But it's hard to see this happening without help from either Peking or Moscow. The betting is that it's Moscow."

The two talked in the tiny room for another twenty or so minutes before Douglas looked at his watch and stood up. At the elevator the Chief of Station hesitated. "I haven't gotten anything from Headquarters, but the Ambassador

here has been asking me about collecting against the
ROK's."

"Collecting?"

"Yeah. State seems to believe that our friends here
may want to join the nuclear club."

Freeman went through the usual credentials check at
the compound gate. A Korean military policeman in an
impeccable uniform and spit-shined boots escorted him in
silence down corridors whose polished floors and oiled
hardwood paneling spoke of years of comfortable occupa-
tion by the United States Forces, Korea. They passed a
large double door with a gleaming brass plaque identifying
it as the offices of the Chief of Staff. The MP continued
down the corridor, then stopped and knocked at a third
door which had no markings.

No matter how often Freeman had seen him,
Bronowski created the same impression. He wants to hit
something, Freeman thought. Or get hit. It didn't seem to
matter as long as there was a fight and Jack Bronowski could
get in on it. He was an endangered species: an American
who still wore a flat-top haircut. His face, framed by two jug
ears, seemed to have been repeatedly broken and the
pieces carelessly reassembled. Freeman's eyes were drawn
to the master parachutist's badge on Bronowski's chest.
Three small bronze stars were set into the gleaming silver,
each signifying a parachute jump in combat. The first,
Freeman knew, was from World War II. Not with the
airborne divisions, the 82nd or the 101st. But with the
OSS, parachuting into German-occupied France with a
Jedburgh team, months before D-Day.

Bronowski waved his hand at the room. "Nice thing
about being a decrepit desk jockey here. At the Pentagon
they'd have me sharing something like this with four other
guys."

"I think they do a little better than that for major
generals. The stars look good on you, sir."

"None of this 'sir' shit, John." Then, with a little boy's
mischievous grin, Bronowski turned to his left, then right,

glancing at the stars on his shoulders. "It's always a surprise, Johnny. That they made me a general. They could as easily have court-martialed me any number of times." He slapped Freeman's bicep. "Hell, I only joined the Army to soldier. The fun went out of it when they made me a general." Bronowski gestured to a chair. "Sit, John. Goddamn, it's good to see you."

An aide brought a light lunch. They talked about Viet Nam, when Freeman had served in SOG under Bronowski, who was then a colonel; about the disastrous reconnaissance mission that had ended Freeman's service in Special Forces. And of Bronowski in Korea; how the South Korean Army was no match for the North; and how President Park Chung Hee had the Blue House in an uproar, searching for a way to reverse the Carter troop withdrawal. Freeman outlined the estimate and suspicions of growing Soviet involvement. He told Bronowski of the dinner the previous night at Douglas's and of the fear and anger of the Korean intelligence officers over the Carter intention to leave them to face Kim Il-Sung alone.

"Damnit, John, you people back there have got to do something. The Russians have us by the balls. We're not up for another war, but we can't afford another retreat." Bronowski hit his thigh with a clenched fist. "They've got to be stopped."

Bronowski got up from the chair, moving slowly, stiff from sitting so long. He stood looking at the map on one wall of his office.

"I'm an old man, John. I don't know when it happened. It seemed that years went by and nothing changed. Then, all of a sudden, one day . . ." Bronowski shook his head free of the thought, then continued. "There used to be a brightness about living, Johnny. Great things needed tending to. And I was a part of all that.

"But now . . . now I look around and it's all gone. Suddenly all the expectations have disappeared. There used to be giants. Roosevelt, Churchill . . .

"I took part in great things once, things that changed the course of history. We stood up against those who would enslave us, John. And we beat the bastards. But those days are gone."

He turned and stared at Freeman. "Sometimes . . . sometimes, sitting at this damned desk, I fall asleep over the goddamn papers they send to keep me busy."

Freeman got up to leave. He wanted to touch Bronowski. To say something. It was something he couldn't do. That he knew he'd never do. He walked to the door.

"John." Bronowski's back was toward him as he stared at a wall map.

"Yes, sir?"

"John, there's a need for us." Bronowski swiveled around, his chair creaking angrily. His eyes flashed at Freeman. "For people like you and me. The others, they look at us and sneer. They're partly right, you know. We gravitate to the unknown side of things because we have to go into the fire and come out again, cleansed and pure.

"They need us. But they deny it. They always deny it. They believe all that's needed to ensure peace is understanding. They believe it's all a communications problem, you see. People like you and me, John, we get in the way of fellowship with the well-meaning barbarians in the Kremlin. They thought that way in the thirties about Adolph Hitler. They screwed that one up to a fare-thee-well, then turned it over to us. And we bled for their stupidity. How we bled."

Again John Freeman felt the urge to throw an arm over Bronowski's shoulder, but the stocky general was now lost to him. His eyes shifted to the mid-distance, remembering times of greater clarity. Freeman gave a slow, informal salute. "Good-bye, sir."

Chapter 3

John Freeman surveyed the remains of curried lamb and *aushak*, then looked at Susan Forbes. "After Korea, my stomach thought it was coming back to something more placid." He raised his hands. "Hot, but good." The return trip from Korea had been tiring, and he had been avoiding the tasks of unpacking and sorting through a stack of accumulated mail when she called. He'd been tempted to beg off her invitation to dinner, but was suddenly seized by a powerful desire to see her.

He dipped a *chapati* bread chip in the chutney and outlined Douglas's concern about mounting an espionage operation against the South Koreans.

She nodded, the light giving a warm sheen to her hair. "It seems there's more in the papers about South Korea. While you were gone, the Justice Department started a probe of Seoul and its relations with Congress. The newspapers are already calling it Korea-Gate."

Freeman sipped his beer. "The White House knows what it's doing. That kind of thing fires a shot across Congress's bows. If Justice can turn up a couple of congressmen on the take, the South Koreans become pariahs. Nobody on the Hill will come to Seoul's defense after that. The folks back home might get the impression that their guy's also on the take." He speared another sliver of lamb. "How's the analysis coming along?"

"It looks like the truck-park changes took place some-time after 1973. If we can come up with more photography, we can get a better fix on the date. Peter Smith has been making progress on the tank and artillery counts. Eleanor's called a meeting for Tuesday."

The waiter brought the check.

"Mine." Susan handed over a credit card.

Returning, the waiter gave Freeman Susan's credit card along with the slip to sign.

She sighed and reached for the credit card and check. "They always do that. Women can vote but we're not supposed to pay for dinner."

"Buy fellas dinner often, do you?"

She smiled. "Not many. Not often. Let's go."

Susan Forbes lived in the Old Town section of Alex-andria. A plaque near the front door said the house had been built during George Washington's days at Mount Vernon, just a few miles south.

"There's beer in the refrigerator," she said.

"Who's this?" Freeman pointed at a huge animal making its way past Susan.

"John Freeman, meet Bandit. He's been with me for more than fifteen years. He's part Siamese."

"And part German shepherd? That's the biggest cat I've ever seen."

Bandit paused, looked Freeman up and down, then judging the new human to be inconsequential to the serious business of cats, continued on toward his bowl in the kitchen.

She showed him her home. The narrow three-story row house was furnished with period antiques, the walls covered in a small print Colonial paper. Plastered surfaces were painted an off-white, and the floors were well-waxed wide-board pine. He finished his beer as they returned to the living room. He glanced at his watch, came close and kissed her softly. "Better be going. I'm beginning to drag."

She put her arms around him and kissed him back. Pulling away, she stared at him with wide eyes and a crooked grin, still holding him tightly. His hands had dropped to her hips. "I'm glad you're here, John, and I'm glad I called you."

"Are you awake?" she whispered in the dark.

In response he moved closer, bringing her musky warmth along the length of him, cupping a breast in his hand and muttering in her ear.

"What did you say?" she asked.

"I think my very brains have been fucked out."

Her finger traced the puckered scar on his belly. "Tell me about it."

He was silent until she began to wonder if he'd answer. Finally, "We were in a small camp near the Laotian border. It was a launch site for long-range patrols into Laos and up the Ho Chi Minh trail." He shifted, rolling onto his back to stare at the ceiling. "They hit us just at dark. I didn't realize it, but I got some shrapnel in my stomach, a tiny splinter. They were too much for us, and the launch site hadn't been built as a defensive position. We slipped out and made it down into the valley. We dodged them for two days. I got peritonitis. One of our choppers spotted us on the third day."

"When was this?"

"Nine years ago. Nine years ago this month. Funny how it seems like yesterday, yet it was years ago." He fell silent.

She moved up against him. Her head was now on his shoulder, lips and teeth nibbling at his neck. She began fondling him lovingly, insistently, until he responded.

"You know," she whispered, "you're still a very smart guy."

Seoul, Republic of Korea

Mark Douglas had been summoned by Thomas Graves Fyleman, the American ambassador to the Republic of Korea. Fyleman was seated in an overstuffed reading chair.

To his right on a sofa was Richard Palmore, the embassy Political Officer. Fyleman was a professional Foreign Service Officer. Washington rarely assigned political appointees to Seoul, since few big-money backers—whether Democrat or Republican—looked on Korea as a fitting reward for their contributions to the winner's campaign chest. Fyleman's candor and lack of subtlety were the stuff of legends. At Foggy Bottom many of his more cautious colleagues thought it unlikely that he would rise much higher. Fyleman knew this and didn't care. He was proud of his career in the Foreign Service.

"Mark, Richard here has something you ought to read."

With a small smile playing around his thin tight lips, Palmore offered a two-page document to Douglas. "I've translated this from the original Korean. Of course, you're welcome to a copy if you want."

Douglas saw that it was an internal Blue House memorandum from Shin Yong Su, a senior staff assistant for research and development to President Park Chung Hee. He scanned the contents, then reread the document from the start. Nausea tugged at his stomach.

"Tom, this seems—"

Palmore interrupted. He had a prissy, wimp voice. "It doesn't 'seem' anything. I think it's quite clear. It's a progress report on a clandestine weapons-development program."

Douglas forced back his irritation. From the first day in the embassy, Palmore had let his animosity toward CIA be known. He hardly ever missed an opportunity to denigrate the station's expertise in Korean affairs. On one occasion Douglas had had to go to Fyleman to protest Palmore telling a Washington visitor at a crowded cocktail party that Marty Horton "wasn't really" a Foreign Service Officer, thus threatening her nominal cover.

Douglas frowned at Palmore. "If you'll let me finish, please. What I was going to say, Tom, is that this seems . . . well, it seems abrupt."

Fyleman tilted his head. "How do you mean?"

"I mean, it's out of the blue. Too much so. We have nothing that precedes this—"

Palmore sneered. "There's a first time for everything, Douglas."

"Richard, let him finish," Fyleman scolded.

"Tom, it strikes me as awfully suspicious that we've heard nothing, absolutely nothing, about any kind of ROK secret weapons development. Not a whisper. Not a rumor. Now we suddenly have in hand a memorandum to the President of the Republic of Korea that talks about machining a high-explosive sphere and figuring out how to manufacture the explosive lenses and a precise-detonation wiring harness. It's too neat a fit. I mean, the only thing this document doesn't do is come out and say, 'Dear Mr. President, we now know how to put together the most technically challenging components of a nuclear weapon.'"

"Richard is confident of his source for this document."

Douglas turned to Palmore. "Who's the source?"

"I can't say. I won't say. You protect your sources for good and sufficient reasons. I have people who trust me, and I have to protect them."

"Is the document you have, the document your—your 'source' gave you . . . is that document the original?"

"Of course not. It's a photocopy."

"And so any kind of analysis of the paper wouldn't tell us anything. And there wouldn't be any fingerprints. Very neat."

Palmore took the translation from the CIA officer. "I think I smell the odor of sour grapes, Douglas. It won't look very good back in Washington. Your superiors at Langley will wonder how you people in Seoul Station got scooped—and by one of the boys in striped pants."

Douglas's jaw clenched, his face flushed. "Goddamnit, Palmore, I don't really give a good rat's ass who finds what. But this thing stinks. And there could be some pretty heavy consequences if we accept that thing without establishing its bona fides."

Fyleman cleared his throat and stood. "How would you go about that, Mark—the bona fides and all?"

"Obviously, we just can't walk up to the Blue House

and ask Park if that memo belongs to him. We would have to get some kind of corroborating evidence."

"Haven't we discussed this before?" Fyleman asked.

"We have, Tom. But starting up an operation against an ally is something I can't do on my own. And I have to tell you quite frankly, I oppose doing that in principle. It's just too damned dangerous. The KCIA covers this country like stink on a manure pile. We'd run a high risk of getting caught—"

"Do the ROK's worry you more than the Russians?" Palmore asked.

"The risks, Palmore," Douglas hung contempt on the name—Pawl-more—"are high working against the Russians—very high. It's just that the risks of *not* working against them are even higher. That's because they're our enemies. And whether you believe it or not, the South Koreans are our friends."

Douglas turned to Fyleman, who, still standing, was obviously deep in thought. The Ambassador was caught. If he did nothing, Palmore doubtlessly would find a way to go behind Fyleman's back to Foggy Bottom. There'd be serious questions asked as to why Fyleman had sat on something as potentially incendiary as the Blue House memorandum.

Fyleman looked at Douglas, slowly shaking his head, a man finding no palatable way out of his predicament. "Mark, if this were a hundred years ago, the lack of communications would force us to go slow on this. But as I see it, I have no choice." He gestured to the Blue House memorandum. "I've no choice at all. I've got to send this back to Washington by our channels along with my recommendation—my reluctant recommendation—that the Secretary ask Langley to get to the bottom of all this."

Washington, D.C.

Building 312 never failed to exasperate Eleanor Trowbridge. Standing in that tiny room with the Marine—a mere child—peering at you through the glass with those gas vents overhead, why, it was something out of the concentration camps. Did they really believe the KGB was going to shoot its way in, grab off a batch of satellite film strips, then hotfoot it out of the country like Bonnie and Clyde?

Somehow, everything was on a more human scale in World War II, when the OSS was in those flimsy temporaries on the Mall, where you were let in by a guard who knew you by your first name.

Now the world and its wars were more impersonal. The computer and instant communications create the illusion that events can be understood and managed down to the smallest detail by "experts" thousands of miles away. And so those on the scene become little more than clumsy marionettes, unable to do anything on their own without looking over their shoulders to Washington—or Moscow.

She saw John Freeman ahead of her in the corridor. There was something new there. Yesterday, his first day back in the office, he looked terribly smug. Almost silly, she thought. It might have something to do with the Forbes woman, who had called to find out when he would be back and to get his home telephone number.

"In here, Eleanor." Peter Smith's conference room was next to his photographic-analysis center. John Freeman took a chair next to her.

She reached down inside the canvas shopping bag and pulled out a yellow legal pad, a couple of stubby pencils, and a cheap government-issue ballpoint pen.

"We didn't circulate a written agenda," Eleanor began, "but I think that part of it is relatively simple. There are four questions:

"First, what do we know *now* about the Korea military balance?

"Second, what *don't* we know?

"Next, how do we get what we must know?

"And last, is there a deadline for our understanding of the answers to the first three questions?

"Let's start at the beginning, and let's hear from you, Moe."

Moe Hirsch had been one of the first senior analysts when the National Security Agency was founded in 1952.

He'd turned down promotions that would have moved him out of substantive work and into management. It was not from any lack of desire for better pay, but Moe's consuming passions—compulsions, some would have said—were his work and billiards. A great, large, shaggy heap of a man who resembled nothing as much as a vast unmade bed, Moe couldn't conceive of randomness. For him there was always a pattern, if only one were smart enough and patient enough to sort it out. It was said throughout the intelligence community that if God ever created two snowflakes alike, Moe would be the first to know about it.

"From recent reporting, we know that there are approximately thirty Soviet *spetznaz* advisors assigned to the headquarters of the 280th Commando Brigade at Yongyon-ni. There is a definite . . ."

Eleanor listened as the big man described the growth of Soviet presence. Apart from herself, only Parsons and Freeman knew that Hirsch was briefing the others based on the information gathered from Algernon, the tap on the landline near Kosan. The most treasured secrets of intelligence frequently were not so much the information itself, but the sources and methods—how the information was obtained. And of the American intelligence agencies, NSA was the most secretive, hiding its tradecraft even from its colleagues.

". . . we do know that the *spetznaz* personnel at the 280th are directly controlled by elements in the Soviet Embassy in Pyongyang, and that the 280th, under Soviet direction, has been conducting significant infiltration field exercises."

Susan Forbes, sitting beside Charlie Evans, the senior Defense Intelligence Agency officer, raised her hand. "What kind of infiltration exercises, Moe?"

Eleanor glanced at John Freeman, who was totally absorbed by the Forbes woman. No doubt about it. Something was definitely going on there.

". . . parachute drops of five- and six-man teams from AN-2's at very low altitudes. The AN-2 is an old fabric-covered passenger biplane, but they have lots of them. They can take off from grass strips or highways, fly low, and are next to impossible to see on radar. Ideal special-operations airplane for short hauls.

"And then there're the tunnels." By 1976 the Americans and South Koreans had discovered two long tunnels, cut through granite, extending from North Korea below the Demilitarized Zone and into the South. One of these was large enough to drive a small truck through; both could have put large numbers of commandos behind South Korean defenses, and the suspicion was that scores of other tunnels remained undetected elsewhere along the DMZ. "The 280th has a number of twenty-man units that appear to be intended for long-range infiltration on foot."

Moe Hirsch rose from his chair and lumbered to the projector, a single transparent slide in hand. "This shows the communication channels we've gone back and looked at to see if we could detect any meaningful patterns." Knowing Moe, Eleanor thought, he wouldn't be telling them this unless he'd found something.

". . . looked at the internal communications, that is, the Russians in Moscow talking to the Russians in Pyongyang—diplomatic, military, and intelligence comms. Then there're the North Koreans in Pyongyang talking to the North Koreans in the USSR. And we shouldn't forget another important link, and that's any traffic anomalies in communications between the Soviet Embassy in Tokyo and Pyongyang and Moscow.

"Reviewing our tape library, we found that the volume of diplomatic communications has remained constant since the mid-1960s. But the military and intelligence traffic have increased to a level we haven't seen since early January 1968." He's hesitating for effect, Eleanor thought. He knows how to sell his wares. "And that peak was just before the North Koreans grabbed the *Pueblo* and its crew."

"Moe, when did the increase begin?" asked Evans.

"We're still refining the data, Charlie, but it looks now like it was sometime in 1974."

Peter Smith spent the next thirty minutes outlining the progress on the location of "new" North Korean tank and artillery units that had previously gone unnoticed on the order of battle lists.

"The tank and artillery units are easier to count simply because tanks and artillery pieces show up well on satellite photography. Infantry units are tough because they just don't have large-signature equipment. The KH-11 is good, but it can't spot rifles or boots. But we have done some research that's paying off."

Smith put a transparency on the projector. "Here is a shot taken the day before yesterday of an area near Haeju. We'd detected some of the new tank outfits there. Look in the upper right-hand corner and you'll see what we identify as a small-arms practice range.

"We've gone back in our photography files, and we've found that such ranges are standard items for each brigade within an infantry division. So if we see the practice ranges, we start a more detailed search for other things such as barracks, kitchens, latrines, and so on. What we have so far points to a significant growth of North Korean military power. And to anticipate your question, Charlie, the trend began sometime in 1974."

Jeremiah Scruggs, Chief of the Foreign Broadcast Information Service, made the next presentation. FBIS was the arm of CIA that listened to and read the public media of most of the world's literate nations. Scruggs, a small black man born on a hardscrabble Alabama farm, was the son of sharecroppers. From early childhood his parents had known that Jeremiah would never become a farmer. The little boy had somehow developed an insatiable thirst for reading. And his talent for languages was precociously demonstrated when, by the age of five, he'd picked up Spanish—street language and all—from itinerant Chicano laborers. He waited tables at Tuskegee, where he attracted the attention of a roving CIA recruiter who'd been told to fatten up his intake of blacks.

"Analyzing Soviet media is more complex than, say, analyzing that of the Western democracies, or even non-Communist dictatorships. I might add, too, that the Soviet leadership is more direct when expressing itself in secret documents than when it is attempting to communicate with the Russian public. This results from the fact that the Soviet media must in all cases not only act as a faithful mouthpiece for a centralized totalitarian regime, it must also be a witness to the infallibility of Marxist ideology as interpreted by a gerontocracy in the Kremlin."

Evans snorted. "Jerry, do you provide a translation for us mortals?"

"Charlie, it boils down to the fact that they're a bunch of old men who're scared to death of their own citizens; who have absolute control over the media, which they use to set the stage for what they plan to do next."

Scruggs checked his notes again, then resumed. "We examined the output from the usual sources: *Izvetsia*, *Pravda*, and Radio Moscow. In addition, we looked at the domestic media—that which is intended solely for use within the Soviet Union." Scruggs passed papers around the table.

"I have the numbers here on these handouts, but to cut it short, we found that since the end of 1974, Soviet treatment of Northeast Asia has generally increased. We found that the particular attention paid to Korea accounted for the majority of that increase."

"Jeremiah, what are they saying?"

"There's the normal socialist-solidarity folderol, Eleanor. But the new theme is to hammer on Seoul. In any number of ways, they attempt to paint the South Koreans as bloodthirsty and irresponsible. Quite specifically, they target Park Chung Hee. What economic progress that has been made, they say, has been at the expense of the working class and has benefited the military through massive diversions of labor and foreign aid into the armed forces and defense industries."

Lew Parsons finished the presentations. The DDO officer gave a short discourse on a group which claimed to be a nonpolitical cultural and self-help emigré organization devoted to assisting the large Korean community in Japan. In reality, Parsons explained, the Chosen Soren was funded and controlled by Pyongyang. Parsons described how the organization had recently stepped up its newspaper attacks on the South Korean government's human rights policies, and that reliable Japanese sources reported increased contacts between liaison officers of the Chosen Soren and the cultural secretary of the Soviet Embassy in Tokyo.

Eleanor looked around the room. "Anybody else?" She paused. "I think the notes of this meeting are going to show that we see a buildup in North Korea's military—a buildup supported and probably directed to a great extent by Moscow. It is something that began sometime in 1974. As usual, all this effort only leads us to other questions.

"What is behind all this? What is the exact nature of the Soviet role? Is this something Pyongyang initiated and the Soviets have taken advantage of to get more of a foot in the door in Northeast Asia?

"Or have the Soviets cooked this up and persuaded the North Koreans to go along?

"And a last question: How much time do we have left?" Eleanor looked around the table; a look that said she expected contributions from all. "Discussion."

The next hour was spent in a free-for-all. Guesses and theories were brought up, twisted, reshaped, discarded. Eleanor knew they wouldn't—couldn't—come to a solution, but she knew also that it was important that they find that out, through the frustration of argument and debate.

Susan Forbes reached forward and tapped on her water glass. "Eleanor, I think the last question we can answer or at least approximate, but the first three are impossible right now.

"We ought to be able to get some rough estimate of a deadline by figuring out just when the North Korean military buildup might be completed. To do that, we need to do two things. First, we find the rate at which these new units are being equipped. We can watch the tank factory and the artillery plants through photography. The Navy can put some of its ship-watcher talent to work to spot exports to Pyongyang.

"The second thing we do is draw up what we believe to be the structure of the armed forces Pyongyang is driving for. Imagine we have an aerial picture of a housing development just breaking ground. We can spot the number of homes that will be built from the clearings. If we trace the lumber and building material into the development, we can estimate how long before they have the job done." Susan Forbes cocked her head toward Eleanor. "For North Korea, we know that each of their divisions has so many tank units. We know what their artillery doctrine says they should have in terms of heavy artillery. What we do is sketch the numbers of skeletal divisions they're now building. Then, with the rate of weapons production and imports from the USSR, we can calculate how long it'll take to fill all their units up with a complete complement of equipment."

Eleanor looked at the younger woman. Perhaps the good Colonel Freeman had gotten lucky. "And why can't the first questions be answered?"

"Because they all have to do with intentions. That's something that satellite photographs can't tell us. And Moe, with all due respect to your field, policy decisions are rarely made over the telephone or radio. We need a human source to know the why of this thing, and I haven't heard anything here today to indicate we have that." She looked expectantly at Lew Parsons, who said nothing.

Eleanor pushed her chair back and stood, scratching her head absentmindedly. "Well. We do have more work to do. I think the time estimate Ms. Forbes suggested is a good one. And we do have to come up with at least an informed judgment on the motives of the Soviets and North Koreans.

"To keep us from feeding off each other, I want to divide you—and the resources you have back at your home organizations—into two teams. Say, Team Alpha and Team Omega. Each of you will have access to the same raw information. But you're to keep your work from each other. I want two independent assessments."

After the meeting, Jeremiah Scruggs approached Eleanor. They traded small talk for a minute or two. As he turned to leave, Scruggs smiled. "We seem to be missing our friend Mr. Portale from State, Eleanor. Didn't you want him carrying tales back to Foggy Bottom?"

"Oh?" She blinked innocently. "I must have forgotten—old age, I guess."

In the hallway, Susan Forbes waited for John Freeman. "The flowers were beautiful, John."

He smiled, and she saw his ears redden. "Come on, I'll walk you to your car."

Once in the parking lot, he took her hand. "I shouldn't have trouble saying this, but I . . . well, it was more than a wonderful night. I'd like to see you again, and I'll be damned if I'm going to walk away from here with you saying you'll call. How about dinner? Tomorrow night?"

She squeezed his hand. "How about tonight?"

Langley,Virginia

There had been some sparring around, but it was finally agreed that David Cummings would come out to Langley for lunch with Roswell Franks.

The Director's private dining room offered a view of the green forest along the banks of the Potomac. Cummings and Franks sat at a round table suitable for eight.

As they ate, Franks carried on a desultory, almost disjointed conversation, punctuated by chin thrusts. He's unsure of himself, Cummings thought. Practically scared shitless.

In the middle of Franks's discourse on the fighting in the Ogaden, Cummings interrupted. "I've got to brief the Secretary later this afternoon. What is it you wanted to see me about?"

Caught off balance, Franks lamely said something about Somalia to close out the Ogaden discussion, then grabbed at the folder by his side so clumsily that he spilled several papers on the floor. Among them was a lined sheet almost three feet long with scratchings in various color inks.

"It's young Mr. Squires, Dave." It was characteristic of Franks that he never bothered to check to see if Cummings was indeed "Dave," or if, as was indeed the case, Cummings preferred to be called David. Cummings, for his part, never corrected Franks, preferring to keep the clumsy attempt at familiarity and intimacy as still more evidence of Franks's ineptness. He said nothing, but captured Franks in eye contact.

"Aah . . . we . . . ah . . . they . . . that is, after you recommended Mr. Squires as the National Intelligence Officer for Nuclear Proliferation, I asked the Office of Security to expedite his background investigation. Since Mr. Squires had never held a government position, and since he would have to have some very sensitive compartmented security clearances, our people had a lot of work to do."

"Ros, I know how the clearance game works. What's the problem?"

"He . . . well, he didn't do well on the polygraph. Not well at all, I'm afraid."

"How do you mean?" asked Cummings, an edge in his voice.

Franks consulted the folder. "The examiner says that there are distinct indications of evasion when the questions involve Squires's relationships with other governments. There also appear to be extreme reactions to questions about vulnerability to blackmail."

Cummings flushed. "Senator Ervin was right about that goddamn machine—it's the twentieth century equivalent of witchcraft. Did you go back over the test?"

Roswell Franks's eyes widened in fearful anticipation of Cummings's next outburst. "Dave, we spent a total of twenty-nine hours with him on the polygraph—spread out over two weeks, of course—and used three different examiners. None of the three had contact with each other—completely independent. All three said the same thing." Franks was perspiring heavily.

"You have the authority as DCI to waive all that, don't you? Or can some GS-11 polygraph examiner tell you who can be your senior executives?"

"Well . . . well . . . certainly I can . . ."

"Then, goddamnit, *do it!*" Cummings snarled. "I know this guy. Known him for years. He's straight—no little boys or dope. Doesn't beat women and isn't in debt. Jesus Christ, what are you guys looking for here? Does he have to walk across the Potomac for you?"

Franks seemed to shrivel. "The field investigation—interviews and records checks—put him in the middle of the Viet Nam protest movement. He was on a boat that sailed medical supplies to Hanoi and was with the Berrigans—"

"Sonofabitch!" Cummings threw his napkin on the table. "I can put up with security checks, but what are you running here? The fucking Gestapo? Don't your guys in the leather overcoats understand where this administration is? One of the first things Carter did was to pardon most of the draft resisters. And what Alan did was far short of breaking the law. Like a lot of us, he opposed a wrong-headed policy. He did it openly. And he did it when it was the duty—the goddamn *duty*, Ros—of thinking Americans to stand up against the stupidity of Washington."

Desperately hoping to placate the angry Cummings, Roswell Franks took on a wheedling tone. "Dave, this puts me between a rock and a hard place. To do his job, Squires has to have access to all the files, all the knowledge, all the memories. That kind of access has to be given willingly. I can order Squires hired. But those bastards in Security will leak this out," he tapped the folder, "and the whole building'll know. Even if he gets the formal clearances, they'll stonewall him. And you said we need a—"

"Ros, I said you people need a senior executive to direct intelligence efforts toward finding out which of our little friends may be building nukes behind our backs. I said that, goddamnit, because that's what the President of the United States wants. Now, either you run this Agency or it's going to run you." He looked at his watch. "I'm going to be late. I suggest you think very seriously about this, Ros. You know the President's concerns about this place and getting it under control."

Franks stood staring blankly long after the elevator doors had closed on the Assistant Secretary of State. Shit, shit, shit. What to do now? Whatever to do?

At four-thirty that afternoon, Roswell Franks was being briefed on changes to the fiscal year 1978 budget request that would allocate more money to satellite systems. Jay Mathias tapped him on the shoulder. "Sir, the White House is calling."

Franks excused himself and took the call in his office. The moment he heard the accent, he knew it was political and it probably wouldn't be pleasant. The Georgians who'd made the long march with Jimmy Carter were a stubborn, opinionated bunch. Their loyalty to their President was exceeded only by ignorance of Washington. They rode roughshod over jealously guarded plots of political turf, not only confirming the worst suspicions of their enemies, but angering friends and important supporters as well.

". . . an' I unnerstan' there's some opposition to movin' fohwad on this nukleer proliferation bidness."

Franks assured the Georgian that "opposition" was an overdrawn description and that the President's policies were being implemented with enthusiasm and dispatch. While talking, Franks unconsciously assumed the military position of "attention," his shirt sticking to his sweaty back. Hanging up, Franks cursed that smartass bastard Cummings and the crowd of snotty White House aides. He punched Mathias's intercom. "Get the Deputy Director for Administration. Get his ass in gear on hiring Squires. Now. Not tomorrow. Now."

Moscow

For at least the hundredth time Gregori Romanov checked the courier case, making certain the charts and documents were in order and that the combination lock did, indeed, work. He'd been summoned to Moscow Center on the personal instructions of Yuri Andropov himself, and he wanted to ensure all went well.

Vasili Kiktev surprised Romanov. We're about the same age, Romanov thought. He could even be younger. His old man must be one of the party bigshots. That, or his mother's the daughter of one. The *nomenclatura*—the privileged class in a classless society. Just choose the right parents and it falls in your lap. The best schools, spacious housing, special clinics, travel—and jobs working for the truly powerful, who would help you up the ladder without having to run risks or suffer discomfort. Bastards.

Romanov was further surprised when Kiktev immediately put down the papers he'd been reading and with a warm smile came around the large desk to shake hands and offer Romanov a seat.

"I hear you're the best at what you do, Comrade Romanov."

Romanov was uncertain. What the hell, it's only a small gamble. "Did you hear that from my boss or from my wife, Comrade Kiktev?"

Kiktev was momentarily startled, then broke into loud laughter. "Rare. A technical specialist with a sense of humor." He sat down, swiveled around to a safe behind his desk which he opened, pulling out a thick file. The outside of the file was a dark green with four broad red diagonal stripes signifying the level of security clearance required to have access to the information inside. Romanov had seen but one folder with three stripes in the years he'd been in the KGB's Scientific and Technical Directorate. He knew his pulse had quickened.

Kiktev opened the folder. "They told you what I want?"

"In general terms, yes." Romanov opened the courier case. Kiktev left the file on his desk, dragged a chair to sit beside Romanov. A uniformed orderly brought in tea in glasses.

"To start with some details, Comrade Kiktev. We have a small satellite nicknamed LIMPET. It monitors the satellite the Americans call KH-11. As far as we know, the Americans haven't detected LIMPET."

Kiktev raised a hand. "What is KH? Does it have a meaning?"

"It stands for Keyhole. The KH-11 transmits its pictures by television."

"And LIMPET intercepts the television pictures."

At least he's eager, Romanov thought, and not stupid. "Not exactly. The Americans code their television transmissions using a device that changes the broadcast frequency hundreds of times per minute. Breaking that code would be nearly impossible. And unnecessary." Kiktev fidgeted and Romanov rushed on. "LIMPET tells us *when* the KH-11 is

taking pictures. Since we know *where* the KH-11 is, we
then can tell the areas on the earth below that are of
interest to the Americans."

"And those areas, Comrade Romanov?"

Romanov pointed to a graph. "For the first seven
months after its launch, much of the KH-11 time was used
to map our strategic rocket forces, particularly our missile
deployments such as the SS-18's at Uzhur, Aleysk, and
Dombarovskiy. There was also activity directed toward
Ramenskoye, where we are building the prototype of our
new intercontinental bomber, as well as the Severodvinsk
Shipyard, where we are constructing the second of our
titanium-hulled submarines."

Pointing to a second chart, Romanov continued. "As
you might suspect, there was a brief flurry of KH-11 activity
over northern Korea when the Americans were killed in the
demilitarized area. That quickly subsided after they sal-
vaged their honor by cutting down a tree." There was the
expected laughter, then Romanov saw the frown of concentration return to Kiktev's face. Back to the point. "But then
there was an abrupt resumption several months later."
Rummaging in the courier case, Romanov came up with a
third chart. "The kind of coverage is as interesting as the
frequency."

Kiktev's intercom buzzed. Annoyed, he picked up the
telephone and told his secretary that he was not to be
disturbed. As he hung up, Romanov was struck by the
change in Kiktev. No longer impatient, Kiktev now had the
air of a hunter who finally had his quarry in sight.

"Go on, Comrade Romanov. Tell me what you find so
interesting about this."

Romanov paused, choosing his words carefully. He
had no idea what was going on, but he had a sense that it
was something worth four red stripes and perhaps even
more.

"I suspect someone's looking at the North Korean
military forces that are behind the front-line units on the
demilitarized zone. It's a steady, plodding thing they're
doing." Romanov rhythmically pounded his fist into his
open hand. "Up to now, American intelligence has been

primarily interested in the Korean forces closest to them—those right on the cease-fire line. This step-by-step approach in the rear areas suggests they're doing a detailed quantitative assessment. In short, Comrade Kiktev, I think they're counting."

"Counting?" Kiktev's voice rose. "Counting what?"

"Large things. Things that're easy to see. Artillery. Tanks. Engineering units." Romanov paused. He leaned forward and spoke more softly. "And, Comrade Kiktev, they'll find that Kim Il-Sung has prospered over the past two years."

It made Kiktev uneasy that Romanov was nibbling around the edges of the plan. But Kiktev couldn't shield Korea from the KGB's own analysis without causing more curiosity.

"How long? How long before they can get a good count? Before they can put it all together?"

Ah, there! There *is* something going on, thought Romanov. There's something up with the Koreans or in Korea, and the Center's worried about the Americans finding out. "It depends. Satellite orbits don't carry them over the target every time, so you wait for that. But weather's the greatest natural obstacle. Korea has heavy cloud cover much of the year." Romanov paused as he saw Kiktev making notes.

"So when will they be able to finish this counting process?" Kiktev asked with some impatience.

"There're other factors. The KH-11 priorities, for example. It's the only satellite of its type in orbit. The demands from other American intelligence agencies must be tremendous. If they keep at it without interruption, they will have all the photography they need within three to six months. Analysis will take longer, but if they're any good, they could have a complete picture of the Korean force structure a couple of months after getting the photography completed."

Kiktev crossed his legs, drank some tea, and looked again at his notes. "So the orbit path and weather are constants. Nothing much we can do to change them. The variable is the emphasis Washington places on the search and analysis." Kiktev jotted more notes, then stood and thanked Romanov.

As he was leaving, Romanov heard Kiktev calling for Belenkov, who, Romanov knew, was responsible for KGB operations in the United States.

Langley, Virginia

". . . and that's where we find ourselves." Eleanor Trowbridge faced Andrew Cabot and Adam Wolfson, who had replaced Cabot as head of the Directorate of Operations when Cabot had been promoted to become Deputy Director of the Agency. She was flanked by Lew Parsons and John Freeman.

Andrew Cabot was the first to speak. "And so, Eleanor, what we're down to is the why of the matter. But is it so important to know that?"

Eleanor heard John Freeman sigh softly and edged her foot over and nudged his. Patience, young man. This is all part of the mating dance. Patience. The one to be wooed was Wolfson. He'd been chosen by Cabot to run DDO when Cabot had moved up to become George Bush's deputy. Nonetheless, Wolfson was his own man and would make up his mind independently of Cabot.

"I think so. We know the North Koreans are building a military force far in excess of what even the paranoids around Kim think is necessary for self-defense. And we have good evidence that the Kremlin's somehow got a hand in this."

Eleanor leaned forward, looking directly into Wolfson's eyes, emphasizing each word with a soft slap on the polished table. "But . . . we . . . don't . . . know . . . why." Her New England accent then sharpened and the pace of delivery picked up. "If this buildup—and we don't yet know the extent of it—was started by the Kremlin, it would mean that the Soviets have in mind something unpleasant for us in Asia."

Cabot had been watching Wolfson during Eleanor's

presentation. He'd shown no emotion, his hands remaining still, clasped before him on the table. "Eleanor, we have some talking to do." He waved his hand to dismiss Eleanor and John Freeman.

Eleanor rose immediately. Freeman, surprised, remained seated. Eleanor tugged at Freeman's shoulder. "Come along, John, come along."

In the hallway, Freeman asked, "What the hell was all that?"

Eleanor didn't break stride, and staring straight ahead, reached up with her index finger to push up the glasses that had crawled down her nose. "Wait till we get back to the office."

Cabot and Wolfson remained seated. Parsons got up, stretched, and refilled his coffee cup.

When Parsons sat down, Wolfson pointed a pencil at him. "Lew?"

"She's right. And there's more." Parsons raised his index finger. "First, I called Seoul Station last night. Douglas says the embassy is under heavy pressure to dig up dirt on the ROK's. Foggy Bottom claims we aren't watching the ROK nuclear energy program closely enough—that the South Koreans could be up to their elbows in a clandestine weapons program."

He raised another finger. "Secondly, some of the 'nonpartisan' human rights organizations have started raising hell about Park Chung Hee—they've discovered he's not Tom Jefferson. State's going to focus on South Korea in their annual report on human rights to the Congress.

"And then there's the interesting case of Mr. Alan Squires," Andrew Cabot added. "State and the White House made Franks hire this fellow to handle nuclear proliferation. He's got a spotty background. Ties into the British Labor left wing and the far left of the German SPD."

Wolfson sighed. "You guys don't have to draw me pictures. So the guys on Dzerzhinsky Square are running an op against us. It's happened before."

Parsons face flushed. "But Adam, the scale, the timing—"

Andrew Cabot spoke up. "Lew, I think Adam and I need to be alone."

After Parsons left, Cabot checked the electronic monitor. Satisfied that it was working, he sat down.

Wolfson preempted Cabot, holding up a hand. "No need, Froggy. You're all set to twist my arm about Hotspur . . ."

"Adam, I think the time's come."

"As I said, no argument." Wolfson got up, stretched, and walked the room, hands in pockets, looking down at the floor. "I guess I always knew it'd be for something like this. But I always had a fantasy we'd keep him until there was some goddamn dramatic situation. You know—Gabriel's about to blow his horn. Then we activate Hotspur, he'd do his job, we get him and his family the hell out, and the white hats would win and we'd all live happily forever."

Cabot smiled ruefully. "Amen, brother."

The Director of Operations paused, then asked Cabot, "When was it you recruited him? Nine, ten years ago?"

"Fifteen," Cabot answered. I was on my third assignment. Bonn Station. They were dark days. Oleg Penkovsky'd just been discovered and shot. But this guy still came over. Not for money. Just a very smart guy who saw the rot."

"When'd you see him last?"

"Two years ago. He's doing well. Promotions. He and his wife are still in love with each other. Kids staying out of serious trouble."

"You think he'll—"

"He will." Andrew Cabot looked at his watch and thought of his appointment calendar. He rose to leave.

"One last thing, Froggy," Adam Wolfson called to him. Cabot stopped at the door and turned. "Yes?"

"Are you going to get Franks's authorization for activation?"

Cabot took a deep breath, closed his eyes for a second, then looked steadily at Wolfson. "No."

Wolfson nodded.

* * *

Eleanor tilted back in her chair and propped her stockinged feet on the desk. "Not exactly the most ladylike position, I suppose, but my feet hurt something awful. I wonder if some of us begin to deteriorate from the bottom up?"

"Eleanor, what the hell's going on?"

Eleanor swung her feet down. "Our friends are talking about 'assets.' We presented our case and now they're going to decide whether they have somebody who can help us, and if they do have that somebody, *if* they'll endanger him to help us with our little problem."

"*They* decide? Why not cut us in on the goddamn decision?"

She said patiently, "It's because those assets of theirs are human beings, John. But some come over because they believe in what we say we stand for. And those are the ones you become emotionally wrapped up with. What Cabot, Parsons, and Wolfson know is that sooner or later an agent who's active is going to make a mistake. And the place where our agent would have to be to find out what we want to know is a very dangerous place indeed."

"But—"

It was one of the few times Eleanor interrupted him. "The DDO takes these things seriously because their agents are human beings, John, not satellites or intercept stations. And I've just asked them to put one of those human beings on the block."

Eleanor Trowbridge trudged through the underground pedestrian tunnel to the bus stop. The Blue Bird would take her to State for her meeting with young Mr. Cummings.

The dusty blue bus wheezed up in a cloud of diesel fumes. The Agency ran the shuttle to the Pentagon and State Department as well as to several of the Agency's facilities that hadn't been centralized out at Langley. At least weekly, KGB officers working out of the Soviet Embassy trailed the Blue Bird, taking telephoto pictures of its passengers. The Agency's clandestine employees such as Lew Parsons didn't ride the Blue Bird, and those under "deep cover" never came near Langley or any of the overt Agency offices.

The bus ride was too soon over, and she found her way up to the East Asia Bureau offices on the sixth floor of New State.

Cummings's office was familiar; it had served previous Assistant Secretaries with whom she'd dealt on East Asian matters—their fading pictures hung on the walls in cheap black frames. She sat on the same leather sofa where she remembered McGeorge Bundy sprawling after an acrimonious confrontation with Pentagon representatives during the Viet Nam War. David stood at his desk, where he acknowledged Eleanor with a smile and then went on to finish explaining changes on a draft speech to his secretary.

She'd first met David in the mid-sixties, when he'd come back from Saigon with Max Taylor for policy conferences with Lyndon Johnson. She'd found him likable and smart—a young man obviously on his way up. She understood his leaving the Foreign Service, although she had disagreed with his ideas about Viet Nam. Certainly, the dreary parade of greedy and incompetent South Vietnamese generals didn't lead that country closer to real democracy, but it seemed to her that they were the only realistic alternative to an infinitely more hideous and pervasive oppression.

Cummings disagreed. He believed that a Vietnamese Abraham Lincoln was somewhere in the bush with the Communist opposition—a liberator-reformer who would cast off superficial Marxist trappings to emerge in democratic splendor, if only the Americans would get out of the way.

He dismissed his secretary and sat next to Eleanor. "It's good of you to come over, Eleanor." He pointed to the disappearing secretary. "I never knew mere Assistant Secretaries made so many goddamn speeches."

"The burdens of office, David." She commiserated, then added, "You said you wanted to talk about Korea."

Cummings got up, walked to his chair behind the desk and sat down, making a show of searching for something in the pile of papers. "Yes. Here it is." Not offering to show her the single page, he studied it intently, as if to reacquaint himself with the contents. "Yes. Yes. The President," he wiggled the paper to the right of his face, "the President is particularly interested in human rights. As you know, Eleanor, he's taken the Kremlin to task on this, and he believes that our allies ought to be more concerned as well.

"And so the Secretary's going to be sending a formal request to Roswell Franks, tasking the Agency to establish contacts among the South Korean dissidents. We must develop sources within the Blue House that can give us some idea as to what Park has in mind regarding his political opposition, and, more important, tracking down reports we've been getting to the effect that the ROK's have started a secret nuclear-weapons program."

"It sounds as if it's all been decided, then," Eleanor remarked dryly.

Cummings looked around his cluttered desktop as if he might find something else there to wave in the air in support. "Yes. Yes, it has."

"Then why are we talking about it? You knew I'd have reservations, David. But since it's been sold already to the Secretary, there's not much sense in going over it here."

He came around the desk and made a show of checking that his door was closed, then sat on the sofa. "Eleanor. You're one of the senior professionals at the Agency. Most of the Directors of Central Intelligence have been professionals. It was only recently that the White House"—here he quickly added, "both Republican and Democratic Presidents—have put in outsiders, political appointees. Carter wants to put a professional in charge. He realizes Franks is incompetent. And under Carter the Agency will have a major role, especially in making certain the Soviets stick to arms-control agreements."

"What does all this have to do with me, David?"

"As I said, Eleanor, the President thinks Franks is a boob. He wants to put a professional in charge of the Agency. And you, Eleanor, are a very competent professional."

Outside, the heat was a suffocating blanket. Washington's afternoon rush hour was building up, and the Blue Bird from Langley was late. Eleanor looked again at her watch, then hailed a cab that took her home to a small house in northwest Washington. There she made a pot of tea, and fed the canary.

Fairfield Perkins and Sam Benezra had kept surveillance on the house on northwest Washington's Foxhall Road for two weeks. They had built a schedule of the comings and goings of the owner, his friends, and the help. At about nine o'clock on Thursday morning of the third week, a Chesapeake and Potomac telephone repair truck parked on a sidestreet, set up the usual traffic-orange rubber cones and warning flags, and a crew of two or possibly three men began work. The problem was apparently between the telephone lines behind the Foxhall house and an underground conduit. The men worked through the morning, passing back and forth between the backyard and the side street. A casual observer would have missed the fact that Fairfield Perkins, wearing a yellow hard hat over a conservative Afro, hadn't been seen for nearly an hour. By noon the work was apparently completed. The crew packed up the cones and warning flags, replaced the conduit cover, and drove away.

"Holy shit, where did you guys— "
"Never mind the totally unoriginal expressions of delight and wonder, Lew, read on." Adam Wolfson sat back and watched Parsons, waiting for his reaction. Parsons propped his feet on a coffee table and continued to read.

CUMMINGS: . . . met with her this afternoon.

SQUIRES: Did you mention me?

CUMMINGS: No. I stuck mainly to human rights, although I did mention our suspicion that Seoul was working on the bomb. I didn't say much. There'll be time enough to get into the nuclear business when you start work out there.

SQUIRES: She's going to be possessive about Korea. . . .

CUMMINGS: We can handle that. She can't shut you out of the nuclear-proliferation account. Hell— that's your title. And we'll make certain that a couple of weeks after you're on board, the National Security Council generates some kind of requirement for a study of Third World nuclear capabilities. And you, in turn, make certain Korea gets the attention it deserves.

SQUIRES: (laughter) If someone'd told me in 1968 that you'd be at State and me (laughter) at CIA, I'd have probably had them committed. All we need now is Chebrakin. . . . (laughter)

Parsons looked up from the transcript. "Chebrakin?"

Wolfson turned to a paper in the file in front of him. "Vladimir I. Chebrakin. Sweden, 'fifty-five to 'fifty-nine. Netherlands, 'sixty-three to sixty-nine. Finally expelled. Originally GRU, transferred into KGB sometime in the early sixties. It's possible he recruited Squires in Vienna, although we have no evidence of it. At the time, Chebrakin was operating under the cover of cultural affairs reporter for a publication of CPSU that in translation is *New Times*. The first file entry is in the Hague at a conference of Third World journalists." Wolfson closed the file and looked up. "It seems Chebrakin is currently assigned here. In Washington."

"Has Squires made contact with him?"

"Don't know."

"How about Cummings? Is he witting?"

"We don't know that either."

Parsons handed the paper over to Wolfson, who put it in the large metal ashtray and struck a match to it. The flash paper was ashes in an instant. Wolfson stirred the ashes with a pencil. "Only copy."

"How'd we get it?"

"Entered Cummings's house."

"Christ, Adam. They throw you in jail for operating against American citizens in the States—much less against a goddamn Assistant Secretary of State." Parsons looked at the ashtray, shaking his head. "And if they find out you did a surreptitious entry, then they'd throw away the key and forget you're in there."

"There's something else, Lew."

Wolfson had a slight, teasing smile. Parsons's hand suddenly trembled.

"Somebody's been there first. Our people found another bug in Cummings's house. In the library. It's active."

Chapter 4

National Military Intelligence Center—The Pentagon

"The principal conclusions are as follows." John Freeman stood at a podium whose buttons, switches, and knobs looked like the cockpit of a small jet. Since the Defense Intelligence Agency had done most of the drafting of the various components of the estimate, Eleanor had thought it best that the briefing on the results be done at the Pentagon.

She and Freeman had constructed the estimate from the contributions of DIA, CIA, NSA, and the military services. They'd structured the work by opening with an executive summary that contained a number of terse one- or two-sentence statements—the major findings. While brief, the summary was perhaps the most important part of the thick document. It was the one section that would be most widely read by an audience with an uneven knowledge of Korea. You couldn't assume, Eleanor insisted, that those responsible for war and peace would take the time to read anything more than two pages long. Bismarck's warning that the squeamish should never watch sausages or laws being made applied to foreign policy as well.

The second section was the study itself—the evidence on which the executive summary rested. There was an introductory chapter on the political history of the two Koreas, followed by others on the military geography of the peninsula, the military industrial capacity of each nation, and detailed analyses of their military forces.

Finally, the last section was a rehash of the executive summary in which the conclusions were again presented, but in greater detail and depth than at the outset. It was a variation of the old but effective Army rule of: "Tell 'em what you're going to tell 'em; tell 'em; and then tell 'em what you told 'em."

Finding the right button, Freeman's first slide came on the screen.

THE MILITARY BALANCE ON THE PENINSULA HAS SHIFTED DRAMATICALLY TO FAVOR NORTH KOREA

Pausing, Freeman left the first slide on and signaled for a second, more detailed slide to be shown on an adjacent screen. "We've seen an increase across the board in North Korea's army, navy, and air forces, as well as in her industrial capability. In our 1973 estimate, we counted twenty-five infantry divisions. Today we see thirty-nine divisions. Two of these are motorized infantry, and, most ominously, two are armored divisions. The estimate reveals similar growth in North Korea's tactical fighters and naval forces.

"South Korea does not do well in comparison. Her army consists of twenty infantry divisions. No armored divisions. Total holdings in tanks are about twelve hundred obsolete American M-47's and M-48's."

In the white glare of his slide projector, Freeman saw that besides intelligence specialists, his audience consisted of a large number of senior operations officers, some of them generals. The numbers on the North Korean army divisions had gotten to them. Whatever their background, these staff officers—still trying to digest the lessons of the defeat in Viet Nam—knew about divisions: the ground gainers and ground keepers of any military. They knew it took time and money to build divisions, to train them, to keep them in battle shape.

Freeman nudged the projector button again.

THE GROWTH OF
NORTH KOREA'S FORCES
HAS TAKEN PLACE OVER A
RELATIVELY SHORT PERIOD

He slapped the screen with the pointer. "Gentlemen, the North Koreans have added *fourteen* divisions since 1973. They have built from scratch the two tank divisions and the motorized infantry divisions." Freeman paused again because of the whispering. Let them talk. Let them tell each other what a task the North Koreans had faced. How much they must have sacrificed.

When the lull came, Freeman put on the next slide.

COST OF BUILDUP = 15–20% OF GNP

"The North Korean military forces totaled about 467,000 in 1973. By early this year that had increased to about 672,000. The South Koreans, by contrast, have 160,000 fewer people in their military, even though South Korea has more than twice the total population of North Korea. Our economists looked at the diversion of resources from the nonmilitary sector to the military—the people as well as the material assets—and have come up with this figure." Freeman pointed to the adjacent screen. "This second slide shows the U.S. defense budget proposed by President Carter amounts to less than five percent of our Gross National Product. Soviet military funding is approximately eleven percent of their GNP. South Korea is spending about seven percent of its GNP on its military." Freeman paused again to let the figures sink in.

BUILDUP ORIGINS = 1974–1975

"We have done a thorough back-analysis. We went through old files of photography and signal intercepts to find a time when these units didn't exist. The best fix we can get—and are likely to get—is that they began to come into the North Korean force structure sometime between the fall of 1974 and early spring of 1975."

THE SOVIET UNION PROVIDED
70–80% OF MATERIEL ASSISTANCE

"Although North Korea has its own tank and artillery production facilities, it is totally reliant on the Soviet Union for aircraft and sophisticated electronics such as radars and microwave communications. Soviet advisors, particularly from the elite *spetznaz* units, have become more numerous; their increased presence corresponds to a quantum growth in North Korean commando units.

"A footnote: Following the example of their Cuban friends, the North Koreans are paying the Russians back by sending North Korean specialists to Third World nations where a Caucasian Russian might not be welcome. Pyongyang has military specialists and advisors mainly in black Africa: some one thousand in Angola, one hundred in Mozambique, fifty or so in Uganda. A handful are helping the Sandinista movement in Nicaragua. North Korea also manufactures for export a considerable amount of weapons, particularly artillery and small arms."

Freeman called for the last slide.

THE BUILDUP OF
NORTH KOREAN FORCES
IS IN ITS FINAL STAGES

"To estimate when the buildup will be essentially complete, we've checked the level of equipment and personnel presently in these new units and matched this up against the rate at which Soviet aid and North Korean resources are filling up those units."

So this is what they mean by dead silence, thought Freeman.

"We then added the training time necessary to bring these units to a level of competency where Pyongyang would be confident they were battle ready."

Get on with it, they seemed to say. Tell us, even though we don't want to know.

"We estimate that North Korea will be fully ready to invade the south by this winter."

Washington, D.C.

Susan Forbes and John Freeman had both been working late at Langley. The question of where they would spend the night had become a routine one. That, in turn, brought with it the inevitable issue of living logistics. His small apartment was closer to the Agency and Arlington Hall. But there was Bandit to be fed, and the huge cat became grumpy when forced to be alone. And so, as increasingly was the case, they were on their way to Susan's home when, on a whim, they crossed the Potomac and parked near the Lincoln Memorial.

"Ten sentences. Two hundred sixty-seven words." John Freeman pointed to the words chiseled in the wall. "It's such a powerful statement. I never realized how short it is."

Susan Forbes, arm linked with John Freeman, moved closer against the cold. "He said what had to be said. The remarkable thing is that he left it at that."

Over her shoulder the statue of Abraham Lincoln was a luminescent white. The outside lights had been turned off at midnight. The late winter night left the two alone in the Lincoln Memorial.

Still looking at the Gettysburg Address, John Freeman asked, "You like that, don't you?"

"Like what?"

He squeezed her arm against him as he turned to kiss her lightly on the cheek. "Directness. No frills."

She laughed. "I suppose so. But don't think that gets you out of foreplay."

"Wouldn't miss it for the world." He kissed her again. "Or the afterplay either," he added.

Walking out of the Memorial, John tugged on Susan's arm. "Let's go around back."

"Back?"

He laughed. "I'll behave myself. There's a good view. Not too many people go there."

They stood looking over the Memorial Bridge into Virginia. The twin rows of golden yellow bridge lamps traced a path toward Arlington Cemetery.

"I didn't realize you could see it so clearly from here." Susan pointed to a tiny flickering light on the black hillside across the river—the flame on Kennedy's grave.

Each was lost in their thoughts of two assassinated Presidents. Susan rubbed her hands together. "Washington's almost too much to bear sometimes."

"How do you mean?"

"Oh, everywhere you turn there's a constant reminder of history. But it's grand history—not the history of human beings. I sometimes wonder where the people were. All the statues, memorials, make everything seem so abstract. So lifeless."

John smiled. "In the midst of the great upheavals of our times, there's always some bastard oblivious to it all, sitting in a corner, stringing beads or practicing his handwriting."

Susan laughed. "Bravo."

"No," John retorted smugly, "Not Bravo. I think it was Voltaire."

"Voltaire? Talking about oblivious bastards?"

"Well," John admitted, "I guess I took liberties. . . ."

Susan huddled up against him. "Seriously, John. I . . . I wonder if we—you and I—if we . . ."

"If what?" He cupped her face in his hand, his thumb caressing her cheek.

She turned and looked up into his face. He recognized the small frown that came to her when she was concentrating. "I wonder if this Korea thing hasn't thrown together two people who wouldn't have ordinarily . . ."

He put on a mischievous grin. "You mean Eleanor and Roswell Franks?"

Shaking her head in exasperation, Susan still let a smile escape. "No. Us." She felt a twinge of panic. She hadn't intended to get started on this. After all, neither of them had opened the ritual—the "what shall we do about all this" groping to sort out whether one would—or indeed, would want to—become someone of relevance in the other's life. God, she thought. I want to know how he sees us, but I'm afraid to ask. Afraid because of what he might say. And afraid because he'd then expect me to tell him how I feel. And I just don't know. Not now. Not yet . . . oh, shit. How'd I ever get into this?

Sensing Susan's ambivalence, John nudged the conversation away from the future. "I don't know that being thrown together because of our work is any worse—or better—than couples who meet anywhere else."

"But it seems like such a strained atmosphere."

"Ever been in a singles bar?" he countered.

Susan laughed. "Your point, Mr. Freeman."

Freeman looked at her laughing. "You know, you're the most beautiful woman in the world."

Still laughing, she protested. "You simpleton. My knees are ugly, my boobs are too small, and my ass—"

Freeman pulled her to him. "Your ass is a thing of beauty. A work of art. That from the world class T and A man, Lew Parsons."

"Parsons?" Susan sputtered, "That dirty old man, why—"

Freeman held her even closer, then kissed her. Breathing more quickly, he looked at her. "I wasn't describing your tits and ass. I was talking about *you*. And you *are* the most beautiful woman in the world."

What is little understood about American secret intelligence is that the Director of the Central Intelligence Agency has another job. Under a second title, Director of Central Intelligence, he heads the Intelligence Community, the community being composed of CIA, DIA, NSA, the intelligence offices of the Army, Navy, and Air Force, as well as the Department of State's Bureau of Intelligence and Research. It also includes the smaller intelligence operations of the FBI, Treasury, and the Department of Energy. In this second responsibility the Director of Central Intelligence is supported by a small staff—the Intelligence Community Staff—that sees to everyday housekeeping chores such as budgeting and the apportionment of intelligence collection tasks among its members.

Before he left government services in 1977, George Bush, in his capacity as Director of Central Intelligence, moved the Intelligence Community Staff from Langley to an ugly gray-brick building on F Street in northwest Washington which used to house the irascible General Hershey when he commanded the Selective Service.

On becoming Director of CIA as well as Director of Central Intelligence, Roswell Franks chose to be briefed on National Intelligence Estimates in the F Street office's conference room on the top floor. He did this to make the point that NIE estimates were not the product of CIA alone, but a community effort. More importantly, he did it to show that it was he, Roswell Franks, who had the last say over the ever-growing empires of the Defense Intelligence Agency and the National Security Agency. Both DIA and NSA increasingly suffered from delusions of grandeur— they had the audacity to believe they should talk directly with the White House. Franks found F Street to be a convenient cork in the bottle, a way to slow DIA's and NSA's end runs until he could mount a counteroffensive by grabbing control of their budgets. Franks justified the vast energy spent in these turf battles as an investment in better coordination and increased unity.

"The Korea estimate isn't going forward, Mrs. Trowbridge." Franks toyed with a silver letter opener, placing it point down on his desk and, holding it upright with his left index finger, spinning it by flicking the blade with his right hand.

Sitting in front of the desk in a straight chair, Eleanor squinted into the light coming over Franks's shoulder, unable to see the man's face. She said nothing. The briefing had been intended to acquaint Franks with the Korea estimate before it would be considered by the Intelligence Community principals. It had not gone well. Franks was running late and kept looking at his watch during John Freeman's presentation. Freeman had barely gotten into the first slides when Franks called everything to a halt. She had told Freeman to pack everything up and return to Langley. Franks then kept her waiting for well over two hours. She said nothing, preferring to let Franks shape his own justification.

"The estimate is an alarmist view of Korea."

"Alarmist?" Eleanor clenched her left hand, jamming her nails painfully into her palm. "In what way, General?"

Franks tilted back in the large leather chair. "The whole damn thing is slanted toward an inevitable conclusion—the Commies are coming. And what's more, State objects to your estimate. Objects to it in its entirety. Why, Cummings himself called me on it. He said—and I agree with him—that it's totally unbalanced. You don't take into account the South's stronger economy—"

"Excuse me, General," Eleanor interjected. "Are you surprised that State objects? The estimate upsets the party line at Foggy Bottom. Did you really expect State to stand up against Cummings, Vance, and the White House? State was given every opportunity to provide dissenting views in that estimate. They refused to do so. They don't object because of the evidence. They oppose it because the reality of the situation would get in the way of their objectives. Cummings wants to kill the estimate because it makes him look foolish. He and his friends care nothing for this country's security, only their agenda and their reputations."

She gulped a breath, then continued her assault before Franks could react. "We aren't talking about economic competition. We're talking about comparative war-fighting capabilities. The North has a military that it built largely on its own, admittedly with significant Soviet help, but one that stands alone. The South for years has been kept dependent on an American military partnership. We persuaded them not to get into certain military areas because we'd take care of it. With us gone, they'd be—"

Franks, recovering from his shock, counterattacked, fairly screaming. "Madam, don't lecture me on how to analyze comparative war-fighting capabilities. I've been in the Air Force through two wars, and I've been up against the Soviets ever since they developed an air force. I may not be one of the life-long intelligence professionals around here, but I've seen the real world out there. And I'm not so naive as not to be able to recognize what's going on here."

Eleanor felt his anger buffeting her. He was trying to bully her—something he'd never dare attempt with a man. "And what *is* going on, here, General?"

Franks's facial muscles were locked, rigid. He'd taken the letter opener in a closed fist with whitened knuckles. "This estimate is one of the Agency's gambits, Mrs. Trowbridge, a gambit to torpedo this President's policies. And I won't have it."

Eleanor stood and stepped toward the desk, forcing Franks to look up at her. In a surprisingly strong but unemotional and measured voice, she faced Franks. "You can't accept us, can you? Instead of leading us, instead of making best use of our talents, you seem intent on shaming us, on grinding out any spark of creativity. Do you really want the truth, General? Or do you want a cheering section for the White House?"

Franks was on his feet, his face beet red. "Goddamnit, lady, I won't have you talking to me that way. I'm not going to put up with you or with that," he pointed a quivering finger at the estimate, "that garbage about Korea."

Their eyes locked. Franks's nostrils flared. Eleanor returned his stare, willing herself to be calm. Franks sneered, tossed the letter opener on the desk, then sat down and swiveled his chair away from her. "That's all, Mrs. Trowbridge."

She met Andrew Cabot on the tree-lined towpath of the Chesapeake and Ohio canal, which parallels the Potomac for nearly two hundred miles. She recounted the clash with Franks.

Cabot, dressed in a blue parka, resembled a short, round monk. "What do you think he's got in mind?"

"I don't know exactly. Certainly, the estimate isn't going forward. My guess is, he'll probably kill it. He's got State in his corner. Even with the military and NSA with us, he and David Cummings could tie the estimate up so it

never sees light of day." Both remembered other contro-
versies that had run counter to the conventional wisdom of
the State Department; how State had buried other appraisals in endless bickering and "coordination problems."

They walked along the red-clay path in silence, the
canal just to their right, and on the left, the steep tree-
covered embankment that fell away down to the river. The
path stretched endlessly before them, deserted, covered
with a slight dusting of snow.

"I think, Andrew, that you and I ought to have lunch
with a friend of mine on Capitol Hill."

The Capitol—Washington, D.C.

Frank Church, Senator from Idaho and the second
most senior Democrat on the Senate Committee on Foreign Relations, scanned the hearing room. It was a huge
white-marble cavern in the Dirksen Senate Office Building.
The Foreign Relations Committee was assigned S-116 in
the Capitol building itself, a resplendent rococo room
complete with chandeliers and a green baize-covered table
at which the places of the committee members were
marked by engraved brass plaques. But S-116 was too small
to accommodate the press, much less the TV crews with
their banks of blinding lamps, and the media—particularly
television—were becoming indispensable to Washington's
politics.

Since the networks were banned from covering the
floor of the Senate, hearings became an important political
stage. Originally intended as a way for Congress to root out
the relevant facts about important issues, hearings increasingly lent themselves as platforms for self-promotion
where, by subpoena if needed, witnesses could be forced to
appear. Then, intimidated by possible charges of contempt
of Congress and handicapped by hearing rules that mocked
First Amendment rights, witnesses could be bullied by
grandstanding Senators who carefully rehearsed their
thirty-second "sound-bites" of outraged opposition or enthusiastic support for this or that policy. And so it was

important that the hearing room be large enough for the media and that the timing of the hearing be such that the networks could broadcast snatches of the proceedings and interviews on the seven o'clock evening news.

Church stood behind his chair at the top of the U-shaped table. John Sparkman of Alabama, the present committee chairman, had already announced his intention to retire. It hadn't taken much to persuade the courtly old Southerner to let Church chair today's hearings. The witness would sit at a table within the open portion of the U, with the committee members and staff looking down from the elevated table. Staff had put copies of Assistant Secretary of State Cummings's opening statement at each member's place. While it wasn't unusual for witnesses to omit reading a prepared statement and have it inserted into the hearing record, Cummings, his eye to the media, would read his statement in its entirety.

Church looked at his watch and walked back to his nearby office. He would be called when the witnesses were in place and all was ready.

". . . and accordingly, the President believes . . ."

Cummings was coming to the end of his statement. In it he'd outlined the Carter policy to withdraw the American army from South Korea. Adroitly playing to the cameras as much as to the committee, he portrayed the move as one that would strengthen the stability of Northeast Asia. Amplifying his enthusiasm and sincerity, he assured the network news that the initiative had the full support of both Seoul and Tokyo.

Church began the questioning. Under committee rules, the questioners would work downward in seniority, alternating between Democrats and Republicans. The Idaho Senator asked each member to hold his questions to ten minutes, with the understanding that time left over would be divided equally. Only Jess Starnes, the conservative Republican from North Carolina, and Laurence Mitchell, the freshman Democrat from Missouri, had been present from the start. But when the questioning started, the absentees would be summoned by staff, and so appear in an attempt to capture some air time on the evening news.

Church looked at the paper before him. He'd personally met with Cummings to make certain that he brought out the points that Cummings wanted emphasized.

"Mr. Secretary, thank you for appearing here this morning. And thank you, too, for the lucid and articulate opening statement." Church went on to give Cummings the openings he'd asked for—the opportunity to emphasize that the troop pullout wouldn't tempt the North Koreans; that Washington's increased military aid to the South Korean military would compensate for the American withdrawal.

Starnes cleared his throat. With the bravado of an actor facing a mock firing squad, he glared into the white heat of the television lights. A large man with rimless glasses and nicotine-stained fingers, Starnes adamantly refused to dull his shiny bald scalp with television makeup. One CBS cameraman who had covered the committee for years swore that Starnes actually polished his head to better reflect glare into the cameras.

"Mr. Secretary, I join with my chairman, the esteemed Senator from Idaho. I agree with him that you've given a very clear picture of your . . ." Starnes paused, looked directly into the cameras—and hopefully into America's living rooms—and fairly shouted, "*your* policy toward Korea. A very clear presentation indeed, Mr. Secretary. *A recipe for disaster! A prescription for war!* It may be *your* policy, Mr. Secretary. And it may be the policy of *your* President. But I want to go on the record before these assembled here and before the American people: It is a policy with which I will not, *will not be associated.*"

Frank Church looked at his watch: twenty-nine seconds. Starnes might not be the smoothest article on the Hill, but he had splendid timing. Cummings, fully expecting such an outburst, sat without expression, looking straight at Starnes. Church waited for Starnes to pause. "Does my colleague have questions of the witness?"

Starnes, satisfied he'd given the cameras his best shot,

became more judicious and diplomatic. His questions and those of the other Republicans who wandered in during the rest of the morning concentrated on laying the cornerstone for later opposition to the troop withdrawal. They did so on the grounds of the Communist menace and that South Korea was a model developing nation, just around the corner from democracy.

For their part, the Democrats countered with much emotion, casting South Korea as a military dictatorship, with many echoing George McGovern's sentiment that Seoul was "unworthy" of the commitment to spill American blood in the event of war.

Laurence Mitchell listened. In 1942 he flew Corsairs as a Marine pilot, downing two Japanese Zeros. At war's end he'd gone back to Missouri, married his childhood sweetheart, and finished his degree in aeronautical engineering. He had just settled down to work for McDonnell Aircraft in St. Louis when the Korean War broke out.

Major (USMCR) Mitchell earned the nickname of "Lead-Ass." It wasn't that he was slow. It was because he insisted on flying lower than his wingmates on close-air support missions against Chinese and North Korean troops. That way, Mitchell argued, you could more precisely deliver bombs (and napalm) against the hordes of enemy troops as they came up the hills at the outnumbered Marine infantry positions. His F-9 was regularly laced with shrapnel, and he kept a box of lead fragments that had torn away half the tail of his plane. Mitchell's love of flying and his competitiveness drove him to make repeated attempts to transfer to flying against the MiG's.

He got his chance above the Yalu River. In one day he shot down two enemy aircraft. But it was the third kill the day after that revealed a hidden side of Mitchell. It was the day before the Korean War ended, when the stick-to-the-book Marine disobeyed standing orders and flew into China alone to chase down the MiG pilot who'd jumped Mitchell's wingman from out of the sun.

Laurence Mitchell stayed in the Corps until retirement in the mid-sixties. Only his wife and the kids had kept him from attempting to return to active duty to fly in Viet Nam. While vice president of operations of what was now McDonnell-Douglas, he followed Viet Nam as an angry spectator, enraged by the Byzantine politics that dictated Washington's gradualist military strategy. It seemed to him a war in which Ivy League professors determined with exquisite precision the rules of engagement for infantry squads in combat half a world away.

Mitchell's impulse to get his hands on the controls of things got the better of him. He gave up a comfortable life in St. Louis to run for the United States Senate in 1974. To everyone's surprise except his own, he won. The professionals said his speeches were "brown and boring," but sixty-five percent of the voters of Missouri saw it differently.

"Mr. Secretary, thank you for coming here. You were kind enough to drop by my office before this hearing and so you know that I've got reservations about pulling our troops out . . ."

Cummings had successfully hidden his contempt for Mitchell, whom he considered a clumsy politician whose Presbyterian wholesomeness had gotten him into the Senate in spite of a pedestrian intellect.

Cummings easily handled Mitchell's questions. Starnes was whispering to a staffer, about some matter not related to the hearing. Church looked at his watch for perhaps the fifteenth time since Mitchell began. "Is the Senator from Missouri finished?"

"One more question, Mr. Chairman." Then, turning to Cummings, he said, "Mr. Secretary, can you tell me what analysis you've done about the military balance in Korea?"

Cummings had been thinking about the afternoon's meeting with Vance and was caught unaware. "I'm sorry, Senator, could you repeat the question?"

"What do your intelligence people tell you about the balance between North Korea and South Korea?"

Cummings fumbled in his briefing book, then turned in his chair to look back at the two rows of Foreign Service officers he'd brought to support him. There was much shaking of heads and thrashing through other briefing books. He turned again to Mitchell. "Senator, the Department of Defense fully supports this policy—"

Mitchell cut Cummings off, placing exaggerated emphasis on each word. "That's not what I asked, Mr.

Secretary." Mitchell held up a restraining hand as he saw Cummings prepare to speak. "I want to know what kind of work's been done to tell us just how much the North has in terms of military forces as opposed to the South."

"As you're well aware, Senator, that kind of thing isn't the specialty of the Department of State. I think I can, however, assure you that we—the administration, that is—that we've looked at that—"

Mitchell gently tapped his water glass. "If I may interrupt, Mr. Secretary. While I respect your assurances, I want some more specific information."

The CBS man paused and saw that Mitchell's face was tensed, that he held his pencil upright, thumb over the eraser as if resting on the trigger button of his F-86 somewhere long ago over North Korea. The CBS man looked around. The light bank was still set up. He scrambled to retrieve his camera.

That night some eleven million Americans saw Senator Laurence Mitchell, obviously intense, score a kill.

MITCHELL: (close-up on right hand, maneuvering pencil). . . what you're telling us, Mr. Secretary, is that even before you became Assistant Secretary of State, you were advocating this troop withdrawal?

CUMMINGS: (close-up on face, perspiration) Well, I wrote—

MITCHELL: Before you even had access to CIA and DIA appraisals of Korea?

CUMMINGS: I have access now and—

MITCHELL: How recent is your information, Mr. Secretary?

CUMMINGS: Senator, I assure you that our information is the most recent available. . . .

MITCHELL: Give us a date, Mr. Secretary. What's the date of the latest CIA estimate on Korea?

CUMMINGS: I—We . . . we don't have that precise information at our fingertips. . . .

MITCHELL: (turning to Senator Church) Mr. Chairman, we need to know more about how this policy came about.

CHURCH: What does the Senator from Missouri suggest?

MITCHELL: That we ask General Roswell Franks to appear as a witness.

CHURCH: We've attempted to do so. The administration refuses on the grounds of executive privilege.

MITCHELL: Then I move we subpoena General Franks to testify in closed session.

STARNES: I second that motion of the Senator from Missouri . . .

Moscow

Leonid Brezhnev looked up from the KGB account of the American Senate hearing and the Mitchell episode. "When is Franks to testify?"

"I can't say precisely," Yuri Andropov answered. "These things are negotiated between the White House and Congress. But within several weeks, I should think."

"Time enough to show our compassionate American friends just how oppressive the South Koreans can be, Yuri Vladimirovich?"

Tokyo

Takeo Amaya, frozen with fear, huddled against the wall of the American Embassy. A long-time employee of the Americans, she was now chief of the bookkeeping and audit section, a position of responsibility and trust difficult for women to attain in the still largely male-dominated world of Japan. She had decided to leave somewhat early. Her husband Masaki didn't have to entertain clients and so

would be home for dinner. She'd asked her parents to take
care of their son Yataro for the night. She and Masaki had
had little time for themselves, and she was looking forward
to the evening.

Leaving the embassy and walking the half block to the
bus stop, she'd noticed the nearly nonexistent pedestrian
traffic. As she stood at the curb, a van pulled up and parked
nearby and television crews began setting up their cameras
and remote antennas. Within minutes, from each end of the
block and the side street directly opposite, came crowds of
angry shouting men, many dressed in makeshift helmets
and armor, some carrying shields, others with banners.

She had seen innumerable street demonstrations,
especially during the years of the American war in Viet
Nam. But none of these banners were in Japanese. To be
sure, there were the usual English posters for the benefit of
American television, but the non-English ones were in
Korean—a language her husband said was unworthy of a
Japanese to learn. The English-language banners said
something about American support of the fascist dictator
Park Chung Hee and repression of freedom and human
rights in South Korea.

Any chance of retreat to the embassy was cut off by the
howling mob, which was now throwing stones, bricks, and
bottles at the compound walls. The Marines had barricaded
the gates and settled down to wait for Tokyo's well-trained
(and well-experienced) riot police.

Takeo dodged one stone, but in so doing, stepped in
front of a bottle thrown from somewhere deep in the crowd.
It broke over her head and the contents immediately
ignited, running down her body, turning her into a screaming human torch. The last thing she felt was an instant of
engulfing pain as her nerve endings were seared out of
existence. She heard sirens, but of course it was too
late.

That evening across America, television news carried
the demonstration. Two networks ignored Takeo Amaya's
death. The sincere, blow-dried anchorman on the third

network did manage to work in that ". . . one death resulted," three words of public acknowledgment that a life had ended before moving on to other news.

The next day there was scattered editorial comment in Japanese newspapers to the effect that the government in Seoul had to undertake reforms in human rights or otherwise expect loss of support from Tokyo; that the outpouring rage of the emigré Korean community in Japan was an understandable, if regrettable, expression of opposition to Park Chung Hee's oppression.

The day following that, columnists in New York and Washington echoed the theme, preaching that supporting dictators such as Park put America on the wrong side of history.

And while the columnists were firing their broadsides against Seoul, Masaki Amaya and his young son Yataro took part in the Shinto ceremony for the dead, with Takeo's ashes occupying a place of honor in an urn surrounded by plum blossoms.

TOP SECRET
NAFAR

Excluded from
automatic downgrading   Copy 1 of 3 copies

MEMORANDUM FOR: Director of Central
                                  Intelligence
SUBJECT: Soviet Activities Against U.S. Embassy Tokyo (C)

1. (TS) The recent riot in Tokyo in which U.S. Embassy employee Takeo Amaya was killed appears to have been instigated by Soviet intelligence.

2. (TSNF) Japanese security services report that the demonstration was planned by the Chosen

Soren, an organization established and funded by the Democratic Peoples' Republic of Korea Research Bureau, Pyongyang's intelligence agency, which is directly controlled by Kim Chong-Il, the son and heir-apparent of North Korean dictator Kim Il-Sung.

3. (TSNF) These same sources also report that the planning sessions were attended by Yuri S. Rylev, who is credited to the Soviet Embassy in Tokyo as commerce attaché. (Rylev is a KGB officer whose last foreign posting was in the Soviet consulate, Lyon, France. He was expelled from France in 1971. For details on Rylev, see OCR File 29K.231JS.)

4. (TSNF) Rylev provided Chosen Soren with detailed information about the security system of the U.S. Embassy, as well as funds for transportation, banners, and compensation to participants for wages lost.

5. (S) Technical analysis of the weapon that killed Mrs. Amaya reveals that the ignition device was a relatively sophisticated impact fuse as opposed to a rag wick normally employed in homemade firebombs of this sort. Moreover, the filler of the weapon was a mixture of gasoline, egg whites, and potassium nitrate: a gelled flame fuel which, like napalm, adheres more readily to the intended target and produces a greater heat concentration than ordinary gasoline.

6. (TSNF) The weapon described in paragraph 5 above is a "standard" in GRU and KGB tradecraft manuals. It is likely that a number of these devices were provided to Chosen Soren by Rylev.

7. (U) You may wish to consider including above

as an item in the President's Daily Brief. DIA of course, stands ready to provide a draft article.

Samuel E. Bartlett
Lieutenant General
Director
Defense Intelligence Agency

Distribution:
Copy 2—DDO
Copy 3—Director, NSA

Roswell Franks was apoplectic. He'd not even finished the Bartlett memo before he'd crushed it into a wadded ball and threw it against the wall. Jay Mathias waited until Franks sat down at his desk, then got up from his own chair, retrieved the memo, and ironed it out on the coffee table with his hands.

"I know what that goddamn no-good bastard's up to," Franks stormed. "If we send some piece of crap like that to the White House, they'll be on my ass again. They'll say I'm fighting the problem. But if I send a memo back to Bartlett telling him I don't think it's worth putting in the PDB, then that sonofabitch will leak it all over town." His voice grew even more shrill. "And there'll be another goddamn article in the goddamn *New York* fucking *Times* that I'm suppressing intelligence to support the White House."

Mathias had served four Directors of Central Intelligence before Roswell Franks. He was treated well by Franks and had no personal complaints. But he heard the mutterings in the halls—this Director's up shit creek, he thought. But a job's a job, and mine depends on coping with this sort of thing.

"General, I think you can deflect this."

Franks looked up at him, giving in to the impulse for a chin thrust. "How?"

"You might call Bartlett. Thank him for the memo. Congratulate him on the tip-off about the relationship between the Soviet Embassy and the Chosen Soren. Tell him that you're going to make it a priority Agency issue.

That way," Mathias explained, "we get out of sending something to the White House and we take that Soviet– emigré group connection away from DIA and put it under your control."

Franks thought for a minute, then picked up the telephone. "Get me General Bartlett on the secure line." He turned back to Mathias as the call was being put through. "You know, of course, what DDO will try to do with this." He waved the wrinkled memorandum.

"But General, DDO's going to be busy circling its own wagons."

For the first time that day, Roswell Franks smiled.

Russell Senate Office Building—Washington, D.C.

Since he wanted the meeting, Frank Church thought it'd be the polite thing to offer to come to Laurence Mitchell's office instead of summoning the junior Senator to appear on Church's home ground. But when he was shown into Mitchell's office, he knew he'd miscalculated.

The place unsettled him. There were no pictures of Mitchell anywhere, nor were there the framed campaign posters or other political memorabilia he'd expected. One wall was taken up by a Rockwell original of Boy Scouts. Church thought the subject fitted its goody-two-shoes owner. And though he didn't recognize it as such, a display box on another wall held a delicate Korean celadon wine cup and stand from the twelfth century Koryo dynasty. Behind Mitchell's desk was another display box containing an American flag, folded in the tricorn.

The two men sat, Church on the leather couch, Mitchell in a worn easy chair. Church surveyed the former Marine. Mitchell had to work to keep the pounds off, but so far he was successful. Slightly under six feet, Mitchell had reddish-blond hair and blue eyes. He carried himself easily, and faced Frank Church with the assurance of a man who knew he'd measured up time and again against other men and had far outdistanced them.

The two traded Washington small talk. Then, crossing

his legs and leaning back into the leather couch, Church brought up the Cummings hearing.

"Laurence, I got a call from the White House on the Franks matter."

Mitchell cocked his head warily. "And?"

"They want us to drop it." Anticipating a strong reaction from Mitchell, Church held up both hands, as if to deflect a blow. "That doesn't mean, Laurence, that General Franks couldn't come over here and talk to you. And they said they'd be glad to set up a briefing out at Langley for you—"

"Not good enough, Frank." Mitchell shook his head. "First, there's Starnes. I doubt that he'd back off. And I don't think he should. No matter what you think about him, this is all to do with foreign policy, and if we really care about bipartisan support, he's got to be included. Second, I want Roswell Franks under oath and I want his testimony on the record."

Mitchell's preachy manner infuriated Church. Of course, this had something "to do with foreign policy"! What did this thick-headed Marine think the Foreign Relations Committee did? Sell real estate? Church managed what he hoped was a straight face. He persisted. "The White House—"

"Frank," Mitchell interrupted, "was it so long ago that Lyndon Johnson railroaded the Tonkin Gulf Resolution through the Senate? Through the world's greatest deliberative body? How many of you voted against that? Two? And then you found it was going to be used to support a no-win policy that killed fifty thousand Americans. Viet Nam divided our country as it hadn't been since the Civil War. We had to go to war in Korea because we let the Soviets and North Koreans think they could get away with it. I just want to make sure that if we have to fight again in Korea, I did all I could to look at the angles before we took off. If we're going to pull our troops out of Korea, Frank, I want to know what the chessboard will look like when that's done."

Church's voice became petulant. "Laurence. The White House wants this Korea thing—the troop withdrawal. They could make this very political. Make it a party issue. Brand you a renegade. The next election could find the President of the United States saying you're not a good Democrat."

Mitchell stood up, angry, his face flushed. To Church's immense relief, his voice was controlled. "Frank, I'm a Democrat all right. But that doesn't mean I'm a rubber stamp for the White House. I don't believe that being a 'good Democrat' and a 'good American' are mutually exclusive. I belong to the party of FDR, Harry Truman, and Jack Kennedy. If that's not good enough for Jimmy Carter and the McGovernites that hang around the back stairs over there, then so be it."

After Church left, Mitchell stood by the door in thought, then turned to look at the folded flag behind his desk. Pausing, he reached for the telephone and punched a number he'd committed to memory.

"Eleanor? This is Bud."

Langley, Virginia

Eleanor Trowbridge and Lew Parsons sat across from Alan Squires. He was a frail man with thin greasy hair, watery blue eyes, and a pallid complexion. At sporadic intervals he'd break into a manic, braying laugh unrelated to what was going on around him. But he knew how to get around in bureaucracies. As soon as he'd gotten his security clearances and badge, he'd come around to call on each of his fellow National Intelligence Officers. He was deferential without being obsequious and, importantly, he knew what he was talking about.

"I think you'll agree, Eleanor, Lew, that even a crude device in the hands of the South Koreans could destabilize all Northeast Asia."

Eleanor swiveled slightly in her chair. "No one will argue that, Alan. But that's a leap unsupported by any credible evidence. And that's something that could be said about the North as well."

Squire's face jerked into a grimace and he gave one of his barking laughs. "Do you really believe, Eleanor, that the Russians would permit that? They know how crazy Kim is."

Parsons leaped in. "Are you saying we're not watching the store in South Korea? Or that Park is even worse than Kim?"

Squires knew he'd gone far enough. At least for now. "I'm simply saying that the South Koreans have the ability and the motive to make the attempt. And there's the matter of the Blue House memorandum—"

"Of doubtful authenticity, Alan," Parsons interrupted.

"Of *unknown* authenticity, Lew," Squires countered. "I think we have to pay close attention to the possibility," he added hastily, "as we undoubtedly have. I've been given this job of looking at nuclear proliferation. Worldwide. Not just at Korea. We've been told by the White House to work this issue, and I'd like to have your support."

Parsons toyed with a paper clip, carefully, precisely straightening it out, then as carefully rebending it back into shape. The swift movement of his fingers was hypnotic. Eleanor watched Squires's eyes become fixed on the shining wire. No one spoke. Parsons kept working the clip back and forth. Finally it broke.

Eleanor cleared her throat. "Alan, Lew and I are merely public servants. We certainly aren't about to tell the White House no. But I know Korea, and, though not as well as Lew, here, I know the ins and outs of human intelligence. Because that's what we'll need. We'll need to set human agents out against the Blue House and the South Korean government to snoop to see if they're trying to build a nuclear weapon. To prove a negative. Our satellites won't handle that and the signal interception people will be of little use to us.

"I'm not posing moral objections to this, Alan," she continued. "We all spy on our friends. The French spy on us, we spy on the Germans, and the Israelis spy on us all. But there are risks. Some friends are more skittish than others. The ROK's are like that. And with good reason. They saw us encourage the coup against Ngo Dinh Diem, and they don't put it past us to try the same against Park. If the KCIA grabs one of our people opening the wrong safe or copying documents, Mr. Carter's administration could be in trouble."

Parsons nudged one piece of the paper clip with the other, pushing it across the tabletop. "Eleanor's laid it out, Alan. We'll do the job. But I hope you understand DDO's reluctance to rush into this kind of thing."

Alan Squires smiled. "I fully appreciate the sensitivities of DDO," he said, trying to give *sensitivities* what he intended to be an ironic emphasis, but succeeding only in sneering. "But I hope you understand in turn that I'm now responsible to General Franks for a major portion of the Korea estimate and—"

Eleanor cut him off. "We're aware of your responsibilities, Alan. We really are."

The Capitol—Washington, D.C.

The United States Senate maintains a special room for sensitive hearings. S-407 is tucked up under one side of the Capitol's massive dome, a sleek, small room without windows, which is guarded twenty-four hours a day and is protected by a variety of electronic and electro-optical intrusion sensors and monitoring devices. All of this is under the immediate control of a large and genial Irishman by the name of George Murphy.

Murphy had duplicated the seating arrangements of other less exclusive hearing rooms, down to the elevated U-shaped table. In seeing to the security of S-407 over the years, George had himself become the witness to and keeper of an infinite variety of secrets. Given the revolving door turnover of most positions in Washington, George's steady stewardship gave him an uninterrupted view of American intelligence paralleled only by Ibrahim Bazdarkian out at Langley, of whom George had heard much but never met. George had seen the probing of Eisenhower's use of CIA in 1954 to overthrow the leftist regime in Guatemala. He'd been present at the agonizing post mortem of the Bay of Pigs.

George cancelled his reservation at Monocle, sensing

the importance of the hearings. First came the CIA's legislative counsel and his assistants, to prepare for Roswell Franks's testimony. They unfolded a screen for use with a VuGraph projector, a fixture at every American government and military briefing, a fixture without which most spokesmen were struck dumb.

Roswell Franks entered, accompanied by Jay Mathias. George showed them back to his private office, where he'd made certain hot coffee was waiting and that his safes were securely locked.

Foreign Relations Committee staff came next, putting out agenda and various background papers for the members. They were still at work when the first of the Senators arrived. George slipped back to his office and got Franks, who came out to chat with Jess Starnes and Frank Church.

Laurence Mitchell, carrying several thick notebooks, came in and went directly to his seat. Church glanced over at him, patted Franks's shoulder, and moved to his chair. Starnes sat to his right, with two other Republicans. At a small table in front of Church and below him, sat the hearing stenographer, dictating softly into a face-mask microphone a transcript of the proceedings. Church took the gavel, tapped it once lightly, and called the hearing to order.

"General Franks, thank you for appearing before us this morning. I understand you've prepared a briefing on the relative military postures of the two Koreas and you've agreed to answer questions from committee members." Church stopped to read a note from Mitchell. He frowned at the Senator from Missouri then addressed Franks again. "I have been asked that you testify after having been formally sworn."

After taking the oath, Franks moved to the projection screen, picked up a telescoping metal pointer, and gave a smooth, well-rehearsed briefing on the military forces of North and South Korea, along with a veritable blizzard of data on production rates, maneuver frequencies, trends of naval exercises, and the usual appraisal of the succession of leadership after the death of Pyongyang's Kim Il-Sung.

When Franks finished, the questioning by Church and the others was brief. It was as if they all wanted to get quickly to the main event: the confrontation between Mitchell and Franks.

Mitchell arranged his notes before him. "I want to join with our chairman to thank you, General, for coming here today. . . ."

Roswell Franks smiled. "I understand, sir, I had a choice of showing up on my own or being dragged in here by the sheriff."

Mitchell smiled back. "We have a saying in our part of the country, General. Something about getting the mule's attention by hitting him between the eyes with a two by four."

"Senator, you got my attention."

"Now, General, I agree again with my chairman. Your briefing was superb. What I want to know is, how recent is the information?"

"Senator, not to be cute, we're continually upgrading intelligence. Some portions of the briefing I gave were less than hours old."

"General, what I'm looking for here is the date you last had a comprehensive effort out at Langley. I want to know when you brought in NSA, DIA, and the rest of the Intelligence Community, to take a fresh look at Korea. At the military situation. I believe that's called a National Intelligence Estimate." Mitchell spelled out the acronym. "N-I-E."

"The NIE isn't the only source of information we make available to the—" Franks began.

"General." Mitchell's interruption was abrupt. "You've said it yourself elsewhere about other subjects, and I quote: 'The National Intelligence Estimate is the highest form of authoritative intelligence. It represents the essence of the best thinking of the Intelligence Community which is intended directly for the President to assist in his deliberations on foreign policy.'

"That quote, General, came from your remarks on *Meet the Press*, Sunday, May 15, 1977. Or at least that's the transcript furnished me by the network. Have you backed off the position, General?"

Franks started to speak, but Mitchell went on.

"I want one date, General. Tell me the date of the last NIE that did an assessment of North Korea against South Korea."

Franks stared at Mitchell. A former *Marine*. "Our last NIE on Korea was published June, 1973. But I believe—"

"Thank you, General." Mitchell turned slightly to his right to make certain Church was paying attention. "So the last NIE came out during the Nixon administration. Years ago. Now here we are, pulling troops out of Korea and you haven't done a new estimate to give us some idea—some inkling—as to whether or not that's a wise idea."

"Senator, I must protest, I—"

Mitchell turned back to Franks, jabbing a finger at the CIA Director. "General, you can protest later. I want to get a point across. I want to know, General Franks, if you now have a new estimate in the works, and if so, when that estimate might see light of day."

Franks's anger overwhelmed him. To have been hauled up before this . . . this Star Chamber was bad enough. But to be harassed by this . . . this *Marine* who had no respect for a three-star general, was enraging. He leaned forward, thrusting his chin toward Mitchell. "Yes, Senator, we do have an estimate being done. As to when it'll be completed, that depends on getting agreements with the other participants about the wording and the major findings."

"By 'other participants,' General, you mean NSA, DIA—the rest of the Intelligence Community?"

"Yes. We put together a draft at staff level and then we have to get formal consensus on what NIE says. That could take a matter of hours or it could be contentious."

"If contentious, how long could this coordination process take?"

"Weeks. Maybe longer. But that's a hypothetical— "

"In the work that's been done on this new estimate, do you see any significant changes from the 1973 NIE?"

Nervously, jerkily, Franks adjusted his tie. Somebody's been talking to him, he thought. He's got something up his sleeve. "There can't be a change until everyone's agreed to it, Senator. And that just hasn't happened. In the process of writing the draft, it's natural to have some analysts come up with differing assessments. They argue about those differences, and if they can't settle that particular issue, they elevate it up to their superiors. If we can't agree, say, between CIA and DIA, then a footnote's put in the estimate that explains clearly the differences to the reader."

"Have you sat in judgment of some of these differences on Korea?"

"Yes," Franks answered. "Just recently an analyst at Langley insisted on a presentation of North Korea navy forces that was clearly misleading. We went back and forth for three days on the issue. I came out on top of that one and we modified the presentation."

Mitchell looked at his notes, then at Franks. "How was the presentation misleading, General?"

"Why, the woman," pausing to let the gender sink in, "the woman insisted on a table displaying comparative numbers of boats only. The North had a large number of small boats." Franks was warming to his story, enjoying the memory of his confrontation with Eleanor Trowbridge. "The South has fewer but larger vessels. It was an example of the doom-and-gloom alarmist school of analysis." Franks became sweeteningly condescending. "It happens when the analyst doesn't have firsthand knowledge of the subject matter."

"In this case, General, a woman who didn't know about navies?"

Franks looked for the first time at the reporter. Over the face-mask microphone, she stared at him. Had her eyes narrowed? Sensing a trap, Franks smiled. "I only cite the incident to show, Senator, why we don't forward the first draft up here to the Hill—or to the White House, for that matter."

Mitchell regarded Franks for a long moment. "My chairman is signaling me that I've exceeded my time, General. Let me sum up." A believer in checklists, Mitchell began enumerating his points by counting on his fingers. "One: We have a policy that calls for withdrawing American troops from Korea. Two: Our last estimate of North Korean strength dates back to 1973. Three: You're working on an estimate now, but can't tell us when it'll be ready."

Mitchell turned in his chair to face Frank Church. "Mr. Chairman, in view of General Franks's testimony before us today, I don't believe we have any alternative but to press for a resolution calling for a halt to the troop withdrawal until the new estimate is completed."

Church was stunned. Jess Starnes was urgently whispering to his staffer to round up the absent Republican members of the committee and get them up to the hearing room. The Democrats, to Church's left, huddled among themselves, excluding Mitchell.

George Murphy watched as CIA people took down the projection screen. It wasn't hard to figure out what had happened—how Mitchell had lost. Church had called for a fifteen-minute coffee break, during which he commandeered George's office. As George was closing the door he heard Church ask for the President. Shortly thereafter, Church talked to each of the Democrats except Mitchell. Probably passed the word that it would be a party issue and the President didn't want any opposition. Since the Foreign Relations Committee had nine Democrats and six Republicans, the Mitchell resolution had failed eight to seven.

Then George looked at his watch. Perhaps he still might make lunch at the Monocle.

Rehoboth Beach, Delaware

Susan drove east out of Washington along the nearly empty Route 50. Slouched beside her, John Freeman scanned that morning's *Washington Post*.

"Replays of the *Times*," he observed, folding the paper and putting it in the back.

"The Carter memo?"

"Yeah. All the talk is that Brzezinski put Carter up to it. Whatever—Franks is on a tear."

Susan fiddled with the stereo and managed to get a tape out of the glove compartment. "I'm not surprised. It isn't often the Director of CIA gets a nasty note from the President."

"Nasty and brutish, but not very short." Freeman laughed, reaching over to squeeze her shoulder. "Roswell's getting screwed for all the wrong reasons. The White House is pinning the Iran mess on him. All along, Carter and his people believed that the Shah would be around forever. It's blown up in their faces, and they're trying to make Franks the scapegoat.

"Hell, I don't know how long Franks will last. Getting hired or getting fired at that level is so goddamn complex. Franks still hasn't started the purge everybody says is coming. I imagine they'd like to have him do that before they throw him overboard."

In summer Rehoboth is a crowded boardwalk beach of tacky motels and weekly-rental cottages, stand-and-eat hot dog stands, cotton-candy vendors, and T-shirt shops.

It was late fall, and the boardwalk was shut down and deserted. Holding hands, Susan Forbes and John Freeman walked into a clean, cold north wind. The afternoon sun, already low on the horizon, was veiled by a haze of clouds, turning the sea, sky, and shore into a salt-sprayed monochrome of grays and silvers.

Susan had suggested Rehoboth. As long as she'd lived in the Washington area, she'd never been there. "I want to go somewhere that's new for both of us," she'd told him.

She took his arm, slipping her hand into his jacket pocket, making a secret warm mingling of flesh that excited both of them. They stopped and turned to face each other. He moved his free hand to caress her cheek and softly kissed her.

She looked at him and smiled. "I love you, John Freeman. I didn't want to tell you in Washington. I didn't want it mixed up with all that back there." She put her hand over his mouth. "Don't say anything. I didn't tell you to get something in return. I just wanted to do that for myself."

Walking for another quarter hour, they found a small restaurant whose bright white plaster walls and light oak tables set with fresh flowers were a cheerful contrast to the gray afternoon. They ordered lunch and Bloody Marys.

They finished lunch. He reached over and touched her hand. "You got me here to tell me you love me." She looked at him, smiling. He reached deep into an inside pocket. "I brought something to Rehoboth too." He opened the small box and the diamond caught fire, reflecting in her widened eyes. "Time to go back. I'll drive."

Chapter 5

Camp Peary, Virginia

Camp Peary, on the James River in southern Virginia, is but a few minutes drive from the tourist attraction of Colonial Williamsburg. Passersby are advised that the camp is a Department of Defense experimental training facility. The locals, however, as well as most of the intelligence agencies around the world, know it as the Farm—a venerable part of CIA mythology.

Sprawling over thousands of acres, the Farm has numerous barracks, ammunition dumps, and firing ranges. There are also exercise areas where carpenters, electricians, and other craftsmen can duplicate any building or location in the world for practicing special operations.

Near the southern boundary, away from the noise of the demolitions and small-arms ranges, are a series of rustic lodges, named after trees, which are used by the upper-level management of the Agency for retreats and planning sessions away from the distractions of Langley. Scattered along broad sand paths that wander through tall pines, the lodges and cabins are simply but comfortably furnished. Meals are prepared and served in a pine-paneled central dining room run by José and Fatima Rodriguez, an elderly couple who had once owned a three-star restaurant in Havana. José and Fatima's restaurant also served as a front for the Agency until Castro's DGI—the Dirección General de Intelligencia—caught on and closed the doors. José was subjected to two months of brutal interrogation before he escaped La Cabaña prison with the aid of the Agency and fled with Fatima to Miami.

Andrew Cabot and Eleanor Trowbridge had been the last to arrive at Evergreen lodge, just missing lunch with John Freeman and Lew Parsons, who had flown in together on an earlier plane.

Parsons knelt before the stone fireplace and put another log on the flames, making certain it was properly in place by poking about with bronze tongs. All were quiet, as if their attention were needed to make certain that Parsons went about everything right. Finally, Eleanor stood, breaking the spell. Firelight glinted from her glasses. Cabot had taken a seat on a cushioned bench. Dressed in a rough wool shirt and twill trousers, he seemed harder, more angular. Freeman had saved sandwiches from lunch, which he put on a low table between Eleanor and Andrew Cabot.

John Freeman came to the fire, handed another log to Parsons, then turned to Cabot. "How is it, Andrew?"

Cabot didn't acknowledge Freeman. He shifted on the bench. Still Cabot said nothing. Freeman wondered if he'd been heard.

At last Cabot responded in a low whisper. "It's bad, John." Suddenly restless, Cabot stood and moved to Parsons's side at the fire. Taking up the poker, he stirred the hot embers and made minute adjustments to Parsons's work. "It's very bad. Franks has started the purge."

Putting the poker aside, Cabot told them how it had begun. He'd been summoned to Roswell Franks's office. With the admiral was the ever-present Mathias as well as the Agency's general counsel.

"Franks gave me this." Cabot produced and held aloft a blue binder about three inches thick. "'These are the details,' he told me, 'you can read them later.' Then Franks launched into a rambling monologue. It almost seemed as if he were rehearsing lines from a script, lines we'll no doubt hear later. Claimed that the reduction of DDO was something that'd been in the works long before he came on board as Director. He told me he was only moving along a course that had been charted—he actually put it that way, 'charted'—by Bush and others, to include DDO itself."

Parsons cursed. "We planned a gradual reduction after Viet Nam, but we never intended a massive—"

"Goddamnit, Lew—" Cabot's voice cracked. "There's no sense in dwelling on the past. It's gone. This is now, and this bastard's gutting the Agency."

Parsons, taken aback by Cabot's outburst, hesitated, then suggested quietly, "Tell us, Froggy."

"He's wiping out over eight hundred jobs," Cabot blurted. "They aren't all firings. The jobs will go immediately. The people in them we can move to various other positions—mostly support—in DDO. Others we can probably find room for in Admin or in Analysis."

"What it means," Eleanor explained, "is that Franks is taking DDO out of doing some of the kinds of work it used to do. This isn't a reduction in *people* to save money or anything like that. It's a restructuring. It's Franks and the White House putting more emphasis on the technical collection and less on the human intelligence."

"Froggy, there's something else, isn't there?" Lew Parsons asked.

"I—"

Quietly, Eleanor rose and went to Cabot's side. "Let me, Andrew. It's better if I do it." Cabot's shoulders sagged. His lower lip trembled and he turned to put the binder on the mantel. Eleanor stood, back to the fire, hands clutched, feet slightly spread. "The Director, in addition to eliminating the DDO positions, has requested the immediate retirement or termination of certain senior officers in the Agency." She looked around the fire. "We are all on that list except for Andrew."

Parsons broke the silence. "This is a long way to come to learn that."

"What we came here for, Lew," Cabot's voice was surprising for its force, "is to talk about where we go from here."

Editorial
The Washington Post

. . . and we applaud the recent initiative by
General Franks at CIA to reshape that troubled
agency. By pruning back the super-secret Directorate of Operations, which has all too often
considered itself to be the only law west (or east)
of the Potomac, the General—if belatedly—
recognizes that the bloated corps of spooks recruited during Viet Nam is no longer needed,
and, indeed, sends a signal to the world that
America is at last moving beyond its self-
destructive infatuation with covert operations.

Chelyabinsk

Vasili Kiktev had gotten the report before dawn but
decided to wait until Andropov had a break in the tour of
the special production unit. They had flown to Chelyabinsk
from Moscow the day before in a TU-154A that Aeroflot
maintained exclusively for the travel of Politburo members.
Kiktev had been kept busy during much of the three-hour
flight, shuttling between the communications center and
Andropov's plush cabin, which took up the rear half of the
airliner. Nonetheless, he'd been able to steal a few moments to nap in the wide seats up front.

Dinner had been a small affair. Andropov and Kiktev
had been hosted only by the director of the Chelyabinsk
weapons facility, a fat Ukrainian named Porsynko and his
equally somber military counterpart, a totally unre-
markable—and dull—lieutenant general of the Strategic
Rocket Forces. Normally, a Politburo member traveling
outside Moscow could expect a reception by a whole
retinue of party and government officials, but Kiktev had
arranged for the trip to be made under conditions of

strictest secrecy. Few would be so foolish as to contradict such explicit orders from Dzerzhinsky Square.

Kiktev whispered instructions to their guide, and as a result, had a few moments alone with Andropov before lunch.

Andropov sat, his elbows resting on the wood table. "They are doing well, Vasili Petrovich." Andropov gestured to the thick ring binder he'd been given at the beginning of the briefings. "I must confess their technical explanations are sometimes too deep for me, but I have a better grasp of the design problems. I had thought all nuclear weapons were alike—at least after they went off. There are complications. But nothing we can't overcome." He pushed the book away. "But obviously you have something on your mind besides this."

Kiktev handed Andropov a two-page telex flimsy, a report from the KGB *rezident* in Washington. He read with deliberation, a look of incredulity growing on his face.

"He's done it, Vasili Petrovich. I can't believe it, but he's really done it. To think, a Director of CIA setting about dismantling his action arm."

"It's not only the operations, Comrade Andropov. This," Kiktev excitedly tapped the telex, "has eliminated the faction that has been the mainspring for their interest in our Asian plan. At the very least, we've gained months. If we're fortunate, very fortunate, this could do it for us."

Yuri Andropov nodded without enthusiasm and looked at the telex, searching for implications that reached beyond the fate of CIA's clandestine service.

Portland, Maine
Washington, D.C.

The Army gave John Freeman two weeks administrative leave following his dismissal from CIA. Completing his necessary debriefings and outprocessing from Langley, he and Susan visited her parents on their farm near Portland, Maine. Freeman and her parents meshed instantly, and days of long runs down country back roads and exploring

New England eased his apprehension and foreboding. On the drive back to Washington, he and Susan had been relaxed and happy.

Monday, after returning from Maine, Freeman was back in uniform and reporting to the Army's Military Personnel Center in Alexandria for reassignment. A dumpy, grim-faced female clerk left him in a stark waiting room. On one wall a cork bulletin board bore witness to the Army's penchant for publishing directives to cover every contingency. He had just worked through summer water-safety tips, the hazards of winter driving, and was finishing the instructions on nuclear-attack survival (to which someone had appended the inevitable last step, "Bend over, grasping the back of your knees, and kiss your ass goodbye!") when the door opened and a rumpled older officer beckoned him to come in.

The next job—"duty station," as Colonel Thomas Lynch put it—would be in an administrative capacity as special assistant to the commanding general of INSCOM, the Army's Intelligence and Security Command. Lynch looked at Freeman's personnel file before him and shook his head. "You certainly haven't fit too many patterns, Colonel Freeman." He smiled as he handed Freeman his orders. "But it looks like you had a good time doing whatever it is you do."

Freeman slipped the sheaf of orders into an envelope. "Who's the commander at INSCOM, Colonel?"

Lynch showed surprise. "I thought you knew. He asked for you specifically. Bronowski. Jack Bronowski. Came here from Korea just last week."

Mineral'nye Vody

Although Leonid Brezhnev's train would not show up until early evening, the station at Mineral'nye Vody had been cordoned off since mid-morning. The militia had allowed only the stationmaster, telegrapher, and three engine-maintenance workers to remain, and they had to go about their work trailed by humorless armed escorts. While only mid-September, the air was chilled by the wind off the snow-covered mountains of the northern Caucasus.

An hour before the train was due, a Zil limousine arrived, accompanied by a battered military truck. Two men in topcoats and hats got out, returned the salute of the militia major, then walked through the station and out onto the platform. The KGB troops in the trucks reinforced the militia, keeping the men on the platform in view, but from a distance. The younger man was about two inches shorter than his companion. The two walked the length of the platform without speaking.

When the General Secretary traveled, it was expected that he would be met by the senior party officers wherever he stopped. Even so, it was obvious to the younger man that Yuri Andropov didn't relish the interruption of his holiday.

Aware of his friend's disquiet, Andropov smiled disarmingly. "Ah, Misha, the air is good up here. And it will be beneficial for you to spend some time with the General Secretary." Andropov clapped his companion on the shoulder. They talked together with an easy confidence nurtured by years of companionship, with an understanding springing from their common roots in the Stavropol region, where both had been born and raised.

"There is talk, Yuri Vladimirovich, about the manner of the General Secretary's travel."

Andropov searched his companion's face. "The manner? By train, you mean?"

The answer was cautious. "Yes. Some say . . . I have heard it said that . . ." The younger man pursed his lips, cocked his head slightly and shrugged, now clearly wishing he'd not brought the subject up.

Charitably, Andropov finished the sentence. "That the General Secretary's health isn't what it used to be? Is that it?"

The younger man nodded.

"You have good sources, Misha. Do they dare predict who will follow our leader?"

Since learning of this meeting, the younger man had thought about a move. A small venture. A conversational pawn. He'd rehearsed it repeatedly, polished and discarded a dozen variants. Now, Andropov himself had provided the opening. "No one is so foolish," he answered. He looked closely to catch Andropov's reaction, then added: "But many believe Comrade Brezhnev has brought us to a fork in the road."

Andropov's expression remained stolid, unreadable. The two completed another turn and had almost gotten to the end of the platform again when Andropov finally spoke.

"Very good, Misha." Andropov chose his words carefully, knowing precisely where he wanted to go but having to pick his way, as if he had thought much about the matter but he had spoken about it to no one. Which was the case. "Let us begin with the basics: Our principal enemy is the United States. We cannot coexist indefinitely. One of us must emerge superior to the other."

"There are those who speak of historical inevitability, of the correlation of forces . . ."

Andropov frowned. "Historical inevitability and the correlation of forces are intellectual bomb shelters for the lazy and inept—the slugs who would sit on their fat asses and not plan, sacrifice, or dare. Action on our part," he smacked one fist into the palm of the other hand, "decisive action on our part makes things happen—shapes the correlation of forces. We cannot sit and expect everything will fall into our laps merely because we are good Communists. We have to have the vision to look into the future."

"And that future, Yuri Vladimirovich?" prompted the younger man.

"Listen. There are things we have done well. One of them is that we've built a military force without peer. And that is Leonid Brezhnev's greatest accomplishment. But like many men who have achieved much, he clings to past successes, and they are his only blueprint for the years ahead. More of the same. That's Leonid Ilyich's intention: more. More missiles, more submarines, more tanks." Andropov shook his head in disparagement. "It is a ponderous strategy; one of mass. It is without intellectual basis or flexibility. He wants a broadsword when we need a stiletto."

The two men stopped. Andropov signaled an aide who had remained discreetly out of earshot. Tea was poured from a thermos. They sat on a nearby wooden bench.

"We must keep our military advantage over the Americans," Andropov continued. "There is no doubt about that. We have paid a great cost to get to where we are today. We've paid the kinds of costs the Americans are increasingly unwilling to bear." He sipped his tea. "And we have gained a certain measure of success. Never again will they lord their nuclear superiority over us. They have lost that advantage. We know it, they know it. And most importantly, the rest of the world knows it.

"But there are perils in the years ahead. Dangers to which our beloved General Secretary is oblivious. One of these is the explosion in technology. The Americans are pulling away from us at an exponential rate. They could develop a society and an economy with which we could never compete. That is, if we continue on our present course. And this in turn could give them new weapons— weapons based on principles undreamed of today.

"But Leonid Brezhnev is blind." Andropov made a gesture with his teacup of throwing out something he'd found distasteful. "More interceptors and air-defense systems—all built with yesterday's technology. Why, Misha, the Americans are experimenting with airplanes that are invisible to our radars! He wants to stack even more nuclear weapons on ballistic missiles while the Americans build satellites that can pinpoint silos to within a few centimeters. And soon—within a few years—they will be able to destroy our missiles in flight.

"Brezhnev and his kind represent the ancien régime. Dinosaurs. They fear the computer and the photocopier. They haven't the imagination to cope with these things, so they try to keep them out, as they still secretly use garlic to ward off the evil eye. They believe the computer will break their control of the people, when, with some forethought, they would see that it offers new opportunities to consolidate social and political controls in ways undreamed of."

Andropov beckoned the aide to come collect the teacups. "If Leonid Brezhnev has his way, his successor will make us into a nation destined to be forever inferior to the West."

The younger man was silent, then turned to Andropov. "You and I have talked before about the General Secretary's plan to assist the Koreans. Might that not have some influence on who succeeds him?"

Andropov hesitated, debating the wisdom of continuing the discussion. His deliberations were interrupted by the aide, who handed him a slip of paper. The General Secretary's train was on time and would be arriving in ten minutes. Andropov showed the paper to the younger man. They both stood and stretched.

"The Korean affair could affect many plans, Misha. Many plans and many people."

One hundred and ten kilometers north northwest of Mineral'nye Vody, Andrei Brezhnev knocked impatiently on the door of his grandfather's private compartment. The old man took longer and longer to get ready, Andrei thought. Behind Andrei Brezhnev stood Leonid Brezhnev's personal servant of fifteen years, a stoic and generally uncommunicative Tartar who would see to a shave and gentle massage before dressing the General Secretary.

Twenty minutes later, Brezhnev joined Konstantin Chernenko in the forward section of the extended railroad car, a painstakingly restored relic of the last of the czars, a walnut-paneled cabin that served as a sitting room and office. Immediately forward and aft of Brezhnev's car, security forces ceaselessly scanned the flanks and maintained contact with the armed HIND helicopters that covered the train from an altitude of three hundred yards. The train was in constant communication with the administrative offices in the Kremlin and the underground command centers just outside Moscow and their alternates deep in the Ural Mountains. The Swedish diesel locomotive pushed ahead of it a flat car weighted with large sandbags to set off pressure mines. And yet another car carried an American Cadillac, a gift from Richard Nixon.

Konstantin Chernenko stood when Leonid Brezhnev

entered the compartment. Chernenko's flushed square face was framed by a mane of snow-white hair. He'd spent much of his life at Leonid Brezhnev's beck and call, seeing to the endless administrative details so necessary for the running of the party, the governing of the nation, and the handling of sensitive personal matters. Leonid Brezhnev's years in power had been marked by a steady accretion of relatives and friends in government and party positions.

Only because of Brezhnev, had Chernenko become a full member of the Politburo. Similarly, Brezhnev had rewarded his personal physician with a membership on the Central Committee. Brezhnev's son Yuri—young Andrei's father—was a deputy foreign-trade minister, which gave him access to luxuries of the decadent West and the government funds to enjoy them. A son-in-law was quickly promoted to general and deputy minister of interior. And then there was Brezhnev's brother-in-law, Semen Kuzmich Tsvigun, made deputy chairman of the KGB in the futile hope that he would keep an eye on the ambitious Andropov. In finding positions for a constantly growing and ever more greedy horde of relatives, Konstantin Chernenko had his hands full as the major domo for this latest reincarnation of the Russian royal family.

"Who is meeting us at the station?" asked Brezhnev.

Chernenko, who was answering the same question for the fourth time that day, pulled a small card from his coat pocket and handed it to Brezhnev, who squinted at it through his heavy glasses.

"And so Yuri Andropov waits for me." Brezhnev stared out the window. He remembered his own fearful excitement when he'd become one of the inner circle in the furtive conspiracy that threw Nikita Khrushchev out the Kremlin door. "Our professor wishes to subdue the West by guile. Intellect."

Andropov was weaving a net for him, he was certain of it. Whenever he was in a room with Andropov, he would catch the sidelong glances from the KGB chairman—sizing him up, calculating, always calculating. Timing was everything, and Yuri Andropov was good at that. The old man sighed deeply. "Perhaps we ought to challenge the Americans to a ballet contest or a vigorous poetry reading." He gave a small gurgling laugh at his own joke. Finished with his reflections, Brezhnev turned to address Chernenko straight on. "Why is he so afraid of the Americans? Does he not see they are rotten to the core?"

Chernenko nodded in agreement.

Brezhnev picked up the card Chernenko had given him and, frowning, tilted it one way then another, having obvious difficulty reading in the fading light. "This other man, the local party leader, the one with Andropov . . . His name . . . ?"

"Gorbachev, comrade. Mikhail Sergeyvich Gorbachev."

Arlington Hall Station—Arlington, Virginia

Arlington Hall, west of Washington, used to be an exclusive girls' school. In the spring of 1942 it was taken over and made the headquarters for the Army's Signal Intelligence Service, a forerunner of the National Security Agency. At the beginning of the Carter administration, Arlington Hall Station housed the Army's Intelligence and Security Command, INSCOM, as well as parts of the Defense Intelligence Agency.

"Johnny, sometimes I think I was put here by the Army to take care of you." Jack Bronowski took Freeman's hand with both of his, renewing Freeman's memory of broken knuckles, a hard ridge of callus along the edge of the palm, and an iron grip.

Bronowski motioned Freeman to the sofa and took the chair nearest him. Bronowski sat on the edge of the chair with his elbows on his knees, leaning forward, softly hitting the palm of his left hand with the fist of his right. He grinned at Freeman. "I suppose you wonder what this is all about?"

"It did cross my mind." Freeman smiled back.

Bronowski got up and began to pace the room. "Some people, shit, a *lot* of people, are worried, John. They think that the President's getting a sugar-coated view of the world out there." He waved toward the windows without breaking stride. Bronowski went on to describe how Freeman's Pentagon briefing on the estimate had been summarized and sent "back channel" to senior American military commanders around the world, and how DIA's Sam Bartlett had reported on Roswell Franks's bottling up of the estimate. "The massacre out at Langley was the last straw. When they saw you people canned, they figured that Franks was going to sit on the Korea bad news until hell froze over."

"And so?"

Bronowski stopped pacing and turned to face Freeman. He pointed to Freeman. "And so you're here, young colonel. And so I'm now the commanding general of INSCOM. And so," he smiled, "I have my own discretionary funds. Funds that have been earmarked to establish something we'll call the"—he consulted a pad of yellow legal paper—"Pacific Studies Group."

Bronowski put the pad back on his desk and sat next to Freeman on the sofa. "The group, John, is going to work under some of the best experts in the field. Through INSCOM you'll be able to task the collection assets of the entire Intelligence Community, just like you did at Langley. The first project will be a highly classified study of Korea. And—"

"And, General, the head of the group . . ."

"Eleanor Trowbridge. Sam Bartlett gave me her name. Know anybody better qualified?"

Freeman looked at Bronowski. It could be done. None of the dismissed CIA people had lost their jobs under circumstances that would prevent getting new security clearances. Arlington Hall was just far enough off the beaten track that Eleanor and others wouldn't be running into any of Franks's people. And the intelligence budgeting process was such that the Army could hire "consultants" under pseudonyms. Working under the cover of Bronowski's Pacific Studies Group, the assessment of North Korean military capabilities could be completed and the matter of intentions probed.

John Freeman nodded. "It'll work. Up to a point. And

that's when—if—we build a plausible case on what Pyongyang is doing and why they're doing it. The tricky part comes if Franks still tries to stand in the way, or worse, if the White House itself tries to stop us."

Freeman raised his voice. "Have the generals ever considered the possibility that Carter's getting exactly what he wants to hear?"

Bronowski said nothing.

"You better watch your ass in this, Jack," warned Freeman. "The generals might be willing to take on someone like Franks, but do you believe they're willing to go up against the President himself?"

Freeman didn't give Bronowski a chance to answer. "And another thing. You know how all this INSCOM arrangement's come about, the Pacific Studies Group and all, but I bet no one above you knows—or wants to know. If the shit hits the fan about this, they'll hang you out to dry. The newspapers and the networks'll make you out to be another Gordon Liddy. I can see it now—a crazy right-wing general out of Strangelove, who tried to kick off World War Three from his headquarters in a ramshackle girls' school."

Bronowski stood, signaling the end of the meeting, and again took Freeman's hand. He was still smiling. "Johnny, you do go on. At least there's no guessing about where you stand." He gave Freeman's hand a squeeze. "I never said it'd be easy. Just fun."

Within two weeks the Pacific Studies Group was settled in an old two-story classroom building whose ground-floor windows had been long since bricked up. Entry was gained through a basement garage, a procedure that duplicated Building 312: bullet-proof glass, Marine guard, gas nozzles. The previous occupants, specialists in Soviet biological and chemical warfare, had been evicted almost overnight, grumbling about having to give up their spacious offices to a Johnny-come-lately crowd.

Eleanor Trowbridge had taken up an office on the second floor, along the southern side of the building. In had come the rolltop desk, the framed batiks, and, of course, the ferns.

Her table was meant for small conferences, but it had become a gathering place toward evening for coffee, carry-out Chinese food from the Hunan Gate. The scarred table was the scene of long rambling sessions that usually began and ended with the Korea problem. It became a sanctuary, a neutral ground where one could sit down and join in any discussion in progress, and where new confidences were revealed in the unspoken hope that they would forge substitutes for those supports that'd been destroyed by the brutal dismissal from the community they'd known at Langley.

Early one Thursday afternoon Eleanor had called for Freeman. "Don't you think, John, it's time we had your General Bronowski over?"

Later, a secretary ushered the chunky general into Eleanor's office. Bronowski and Eleanor talked for the better part of an hour about inconsequential things, warily circling each other. Eleanor lost no opportunity to assure him that the support was splendid. They explored each other's careers and found mutual friends from the OSS when both had spent some months in London Station, he before parachuting into Vichy France, she while exchanging intelligence with MI-6 about Sumatran oil production for the Japanese war effort. She was surprised that he could be as subtle as he was direct; for his part, he found it refreshing that she wasn't given to female affectations.

"We'll be starting our progress briefings tomorrow, Jack," she told him. "But I'm glad we had this time to talk alone."

Bronowski nodded, his eyes fixed on her.

"I don't like having to work this way. I'm uncomfortable with this . . . this subterfuge."

Bronowski began to interrupt, but Eleanor waved a hand at him. "Hear me out. It's important that you do. I want to say this, then I'll not mention it again." She looked at the backs of her hands, palms down on the tabletop. "I wouldn't be here if this was just another bureaucratic contest. God knows, I've been in government long enough that I've learned how to lose and get up the next morning and go out and find something else to work on. But this," she held her hands out in a gesture of supplication, "this simply isn't another issue that will be lost in history a year from now. I know . . . *I know* that this is more than that. The stakes are such that I've had to put aside the only thing of value to me—my integrity. I find myself in a place from which there's no way out, except to walk close to insurrection. I can only justify that, Jack, by believing that in this one instance, the ends *do* justify the means. I will see this through, Jack. But I'll never be proud of my part in it."

Bronowski sat in silence, then asked quietly, "Where do we go from here?"

She picked up her coffee mug, then set it down again. "The North Korean Order of Battle. We've got a fairly good picture, but our people say they need to do more work on the armor holdings and some of the commando units."

Bronowski looked surprised. "I thought that'd been done."

Eleanor shook her head. "When this surfaces, it must be watertight. It not only has to be persuasive, it has to be nearly perfect. We're going to have only one chance with this, and if the administration can find any weak spots in it . . ."

Bronowski nodded in agreement. "They'll crucify you."

"The next thing is intentions. We still have no idea what Pyongyang is up to, and more important, what Moscow is up to."

"How're you linked into DDO?" Bronowski probed. "How do you avoid Franks?"

Eleanor pursed her lips. "That's tricky. Andrew Cabot will be our contact." Seeing Bronowski's look of concern, she added firmly, "He's been in this from the start. He's a professional. He also knows the risks he'll run. We pass our requirements through Lew Parsons to Andrew. Between them, they've set up a series of safe houses to handle our meetings with the DDO people Andrew trusts."

"You're not meeting them here?"

"No. No sense in pushing our luck."

"How do you work the photography and SIGINT requests?"

"Through Peter Smith at the Navy Yard. He can task the KH-11 and other photo collectors. I deal personally with Moe Hirsch. I suspect NSA knows what's going on, but they've lost no love for Franks."

Bronowski looked at his watch and then to Eleanor. "I've got to be going. Anything we can do for you?"

"I was going to have John Freeman talk to your documents people. We're going to need several passports made up."

Munich

Andrew Cabot took the evening Lufthansa flight from New York's Kennedy Airport, landing in Munich early the next morning. Lew Parsons flew on TWA to Frankfurt, where he would rent a car at the airport and drive to Munich, arriving later that same afternoon.

A week before, Andrew Cabot had called Parsons. He set up a meeting in a dingy efficiency apartment in south Arlington. Hotspur, Cabot told Parsons, would be participating in the upcoming Mutual and Balanced Force Reduction arms-control negotiations in Vienna. Hotspur, moreover, would be a member of the Soviet delegation to Munich which would confer with Western military representatives on procedures for estimating the manpower of the NATO and Warsaw Pact ground forces. Cabot and Parsons worked late into the night, developing a detailed list of questions about the Soviet delegation's stay in Munich: their lodging accommodations, transportation arrangements, composition of the Soviet group, and location and schedule of the conference sessions. Cabot took the questions back to Langley for transmission to CIA's Bonn Station. Parsons gathered all evidence that had been in the apartment, put it in a heavyweight paper sack, and carried it back to the Arlington Hall incinerator.

Two days later they met again, this time in a motel in suburban Maryland. Armed with the responses from Bonn, they put together the contact plan. The Soviets would be staying in the Bayerischer Hof, a stately old hotel in the center of Munich. A member of the housekeeping staff, a reliable Agency asset, would pass an authenticated coded message to Hotspur, giving him a primary and several alternative meeting times and places. Agency officers would also support the operation by keeping the meeting places under surveillance. West German intelligence, the BND, had agreed to share with the Americans the reports of the watchers it would assign to the Soviet security contingent. Lew Parsons would be the backup, but would only make contact with Bonn Station or Cabot in an emergency.

The following afternoon, the deputy chief of Bonn Station arrived in Munich and followed emergency-contact procedures to reach Cabot.

Thirty minutes later, on a park bench in the English Garden, Tom Whitmore sat down next to Cabot. The young man carried a newspaper in one hand and a German briefcase in the other. Whitmore, Cabot estimated, was in his late twenties, early thirties. Deputy Chief of Station at that age—the kid's doing pretty good, Cabot thought.

Whitmore read his newspaper for a moment, then, as if commenting on a particularly interesting article, turned to Cabot. Cabot took the paper, scanned the column Whitmore pointed to, nodded, then returned the paper. The park pathway was deserted, but Cabot knew that Whitmore had a couple of his people somewhere close, where they could keep the bench in view. Whitmore put the paper down between them. That probably told his watchers that I passed identification, Cabot thought.

"The BND reported this afternoon that the security around the delegation's tight. Tighter than they've seen it in years." Whitmore spoke with assurance in a clear, steady baritone.

"Were you able to pass the instructions to him?"

Whitmore nodded. "He has them. I'm certain of that. But . . ."

Cabot studied a woman approaching on the pathway to

his left front, walking a long-haired dachshund. "It's settled, then. We make the meeting."

"The BND report . . ."

Cabot faced the younger man. "It means nothing, what the BND says about the Soviet security. We can't make a decision to continue or not. That's up to him, to our man. He knows what he can do and what he can't. He knows better than the BND or us just how much play he has." Cabot's voice became more intense, rasping. "We do our part. We watch the meeting place. We make certain of the recognition and warning signals. You know the procedures. Follow them." Cabot looked again at the woman with the dog. Cabot felt the need to soften his harsh lecture. "We do our part, he'll do his."

Whitmore knew it was rare that a senior officer like Andrew Cabot would become involved at this level in an operation. Whitmore, moreover, hadn't needed to make the emergency notification. The after-action analysis would probably point that out. They'd cut him a point or two on the informal but very real rating scale that measured him against his contemporaries. But he'd wanted to see Cabot before the meeting; to see if the Deputy Director was still the field man he'd been reputed to be. To see himself twenty or thirty years from now.

When first proposed by Bonn Station, Andrew Cabot had objected to the meeting plan. An arrangement in the Bayerischer Hof, literally under the noses of the Soviet delegation staying there, seemed at first to be a high-risk venture. But after detailed walk-throughs and rehearsals, Cabot agreed. A number of shops formed a mall in the old hotel's basement. A short hallway connected the mall to the underground garage. There were three doors along the hall, the men's and women's *toiletten* and a small windowless office for the manager of hotel maintenance. The office would be empty for two hours between two and four P.M. That the room and vicinity were safe would be signaled by a malachite globe, pierced by a golden arrow, which would be placed in the display case at the entrance of the mall.

Standing well back in the darkened room, Andrew Cabot looked out the window onto the street running behind the Bayerischer Hof. He'd moved into the small *pension* just after lunch. There'd been a communications check on his telephone. He would now wait until the watchers called, telling him that Hotspur had entered the meeting room. He would then leave the *pension*, cross the street, and walk down the ramp of the Bayerischer Hof's parking garage. There would be one last signal in the garage: a red rose in a white ceramic vase in the glass cage of the parking attendant—a "go."

How hard waiting is, Cabot thought. I'd forgotten it's so difficult. Waiting's a skill. A tough one to master. Some never do. The best in this business are the young who can wait. I've never understood why the old are supposed to be patient. God, I couldn't do this the way I used to when I was Whitmore's age. Perhaps time has become more precious. Or have I become bad company for myself? He sighed heavily, pulled an easy chair toward the window, and continued his watch.

At two Cabot had a feeling he'd had many times before. It's like a sailplane, he thought, just after they drop the towline. Now it's you alone in this thing. Others are out there. Friends. But they can do very little.

He grew alarmed when, at two-fifty, a large van stopped in the street below. A man in faded blue coveralls got out of the passenger side of the cab and directed the driver as he backed the truck into the Bayerischer Hof ramp. Anything that the van would drop off or pick up had to come down the hallway off which the manager's office opened. The van disappeared down the maw of the ramp.

Instantly, Cabot could imagine Hotspur, drugged in the hallway, being dragged into the van; the first stage of a journey back to Moscow and the interrogation cells and "forcible treatment" at a mental institution.

With binoculars he studied the dark opening of the hotel garage. Then, with a muttered curse, he dialed the trouble number of the temporary operations center Whitmore had set up in a rented house nearby.

"Tell me again, Mr. Whitmore."

"It was a legitimate delivery."

Cabot had hailed a cab that took him across the Isar River to the Bogenhausen, where he met Whitmore in a private dining room in Kafer's. The younger man was shaken and pale.

"Did you think to check with our people in the hotel about any activities in the garage during the time we'd planned for the meeting?" Cabot asked sharply.

A grim Whitmore looked squarely at Cabot. "No. No, I didn't."

"Perhaps one of your subordinates needs—"

Whitmore drew himself up, squaring his shoulders. "It was my responsibility to make certain. I didn't do it."

Cabot thought back over the decades in the field, of botches and bungles, then looked again at Whitmore. "That's right," Cabot agreed with firmness. "It was your responsibility. You're responsible for everything you and the people assigned to you do or fail to do." He's taking it well, Cabot thought. No pettifogging. He knows I could get this back to Headquarters and he'd get it into his 201 file.

"There's a myth about us, Tom," Cabot began, then hesitated, finding words for years of private thoughts. "Not just the Agency, but about the others too. MI-6. The Mossad. The KGB. We're all-seeing, all-knowing. Pull off the most complex operations without a hitch. We encourage it—the myth. We do it for all sorts of reasons. Ego. Self-preservation.

"But the myth takes its toll. Especially for us Americans. We're more exposed than our friends. Hell, the *Post* and *New York Times* have reporters that make a career—and good money—covering the Agency. Most of what they know about intelligence comes from Fleming and Le Carré. The media know in their heart of hearts that much of the stuff they put out is garbage. Nothing but garbage. But who's going to prove them wrong? And do you think their newspapers would ever publish retractions?"

Cabot continued. "We shouldn't pay attention to the junk they write, but we do. We do because we've come to care what they say about us. Their scrutiny makes us fear failure. We lose our daring. We go for the sure thing. We play to our critics, the sleek and assured second-guessers. Instead of concentrating on the mission before us, we approach things wondering how we'll come out on the evening news."

Whitmore, still through Cabot's discourse, seemed entranced by the flame of the small oil lamp between them on the table. Cabot watched the younger man. How did one sort out the simple missteps from the mistakes that were the symptoms of ineptitude—clear warnings of flaws that could later lead to disaster? Like patience, wisdom was supposed to come with age. If so, Cabot reflected, it had eluded him. All the sophisticated testing—the batteries of psych tests, the polygraph—none of it is certain. Whether or not someone's going to make it in this game always comes down to chemistry. To intuition.

Whitmore, mouth set, looked from flame to Cabot.

Cabot, impassive, met his eyes. Then Cabot smiled and raised a glass of white wine to Whitmore. "I didn't think of checking deliveries either, Mr. Whitmore. I will from now on." He cocked his glass slightly toward Whitmore. "To old dogs."

Whitmore's smile of relief, though restrained, was quite evident. His glass met Cabot's. "To learning, Mr. Cabot. *Prost.*"

Andrew Cabot walked down the narrow lane of Maffeistrasse. The small exclusive shops were just opening. He paused in front of a chocolate store, considered the display for a moment, then went inside to buy a small assortment which the clerk wrapped in waxed paper and put inside a white parchment bag. Continuing down Maffeistrasse, Cabot again stopped, this time at a Dunhill shop. An antique edition of the collected works of Dickens served as the display for an English straight razor.

Noting that the book was opened to the *Tale of Two Cities*, and that the straight razor was folded shut, Cabot entered the shop, nodded to the clerk, then went to the back room.

A muscular man of medium height and a thick shock of dark hair cut close on the sides stood facing him, his hands thrust deeply into the pockets of a badly tailored topcoat. "Good morning, Andrew Cabot." Petr Aleksandrovich Korznikov extended his hand. The right side of Korznikov's coat, freed from his hand, fell quickly against his body.

Cabot took the Russian's hand. "Carrying heavy artillery, Petr Aleksandrovich?"

The Russian smiled broadly, showing poorly made dentures. He dropped Cabot's hand and patted his bulging pocket. "As you Americans say, Andrew, it goes with the territory."

"Would you prefer Russian?"

Korznikov sat in one of the chairs, unbuttoning his coat. "No. English or German. It seems . . . more fitting." He reached inside his coat and came out with a pack of Marlboros. Offering one to Cabot, he smiled. "You Americans make the best cigarettes, then you insist on telling the poor smoker how deadly they are."

"I called off the meeting yesterday, Petr. There were complications."

"Not from our side?"

"No. Ours. We overlooked a delivery van."

Korznikov laughed, blowing smoke to the ceiling. "I had problems once with a stalk of bananas in Delhi—but that's another story."

"You didn't have trouble with this . . ."

"No. That, Andrew, is one advantage to my job." He arched an eyebrow, then winked. "Although, as the saying goes, 'Who watches the watcher?'" Korznikov pulled deeply on his cigarette. "I didn't think we'd meet again. Moscow Center predicted your demise at the hands of your new Director. But then I was contacted in Moscow by your people. Your name was used. And here you are, obviously with good support." Clearly, Korznikov was angling for tidbits from inside Langley. Not to use them, of course. But from his own curiosity about the Agency, a curiosity about the opposition that was shared throughout Moscow Center.

"There isn't time here, Petr." Cabot waved his hand in dismissal. "It is a complicated thing." He went on to brief Korznikov of the outlines of the buildup of North Korean forces, taking care not to reveal the sources and methods used in developing the information.

Korznikov listened without interruption, rising only to take off his overcoat. He carefully folded it, placing it on the floor near his chair so that he could easily reach his pistol. He sat back and lit another cigarette.

Cabot brought in the evidence of Soviet support and the assessment that this support had derived from a Kremlin decision made in 1974. Done with the background, the American moved to specifics—the matter of intentions, of the motivation for the decision, the players in the Politburo, the timing.

When Cabot finished, Korznikov got up, stretched, and walked about the small room, examining as if with some interest the desk piled high with orders and business correspondence. "You know my job, Andrew. And you know compartmentation. You call it 'need to know.' For what you ask, I have no 'need to know.' I have no access. I will have to make access, and that, as you also know, is a difficult thing." Korznikov stopped in front of Cabot's chair and looked somberly at him. "It is something that the smallest mistake would mean the end for me. There would be no mercy."

Cabot started to speak, but Korznikov shook his head. "Let me finish, Andrew. I worry about this. I am increasingly concerned about the ability of Langley to keep its activities out of the newspapers. I do not wish to be theatrical, but you Americans depend on me and others like me. And then you spill the most sensitive information in your petty intramural squabbles. How do you expect to keep friends who will risk their necks for you, not knowing if some morning their name or the information that was uniquely theirs won't show up in the *New York Times*?"

Korznikov resumed his pacing. His voice grew thicker. "And then there is your Director, who says that he wants to 'open up' CIA to your public. There are even to be sightseeing tours! How can a secret intelligence agency be open? Have you all gone crazy? What are your national priorities? Do you care about survival at all? Do you believe you can continue to do all kinds of foolish things and still remain free? What kind of world do you think you live in?"

The Russian stopped, then grew reflective. "I live well, Andrew. The *nomenclatura* takes care of its own. I can retire one of these years, knowing that I will want for very little, that my children and their children will be rewarded also. Rewarded, that is, unless a little thing like spying for the Americans gets in the way."

He sat down in the chair, leaning forward, hands out in supplication to Cabot. "But you know that isn't enough, don't you, Andrew?" He slumped back in the chair, sighing deeply. "You know I cannot stand the smell of the garbage—the stench of a revolution gone wrong. That great literary terrorist, that Kropotkin of letters, Solzhenitsyn, likened the party to doctors on a cancer ward, with the Russian people the inmates. A patient revolted. He was not willing, he said, to pay *any price* to be saved by the doctors. But that's what our Politburo physicians demand—they demand it all."

He looked at his watch, then stood. He moved like a man deadly fatigued. He pulled on his coat. "I'll do what I can, Andrew. You knew that all along."

Andrew Cabot stood. The two men embraced. Korznikov would leave first, Cabot would go out the back door five minutes later.

"Good-bye, Andrew."

"*Nu vsevo, Petr, nu vsevo.*"

Moscow

"They are waiting, Comrade Kiktev."

Kiktev acknowledged the intercom. Standing, he searched his cluttered desk for the notes he'd prepared, finished a glass of now-cold tea, and walked down the corridor toward the meeting. After word had come of the Korea briefing at the Pentagon, he'd convinced Yuri Andropov that the Americans had to be watched more closely. This, in turn, would require the melding of various offices within the KGB—offices that normally would be separated from each other by compartments—security bulkheads to prevent the spread of sensitive operations or information to an inordinate number of people, which, obviously, increases the risk of exposure to prying eyes. A compromise, of course, was to create another compartment, a room into which only certain specified members of the KGB would be admitted, and the information divulged within that compartment would not be shared back in the home office.

If all the compartments were drawn as if in a house plan, Kiktev had thought, what would the KGB look like? Or the GRU? When Andropov had taken over at Dzerzhinsky Square, bringing Kiktev with him, Kiktev, though a career intelligence officer, had been astounded at the pockets of exclusive access he never guessed existed. Often he wondered if there weren't yet other doors leading to still yet other rooms they hadn't told him about—or even Andropov. For that matter, did any single person really know them all? Had the house been added to, willy-nilly, until it rambled all over? With no one aware of where the compartments led? There were times when Kiktev mused about finally gaining access to the ultimate compartment— one in which he opened a door only to find an American on the other side, in what the American thought was *his* ultimate compartment.

"We have helped Pyongyang create a fictional front organization in Tokyo. It ostensibly is formed of South Korean students who've fled to Japan from the repression of the Seoul government. Under the imprimatur of this organization, we have published a book of poetry linking Washington to Park Chung Hee's dictatorship. One such poem, for example, makes good use of the American U.N.

ambassador's admission that the United States itself has hundreds of political prisoners. The book has been circulated through the World Peace Council and affiliated organizations. The poems have been read at gatherings in New York and Washington. And in Cambridge, professors and students at Harvard have taken up collections and staged demonstrations denouncing American support of South Korea."

Vasili Karpovich Okolovich, deputy director of Service A, stood at the podium, speaking from his notes. The chubby Georgian was the special group's authority on *dezinformatsia* matters. "In the same part of the world," Okolovich continued, "we have persuaded our comrades in the Japanese party to mount a campaign calling for a nuclear free zone in Northeast Asia. A nationwide petition is being circulated and will be presented to the American ambassador in Tokyo just after Congress reconvenes in Washington and resumes hearings on the Nuclear Nonproliferation Act."

Mikhail Belenkov, chief of KGB operations in North America, rapped the tabletop with his knuckles. "At our last meeting, Comrade Okolovich, you talked about building a connection between the South Koreans and the South Africans. . . ."

Okolovich frowned. Belenkov was a boor. And incompetent. That one as inept as Belenkov occupied such a sensitive position was a constant in whispered conversations after a vodka or two. Most agreed that his wife, the daughter of a Marshal of the Soviet Union, had something to do with him getting his job—and that his own boot licking and bullying had something to do with keeping it.

"We are going about that, comrade," Okolovich answered. "First, there is the letter from the General Secretary."

Kiktev knew all too well the problems Okolovich was encountering with that letter. Service A had come up with the idea, a straightforward deception that could pay great dividends. In a personal letter Leonid Brezhnev would tell Jimmy Carter that Soviet intelligence had uncovered South African preparations to explode their first nuclear device.

Brezhnev would then ask the American President to use his influence to persuade Pretoria not to go through with the test.

Okolovich was convinced the ploy would cut two ways. Carter, eager for rapprochement with the Soviet Union, would cite the Brezhnev letter as evidence that the Soviets were eager to work with the Americans to stop the spread of nuclear weapons. More immediately, the Brezhnev letter would buttress American suspicions that Pretoria was on the verge of becoming a nuclear power, a prerequisite in the Korea plan.

If the Americans swallowed the bait and pressured the South Africans, so much the better: Pretoria's relations with Washington would be worsened, and obviously no nuclear test would take place, because Pretoria never intended one in the first place. But the Americans undoubtedly would enjoy the opportunity to thrash the South Africans, and would chalk up the explosion that never happened as a milestone in a new epoch in Soviet-American relations. Okolovich's difficulty lay in manufacturing evidence that was credible enough for the White House but which could not be proven false by American intelligence.

". . . and there are, of course," Okolovich continued, "the forgeries, both those purportedly coming from within the South Korean government as well as the shipping documents between Germany and South Africa. These have been successfully injected into the American system."

Okolovich paused to refer to his notes. "We are also taking advantage of the Americans' own blunders. We have, for example, exploited the study released by the Central Intelligence Agency to the effect that another American puppet, Israel, has produced nuclear weapons as far back as 1974. And, too, we will use the fact that the South Africans have expanded production of enriched uranium because they fear the Americans will not supply them in the future."

As Okolovich gathered his papers to return to his seat, Kiktev spoke up. "Stay on the South African connections, Vasili Romanovich. The experts at Chelyabinsk assure us we'll need them."

Kiktev had included Gregori Romanov in the group largely because he'd come to value the analyst's keen judgment, which extended beyond the narrow scope of satellite photography. Romanov had proven himself an enthusiastic ally, and now frequently served as a sounding board for Kiktev, often laughing in derision at the suggestions and proposals that reached the outer offices of Yuri Andropov himself. Romanov had busied himself the past few weeks with the latest batch of tapes from LIMPET. On the way to the podium, he put a chart on the easel.

"Comrade Kiktev." He nodded. Sitting beside Kiktev was a new face. Judging from the reactions of Belenkov and Okolovich, it was apparent they didn't know him, nor had Viktor Lessiovsky, director of KGB operations in English-speaking portions of Africa, spoken to the newcomer either. "You are now familiar with this chart. It shows the frequency with which the American KH-11 satellite photographed North Korea. The drop-off here," he pointed to the right edge of the chart, "shows that the missions over Korea nearly ceased just after the elimination of those elements in CIA that—"

Kiktev nodded. "Yes, Comrade Romanov. We discussed that at our last meeting. Do you—"

By now Romanov felt comfortable interrupting Kiktev. "Do we have something new?" He placed a second chart on the easel. The downturn in KH-11 Korea missions showed a sudden reversal—a near-vertical increase to a point higher than the previous peak. Following the rise was a plateau representing a sustained level of activity. Romanov left them alone with their thoughts. Seeing that Kiktev had absorbed the chart and was about to ask the inevitable, Romanov nodded to Belenkov, who strutted to the podium, a smile playing at the corners of his heavy mouth.

"Comrade Romanov came to me with this. 'Why the sudden changes?' he asked."

Romanov forced a neutral expression. The arrogant bastard. I had to practically teach him that the earth was round before he understood what the LIMPET data meant. It was *I* who explained it to *him*! Now he stands there, acting as if he unraveled the whole thing, and I'm the simpleton.

". . . and so we tasked our most trusted source," Belenkov related with great authority, wrapping mystery around *trusted source*.

Kiktev was the only one present who knew that Belenkov was referring to Birch. He wondered idly how long it'd be before Belenkov would compromise Birch in a fit of vodka-fueled braggadocio. Kiktev made a note to remember to put his concerns into the private file he kept on Belenkov. If Belenkov started slipping, Kiktev could thus join the lynch mob. If Belenkov's star began to rise, why, the file could be consigned to the shredder in an instant.

". . . the requests for Korean photography must go through COMIREX, the Americans' clearing house for all satellite and SR-71 photography."

Kiktev stirred. "Thank you for refreshing our memories as to how the Americans process requests. Did we find out which of the intelligence agencies asked for the Korean coverage?"

Visibly chagrined and somewhat angry, Belenkov bridled. Then, smiling expansively, he adopted the smug air of a child beseeched by his playmates for a piece of candy. Hesitating just long enough to savor the moment, he stood back from the podium and folded his arms across his chest. "Of course, Comrade Kiktev. It was a new organization, a subordinate to their Army intelligence. Something they call the Pacific Studies Group."

Romanov saw Kiktev and the stranger exchange a few sentences after the rest had gone. The stranger then left; Kiktev caught Romanov's eye and nodded toward the open door. Outside in the deserted corridor, the two men walked in silence.

"Well, Gregori Stepanovich?"

Romanov shrugged. "Boxes within boxes, Comrade Kiktev. And our visitor today?"

"No visitor," Kiktev replied. "He is Aleksi Erzin. He'll be a regular from now on."

Tired, but looking forward to dinner with Lydia and perhaps even making love, Gregori Romanov waved his driver good night at the entrance to his apartment building. The elevator, as usual, wasn't working. As he climbed the stairs, he thought about Erzin. He'd heard the name before in Center gossip. It was said that he was the director of Department V. Department V or "Viktor," specialized in *mokrie dela*: "wet affairs," the spilling of blood.

Washington, D.C.

As he usually did on Tuesdays, Laurence Mitchell left Potomac, Maryland, at 5:45 A.M. and drove to the Pentagon's north parking lot, where, carrying his athletic bag, he walked toward the underground entrance of the athletic center for an early morning handball game. A car was double-parked near the pedestrian crosswalk, motor running. Glancing quickly around, Mitchell opened a rear door and squeezed in.

"Eleanor, I'm not easy with this." Mitchell looked at Eleanor Trowbridge, who sat back in the corner of the car. She nodded but said nothing. Mitchell had said the same thing when she'd first told him about the Pacific Studies Group; he'd questioned the legality, then the ethics of the operation. He'd been mollified, but far from totally satisfied with her explanation that PSG was operating under an appropriate charter, that PSG was conducting classified military studies for the Department of the Army, and that everyone had been properly cleared.

"I know the arguments, Eleanor." Mitchell held up a hand to preempt her protest. "But if everything's on the up-and-up, why the pickup in a parking lot at oh-dark-thirty in the morning?"

"Because we aren't supposed to be briefing members of Congress on something as big as this without White

House clearance. And we can't get White House clearance because they don't know what we're talking about. . . ."

". . . and the White House doesn't know because Roswell Franks doesn't agree with you," Mitchell finished. "I understand. But I still don't like it."

John Freeman's briefing at Arlington Hall Station was essentially the one that he had given earlier at the Pentagon; the briefing Franks had refused to endorse. The small briefing room was crammed. Moe Hirsch from NSA sat with Peter Smith and Susan Forbes. Jeremiah Scruggs, having heard over the grapevine of the meeting, had gotten Eleanor's permission to attend. Lew Parsons sat by Eleanor. Laurence Mitchell probed each major statement, engaging Freeman, Eleanor, and the rest of the group in discussions that lasted until mid-morning. But the work at PSG had filled in details and had arrayed supporting evidence in such a way to make the conclusions irrefutable. Finally Freeman finished, and Mitchell sat silently.

Once in the car again, Mitchell called his office and had his secretary cancel appointments for the next hour. In Rosslyn the driver turned south, headed toward Memorial Bridge, then, instead of going across the Potomac into Washington, swung back toward Virginia. At a word from Eleanor, the driver stopped the car just inside the gray granite gates of Arlington Cemetery. She and Mitchell got out and walked up the hill toward the Custis-Lee Mansion.

The Kennedy grave site was deserted. Eleanor and Mitchell stood for a time, silent. They turned and walked to the parapet of the site and stood looking from the slope of Arlington Ridge into Washington, the Lincoln Memorial, Washington Monument, and Capitol nearly in alignment.

As she had so many times before, Eleanor was absorbed by the excerpts from Kennedy's inaugural address, cut in the granite before them. ". . . we shall pay any price, bear any burden . . . support any friend, oppose any foe to assure the survival and success of liberty."

They walked to a nearby bench.

The sky, save for a few white puffs, was a deep blue. The light breeze had a cool, sweet moistness about it, the freshness of new life.

"Eleanor, your people put on a good show. You know the strength of the evidence that went into it. Where are the weak spots?"

Eleanor turned slightly away from Mitchell, looked out on Washington for a moment, then turned to face him. "It's the strongest case I've seen. We divided the analysts into two teams. Each had the same raw data. Both came up with the same conclusions independently."

"There's bias . . ."

"Certainly. A good intelligence officer automatically asks how the information he has can be made into the worst case. We're not in the business to predict peace and prosperity. We're here to be suspicious, to warn of war, of danger. Good news can't kill us."

"Franks—what's his problem with this Korea thing? Why does he fight it?"

"I'm not objective, Bud." Eleanor shook her head as if reproving herself. "I'm not objective at all," she admitted. "I dislike that man intensely." Satisfied she'd given fair warning, she continued. "Franks is complex. One certainly shouldn't underestimate him. I think a number of things are influencing him on Korea.

"First, there's his very natural and admirable inclination to serve his President—to make the things happen that Carter wants. But there you run into problems. I don't think Franks has it very clear just what the obligations are of a subordinate to his superior in government. Certainly, there's the need for loyalty, for obedience—you learned it at Quantico. Take that hill. A snappy salute and a quick 'Yessir.' Franks has that. I don't think the President truly appreciates Franks's loyalty.

"But there's the other obligation. Of a subordinate to lay out for his superiors the downside—to think and give them the benefit of his best judgment. It's important that the commander realize this, and it's important that the commander encourage the—what did Harry call them? Grunts? Yes, that the grunts report back without fear."

"And Franks ignores the grunts," Mitchell prompted.

"Worse. He's terrorized and demoralized them. The grunts—the analysts of the Agency—started out enthusiastically enough with him. Then he browbeat them, telling them in effect that he didn't trust them to interpret what they saw from their particular foxholes—that the only thing they were good for was to pass the information back to him and he'd decide what it really meant. He turned good analysts into information gatherers. He was contemptuous of their intellect, and so they've hidden it from him."

"But why?"

"Oh, I don't know. I'm not a psychiatrist. But I suspect our General Franks lives in a world where all-powerful superiors make every decision for those beneath them. Where high rank is proof of greater intellect. The military is a funny place. It has room for imagination, initiative. You know yourself that somehow one or two nonconformists manage to do quite well. On the other hand, the military also rewards the lock-steppers."

"You said there were other things about Franks," Mitchell persisted.

"Yes," Eleanor replied. "I think you have to consider the picture Franks had . . . has of the Agency. Another thing—he can't deal with women." She gestured toward her bosom. "I'm no virulent feminist. I can't get used to the idea of women carrying rifles or sleeping in foxholes. But I think it bothers Franks terribly when a woman tries to deal with him as an intellectual equal, particularly on military issues. I suspect he'd be more comfortable with me as a third-grade teacher than he was with me as one of his senior officers."

Mitchell saw the driver trudging up the roadway toward them. He took Eleanor's elbow as he stood, helping her up. They looked at the Kennedy grave for a moment, then turned to follow the driver, who was now walking back toward the car. Down the hillside to their right, the Third Infantry honor guard was concluding a funeral service. The mourners were standing as a bugler sounded "Taps." The

driver continued toward the car. Mitchell and Eleanor
stopped and put their right hands over their hearts: Mitchell in the hesitant and reluctant way that military men do
when they prefer to salute but cannot because they are in
civilian clothes.

The ceremony over, they continued down the road and
drew opposite the grave site. The mourners were getting
into cars, leaving the coffin to those who would lower it into
the red Virginia clay.

"We paid once before in Korea, Eleanor." Mitchell
stared at the grave, recalling other deaths. Then, thinking
of one day in the skies of Korea, he whispered hoarsely,
"He managed to warn me. Then he was gone. I still blame
myself for that." Mitchell's voice quavered. "I have a
nightmare. That he didn't die right away. That he was alive,
all the way down." Mitchell and Eleanor walked several
yards in silence.

Eleanor put her hand in Mitchell's. "Bud," she
pleaded, "it was a long time ago. It's over. Let it go."

Almost to the car, Mitchell stopped, turning to her,
overcome with Arlington and with the memory of a laughing wingman, Harry Trowbridge, now twenty-five years
dead. "He was the best of them all, Eleanor. They killed
him. I'm not going to let that start again."

The Washington Post

HOW WEST, SOVIETS ACTED TO DEFUSE
S.AFRICAN A-TEST
by Murrey Marder and Don Oberdorfer

In the midafternoon on Saturday, August 6,
the acting chief of the Soviet Embassy, Vladillen
M. Vasev, called at the White House with an
urgent personal message from Leonid I. Brezhnev to Jimmy Carter. South Africa, according to
Soviet intelligence, was secretly preparing to
detonate an atomic explosion in its Kalahari

Desert. Brezhnev asked for Carter's help to stop it.

The Brezhnev message, still in its original Russian, enclosed the text of an announcement scheduled to be made public two days later by Tass, the Soviet news agency, reporting South Africa's preparations. There was no reference in either document to the Russian spy-in-the-sky satellite photographs that played a key role in Moscow's alarm. . . .

For the first time since the dawn of the nuclear age in a blinding flash over Hiroshima on August 6, 1945 . . . the world's leading powers, east and west, worked in concert to back away a lesser nation from the threshold of entry into the nuclear weapons club. If this cooperation can be buttressed and extended—and if timely warning through intelligence is available in the future—what happened without much public notice in these past weeks may set a pattern of historic importance. . . .

. . . the Soviets publicly blamed the West for atomic collaboration with South African "racists" even while privately consulting the West on ways to block a nuclear explosion. The dichotomy was characteristic of the two faces of today's superpower détente, where bitter rivalry coexists with wary cooperation in pursuit of shared objectives.

"Bud, what you want to do'll be difficult." Henry "Scoop" Jackson of Washington State was the second-ranking Democrat on the Senate Armed Services Committee. He had served in Congress, first as a Representative, then as a Senator, for over forty years. Scoop's consistent stands for common-sense toughness about American security and concern for human rights were well known to Mitchell even before he'd entered politics. Jackson had been a beacon to Mitchell, and on getting elected, he'd wasted no time getting to know the flinty man from Everett, Washington.

After the Arlington Hall briefing, Mitchell had spent several hours with Jackson. The two went over the details of the intelligence assessment, then the politics of the Senate.

"There're some that're already worried. Most of the Republicans." Pulling from his coat pocket a small notebook, Jackson peered through half-frame reading glasses, warming to the task of counting votes. "Then you've got a lot of Democrats too. Stennis. Nunn. Hollings. Glenn." Jackson scribbled for a moment then looked up. "Yes." He nodded. "It can work, but you've got to hustle, young man. I'll help. But this is your wagon." The two talked some more. Mitchell thanked him, shaking hands. Jackson called to him as he got to the door. "And Senator Mitchell," Scoop Jackson shook a warning finger at him, "never forget who our enemies are."

David Cummings came up through layers of drugged sleep. At first he didn't know what had woken him or where he was. The bedside clock said it was three-thirty A.M. Only then did he realize the telephone was chiming.

"David, this is Sanford Lindsay." Lindsay was the Assistant Secretary of State for Legislative and Intergovernmental Affairs. What's he calling me for, Cummings asked himself, struggling to clear his head.

". . . deep shit, David. Really bad."

"What . . . what the hell's going on?" Cummings said, still disoriented.

"David. I didn't know anything about it. It wasn't anything of ours. . . ."

"What in the hell are you talking about, goddamnit? Start at the goddamn beginning."

Lindsay was silent, presumably searching for the beginning. "I'm in the Senate, David. The DOD authorization bill was on the floor." The annual spending bill for the Department of Defense was only of peripheral interest to the State Department, and so the monitoring of the bill's passage and the accompanying debate over amendments was left to Lindsay's counterpart from the Pentagon. As was generally the case, the DOD bill was contentious, since it involved so much money. And it wasn't unusual for the Senate, in its rush to get out for the weekend, to spend several late-night sessions to finish off the votes.

Scoop Jackson had waited until two-thirty and then withdrew a motherhood amendment he'd submitted to give the floor to "my distinguished colleague, the junior Senator from Missouri." Whereupon Laurence Mitchell introduced his amendment, a "sense of the Senate" resolution—one warning the President of the United States against withdrawal of American forces from the Republic of Korea.

Cummings sat bolt upright. "Goddamnit, Lindsay, get to the White House. Get the President to call—"

"David. I got here as soon as I could."

"You shit. Stop covering your ass and get the Pres—"

"David." Lindsay was almost sobbing. "It's too damn late. The bastards passed it, eighty-one to seven. Mitchell saw me after the vote. Told me to wish you the very best."

Alushta, the Crimea

". . . we believe they will persist in this. Vasili Kiktev sat facing Yuri Andropov, having flown to Andropov's dacha on the Black Sea to brief him on the American Senate resolution. A male aide set the terrace table and then poured Turkish coffee. Andropov said nothing, but sat, smoking an American cigarette. He stubbed the cigarette out, then lit another.

"Do we know the specific individuals?"

"Yes, Comrade Andropov."

Andropov continued smoking, occasionally flicking the ashes onto the terrace. "Obviously," Andropov spoke to the smoke curling into the air, "they are out to stop the troop withdrawal." He fell silent again, marshalling the next point toward what Kiktev had already decided would be the conclusion. "That could give our friends in Pyongyang a more difficult time, but Kim could probably prevail, even over the Americans. Our greatest concern must be that this Pacific Studies Group will search beyond. That they will uncover our preparations." Andropov finished his coffee. "And you say they are renegades? That they have no backing from the White House?"

Kiktev nodded.

Yuri Andropov stood and for a long moment looked out on the blue sea. "Wait here. I must talk to the General Secretary." Tossing his cigarette over the low terrace wall, Andropov went inside to call Moscow. Within a few minutes Kiktev heard the sound of Andropov's sandals on the inlaid tiles.

"The General Secretary believes extreme measures are necessary to protect his Korea plan, Vasili Petrovich." Andropov hesitated, then, grim-faced, told Kiktev the rest. "He has directed that Department Viktor be sent into action at once."

Washington, D.C.

At the same time Vasili Kiktev and Yuri Andropov were meeting in the Crimea, preparations were being made in Washington for Secretary of Defense Harold Brown to visit the Republic of Korea to mark the beginning of the first American withdrawal of 3400 troops. Two weeks after the Crimea meeting, President Carter vetoed HR 10929, the Defense Appropriation Act, because Congress had provided $1.9 billion for the construction of a nuclear-powered aircraft carrier. And in a Chicago courtroom ex-CIA employee William Kampiles was found guilty of selling documents on the KH-11 satellite to Soviet agents in Athens, Greece, for the sum of $3000.

Chapter 6

Paris

Severi Chobanian inquired at the *poste restante* window of the small PTT office on Rue Jean Bart. The mail clerk, a sour-faced little Alsatian, as if making an official statement that too many foreigners already infested Paris, sighed deeply, rummaged in a large bin to his right, and came up with a flimsy aerogram which he reluctantly surrendered. Back in his apartment, Chobanian lit the gas oven, then sat at a plain table and opencd the envelope. Without bothering to read the letter within, he smoothed the single sheet of paper over the bottom of a Pyrex dish. Into another shallow dish he poured a few milliliters of household ammonia. Putting both the Pyrex dish and paper in the oven with the ammonia container on a lower rack, he shut the door, checked his watch, and sat back with the newspaper to catch up on the soccer scores.

Fifteen minutes later Chobanian opened the oven and removed the dish, wrinkling his nose at the ammonia fumes. Memorizing the instructions now visible on the back of the letter, he then burned both the letter and the envelope in the Pyrex dish and flushed the ashes down the toilet. From a battered green-metal filing box he took from a nearby cabinet, he selected a postcard, one showing a fog-shrouded Pont Neuf bridge. Two hours later, the postcard in hand, Chobanian set out for the PTT office on Boulevard St. Denis.

Washington, D.C.

David Cummings was suffering from a cold. He'd been kept awake the night before, coughing and hacking. His nose was a raw red around the nostrils, the abrasion of countless Kleenex and handkerchiefs. Alan Squires sat on the sofa, trying to breathe as shallowly as possible, in hopes he wouldn't catch whatever it was that Cummings had.

"I thought, David, it was going well. Seoul still doesn't like it, of course, but the American military's fallen in line. We haven't had any difficulty putting the Trowbridge estimate on ice."

Cummings sniffed, feeling the congestion in his nose and sinuses. "It's not a sure thing. There's the Senate . . ."

"But it was only a resolution. The President just has to nod at it and go on his way."

"It encourages the right-wingers and their friends at DOD. They're foot-dragging. A bureaucratic filibuster. The first increment of troops is due out in a few months. If we can get it started, the momentum'll be on our side. But goddamnit, it's the getting started that's the problem. We've got to make certain we keep our support."

"I talked with Quinn Barnes day before yesterday." Squires went on to relate his meeting with the director of the Foundation for International Relations. Earlier, Squires had suggested that FIR publish a monograph on nuclear proliferation to parallel the Agency's classified estimate on the same subject. FIR, of course, would conclude that South Korea was building nuclear weapons. Then, when the media stir caused by that reached a peak, excerpts of the CIA study would be leaked. The flap would be enormous, Squires argued. Carter would gain support for the troop pull-out, and FIR's reputation would profit as well.

"Quinn's made good use of some of the Blue House memoranda. The World Peace Council research staff has sent FIR an interesting analysis of the collaboration of the physics department of the University of Jerusalem and the South Africans. And, of course, there was the Agency report on Israeli nuclear-weapon production."

David cocked his head. "How did you manage to get that released?"

"We used the Freedom of Information Act." Squires smirked. "If someone asks the right questions, they can spring a lot of stuff loose—even from the Agency."

"And you told Quinn Barnes which questions to ask."

Squires nodded. "The Agency estimate is nearly finished. We're concentrating on Pakistan and South Korea. FIR's going to cover South Korea and tie them in with the South Africans."

"How've you been doing in Seoul?"

"Seoul Station gave in. They've started electronic surveillance of the ROK's. We aren't getting much from that. Usual crap about paying off their friends in Congress. Nothing we can use on the nuclear side."

Cummings doodled on a scrap of paper, then looked up. "What if it gets out that we're bugging them?"

"Bugging the Blue House? But David, I told you, we can't pin anything on them in the way of nuclear—"

Cummings held up two fingers. "We've got," ticking off his first point, "the fact that an ally is bribing members of Congress. And second, we have CIA bugging the office of one of our supposed friends. It cuts two ways. And we win both ways."

"Yes," Squires agreed. A troubled look crossed his face. "But how do we go about—"

David Cummings rolled his eyes upward. "I don't have to draw you pictures, do I?"

Budapest

From a rumpled bed still warm with their lovemaking, Stefan Pomian Csikos regarded Kristina Lukarnos's full breasts as she stood in front of the mirror, slowly dressing. They had met on the flight from Katowice. He was a senior steward and she was a new attendant for Malev, the

Hungarian national airline, and they struck up a conversation while filling out the interminable paperwork at flight's end. He'd invited her to dinner. They'd found each other interesting enough, at least for a night, and so he'd taken her to his apartment.

Pulling on a pair of black-market Levi's jeans and a cotton sweater, Stefan found two not very stale croissants and started coffee. He heard Kristana pad across the floor, then the sound of water running. Taking a key, he stepped out into the hallway and went down two flights to the bank of mailboxes at the entry. He found the pickings slim: a monthly schedule of his soccer club and the postcard of the Pont Neuf bridge. He checked the postmark, then the front of the card again.

Kristina had finally left, having gotten solemn assurances that, why of course, he'd be in touch soon. Stefan poured another coffee, then unscrewed an ornate knob from a post at the foot of the huge wooden bed and removed a small kit. An hour later he'd read the instructions on the microdot that Chobanian had put on the front of the postcard, just under the arch closest to the Seine's right bank. He stashed the kit away, finished the last of the coffee, and called the Malev office.

Simferopol, the Crimea

Thirty minutes before departure, Stefan Csikos left the aircrew lounge and found the toilets. There was no lock on the stall door, and so, sitting on the toilet, he jammed his documents case against the door, holding it with his foot. From his pocket he pulled a folding knife with a long thin blade. The flimsy lock on the toilet-paper dispenser gave way easily; on top of the folded squares of rough paper was a cassette. Quickly, Stefan looked at it. A Beatles tape.

As he was bending over to open his case, the door of the stall shoved open, pushing him back onto the toilet, his head banging into the wall. A KGB internal security guard stood, trousers half down, apparently in extremis, his attention divided between taking care of his galloping diarrhea or making sense of Csikos, pants up, sprawled on the toilet, a knife in one hand, cassette in the other.

Before the guard fully realized what was happening, Csikos lunged forward, right arm stiffly in front, aiming the knife toward a point a half inch above the beltline. The blade slashed into the Russian's heart, tore through the right ventricle and ripped into the left atrium. The guard gasped deeply, his eyes and mouth opened in surprise, then fell backward, slamming to the floor.

Csikos dragged the guard into the stall and, embracing the heavy body, lowered the guard's trousers, now stinking of excrement. He eased the Russian onto the toilet, leaned his head back against the wall, then backed out of the stall, shutting the door. *"Viszontlatasra, orosz kutya,"* he whispered softly.

Running water over the knife, then checking his own uniform for stains, Csikos returned to the lounge, feeling all eyes were on him and certain that his face and trembling hands would betray him.

Considerably calmer on reaching Belgrade, Csikos slipped the tape into a small handbag that was filled with the normal assortment of clothes and toilet articles a man would carry for a short trip. On the tarmac he casually put the bag on the luggage cart that was loading up beneath his plane. The luggage tag on the bag said it belonged to one Spiros Vessilades, who duly claimed it in the terminal. The following day a tall dark-haired young man named Spiros Vessilades flew to Rome, where, among other things, he mailed a small package. SISMI, the Italian security service, far more efficient than generally realized, noted that the package was destined for a post-office box in Baltimore, Maryland. Careful examination of the contents revealed nothing of interest, and so it was rewrapped and sent on its way to one Adrian Tabrizian.

Washington, D.C.

Taking his eyes from the Washington traffic, John Freeman glanced at Eleanor, who was making corrections to a manuscript. He asked a question.

"What?" Eleanor looked out the window to see if his question had something to do with the trip to Capitol Hill.

"I asked how you and Laurence Mitchell met."

She closed her eyes and leaned back against the headrest. Finally, almost reluctantly, she spoke. "He and my Harry were Marine pilots. Both had volunteered from the reserves when the Korean War broke out. They met in refresher training in North Carolina. I was just out of a job at State and followed Harry until he and Laurence— Bud—shipped out to Korea. They stayed together nearly to the end of the war. They were surprised one day while they were on patrol near the Yalu." Eleanor's voice caught. She felt again the disbelief, followed by the dark emptiness that had engulfed her when she'd opened the apartment door to the two somber Marine officers who'd come to tell her of Harry's death. "They never found his body. I suppose he's still there, somewhere."

Over the next hour in Laurence Mitchell's office, Eleanor added details to several questions the Senator had asked during his briefing at Arlington Hall, and inevitably the issue of intentions came up.

"I don't think we can consider the Politburo united in purpose behind something like this." she explained. "There're likely to be all kinds of reasons why the Korea operation would be supported or opposed."

Anticipating Mitchell's question, Freeman raised a hand to make a point. "I don't go along with those who say there're hawks and doves in the Kremlin. The guys who make it to the top over there make it because they conform. But that isn't to say there aren't factions. And different factions could have different motives—based strictly on a desire for power."

Mitchell sat, thinking, "What about the Koreans? Pyongyang?"

Eleanor stood, walked to the windows and turned to Mitchell and Freeman, leaning against the sill. "Same there. But with a twist. Kim Il-Sung is trying to make his son, Kim Chong-il, his successor. That kind of dynastic maneuver isn't new to Korea, but it's out of place in a Communist society. There've got to be orthodox Marxist-Leninists who don't like it, and it causes certain embarrassment in dealing with other Communist governments.

"We have to worry about the elder Kim right now. He's old and his health is deteriorating. If he's talking succession, he's thinking about his own death. And he would like to see Korea united before he goes."

Mitchell turned to Freeman. "And the Soviets?"

"It's much like Korea, Senator. We have to speculate, even though we know more about the Russians. A number of our people believe there's a struggle going on between Brezhnev and Andropov."

"The KGB guy?"

Freeman nodded. "We know Andropov made a stink about the Shevchenko defection at the U.N. and has been saying some snide things about how Brezhnev has let the Chinese get out of harness. Just recently Brezhnev promoted several of his backers in the Central Committee, including Konstantin Chernenko, who some say Brezhnev's grooming as his successor."

They were interrupted by a series of rasping buzzes from a wall clock, signifying an imminent vote on the Senate floor. Without knocking, a staff assistant came in, nodded perfunctorily to Eleanor and Freeman, and handed a single sheet of paper to Mitchell.

Mitchell walked them to the First and C Street entrance of the Russell building. Good-byes were exchanged. The Missouri Senator then turned down the high-ceilinged marble hallway toward the Senate subway, his staffer lugging a bulging folio of papers and background information, briefing him as they walked.

Eleanor and John Freeman stood for several minutes at the corner of First and C. They decided that she would catch a cab back to Arlington Hall while he drove to the Navy Yard to talk with Peter Smith. Looking down toward Union Station to find a cab, Eleanor saw Freeman cross First then C streets on the way to his car, which he'd parked several blocks away. Frustrated by the lack of cabs—there's got to be a conspiracy among cab drivers, she thought—she noticed Freeman talking to someone in a parked car, apparently giving directions, from the way he was pointing toward the Mall.

John Freeman straightened up and staggered back from the car. Then, tires squealing, the car accelerated across the intersection. As it passed her, Eleanor saw there was only the driver. Freeman lay on the pavement, his hand clutching at his chest.

Seconds later Eleanor knelt beside him. His pupils were dilating, breath coming in short gasps, face flushed and darkening. She shouted for help to a nearby Capitol policeman, cradled John's head with her raincoat and began to loosen his tie.

She paid no attention to the screech of tires down the street. Freeman, rapidly fading, looked past her. "He's coming back," he whispered.

Pushing through the double doors, he saw the older woman sleeping curled in a chair. Someone had put a blanket over her. A younger woman sat beside her, and when she saw him, she gently shook the sleeping woman awake.

Eyes blinking rapidly, Eleanor gained her bearings. "Doctor?"

"He's alive. He's had a bad time of it, but he'll live."

"What was it, Doctor?" asked Susan Forbes.

"Some sort of cyanide aerosol. Apparently the driver fired it into his face. He didn't' get a full dose. Wind, perhaps. The stuff contracts the blood vessels. After death, the vessels relax. All the symptoms of cardiac arrest." Commander Vogel of Bethesda Naval Hospital was a specialist in toxicology; even so, pulling John Freeman (registered as John Kester) through had been a near-run thing.

* * *

Two days later John Freeman regained consciousness. A drawn Susan Forbes told him what had happened. Bronowski's investigators had found the weapon in the wreckage. A slender aluminum tube, perhaps seven inches long, had held a glass phial containing five cubic centimeters of prussic acid. "When the trigger was pulled," Susan explained, "a small powder charge breaks the phial and vaporizes the acid, giving off cyanide gas. The KGB used the same thing to kill Bandera, the Ukrainian nationalist, some years back."

To Freeman, of course, the episode would never be entirely clear. All he remembered was a patchwork of impressions, of scenes. The last being as if in stop-motion: Eleanor trying desperately to drag him out of the street, then giving up. Her fumbling in the shopping bag. Then the staccato crashing blasts as she stood over him, feet widespread, both arms extended to hold the .357 magnum revolver, thumb cocking the hammer back for each shot— each shot smashing into the windshield of the oncoming car.

Andrew Cabot had the cab drop him on Connecticut Avenue. He hurriedly crossed the street against a light, then walked north. At the next intersection he crossed again against the light, then proceeded south to Calvert Street. Turning left, he passed, then doubled back to the Calvert Street Café. He went past the empty booths to a back room.

Ibrahim Bazdarkian put down the coffee cup. He wore a dark suit over an old-fashioned white shirt buttoned at the neck, a shirt with neither tie nor collar. The small room was filled with cigarette smoke. Cabot pulled a chair up to the table.

"The room is safe, Andrew. And Mama will be bringing couscous in a moment."

The day before, Ibrahim Bazdarkian had settled himself at his desk, adjusted the lamp just so, and examined the

Beatles cassette before him through a jeweler's loupe. Prising the cassette open, he cut the clear leader from both ends of the sprawl of brown tape. He then discarded the tape, keeping the leaders. These he carefully washed in dilute solution of sodium thiosulfite, following with a rinse of distilled water. When thoroughly dry, the old man carefully spliced them together and wound the result on a tiny plastic spool.

Bazdarkian leaned over the table, having set between them a small Swiss tape player. Cabot was struck by the deep liquid softness of the old man's brown eyes, the tightness of his skin—like a tanned leather—the beak of a nose over liver-colored lips. A translucent finger pushed a button on the player. "This, Andrew, is a conversation between one Vasili Petrovich Kiktev and his master, Yuri Andropov."

> ANDROPOV: . . . could give our friends in Pyong-yang a more difficult time, but Kim could proba-bly prevail, even over the Americans. Our greatest concern must be that this Pacific Studies Group will search beyond. That they will uncover our preparations. (pause) And you say they are renegades? That they have no backing from the White House? (pause) Wait here, I must talk to the General Secretary.

Cabot paled. He listened to the rest of the tape, then motioned for Bazdarkian to play the tape again. He had heard Andropov's voice before. He thought he detected a wariness, a note of caution. He pointed to the tape player. "Where did you get this?"

Bazdarkian poured more coffee from the carafe. Cabot held his hand over his cup. "In Geneva with Dulles I made use of my old friends. We established networks into what is now Soviet Armenia and throughout the *ëspiurk*—the Armenian diaspora. We kept those networks, Dulles and I. And every Director has known of them—" The old man hesitated.

"Except this one?"

"Except this one," Bazdarkian answered. "I came to you with this as soon as I could. I regret it was too late to warn of the attack on John Freeman. But there may be others . . ."

New York Times:

CARTER MILITARY PLANS FOR ASIA RAISE STRATEGY ISSUES
by Drew Middleton

President Carter's proposal to withdraw American ground forces from South Korea and his enigmatic description of the Air Force's future role there have sparked an intense reexamination of the strategic position in Northeast Asia.

South Korea and Japan are the countries most directly and openly concerned. But it is understood from qualified sources that the Chinese government would not welcome any change in the strategic balance that would destabilize the power equation in the area, where the interests of the Soviet Union, China, Japan, North and South Korea and the United States converge.

State Department officials tend to minimize the risks of withdrawal. They say that South Korea's armed forces are better trained and, in some respects, better armed than those of North Korea. . . .

Some American, allied, and neutral analysts believe, however, that the President's measures will shift the power balance in favor of North Korea and its arms supplier, the Soviet Union.

They may be overly pessimistic, but they fear that American withdrawal will encourage a Soviet-supported North Korean attack on South Korea that will end in a victory for the North. This victory, they predict, will provide the Russian Pacific Fleet and Far East Air Force with bases in South Korea on Japan's doorstep. . . .

"I think it's as close as I've come to hearing a death-sentence." Susan Forbes broke the silence. To her right, Eleanor sat quietly. John Freeman was across the table in Eleanor's office, next to Jack Bronowski. Andrew Cabot had just finished playing the Andropov tape. "What now? Are you going to take that," she gestured toward the tape player, "to the White House?"

Cabot shook his head. "We're sending a sanitized report. One that covers up the source or that it was a taped conversation. If those details got back—"

Freeman protested. "But something like that—it lacks credibility. If you sent the tape—"

"The tape, or a copy of it, would be at Dzerzhinsky Square before lunch." Bronowski grunted. "And before dinner, whoever did the taping for Cabot here'd be getting his toenails pulled out."

Eleanor looked at Bronowski, right elbow on the table, the palm of her hand cupping her chin. "I don't think we should expect much from the White House. They've already put it about that the attempt on John was suspected to be a case of some old enemy settling scores; that he'd been mixed up in some sort of shady business in Southeast Asia." She put her hands in her lap and sat back, looking from face to face. "I think we're very much on our own. Except, of course, with a little help from our friends." She nodded to Bronowski.

New York Times:

U.S. IS REPORTED TO HAVE BUGGED KOREA PRESIDENT
Spying Yielded Data on Bribery, Sources Say
By Richard Halloran

WASHINGTON—A United States intelligence agency activated electronic surveillance of the presidential mansion in South Korea . . . and produced specific reports on Korean bribery of American congressmen, according to sources connected with the inquiry into the Korean scandal. . . .

An account of the electronic surveillance of the Blue House, the executive office of President Park Chung Hee of South Korea, was pieced together from information obtained from officials, former officials, and investigators here. . . .

Precise details of the surveillance technique could not be determined. The sources said the operation had to be carefully executed because of the diplomatic risk involved.

Specialists in electronic devices said that it appeared to have been a beamed radio wave, a method that would overcome the problem of getting through the security surrounding the Blue House and the risks of hiring Koreans to enter the executive office.

The technique, a specialist said, does not require an instrument inside the room targeted for eavesdropping. The radio wave is beamed into the room, moved around until it finds an object to vibrate against, and then transmitted back with the voices and noise in the room.

This technique can be used whether or not there is a line of sight between the transmitter and the target, and the radio wave can go through walls and glass. The American embassy and the residential compound of American diplomats in Seoul are close enough to the Blue House to permit use of such a device. . . . the source said the system was producing intelligence for the National Security Agency, which undertakes electronic surveillance missions all over the world.

St. Michael's, Maryland

The small helicopter flared slightly, settling tail first on the grassy lot. John Freeman got out of the passenger seat and walked to the marina office. The day before, Lew

Parsons hadn't checked in from a four-day vacation. John had called around, even to O'Toole's, and hadn't been able to find him. Then, taking the key Lew had left with him months ago, John went to Lew's apartment. Poking about, he'd found no sign that Lew had come back. Calling the various marinas and docks around Annapolis had been fruitless until one operator remembered that Parsons had talked about moving to a berth in St. Michael's, a picturesque Eastern Shore fishing village on the Chesapeake Bay.

The grizzled marina owner, one of a long line of watermen who had lived for generations harvesting the bay, squinted at Freeman's credentials, then grudgingly allowed as how, yes, somebody named Parsons might be paying for a berth. And how, yes, this feller took off a week ago. By hisself. A thirty-one-foot sloop it was. Knew his boat, he did.

Freeman called Bronowski, who in turn made other calls. Within hours the Coast Guard was mounting an all-out search for *The Tove* and her owner.

Agencie France-Press

> TAEGU, SOUTH KOREA—Slogan-shouting South Korean students smashed windows and furniture, then burned the United States Information Service library here in Taegu this morning. In the near-riot, two students were killed and one wounded by military police.
>
> Student leaders say the demonstration was a "spontaneous gesture of opposition" to reports of American electronic eavesdropping on South Korean President Park Chung Hee's Seoul office.

Arlington Hall Station—Arlington, Virginia

John Freeman looked up to see Jack Bronowski enter his office. Bronowski came directly to Freeman's desk, face ashen. "They found *The Tove*, John. She was aground near

Point Lookout—where the Potomac empties into the bay. She was empty; no sign of Lew. No sign of any kind of disturbance."

Ten days later Lewis Parsons's body was dragged from Chesapeake Bay. He had been wearing jeans and a T-shirt. A deck shoe remained on one foot. Forty pounds of diving weights were wrapped around the body. Initial police examination had it that he had been killed by a single nine-millimeter bullet that entered his skull just behind the left ear. A CIA spokesman, according to the Associated Press, refused comment beyond saying, "We are not involved in the investigation in any way, but we will cooperate if asked."

SECRET

FROM: USEMBSEOUL

P R I O R I T Y   I M M E D I A T E

TO: SECSTATE
       EABUREAU

230930ZAPR79

1. (S) ROKG DEMANDS IMMEDIATE, RE-PEAT, IMMEDIATE, DEPARTURE OF EM-BASSY POLITICAL ATTACHE MARKHAM DOUGLAS. DOUGLAS WILL DEPART KIMPO VIA NW FLT 200 AT 1550Z THIS DATE.

2. (S) DOUGLAS ADVISES THAT MARTHA HORTON WILL ASSUME DUTIES AS ACT-ING POLITICAL ATTACHE.

PALMORE

Langley, Virginia

Andrew Cabot knew it would be about Freeman and Parsons. He walked past Roswell Franks's secretary and into the DCI's office. Franks, on the telephone, waved Cabot to the sofa. *At least we aren't going to go through the "stand until spoken to" routine,* he thought.

Franks hung up, found a file folder on his desk, and came around to sit opposite Cabot. "I've read your comments on the Freeman and Parsons matter." He tapped the folder in his lap with his hand. Franks paused, waiting for Cabot to say something in acknowledgment. When Cabot said nothing, Franks cocked his head, was silent for another few seconds, then continued. "I don't agree with your assessment that the KGB's had anything to do with any of this."

"General, we have a very reliable source that ties this directly to Brezhnev himself."

"What is it?"

"The source?"

"Well, of course. If I'm going to believe something like that, I want to know the source."

"It was an independent report through an emigré network with which we've had a long association. That's all I really know."

"And you were the Agency contact for this . . . network?"

"Yes."

"And you didn't bother to question the origins of this report any more than what you've told me?"

"No sir, I didn't."

Franks was incredulous. "You didn't even ask? Why not?"

"If I had, General, I wouldn't have gotten an answer." Franks's expression of disbelief angered Cabot. "They wouldn't have told me, General, because we're no longer trusted. Not by independents such as these people, not by those we used to piggyback on. In case you haven't noticed, we're getting less and less stuff from the Brits, the French, and the Israelis. And the New Zealanders and Aussies have just about shut off sharing their take from Southeast Asia, especially from places like Indonesia and Malaysia.

Cabot leaned forward. Franks was taken back, his

mouth partly opened. "They don't trust us, General, because they aren't sure we'll keep their secrets. We can get a titillating report from the Mossad about a private in Sadat's kitchen, and the new people here think there's no harm done if some Hill staffer or White House aide lets it out at a cocktail party. But if Egyptian counterintelligence picks up that an American official knows a certain bit of information that only a few Egyptian insiders have access to, we could be blowing a source that the Izzies were depending on for their very survival."

Franks, recovering from Cabot's outburst, raised a hand. "That's enough, Cabot. Apparently you're having trouble understanding plain English. This President and"— pointing to himself—"this Director of Central Intelligence believe the Agency has to be opened up. If the American people are going to continue to support an intelligence establishment that spends billions of dollars each year and gets involved in all kinds of potentially dangerous operations, then those people have got to have a better understanding of what it's all about."

"I'm not arguing that, General. And don't think every professional here hasn't wished Americans knew more about what we did and how we do it. We've done a lot of things we can all be proud of. But we still give out our medals in secret. And for good reason. The intelligence agencies of other nations—our friends—believe that too much publicity about us is dangerous to them. Would MI-6 let out a report—as we did—on Israel's nuclear-weapon production? I don't think the Mossad was half as shocked about our snooping as that we told the world about it."

Franks snapped back. "Goddamnit, Cabot, we're not going to open the store for every Tom, Dick, and Harry. But we aren't going to let the so-called professionals here run loose. There's going to be accountability. There's going to be accountability to me, to the President, and, goddamnit, to the Congress."

Franks stood, walked toward his desk and then stopped, turning to Cabot, who'd also gotten up from the sofa. "Let's get back to the Parsons thing, Cabot." Franks took Cabot's report from the desk. "I'm not buying this . . . this tale of the Soviets putting out a contract for some ex-employee of ours. A reprobate whose morals alone should have gotten him thrown out years ago. It's perfectly clear—the man was off balance. He did himself in. And he did it to make it look like it wasn't suicide. That's it. Case closed.

"And another thing. Just what in the hell are those people doing working for the Army? We fired them from here, didn't we?"

"Yes. Yes, you're right. We fired them, General." Cabot's lips curled. He'd rolled the report into a tube which he waved at Franks like a baton. "Freeman went back to the Army, and we gave Parsons his walking papers after years of service. Is there some restriction, some prohibition against them working elsewhere?"

"You know damn well what I'm driving at, Cabot. Is the Army—is DOD—setting up an independent operation?"

"I don't know everything that's going on down at the Pentagon, General," Cabot evaded.

"I thought that Korea business had been put to bed. But here . . ."

Cabot gathered his notepad from the end table beside the sofa. "The military services are still concerned with Korea, General. Should they close up shop? Do you want to make it a test case for the authority of the DCI? Do you want to tell DOD not to worry about Kim Il-Sung? To shut down the warning nets?"

"You're being extreme, Cabot. You know goddamn well that's not what I had in mind. But I'm not going to have the Pentagon or DDO pulling an end-run around me."

Cabot paused in the doorway. "I'm certain, General, that they never had the slightest intention of doing so."

Alexandria, Virginia

He looked at the clock again and felt the lonely despair of the insomniac—that time would be forever frozen between midnight and dawn. Too warm, he pushed the sheet down. His mouth tasted sour. Bandit awoke, mewed softly in reproach, moved to a different spot on the bed, then curled up and went back to sleep.

Susan stirred. "Thinking?"

"I can't help it." He turned to her, talking in a near whisper in the dark.

"About Lew?"

"Yes. And the way they've stacked things to make it look like a suicide. It's not right."

She touched his arm. "Are you surprised? Especially after they spread the rumors about you?"

"The bastards. They smeared him. To keep their train on the track. The shit they gave out about the divorce. *Time* quoted a 'reliable source,' saying he was drunk. Reliable source, my ass. Probably one of those greasy smacks around Franks."

John sat on the edge of the bed. Susan turned on her lamp. She had come home that afternoon to find him at the kitchen table, sitting in front of a white towel on which he'd laid the carefully cleaned and oiled parts of the Browning. They hadn't talked while he reassembled the pistol. She'd never seen him handle the gun before, though she knew he kept it in his nightstand. He had inspected his work, turning the gun to angle the light off the oil-slick metal planes.

She had watched him, suddenly jealous of the way his hand closed on the pistol, as if she were a witness to him fondling another woman's body. Angry at him and angry, too, at herself for the anger, she had gone with him to a small Italian place near DuPont Circle and ate dinner with only desultory conversation.

She went downstairs and returned with lemonade. They shared from the same glass. "Peter Smith has shut down the KH-11 requests." She'd spent the day at the Navy Yard, missing the meeting John had had with Bronowski, Eleanor, and Andrew Cabot.

"Just as well. We've probably got more stuff now than we have people to look at it." He got up and padded, naked, to the bathroom. Returning, he pulled on a pair of ragged shorts. "Cabot told Franks about the Andropov thing."

"The tape itself?"

"No. Just what Andropov said. Franks dismissed it."
Freeman thought for a minute. "I suppose he had to. If he
accepted that, he'd have to accept other things too. He who
says A must then say B." He came to Susan's side of the
bed, motioned her over, and sat beside her.

"We talked about stopping. Disbanding the Pacific
Studies Group. Cabot said there were ways—ways to let
them know."

Susan, puzzled, asked, "Them?"

"The KGB. We let them know we're dropping Korea."

"And that's it?"

"That's it." He took another sip of the lemonade. "We
just walk away from it. Let whatever's going to happen,
happen."

Susan stared at him.

She said nothing, so he went on. "Or we keep going.
Move somewhere else. New cover. More physical security."

She felt the tenseness in him that had begun with the
attempt on him and had ratcheted more tightly with Lew
Parsons's death.

John stood, stretching, straightening his leg. He
looked down at her. "I'm scared." His facial expression was
flat. He raised his hands to say something in motion with
them, then dropped them in futility. He came back to her
side of the bed and sat down again. "It's not like Viet Nam.
No matter how bad it got over there, I felt like . . . like
we had . . . always had something in reserve, one more
card to play. That the others would do everything they
could if we got in a jam.

"I took it for granted. I never realized how . . . what
it meant. You can be brave when you have an
organization—an entire government—behind you. But
we've got nothing now. We're alone in this, and I'm scared,
goddamn scared."

And so the gun today. She looked steadily at him. "Are
we going to quit? Or go underground?"

"No." He stood, took off the shorts and got into bed.
"No, we're not quitting." He reached across her to turn out

the light and then lay back to stare into the darkness and to wait for first light.

Great Falls, Maryland

Andrew Cabot, also unable to sleep that night, dressed quietly in soft corduroy trousers, chambray shirt, and on the way out the door, slipped a worn canvas bird-shooting jacket from a peg in the hallway. Whistling softly, he heard River stir in the kitchen and the sound of claws on the wood floor.

He and the old retriever set off down the moonlit country road. Freeman had been right, of course. It was the only rational response, short of surrender. He'd been somewhat surprised that Eleanor, not Bronowski, had been the first to agree. "It's sensible, Andrew. It's the only way to stop them."

River was coursing along the road's edge, snuffling, running to another new spot, snuffling some more. Cabot found the chewed tennis ball in his pocket. Making a barely audible clucking sound, he got River's attention. The retriever froze in place, his eyes riveted on Cabot. He threw the ball, watching it bounce down the hard-packed clay.

Is there a line, he wondered, not for the first time, beyond which we cannot go, even in order to survive? Is there a line beyond which things set in motion took on an evil life of their own? The line beyond which democracy would destroy itself as surely as if its enemies had prevailed?

Muscles tensed, River waited. Cabot released him with a silent hand signal. The retriever lept forward.

"You're still not asleep," Susan whispered later.
"Just thinking."
"About?" She rolled on her side toward him.
"About Nguyen Van Hai. A Vietnamese; someone I once knew."
She found his hand. His skin was cold and trembling.

Washington, D.C.

Section 2-206. *Physical Surveillance*. The FBI may conduct physical surveillance directed against United States persons or others only in the course of a lawful investigation.

Executive Order 12063,
signed by President Jimmy Carter
on January 24, 1978

Silver Spring, Maryland

Fairfield Perkins checked the dashboard clock, took another sip of lukewarm coffee, then wiped the fog from the inside of the windshield with an old towel. One of CIA's most experienced S.E. men (surreptitious entry), Perkins had learned how to wait. The lights were still on dim in the seventh-floor apartment bedroom. Some overtime was being put in tonight. Perkins turned up the volume on his HF receiver. He thought he could hear panting, but certainly no screeching. Rona baby hadn't yet begun her "Oh, God, give it to me" routine. Perkins stretched his legs, taking care to avoid the plastic milk bottle that now served as a urine container.

A week ago he'd met with an FBI counterintelligence agent at a safe house in Alexandria, Virginia. "I don't know why you guys want this stuff, but it's all here." Ferrando, the FBI agent, had patted the heavy cardboard box that sat on the table. Perkins didn't know, either, what Langley wanted with the watch files. But he wasn't about to admit that to someone from the Bureau. And so he inspected the files, and grudgingly acknowledged with a grunt that they were marginally acceptable.

Two days before Fairfield Perkins sat down with Mr. Ferrando, Andrew Cabot had lunch in a private room at the

Metropolitan Club with Oliver MacKenzie, Executive Assistant Director (Counterintelligence), FBI. Unknown to most Americans, President Jimmy Carter severely limited the Agency's license to operate in the United States. CIA might spot a Soviet spy in the Netherlands and follow him as he made his way toward the United States, but it was the FBI to whom the Agency had to turn over their surveillance once the spy entered the country. And while CIA could monitor the activities of foreigners abroad, it was generally prohibited from checking on Americans overseas, even if those Americans were dealing with known foreign agents. What Andrew Cabot had in mind was to obtain a small exception to the presidential order.

Cabot finished his roast chicken and put his napkin on the table. "If this place weren't hard to get in, nobody'd eat here."

Oliver MacKenzie drained the last of his wine and sat back in his chair, appraising his colleague. He took a deep breath, held it for a moment, then let it out, shaking his head. "Froggy, what the fuck's going on? Franks shitcans half the Agency. Then a guy the D.C. cops can't identify tries to off some former Green Beret. The Green Beret used to work at Langley, and the alleged assassin is blown away by this Annie Oakley character—who, it turns out, has also been fired by Franks. Within the month another one of your unemployed spooks ends up in the bay with divers' weights around him and a nine-millimeter slug in his head."

Cabot quickly told MacKenzie about the Korea estimate, how it ran counter to the Carter troop-withdrawal initiative, and how the Franks firings had threatened to stop all efforts to uncover the Soviet role in Korea and to determine what might lie ahead there.

MacKenzie digested what his long-time friend had told him. "And so DOD sets up this Pacific Studies Group."

Cabot wasn't surprised that the Bureau knew about the Pacific Studies Group. There was the bureaucratic world of formal organization diagrams and legal charters for intelligence organizations. In this world, responsibilities and authority were clearly specified. The FBI, CIA, and military cheerfully cooperated with each other, and there was no claim-jumping or peeking over shoulders of friends.

And then there was the real world, where every American intelligence agency watched its local competition with as much attention as they paid to the Soviets and their satellites; where agency heads stretched legal and executive limits on operations, occasionally reaching into another's pockets. The bureaucratic poaching rarely erupted in openly contentious disputes, everyone preferring to settle their differences and make adjustments in sometimes acrimonious—but always informal—private discussions.

"And so the Pacific Studies Group," Cabot echoed. Cabot then filled in the details of Parsons's death and the attempt on Freeman. Cabot alluded to the Andropov conversation while avoiding the fact that it had been captured on tape.

MacKenzie had known Andrew Cabot since they'd worked as field officers on a Soviet attempt to penetrate the U.S. Agriculture Department's highly sensitive office of grain harvest forecasts. It had been a case that threw the two men together in situations that demanded the utmost in personal trust. Both had come out of the experience with an abiding respect for the other. Both knew that they had risen within their respective organizations as high as they could; the retirement lay just ahead, a time so eagerly sought by so many, but feared by MacKenzie and Cabot as a banishment from a world that never lost its attraction. Doors would be closed behind them forever, and never again would they know the secrets of why things really were.

"What do you want, Froggy?"

"We need the watch files on these guys."

MacKenzie studied the list, then made notes on an index card he found after searching through his coat pockets. He handed the list back to Cabot. He put his fingertips together, making a tent, and fixed his eyes on a spot just over Cabot's head. "Let's just say we agree that the Bureau will train some of your people in counterintelligence techniques for your foreign operations." Cabot listened carefully. "And let's agree also," MacKenzie continued, "that we'll furnish your trainees with copies of certain of our watch files on, say, fifteen Soviet intelligence officers in the Washington area. Just as examples, mind you—case studies. So you can learn how we determine the pattern of a subject's coming and going. Just training. Just interagency cooperation."

Fairfield Perkins heard a rising rush of moans. Making certain the dome light in his car was out, he opened the door and walked around to the sidewalk. Glancing up and down the street, he pulled a twenty-two-caliber Colt Woodsman automatic from a shoulder holster and carefully screwed a long silencer to the muzzle. Checking the street again, he took aim at the streetlamp, let out half a breath, and squeezed the trigger. There was a soft "thut," and the mercury-vapor lamp went out, plunging the area into inky blackness. Perkins made his way back to his car, put the pistol and silencer under the seat, then settled down to wait for Valeri Maksimovich Vuchenko.

When Perkins heard the door close in Rona's apartment, he started his car. As Vuchenko left the building and headed toward the car, Perkins turned on his headlights and pulled away from the curb. Positively identifying Vuchenko, Perkins turned on his left-turn signal then switched to signal a right turn. As he turned the corner, he looked up to the rearview mirror and thought he saw another man on the street, just behind the Russian.

Section 2-202. *Electronic Surveillance*. The CIA may not engage in any electronic surveillance within the United States.

Executive Order 12063

Vladimir I. Chebrakin had been one of the decoys during the evening "scatter." To throw off FBI surveillance of the one or two KGB and GRU officers who wanted to make contacts in the Washington area, perhaps as many as two dozen operatives would drive out of the embassy compound into the evening rush-hour traffic within minutes of each other. A few would go to meetings; others, like Chebrakin this evening, would drive aimlessly, leading his tail on a tour of the Virginia and Maryland suburbs, sometimes stopping, as had Chebrakin, at a bar or restaurant. Chebrakin enjoyed the scatters. It gave him a chance to get out of the compound on his own, eat a decent meal, and at the same time push the needle under the fingernails of the FBI.

He was getting the special treatment tonight. He'd been picked up by a small Caucasian female driving a battered green Plymouth who'd followed him out the Shirley Highway through the creep-and-beep congestion to Springfield and then around the Beltway to Bethesda, where she'd been replaced by a black male in a large white Pontiac who looked to have seen heavy service in the drug trade. The black had stayed with him perhaps only fifteen minutes or so when he was replaced by a third driver, a white male in a gray Honda. Pulling away from the traffic light at Western Avenue, heading south on Wisconsin, Chebrakin was still musing about the FBI buying Japanese cars when his car began to shudder and shake. A flat tire. He turned off to the curb on his right and watched the gray Honda drive on past and disappear in the night traffic. Then, knowing he had no other choice, he prepared to get out, find a pay phone, and call the embassy.

As soon as Chebrakin unlocked the door, a figure moved swiftly to the left side of his car and jerked the door open, pulling the handle from his hand.

Section 2-305. *Prohibition on Assassination.* No person employed by or acting on behalf of the United States government shall engage in, or conspire to engage in, assassination.

Executive Order 12063

Vicinity of Kosan
Democratic Peoples Republic of Korea

Corporal So Chae-p'il was disgusted. The fools in Pyongyang had sent him two signals specialists who were specialists only in avoiding work. He'd sent them to clean his shed. Clearly they'd done nothing but sit out here and smoke. Probably lied to each other about all the women they'd made love to.

So clucked over the dusty transmitter junction box, the trash in the corner. Bending closer, he saw an unfamiliar wire lead running from the transmitting antenna. Curious, he traced the wire toward the back of the shed, where the land-line cables came in from the 280th Commando Brigade.

Moscow

Leonid Ilyich Brezhnev, General Secretary, Head of State, Chairman of the Presidium, Marshal of the Soviet Union, and recipient of the Lenin Prize for Peace, acknowledged Yuri Andropov's presence with a barely civil grunt, then pretended to be absorbed in finishing off a report before him on his desk, pointedly leaving the KGB chairman to stand. Off to Brezhnev's left, Konstantin Chernenko sat, never so much as nodding, his flat face impassive, bright little pig eyes locked on Andropov. Brezhnev fussed over initialing the document before him, stretching further the tension in the silent room.

Brezhnev finally looked up and threw his hand in a curt gesture toward a chair positioned so that it faced both himself and Chernenko. Andropov sat. The chair was low—sufficiently so that Andropov found himself looking up at the two men. The abruptness of the meeting was alone enough to set off alarm bells. Given his relationship with Brezhnev, Andropov dismissed any possibility that the General Secretary wanted his opinion on some matter that had suddenly come up. No. This was a summons to a one-man tribunal at which the accused would stand without a prepared defense.

Brezhnev hunched his hulking body forward, bringing his hands together on the desktop. "We have problems, Comrade Andropov." Brezhnev breathed deeply, then let out a heavy sigh. "We have very serious problems."

Andropov glanced to Chernenko. He could detect no change in the Ukrainian's face, but was there a gleam of anticipation in his washed-out eyes?

Brezhnev consulted the folder from which he'd been reading. "Early this morning, Washington time, Comrade Andropov, the GRU watch officer at our embassy was called by an anonymous person. This same anonymous person, by the way, knew the unlisted number of the GRU *rezident.*"

Brezhnev paused here and looked at Andropov in reproach, implying with his curled lips that somehow the slipped knowledge of the GRU telephone number in Washington was evidence of yet another failing of Moscow Center. He waited another second or two, then went on. "Our man was told that an embassy automobile could be found at a certain address. We located the car. In the trunk were the bodies of Valeri Vuchenko, GRU, and Vladimir Chebrakin, who, I understand, is in your service."

Deciding to bluff, Andropov heaved himself with some effort from the chair. "The losses are regrettable, nonetheless—"

Brezhnev interrupted. "Please sit, Comrade Andropov. What is of concern is not the deaths, but the circumstances. Vuchenko was strangled. With a garrote made of piano wire. Whoever used it nearly took his head off. The garrote was still embedded in his neck. Your man," Brezhnev paused, and looked up from under his heavy eyebrows at Andropov, "died of a bullet wound. A single shot to the head. Behind the left ear." Brezhnev smiled maliciously. "A curious thing, Comrade Andropov. He'd been doused in water, and divers' weights were wrapped around his body."

Leonid Brezhnev shifted. "Ambassador Dobrynin has been instructed to say nothing to the American authorities.

The bodies are being flown back to Moscow under certification of our embassy physician that they died of natural causes."

It was worse, far worse than Andropov had thought it would be. The GRU had obviously known of this and had kept him and Moscow Center in ignorance. And now that flatulent old wreck Brezhnev was playing the prosecutor.

Brezhnev took off his reading glasses and shuffled again through the file. Chernenko now moved slightly, almost imperceptibly leaning forward, his loose mouth opened ever so little, his eyes still fixed on Andropov. Andropov imagined he could detect a sharpness to the air, the smell of a new edge being put to a steel blade.

"You took action against the Americans, Comrade Andropov," Brezhnev intoned, coming at last to the charges. "It was your assessment that they were, how you put it, 'renegades,' men who no longer enjoyed the protection of their government. The subsequent deaths of Vuchenko and"—Brezhnev searched the paper before him— "and Chebrakin indicate otherwise. The Americans targeted us very precisely. They killed our people in the streets of Washington. They apparently did so with sanctions—approval. This was not the work of some independent. It was a well-coordinated operation. They knew our people—their habits, their backgrounds. The Americans have settled a score."

Chernenko was now smiling. Obviously, they had him either way. If he hadn't gone along with the assassinations, and the Americans had kept picking at the Korea problem, Brezhnev could easily have charged Moscow Center with criminal inaction: "wrecking," as Stalin had called it in the show trials of the thirties. They probably already had in mind some stooge to replace him at Dzerzhinsky Square, and then to begin work in earnest on the Dnepropetrovsk Mafia's enemies list. They would use this as an excuse to do what they'd wanted to do for years—eliminate any opposition to Leonid Brezhnev's hand-picked line of succession.

Yuri Andropov felt precariously balanced—standing in the dark at the edge of a deep pit. Nowhere to go save forward, he leapt. "I differ, Comrade General Secretary," he objected, using the formal address. "I believe the Kh.V. files will demonstrate that contrary to a unified American action, the murders were, in fact, evidence of divisiveness in the Carter administration." Andropov's choice of the acronymn was deliberate. Shorthand for *khranit' vechno*— "to be kept in perpetuity"—Kh.V. files were intended for such sensitive matters as the assassination of Lew Parsons and the attempt on John Freeman. They were, as Leonid Brezhnev well knew, the repositories of any evidence, rumors, and gossip of misdeeds by Soviet citizens. And the Kh.V. files for the Brezhnev family, the General Secretary believed, were quite thick indeed. In his years at Moscow Center, Yuri Andropov had seen to the tending of those files.

There was also the direct issue that Andropov had raised. The American response had been out of character for Jimmy Carter. It was an aspect that Brezhnev and Chernenko had not considered. Feeling his confidence slipping, Brezhnev relied on his sense of the ebb and flow of events. Not now the time for the blow against this insolent bastard Andropov. Not yet. He twisted slightly in his chair, not quite catching Chernenko with his eyes, but throwing a command in his direction nonetheless. "Leave us. Comrade Andropov and I have sensitive matters to discuss."

Startled, Chernenko showed open emotion for the first time. Surprise, wonder, then resignation successively crossed his ruddy face.

Chernenko stumped through the door, turning and nodding deeply to Brezhnev before leaving the room, and gave Andropov the satisfaction of a quizzical stare. Andropov noted the two heavily armed guards at the door. Members of the KGB's Kremlin Kommandant. Andropov was nominally their boss, but in reality they were Brezhnev's private palace guard. He noted one was wearing what appeared to be a hearing aid; a receiver that monitored everything that went on in Brezhnev's office. Even had he been able to slip a knife by the inspection, they would have burst in and shot him before he could get anywhere near Brezhnev.

In the silence that followed, Andropov could hear Brezhnev's labored breathing and the rattle of phlegm. Exhausted, Brezhnev settled back in his chair. The old man cleared his throat. "Comrade Chernenko came to me with a rather simple tale, Yuri Vladimirovich." It was not unusual for Brezhnev to put the blame on his chums—why not? Wasn't that what one used subordinates for?

Andropov shrugged slightly, affecting the scholarly demeanor that had stood him in good stead with the Western journalists. (Some years later, the *Washington Post* would describe Andropov as a "well-educated and enlightened man—even a closet liberal. . . .")

Brezhnev looked at the younger man before him. He had let his hatred of Andropov get the better of his judgment. Caution was required. Andropov had proven himself a master of intrigue.

"Yuri Vladimirovich." Brezhnev shook his head slightly, a small smile hovering at his mouth. "We have a splendid opportunity. The correlation of forces favors us over the Americans. All we need is a small push." He illustrated, softly jabbing a thick index finger at Andropov.

Brezhnev straightened up, the smile gone. "My concern about the 'wet affairs' was that they would direct American attention to our Korean operation." Here Brezhnev's voice became silky smooth. "But Comrade Andropov, do not worry much about this"—he made a gesture of dismissal, of brushing away crumbs before him—"this inconsequential matter. Your planning has been superb. Few can find fault with the Committee on State Security."

Andropov quickly noted the reference to fault-finding. Those "few," he wagered, would be those closest to Brezhnev.

"What is left in the Korean plan is a relatively straightforward matter. One that can be handled by the GRU."

Again, within minutes, Andropov faced a probe by Leonid Brezhnev. He smiled, and then, as if to speak for the hidden recording devices, he asked, "I take it, then, Comrade Brezhnev, that Moscow Center's assets are no longer needed? That I may reassign those now working on the Korea matter?"

* * *

It was not until he was safely out of the Kremlin that Yuri Andropov permitted himself to touch the face of the fear he'd kept at bay in Brezhnev's office. They had tried first to eliminate him directly with the absurd charge about the bungled actions against the Americans. Failing that, Leonid Ilyich had taken another tack. Less obvious, but equally deadly in the long run had been Brezhnev's attempt to cut Moscow Center from the Korea operation. Had Brezhnev summoned the nerve to completely isolate the Center, it would have been seen by all as the certain precursor to Yuri Andropov's political demise.

But that had been avoided. He had stood at the mouth of the pit and had managed a reprieve: time—time for Moscow Center and himself. A modest accomplishment. But he was certain it would be enough.

Leonid Brezhnev sat alone in his office. The late sun threw shadows against the damask-covered wall opposite him. It had been only prudent, he thought, to allow Andropov to continue for the moment to play a small part in the Korea plan. The arrogant fool. As if his precious Kh.V. files meant anything. Files could be taken care of. What mattered was that even the most brilliant of plans had moments that required a plump scapegoat. And he'd seen to it that one would be available.

Chapter 7

Alexandria, Virginia

Susan Forbes stood in the kitchen doorway. She'd come home late, and John Freeman had already started dinner. Freeman's smile froze as he registered her appearance. Her eyes were wide and she was breathing heavily, as if from great exertion.

Startled, he was unable to raise his hands before she was on him, fists beating his chest. "Goddamn you, John." She began to cry. "Goddamn you." Bandit, who'd been perched on a stool watching Freeman, gravely regarded the scene before him.

"Eleanor let it out. About those Russians," she sobbed. "She thought you'd told me."

He hugged her, pinning her arms between them. He caressed her hair and neck until her breathing slowed. "Let's go somewhere. I don't want to talk about it here."

They drove in silence to the Capitol, parked on Constitution Avenue, then walked to the west-front terrace and stood looking down the Mall toward the Washington Monument. The warm air was moist with the humidity of southern nights. Around the Smithsonian buildings at mid-distance floodlights were beginning to take up the burden surrendered by the fading western sky.

"I didn't tell you because I didn't want to admit it to myself. Maybe that's not the best way to say it, but . . . I thought that after Viet Nam it was all over—that kind of killing. I thought I could close the door on that. But when they came after us—when they killed Lew—it came back to that again." He closed his eyes and rubbed the bridge of his nose between his thumb and index finger. "I thought I could go back just once more, then shut the door. Walk away. Not get you involved."

"I had no 'need to know,' was that it?" Her voice was cold and furious. "Do you think I'm too delicate to deal with something like that? Or didn't you trust me? Did you think I'd use it against you?"

He turned to face her, his anger rising. "It wasn't that. It wasn't that at all. It just seemed the easier way out. If I didn't bring you in on it, it'd be easier to pretend it never happened, that it wasn't part of our lives. I wouldn't have to see the knowledge of it in your eyes." There had been Helen, who'd found out and had left him shortly thereafter. "I never thought you'd hurt me. I just didn't want it to hurt us."

The hard leather heels of a policeman tapped on the flagstones and echoed off the granite walls of the Capitol.

"If you have to kill for your country," he continued after a moment, "why not limit the killing to those who're in the game? Why slaughter the spectators? A German soldier in *All Quiet on the Western Front* says the guys in the trenches shouldn't be there, trying to kill each other. Get the leaders, he says, the bastards who started the war. Put *them* in the coliseum, make *them* fight while the cannon fodder watch on."

The policeman, having satisfied himself that the two figures were lovers, turned and continued his beat.

"I remember briefing an American general in Viet Nam. I told him how we would target a specific party cadre—a tax collector, an organizer, a terrorist. How we'd then track him—or her—sometimes for days. And how if we couldn't take him alive, we'd kill him. Kill him in close, but kill only him.

"Assassination puts those who start wars in the coliseum. It makes the leaders, the columnists, and the generals liable for their mistakes." John Freeman thought of the sure, certain ones—the staffers in Westmoreland's air-conditioned headquarters, the correspondents covering the war from the Caravelle bar, the sleek embassy salesmen of computer evaluations of the war's progress. Pitchmen who'd never seen a man's guts strewn in the mud because of the snake oil they'd sold. Ball-less wonders, butterflies who never smelled the war as they flitted to their villas to dress for tennis and cocktails at the Cercle Sportif. "It's not so much the dying. It's the leveling effect. Assassination makes them share the burden of the common man. That's why they fear it."

Over the Capitol dome the bright lights lured swarms of flying insects, which in turn attracted the swallows and bats that fed upon them.

Freeman turned and stood looking at the Capitol. "We've lost touch with reality. We're blind to the fact that the world's a dangerous place; that we need people who're able to do what has to be done without sending in the Marines or drafting kids out of high school. We're blind because we elect people who tell us what they think we want to hear: that there's no need for a draft; service to the nation's an inconvenience. The Soviets planning a war in Korea? Why, that's just some paranoid alarmist popping off.

"The professional politicians have all the easy answers—the no-pain solutions. Troubles with the Soviets? Just negotiate. The old men in the Kremlin snuff out human rights because we Americans don't talk to them. Talk's the answer, and God knows, talk's plentiful in Washington.

"And then, occasionally, the real world rears its head. The glib press releases don't work and the politicians come to us with whispers and nudges. 'Do something,' they plead in the back rooms. 'Don't bother telling us the details,' they say. Like fools, we never make them openly commit themselves. We go out and give it a whirl, and if it turns out badly, they disown us. They beg us to clean up a mess they've made, and then want us to go away because they find our odor offensive."

He was silent for long moments, then spoke again, so softly Susan had to strain to hear him. "You, me—Eleanor and the others . . . we're fools. Time after time the politicians send us up the hill, then desert us. And time after time we keep coming back when they call us. It's happened so often, even a dumb soldier finally learns their game." He looked at Susan, a look heavy with resignation and warning. "A time will come when they call and none of our kind will be left to answer."

Susan Forbes took his hand. "Let's go home."

Down below on First Street an occasional car slowly circled the reflecting pool. A green-bronze Ulysses Grant sat on horseback, facing down the long Mall to the memorial to his commander-in-chief, surveying the capital of the nation he'd wreaked such carnage to preserve.

Hains Point is a landfill, an appendix sticking out into the Potomac. It has a nine-hole golf course noted for its flatness and seagulls, and a 3.3 mile loop road that is a favorite of runners.

Alan Squires drove slowly around the point. It was his third circuit. The first time, he'd spotted the watcher, the one who'd make certain he wasn't being tailed. It was a black man sitting in a beat-up silver Mercury, reading the Sunday papers. By Squires's third circuit, the black had put a yellow stuffed dog in the car's rear window: Squires was clear. Squires then drove to the Washington waterfront and parked in the underground lot near Hogate's restaurant. Two rows over he spotted Chebrakin's car. He looked quickly around, then opened the door and got in.

"Good morning, Mr. Squires."

Squires felt a cold rush of adrenaline and a tightness around his chest. "Where's Vladimir?"

Yakov Lishinsky, the KGB deputy *rezident*, smiled disarmingly. "Vladimir was called home unexpectedly. An illness in the family. He asked me to fill in." Lishinsky could easily have passed for an American. Tanned and slender, with blond hair, Lishinsky drank prodigious quantities of white wine, told delightfully risqué jokes in idiomatic American English, and disarmed Westerners at cocktail parties with easy acknowledgments of the Soviet Union's most obvious shortcomings. Everywhere he went he left the impression that the Soviet Union couldn't be such an awful place if it was represented by good sorts like himself.

Alan Squires was frightened, breathing heavily, his armpits suddenly wet. Lishinsky put the car in gear and drove up the ramp into the glare of the morning sun.

"Stop! Please stop!" begged Squires.

Lishinsky smiled again, but continued, neither slowing nor speeding up. "It'd be better if we drove. Just around downtown."

Lishinsky had arranged the meeting in order to take over as Squires's control. He'd stepped into such situations before, and he knew it would be difficult. If you were successful in running a high-strung agent such as Squires, as Chebrakin had been, it meant you'd established a relationship of trust, or at least one of confidence and predictability.

Lishinsky drove slowly, carefully, watching his rearview mirror. Another watcher, parked on Maine Avenue, had seen them and was now following behind, in position, if need be, to block or throw off an FBI tail. In another mile he would drop off, to be replaced by the black in the Mercury. Lishinsky was not one to give the Americans an easy time.

The story about Chebrakin's family illness had been carefully thought out. Lishinsky, on reading Squires's psychological profile, had reasoned that the truth might cause Squires to break contact altogether. If Chebrakin was merely out of touch temporarily, then the KGB could hold out the promise—or threat—of his eventual return.

Alan Squires turned to look at Lishinsky, whose eyes were on the street ahead. He desperately tried to remember exactly what he'd said after getting in the car. Was this an FBI trap? Had they tumbled to him at last? Or was it a fishing expedition? He felt weak and the need to urinate almost overwhelmed him.

Lishinsky began his monologue. He'd spent days going through the field file on Squires, even sending priority queries to Moscow Center for additional details. He'd then built his approach. Lishinsky had anticipated Squires's first response of shock, followed by fear of disclosure. This reaction he dampened by tidbits he'd culled from the file and anecdotes of his own career as a "journalist" for *New Times*—a fabricated tale of how he and Chebrakin over the years had shared bottles, hardships, and even women.

He could tell Squires was relaxing. The time to tighten the screw, to give Squires a taste of the knout. No sense in letting this one think his work's over. Lishinsky abruptly shifted from the trivia of his relationship with Chebrakin to the spying Squires had done. In short, precise sentences, he spoke of the details of reports Chebrakin had submitted over the years and of Squires's more recent work at Langley.

As Lishinsky intended, this numbed Squires with fear. God! He knows everything! Everything! All along, Squires had wanted to believe that his association with Chebrakin had been a personal one, a unique relationship that transcended the grasping and parochial interests of their respective nations. Lishinsky's brutal recital proved to Squires that he'd been no more than another asset to be recruited, trained, and exploited as Moscow Center saw fit. Squires felt the panic crash on him again, along with the need to piss.

Lishinsky saw Squires tighten. Almost a spasm, he noted. He saw the whitening of knuckles. Ah, we've shown him hell opened up. Now, the last act: the path to salvation.

They reached a traffic light. "Alan, if Vladimir and I hadn't both been prudent, we would not have been such close associates," or even alive, he added mentally. In an obvious and therefore clumsy appeal to Squires, Lishinsky talked on about shaping world events, attempting to engage Squires in a political fantasy in which the American would be a reformer, a revolutionary. There! Can't you see yourself, Alan? There on the barricades, making great things happen!

Lishinsky dropped Squires at Eighteenth and K streets, where Squires hailed a cab that took him to the waterfront. Yakov Lishinsky hummed off-key on the way back to the embassy. It had not been the smoothest of transfers. But it had worked, and that was good enough.

Lishinsky looked at his watch and smiled. There would be time, after all, to take his two sons to Baltimore. The Orioles were playing New York. And how he disliked those arrogant Yankees.

Langley, Virginia

Lieutenant General Samuel Edward Bartlett IV was born into a Rice, Virginia, family that carried its tradition of military service with a well-burnished pride that enabled it to ignore its poverty. It was this pride that prompted a fifteen-year-old Sam Bartlett to lie about his age and run off to join the Army just before World War II. By war's end, still not twenty-one, he had gotten a chest full of medals and a battlefield commission, led a reconnaissance platoon of Merrill's Marauders in the bloody guerilla war behind Japanese lines, and decided to make a career in military intelligence. Over the next thirty years Sam Bartlett mastered Russian, fought in wars many Americans had never heard of, and according to most accounts, became pretty damned good on the guitar. Though time had thickened his waist, he had aged well and carried himself with a courtly assurance that turned women's heads at any gathering. At present he was the Director of the Defense Intelligence Agency.

Bartlett leafed through the black leather three-ring binder on the way up to Langley from the Pentagon. He'd be a fool to think that he'd be able to convince Roswell Franks, but the attempt had to be made. He closed the book and looked out the window at the green of the parkway. It was as if he were at a roulette table and, despite having played wisely, was down to a handful of chips.

He had known that desperate feeling before. Whenever he felt its dark and malignant presence, he remembered the morning in Burma, when they'd had to cross the runway at Myitkyina against the withering fire of the Japanese machine guns. A morning when an eighteen-year-old boy lieutenant knew with rock-solid certainty that he would die. He remembered, too, other times in the intervening years.

Roswell Franks sat back. He'd had major disagreements with Sam Bartlett. When he'd taken over as Director of Central Intelligence, Franks had tried to gain control over the Defense Intelligence Agency's budget, to bring order to the American Intelligence Community—to unite the feuding baronies. Bartlett had fought him with considerable skill and tenacity, arguing that the benefits of competitive intelligence outweighed the shortcomings of having to ride herd on the intramural squabbling—that a behemoth agency would soon stifle dissent and produce only homogenized pap.

The outcome was typical of Washington: there were neither clear victories nor decisive defeats. The issue was never finally decided. It still smoldered below the surface. Faceless staffers who had been on the losing side nurtured their memos and studies, hoarding them in files and safes, and looked forward to using them again to settle old scores once the issue returned, as it undoubtedly would. What came about in the battle between Franks and Bartlett was a murky accommodation in which neither man got everything he wanted, but in which there were sufficient adjustments at the margins so each could claim some measure of success.

As angry as Franks had been that he'd not gotten his way, he came out of the confrontation with a grudging respect for Bartlett and about as much affection as Franks was capable of having for an adversary. Bartlett was hard and tough. But he'd come at you straight on, as he was doing now.

"Sam, I've heard all this before." Franks pointed to the briefing book on the coffee table between them. "This is a rehash of the Korea estimate that that . . . woman did. I thought it was an alarmist piece of"—Franks caught himself about to say crap, but thought better of it—"piece of work then, and I still think it is."

"Ros." Bartlett's voice was patient, calm, almost friendly. "There're only so many ways to skin a cat. No

matter how we've skinned this one, we come up with this."
He nodded toward the briefing book. For a moment both
men stared at the book, as if it were something each
wished, if for different reasons, would just go away. But it
was something both knew they would have to deal with.

Bartlett cleared his throat and gave his sly good-
old-boy grin. "Sorta looks like the proverbial rubber in the
collection plate, doesn't it, Ros?"

Franks, grateful to be able to release the overpowering
tension, laughed hard, closing his eyes and throwing his
head back. "I was thinking the same thing." Franks sat
erect, hands on knees. He tilted his head toward Bartlett.
"What are you going to do with it, Sam?"

Bartlett's chin dropped to his chest, and at the same
time he fixed Franks with a grin. "I suppose I can't get you
to walk it in to the President, can I, Ros?"

Franks smiled back at him. "No, Sam. No, you can't.
And not because of the ration of crap I'd catch. I'd put up
with that. I won't do it because I don't believe it's a
balanced appraisal of all aspects of the Korea problem. I
really don't.

"This administration, Sam, is dead set on getting out of
Korea. If we send that to the White House and up to the
Hill"—he pointed to the book—"it'll leak—no matter how
high we classify it. It'll cause one hell of an uproar, but it
won't stop the withdrawal. Carter's dead set on it."

"Ros, I disagree." Bartlett's voice came with the
realization of defeat. "I'm not as young or as foolish as I once
was, but there comes a time, even in Washington, to come
out and tell the truth, no matter who it pisses off. That little
book there does a damn good job of telling us what the
North Koreans' capabilities are. And with the capabilities
they have, they could roll over the South without us there
on the ground."

As if reluctant to disappoint Bartlett, Franks sighed.
"Sam, I'm not taking it to the White House."

Bartlett nodded, then got up, reaching at the same
time for the binder. "Didn't really think you would, Ros."
He slipped the briefing into an old-fashioned leather
briefcase, snapped the catch and fastened the leather

straps. Buckling the last strap, he shifted the briefcase to his left hand and extended his right to Roswell Franks.

Franks took the hand without hesitation, and was surprised at a sudden surge of regret that he couldn't join with Bartlett. He put his left hand on Bartlett's right shoulder. "I won't ask what you're going to do next. But Sam," he squeezed the shoulder, "good luck."

Bartlett smiled and gave Franks a slow wink. "Thanks, Ros."

Moscow

". . . and so, Vasili Petrovich, they got into North Korea, many kilometers behind the Demilitarized Zone, planted this monitoring device, then left? Without a trace?"

Kiktev nodded.

Yuri Andropov lit a cigarette. "One can never be quite certain of them, the Americans. One moment they're trying to hide behind their oceans; the next, they're popping up where you least expect them."

"Do you think, Comrade Andropov, that they're deceiving us in Korea? Laying some sort of trap?" Kiktev asked.

"If they are, they are much more competent and imaginative than I would give them credit for." Andropov dragged on the cigarette. "No, I think we're seeing the results of an operation that was undertaken without extensive knowledge of those in Washington. Otherwise we would have known sooner." Andropov's voice became brisk. "Did our Korean friends leave the device in place?"

"Yes. When they discovered it, they called the 280th Commando Brigade. One of our advisors with the *spetznaz* investigated, saw what it was. Told the Koreans it was a modification we'd put on the line."

"Good. We can use it for a channel for our friends in Service A."

Kiktev groaned inwardly at the decision. Yuri Andropov intended to keep the tap operational and use it to feed the Americans misleading information. On the face of it a wise and cunning decision. Implementing it, however, would be a nightmare. Specialists would have to be assigned to produce the false material; no easy matter since it had to be plausible to the Americans. Sometimes authentic secrets would be divulged in order to make a larger lie easier to swallow. It was mind-bending work made all the more difficult because it was impossible to judge the American reaction to it; the passive tap on the line provided no response back from its owners. Service A would not know if their work was worthwhile or not. He would take this up with Romanov.

"The GRU will be taking over control of the *spetznaz* unit. Shall I let them know—"

"No, Vasili Petrovich," Andropov stated emphatically. "We certainly will not let the GRU know. Disinformation is our province. The American tap will remain our little secret."

Washington, D.C.

The Foundation for International Relations occupied two adjoining row houses on northwest Massachusetts Avenue. FIR was founded in the mid-fifties. FIR's salad days, however, came a decade later, when Lyndon Johnson opposed Marxist adventurism in the Dominican Republic and South Viet Nam.

Like defense contractors, FIR also profited from the war in Southeast Asia. FIR attracted formidable brainpower from academia and dollars from Hollywood, the churches, and other traditional sources of utopianist support.

With FIR's new fortunes came less obvious but highly significant changes in direction and staffing. The old FIR was a sleepy place, inhabited by the cognoscenti of American socialism, the remnants of the left of the thirties.

The new crowd, many of whom had cut cane for Castro, passionately believed that the underdeveloped nations—the wretched of the earth—could be the cradle of the Marxist millennium that had eluded an earlier generation at FIR.

Quinn Barnes had made FIR an intellectual main-spring of the Viet Nam antiwar movement. Barnes's recruits served their political apprenticeships at FIR, where they crafted the speeches for sympathetic politicians. FIR graduates then moved on, aided by Barnes and a network of FIR alumni, to jobs in other parts of Washington: to the media, and some, like David Cummings and Alan Squires, to government. Even now, in the aftermath of Viet Nam, the cycle was repeating.

If Quinn Barnes found out that Alan Squires had penetrated CIA as a KGB agent, he probably would have shrugged; his only concern would have been that FIR not get any of the splash if things went wrong. Aside from that, he would have gotten immense satisfaction in knowing that CIA was being diddled, although he greatly would have preferred that Alan be working for Castro's DGI or some other Third World intelligence agency rather than the KGB. As it was, Barnes was untroubled by such thoughts as he watched Alan toy with his pasta.

Squires looked up from his plate. "So you think they'll fold?"

Barnes nodded. "It's only a matter of time. Days, perhaps. A week or two at the most. It's too bad. Carter's going to claim it's the new intelligence," Barnes shook his head, "but the right's gotten to him and Vance. The generals and the defense industry have to have South Korea as a customer. Think of how many generals'd be out of a job if it weren't for Korea."

Barnes went on. Squires had heard it all before. How America had sheltered the fascist-industrialist South Koreans, who in turn had destroyed the true Korean culture, which now only existed in the North. Squires's attention wandered. Lishinsky still worried him.

"What?"

Barnes was patient. "I said, Alan, what next? After Korea? What are you going to do?"

Squires gathered his thoughts. "I don't know. Leave the Agency, I suppose. Perhaps get a staff job on the Hill."

"Soon?"

"No. Not until we finish the nuclear thing."

"The estimate?"

Squires nodded. "Yes. I think we ought to get that through. Especially if Carter's going to leave the troops in Korea, it'll be important to show how we've allowed ourselves to become the patsies of just about any tinhorn dictator who claims he's an anti-Communist."

Barnes made a signing motion in the air toward the waiter. Carefully checking the bill, he began, "And there's the Middle East . . ."

Squires, annoyed that Barnes hadn't even asked him about dessert, looked balefully at Barnes.

"I mean, Alan," Barnes gestured with a flutter of hands, "that if we can credibly tie Israel—"

Having given up hope of dessert, Squires interrupted Barnes by standing and motioning toward the door. "I've got to be getting home."

Crossing Connecticut Avenue, Barnes broke the silence, asking Squires, "Do you suppose David will stay on at State? This'll be a terrible blow to him. After all, it was—"

Squires laughed harshly. "David's made the grade. He's now a good Nazi."

Barnes gave him a startled look.

"You know," Squires explained, "the ones after the war who said they were in the secret resistance against Hitler."

Howard Ochsman considered himself a pretty hot-shit journalist. Admittedly, he was rather short and his hair too thin, and his wife of twenty-seven years missed no opportunity to tell him that his round face and rimless glasses made him look like a little owl. Nonetheless, he wrote with dispatch and accuracy about interesting events in other countries. That he did so with a minimum of personal bias earned him the respect of—and a few tips from—those in government who had to take care of those interesting events.

It was nearly bedtime when Ochsman got a call on his private line. The caller hadn't given his name, but said he had certain sensitive information about Korea that might be of use to Ochsman. In spite of the hour, a meeting was arranged in a nearby hotel. Ochsman gently nudged Clara awake, gave her the name and address of the hotel, and told her he'd call her shortly after arriving.

A tall man opened the door just wide enough to identify Ochsman, then closed it again. Ochsman heard a muffled voice—apparently the man talking to someone else in the room—then the door opened to let him in. Instead of standing behind the door and pulling it open toward him, the man stood to one side, pushing the door away from himself. The way the man stood in the doorway, he partially shielded the other person, who sat in a chair toward a dark corner of the room.

A voice came from behind the man. "Hullo, Howard. We're sorry to get you out like this. Coffee?"

Ochsman let his breath out in relief and smiled. "Hello, Eleanor. Yes, I'd like that very much."

Ochsman reached over his sun visor and pressed the remote garage-door opener. He looked at his watch, wondering how he could rearrange his office schedule so he could pick up a little extra sleep. Eleanor and that fellow Freeman had spent two hours briefing him, laying out the substance of the intelligence work on Korea. They'd been open enough, easily answering most of his questions, providing the chilling comparisons between the two Korean military forces. They'd been adamant about one thing, however—nothing about sources and methods. Ochsman was confident he had their story— all of it that they wanted to tell him. None of it, naturally, was for attribution.

When he'd asked them why Roswell Franks was blocking the estimate, they demanded that their response be off the record—he couldn't print what they told him, but could use the knowledge to probe his other sources further. When he'd asked them a natural question—the role of the Soviet Union—they'd refused point-blank to discuss that, which put it at the top of his mental checklist of things to look into. Staying off the record, Eleanor Trowbridge recited a list of the major players and the kinds of knowledge she thought they had. As he eased the garage door down, he realized it would be senseless to rearrange his schedule. He wouldn't be able to get back to sleep after this.

The Washington Post—June 22, 1979

NEW INTELLIGENCE STUDIES CONFIRM HIGHER ESTIMATES OF NORTH KOREAN STRENGTH

Secretary of Defense Harold Brown said yesterday "there clearly is a larger North Korean force than had been thought a couple of years ago," thus conceding that the threat to South Korea is greater than originally admitted by the Carter Administration.

Although Brown refused to give specific figures, intelligence officials elsewhere confirmed that North Korea now has the world's fifth largest army . . .

Rep. Les Aspin (D-Wis.), a member of the House Armed Services and Intelligence committees, revealed that he has reviewed the studies and that they show North Korea has an army of 550,000 to 600,000 troops. . . .

Aspin told the Armed Services investigations subcommittee the estimates have caused him to withdraw his support from President Carter's plan to pull all U.S. ground troops from South Korea.

Arlington Hall Station—Arlington, Virginia

"Here's the interesting stuff." John Freeman handed several sheets of paper to Eleanor. "The first is small talk—when they last met, Ochsman's book on Viet Nam, Cummings, and working in Saigon."

"How'd the meeting happen? We didn't give him David's name."

"I suppose it was Portale. He called me from INR, asking if Ochsman had contacted me. I told him no. So it was probably a case of one lead connecting to another."

CUMMINGS: Yes. Those numbers seem about right.

OCHSMAN: Are they a surprise to you? Did you know about them when you were writing for FIR?

CUMMINGS: Well, the magnitude, I think, sort of shocked everyone. Obviously the intelligence people had been asleep at the switch.

OCHSMAN: But about FIR . . .

CUMMINGS: Well, certainly I had no idea back then. But I think you put too much emphasis on those numbers. The American withdrawal could be done safely. I thought so when I was at FIR, and I think so now.

OCHSMAN: So you're in favor of the withdrawal in spite of the fact that the North would have an overwhelming superiority? That doesn't mean anything?

CUMMINGS: Of course it means something. It means a lot. It means that the withdrawal as I proposed it had to be carried out with some touch of deftness, finesse. It's not just a matter of military balances, it's a question of diplomacy.

OCHSMAN: You said *had*— "the withdrawal as I proposed it *had* . . ." What do you mean by that? Is the withdrawal really a past-tense issue?

CUMMINGS: (laughter) You're persistent, Howard. I can let you have it on deep background. Deep background. These people—some of the ones that've come on with Carter—they aren't capable of managing a sophisticated foreign policy. They couldn't get laid in a Chinese whorehouse with a sack of rice on their backs. Look at how they've botched up the Korea thing already. They have the military in damn near open revolt. The Senate Foreign Relations Committee is putting out a critical press release every day, and the House of

Representatives is in an uproar over the bribery allegations.

OCHSMAN: Don't forget the Blue House bugging . . .

CUMMINGS: Yes. That. I wish I could forget. That idiot Franks was sent out to Langley to keep that kind of thing from happening. Either he's not in touch with what's going on out there—in which case he's incompetent—or they've coopted him. Imagine. Bugging the goddamn Blue House . . .

OCHSMAN: What you're telling me—

CUMMINGS: What I'm telling you, Howard, is that this is the original gang that can't shoot straight. They advise Carter badly on the neutron bomb, and he pisses off every NATO ally of any consequence. . . .

OCHSMAN: So there's a degree of incompetence.

CUMMINGS: Incompetence is charitable, Howard. Their ineptness is why I've rethought my position on the troop withdrawal.

OCHSMAN: Then . . .

CUMMINGS: I'm trying as best I can, Howard, to get this thing turned around. Actually, I've been working behind the scenes now for months.

Eleanor tossed the transcript to her desk, took off her glasses and rubbed her eyes. "He's not much in the integrity department, but you have to admit he's got a keen sense for wind direction."

Paris

Jay Mathias and Roswell Franks sat at breakfast in Franks's suite at the Intercontinental. Mathias had a government-issue briefcase beside his chair, from which he'd taken a folder containing the day's agenda.

He had spent the previous day in various appointments at the Service de Documentation Exterieure et Contre-Espionage (SDECE), the acronym of which Americans pronounced as "suh-DECK." It was an organization that combined the foreign intelligence responsibilities of CIA with the domestic counterintelligence of the FBI.

The SDECE appointment was one of many visits Franks would be making with friendly intelligence agencies while he was in Europe and the Middle East. Andrew Cabot had been right, Franks grudgingly admitted. The quality of information from the foreign intelligence services was definitely getting worse. This trip was intended to help set things aright.

CIA's dependence on shared intelligence resulted from America's relatively late entry into the secret intelligence business. The Agency had been a permanent fixture of the American government only since 1947, while the British Secret Intelligence Service, for example, had been the Crown's right hand for centuries and consequently had flung its net over much of the world by the time CIA came on the scene. And so, Langley benefited greatly from British MI-6 coverage of the Balkans and Egypt. The French were active in parts of Africa and the Pacific, while the West German BND still retained considerable assets in Eastern Europe. The German networks were a legacy from Reinhard Gehlen, who'd stayed in the trade under an American franchise after building a far-reaching intelligence empire for the Third Reich in World War II.

Franks's session with Paul Trinquier, head of SDECE, had not left the American general in the best of spirits. The dour Frenchman had bluntly criticized the American government for its inability to keep others' noses out of its secret business.

"Tell me again who we're seeing this morning," grumbled Franks.

"Jean-Pierre Morand. He's the publisher of a political newsletter." Mathias consulted his notebook. "It's called *Antithesis*."

Franks slumped in his chair and ran his hand over his eyes. He'd still not recovered from jet lag, and was fading after breakfast. "Shit. All's I need is a morning with some goddamn French intellectual."

Mathias walked to the telephone to call for room

service to remove the breakfast trays. He came back and stood expectantly before Franks. "We're seeing him because of Secretary Cummings."

Fifteen minutes later Jay Mathias answered a knock on the outer door and returned with Jean-Pierre Morand, a cadaverously thin man whose few words of welcome were carried to Franks on a stale wine and garlic breath. Franks gestured to a period sofa upholstered in a blue silk brocade. Morand smiled, showing a mouthful of gray and crooked teeth. Mathias poured coffee all around.

In good English Morand described *Antithesis* as a small-circulation publication intended for French government leaders in Paris. "My subscribers include most of the Chamber of Deputies," he explained with a smile, "but only God knows if they really read it or not, or, if indeed, our deputies are capable of reading anything at all." Morand, a Parisian insider, then conducted a scintillating tour of the European political horizon, punctuating his recital with gossip of the peccadilloes, mostly sexual, of leaders from Moscow to London. In spite of his initial distaste for the man, Franks found Morand increasingly charming.

Morand looked at his watch and made a face. "Ah, General, I've taken up much of your valuable time, chattering about the foibles of our notables. A small thing for you, then I must go. I talked with David Cummings first about this and he said I should mention it to you."

Morand dropped his voice and hunched forward. His right hand wrapped around the coffee cup. Franks noticed that the fingernails of his index and middle fingers were missing. The fingers themselves had apparently been broken and badly set. "There are interesting reports from my sources in Germany. Reports about the Germans aiding the South Africans in a nuclear venture. It is all very hazy. The picture I have is incomplete."

"Yes." Franks quickly picked out of his memory a briefing by Alan Squires. A West German source, an export agent from Hamburg, had turned over photocopies of shipping manifests and customs documents. Squires had said that the components, when coupled with earlier shipments to South Africa, could be used in the cartridge assembly of nuclear weapons.

"There is also, General, the matter of the Jews." Franks felt a corrosive anti-Semitism roll over him in the Frenchman's tone and inflection. Morand was a man who truly lamented Hitler's failure, a man who hoped the final solution had only been postponed. "We know that some of the Germans are advising the Jews at the Dimona reactor." The Dimona reactor, Squires had told him, had been built in the Negev Desert not for safety—to get it away from the more populated areas of Israel—but for security. It's nothing but a bomb plant, Squires had argued. They're building the weapons below the reactor.

"It is much the same as it has been, General. *Le boche* are using the Jews, and for their part, the Jews are doing the bidding of their masters in spite of the humiliations of Auschwitz and Belsen." Morand's eyes were glittering. His lips were quivering and wet, and he caressed his twisted fingers with his left hand.

The SDECE tail picked up Jean-Pierre Morand as the journalist left the Intercontinental and walked through the Place Vendôme. Like any good intelligence officer, Paul Trinquier had his store of suspicions. One of those was that Morand was an agent of influence working for the Soviets. SDECE had already mounted surveillance on Igor Kuznetsov, a Soviet official who had attempted to recruit a member of the French parliament. The surveillance on the Russian had paid off with photographs of a meeting of Kuznetsov and Morand. With enough patience, Trinquier was certain that Morand would make a slip. In other times Paul Trinquier would have shared this information with the Americans, certainly with other Directors of Central Intelligence. But not with Roswell Franks; not at this time.

En route to Germany, Roswell Franks, still thinking about the meeting with Morand, directed Jay Mathias to cable Langley, authorizing Alan Squires a higher priority on

KH-11 targeting against suspected South African nuclear weapons facilities.

Headline—The Washington Post:

CHIEFS OF STAFF ASK CARTER TO SUSPEND KOREA PULLOUT

* * *

Report by Senator John Glenn
Chairman, East Asia Subcommittee
Senate Foreign Relations Committee
July 1, 1979:

A recent intelligence estimate has reappraised the North Korean situation and concludes that its forces are considerably stronger than previously believed. It is my judgment based on this new information, that the risks involved in continuing the troop withdrawal demand that we reverse our policy and maintain the 2d Infantry Division in Korea. . . .

Washington, D.C.

Howard Ochsman leafed through his first draft. His colleagues could compose and edit right on the screens of their word processors. He had to have it on paper. Ochsman scribbled on legal pads with a cheap felt-tip pen in a wide, looping scrawl, then pulled it together with a typewriter.

In the past ten days he'd talked to any number of contacts in the Pentagon, State, and elsewhere in the so-called "policy arena," a term he thoroughly detested and never used except as mental shorthand. He'd managed to get an interview with Mark Douglas, who'd recently been relieved as the Agency's Chief of Station in Seoul, and from there the path had led to Fyleman, the American ambassador to South Korea, who, luckily, was in Washington on home leave.

Both Douglas and Fyleman had confirmed the fact that there was general agreement among the Americans about the essential judgments of the Korea estimate. "I think the ROK's have a pretty good idea of the magnitude of the numbers," Douglas had told him, "but I suspect the administration doesn't want to let it out now. That would strip the figleaf off this whole thing. The ROK's as well as the other friends we have left out there would see it for what it is. Another goddamn sellout in Asia."

Douglas had given him permission to use the quote, but without attribution. Fyleman had been more obtuse, but he'd denied nothing. Interestingly, it was from Fyleman, not Douglas, that Ochsman had learned that the pressure to bug the Blue House had come from Cummings. Fyleman, moreover, suspected that it had been a leak in Washington—not Korea—that had blown the operation and implicated the American intelligence community.

Ochsman found the legal pad on his desk and started to draft an additional paragraph, one that hinted at David Cummings's double (triple?) dealing. He got three sentences into it, then crossed it out, tore out the page, and made a mental note to drop it by the shredder. Sordid, it was. Interesting? Certainly. But the story he wanted to write was about CIA and Korea. Another time, another place for Mr. Cummings.

The Washington Post—July 21, 1979:

PRESIDENT DROPS PULLOUT
OF U.S. TROOPS FROM KOREA

President Carter yesterday was forced to abandon one of his most controversial foreign policy initiatives, the withdrawal of U.S. ground troops from South Korea.

Knowledgeable Washington sources agree that the driving factor for this change was the recent increase in the U.S. intelligence estimate of North Korean ground forces.

Carter announced his intentions to withdraw U.S. forces as a distant contender for the presidency, and he stuck to his idea with tenacity throughout his campaign and after taking office. With little support from anyone else and against strong misgivings of South Korea, Japan, the U.S. military and powerful elements in Congress and the American intelligence community, Carter began the withdrawal and strongly defended it against attack. . . .

CIA Moscow Station discovered that one of its dead drops had been filled. Standard station procedure required that drop signals be checked randomly by different officers to make it difficult for the ever-present KGB tail to stake out the signal. Randolph Eddington, a station officer, had spotted the blue thumb tack stuck on the back of a certain bench in Sovetskaya Ploshchad, near the Arts Theatre.

Within an hour the drop area itself—a lane in Gorky Park—was under American surveillance. Satisfied that the drop was safe, one member of the surveillance team pulled a handkerchief from his pocket and blew his nose. Approximately forty yards away a third CIA officer, strolling with his wife, saw the handkerchief and motioned to a grassy area off the footpath. Taking his coat off, he carefully folded it, hanging it over a tree limb. The couple sat on the grass, smoked cigarettes, and watched the children sailing boats on the nearby pond. Fifteen minutes later they got up to leave. Retrieving his coat, the man slipped a small dark plastic box from a hollow in the tree and palmed it into his wife's purse. On their way out of the park, the woman handed the box off in a brushing pass to yet another American intelligence officer who was walking in the opposite direction.

The film arrived at Washington's Dulles International airport by special courier. It was duly receipted for by yet another heavily armed courier who took it to Building 312 of the Navy Yard, where it was developed in a laboratory two floors above Peter Smith's satellite interpretation center.

Andrew Cabot, using the Moscow Foreign Languages Publishing House's 1933 edition of *The Collected Works of V.I. Lenin*, deciphered the book code of the Hotspur report. There followed several hours of discussion with Eleanor and Bronowski; later, the three met with Sam Bartlett.

Meeting with Roswell Franks and Andrew Cabot in the general's F Street office, Sam Bartlett crossed one leg over the other, displaying highly polished black-snake Wellington boots, a breach of Army regulations like the red suspenders he wore beneath his uniform blouse—statements about himself that he considered even more important than the stars on his shoulders.

Bartlett first developed the cover story for Hotspur. "Ros, I met a fellow back when I was the attaché in Moscow. I know the Agency's supposed to be brought in on high-level human sources, but . . ." Bartlett shrugged. "I thought it was a case of me handling the thing or no one. He knew me, and I didn't think he'd have trusted anyone else."

Franks looked at Bartlett in suspicion. The CIA Director had been so battered by the media and the White House that he found it increasingly difficult to accept any story on its face value. Everything new had to be carefully examined for poisoned darts, and the messenger's motives thoroughly probed. "What's your friend have to say, Sam?"

"Like most of these reports, Ros, it's bits and pieces. My . . . my source pulled together some items that he believes are related." Sam Bartlett watched Franks's face carefully, certain of some kind of reaction but unsure of the form it would take. "It's Korea, Ros."

Franks tightened his lips. "I thought we were through with that, Sam. You people've won. The troops are going to stay."

Bartlett frowned. "I don't think it's a situation where there're winners or losers, Ros, but I didn't come here to talk about that." Bartlett leaned forward in the chair. "It's about the Russians, Ros. What they might be doing in Korea." Knowing he had Franks's attention, Bartlett continued. "We have some fragments. Let me tell you the story we see those fragments telling, then I'll give you all I know about the fragments themselves.

"In a sentence, Ros, a case can be made that, having helped the North Koreans build up their conventional military, the Soviets may now be bringing in nukes."

"Jesus . . ."

"I said 'may,' Ros," Bartlett warned. "We picked up administrative traffic on replacements for Russian advisors to Korean commando units—"

"Algernon?" asked Franks, interrupting.

Andrew Cabot took a deep breath, wondering if the memory of Algernon would so rankle Franks that the rest of Bartlett's briefing would be lost. To his relief, Franks's only reaction to Bartlett's nod of affirmation was to reach for a pen and pad of paper.

"For some reason, the Soviets are sending in entirely new *spetznaz* teams. We've identified some of the names from our files. We have high confidence that the new team at the 280th Commando Brigade, for instance, is specialized in SADM delivery." Bartlett pronounced it "SAY-dum."

Seeing Franks's puzzlement, Cabot interjected, "SADM's our acronym for Small Atomic Demolition Munition, Admiral."

Franks looked up from his notes. "You said you had other pieces to add to this?"

Sam Bartlett cleared his throat. He was unable to read Franks thus far. "Some months before the *spetznaz* rotations, Yuri Andropov and his horse holder, one Vasili Kiktev, took two days out of a busy schedule to fly to Chelyabinsk, a major nuclear-weapons facility east of the Urals. They were briefed by one A. Porsynko."

Cabot consulted a folder. "Porsynko is a nuclear design specialist, General. Worked with Sakharov on their H-bomb. He's been at Chelyabinsk for the past six years."

"Once we pinned down the date of the Andropov-

Porsynko meeting, I asked NSA to go back through their tapes. They picked up the establishment of a dedicated high-frequency link between Dzerzhinsky Square and Chelyabinsk."

"Can we read it?" Franks asked.

Bartlett shook his head. "No. All we know is that it's the kind of comm that's reserved for high-level communications."

"It's still active?"

"No. They shut it down several months ago."

"And no more trips for Mr. Andropov to Chelyabinsk?"

"No."

Cabot suspected what was coming. Franks didn't surprise him.

"Pretty thin stuff, Sam." Franks sat back in his chair, crossed his legs and raised his left hand, index finger extended. "We have a *spetznaz* unit replacement in which some of the members have been trained on nuclear demolitions. I recall that in the Air Force we had Air Commando teams that had similar capabilities. We sent the Air Commandos to Viet Nam, but they didn't take their nukes with them."

A second finger. "And the Andropov trip to Chelyabinsk? Hell, I've made it a point to visit the labs at Los Alamos and Livermore. I'd hate for the KGB to leap to the conclusion that we're going to give nukes to Guatemala on that kind of evidence."

Unruffled, Sam Bartlett held up both hands in mock surrender. "Ros, you got me. It *is* thin stuff. And I agree with you, you can't come to any conclusions on the basis of two sketchy reports. But I do think we can't let this drop."

"What do you want, Sam?"

"I'd like to have your support in getting some KH-11 coverage of the main *spetznaz* training centers in the Soviet Union, say, for the next several weeks or so."

Franks frowned. Bartlett was putting him over a barrel. The DIA chief's request was, on the face of it, a reasonable one. If Franks denied it and something later popped, a lot of fingers would be pointed at him. He nodded reluctantly.

Picking up his winnings, Sam Bartlett smoothly dropped the next card. "And I'd appreciate you adding a little weight to my request to NSA to devote some MISER time to the *spetznaz* comms."

Franks choked back the anger of the gulled. What next? Dealing with this man was like haggling in a bazaar. MISER was a signals-intercept satellite whose advanced capabilities resulted in a clamor for missions from every sector of the intelligence community. Assigning MISER to the *spetznaz* target would mean that another customer would have to wait longer in line.

"Okay, Sam. You've got MISER," Franks surrendered. "How about my underwear too?"

Bartlett responded with a bashful smile. He did, indeed, enjoy rolling Franks.

As if to retrieve a shred of dignity, Franks pointed to Bartlett. "I'll give you priority on MISER, but we can't keep it on for any great length of time."

Andrew Cabot walked Sam Bartlett from Franks's office to the Director's elevator and rode with him down to his car, where Sergeant Major Braestrop waited.

"You didn't mention the Service A business, Sam."

"No." Bartlett waited until they were clear of the elevator, standing in the middle of the cavernous underground garage. Bartlett signaled Braestrop to start the car engine, then stepped closer to Cabot and lowered his voice. "Your source thought it was important—the linkage *dizinformatsia* is trying to build between South Africa and Seoul. And I'm sure he has his reasons. But we don't understand the connection, and it wouldn't have meant much, if anything, to Roswell."

Braestrop had opened the front passenger door of the car. Sam Bartlett got in, shut the door, and rolled down the window. "I'll be in touch, Andrew."

On the seventh floor Roswell Franks studied the notes he'd taken, then tore them off the pad, then threw them in a plastic container marked BURN.

Alushta, the Crimea

From his terrace, Andropov squinted into the early morning sun. He sat alone, wrapped in a white terry-cloth robe. Andropov took off his glasses and rubbed his eyes, still heavy from sleep.

He was certain that Moscow Center's skirts were clean—the Politburo had been kept informed of the struggle in Washington. Andropov thought he detected seeds of doubt about continuing the Korea plan now that the Americans would be staying. Even more encouraging was the guarded conjecture that things might have gone better had Leonid Brezhnev left matters to the KGB.

Andropov stretched his legs and called for his aide to bring more coffee and another roll with the English marmalade.

Chapter 8

Lyuh Chun-il stood slightly crouched, legs apart, and shouldered the heavy MC-1 parachute onto his back. Making certain the wide olive-drab nylon webbing was flat, he snapped the chest strap into the circular quick-release buckle. Bending over farther, he reached down, back between his legs, snagged the left leg strap, brought it up and routed it through a loop at his waist, then to the buckle. He repeated the step with the right leg strap. He cinched the straps tight, tugging on each in turn. Lyuh never forgot the time when he'd left a leg strap entirely too loose. When the parachute opened, his testicles had been caught between his leg and the parachute harness. The drop-zone crew said he had alternated screaming, cursing, and midair dancing all the way to the ground. He laughed now. But it damned sure wasn't funny at the time.

The rigger stood before him with the emergency chest parachute. Lyuh looked at it for a moment. Jump altitude tonight would be around 400 feet. If his main didn't open, he'd be a grease spot on the earth before the reserve could work. It would be just extra weight, something else to get in the way. He shook his head and waved off the rigger, who shrugged and took the reserve back to the parachute loft.

Lyuh pulled back his left sleeve and unsnapped the leather cover over his watch. The reception-and-security team would be boarding their airplane in a few minutes and be in the air within the hour. His plane would take off two hours later. Two hours strapped into the parachute before leaving. Flight crews could show up three or four minutes before takeoff, kick a few tires, tell a dirty joke, and fly. The poor bastards who jumped had to get trussed up early, then wait. It never failed: As soon as he had everything on, he felt his bladder swell. It wasn't too bad. He didn't want to have to go twice. Time enough later. Many's the jump with a wet leg, anyway. He found a clear space on the concrete floor of the rigger shed and lowered himself, squatting until he could feel the parachute come to rest against the wall. He then unfolded his legs, sticking them straight out front. He unzipped a leg pocket, found his lighter, and lit up a Marlboro.

Lyuh awoke. The rigger was nudging him with a boot. Ignoring the proffered hand, Lyuh struggled to his feet. His calves were stiff and sore, and he gingerly stamped one foot then the other to restore circulation. While asleep, he'd slipped down in the snug harness, and now the parachute didn't seem to fit quite right. He had to walk hunched over. He reached down, picked up the steel helmet and put it on, strapping it over the point of his chin.

The rigger first checked the front of Lyuh's parachute, running his hands over all buckles and fasteners of the harness, making certain Lyuh's rucksack, assault rifle, and other equipment were securely tied down. To give the rigger complete access, Lyuh clasped his hands together on top of his helmet. Satisfied with the front, the rigger motioned Lyuh to turn around. The rigger inspected the parachute pack, and when finished, passed the static line over Lyuh's left shoulder and slapped him on the buttocks. Outside on the asphalt ramp, Lyuh could hear the coughing sound of engines starting.

The Americans called it a C-47. The "Gooney Bird" had made possible the mass parachute drops at Normandy and had since flown into aviation legend.

Two hours later the load master cocked his head and then said something back into the mike. The plane began a moderate descent toward drop altitude. The load master spoke again into the microphone, and in a few minutes got up. He looked at Lyuh as he walked to the rear of the plane. He held up both hands, palms facing Lyuh, fingers extended.

Ten minutes.

Lyuh got up from the nylon-webbed seat and moved to a container about six feet from the door. Lashed to steel rings set in the cabin floor, it looked like a small beer keg. Lyuh squatted, hampered by his parachute. Annoyed, he beckoned the load master, who apparently was willing to sit back and watch him wrestle with the damn thing all by himself.

The two got the container unfastened from the floor rings and hooked its heavy straps to the front of Lyuh's parachute harness. The round container had handles on the top, which Lyuh used to lift the container off his toes, which in turn let him shuffle toward the door.

No matter how often he jumped, Lyuh was gripped by a wild surging thrill when the airplane door was thrown open. For five or so minutes before the jump, the noise of engines and wind would scream by, and mingled with it, the smell of exhaust fumes.

The load master motioned to the now-open door. Lyuh took the heavy metal snap link of the parachute rip cord and hooked it to the thin steel cable that ran the length of the cabin. He moved into the door. The load master took up the slack in the static line that now connected the parachute pack to the airplane.

Lyuh now stood in the door, his hands on either side of the opening braced him against the pitching and bucking of the airplane. He kept the container in the wind shadow of the airplane, out of the raging gale just inches away, howling by at over 120 miles an hour. The ground below was a pool pitch at his feet—solid inky black. Above him, a clear sky, the stars a dusting of incredibly sharp pinpricks of brightness.

The load master thrust a hand in front of Lyuh, fingers out.

Two minutes.

Lyuh squatted, to be able to look farther ahead under the C-47's wing.

One minute.

Set against the darkness below, Lyuh saw four small lights come on. They formed an inverted L, the pilot made minute adjustments so that the plane was now flying straight up the long axis of the L. The short arm of the L extended out to the left of the airplane's flight path. Unlike the other lights, the one that formed the short arm was blinking. It was international Morse code—the letter C being repeatedly flashed—the all clear signal. As the C-47 came even with the arm of the L, the red light on the doorsill winked out and was replaced by a bright green one, and over the engines' roar Lyuh could hear an insistent buzzer. He did a burlesque bump and pushed the container out into the slipstream, where the wind pulled the container and him into the night. He remembered later being irrationally enraged that the lazy load master, who would sleep this night in a warm bed, had slapped him on the butt as he was leaving the airplane.

Feeling the reassuring tug of the parachute opening, Lyuh quickly glanced up at the canopy, then felt foolish. Even if anything had gone wrong—an inversion or a streamer—he wouldn't have time to do anything about it. He'd wasted valuable seconds, and there was the container to attend to. On seeing the airplane pass overhead, the reception party had extinguished the lights, and once again Lyuh looked down into blackness.

Lyuh reached below his chest-release buckle and felt a round, knurled knob, about the size of an apple. He pulled the safety pin from the knob, then jerked the knob itself. Instantly he felt his burden drop away, and a second later was rocked gently as the container came to the end of the twelve-yard cable. He'd heard of jumps when the container didn't drop and the jumper, coming in at fourteen feet per second, had both legs broken on hitting the ground. Even when the thing did drop, the worries weren't over.

Lyuh felt the container make contact, and an instant later he hit the hard ground, rolling to spread the impact:

balls of the feet, side of the calves and thighs, buttocks, back muscles, shoulders.

By first light Lyuh and the others, eight in all, were far away. They had made certain all traces of their presence had been removed from the drop zone. They moved quickly, noiselessly, to the forest. Lyuh had then opened the container, which had served to protect yet another cylindrical package inside. Lyuh lifted it out, and, using the straps on the package, swung it like a pack onto his back. The now-empty carrying case and Lyuh's parachute were put into a hole dug earlier in the tree line by the reception party. The men quickly filled in the hole, then sprinkled the fresh earth with a tobacco-pepper mixture to discourage tracking dogs, and finally covered over the site with pine needles.

Lyuh scanned the low squat building. Approximately two hundred yards away was the headquarters—according to briefings, the nerve center for this sector of the Demilitarized Zone. The building housed only basic maintenance facilities for the warren of concrete and steel that extended into the granite beneath his feet. Ordinarily, to gain access to the entrance then get below ground would have been difficult. To then destroy the place and escape would have been impossible, even for a team as experienced and talented as Lyuh's.

But Lyuh's burden made all that unnecessary. Digging a small hole for concealment, the team buried the cylinder save for a small access hatch. Lyuh opened the hatch. In the night the luminous dials showed clearly. He set the timer for three hours, then tripped the arming switch. They would be far away when the nuclear fireball engulfed the underground operations center, incinerating its inhabitants and setting the stage for the liberation of southern Korea.

Washington, D.C.

Zbigniew Brzezinski had not chosen Rodgers Thurlow to be his assistant on the National Security Council.

Nonetheless, that the short, pudgy Floridian with the ready smile sat at Brzezinski's right hand was one of the many appointment concessions the Carter political team had made to gain the support of various factions within the Democratic Party. Not that Thurlow was a clod. Even Brzezinski would admit that his deputy was bright. And quick? Thurlow was so quick it was said that his victims walked around for days before they realized the genial red-haired man had cut their throats.

Thurlow's office was in the White House West Wing, next to Brzezinski's. Most of the rest of the NSC staff were over in the EOB—the outrageously baroque old Executive Office Building. Many of them tried to gloss this over, glibly telling outsiders they "worked at the White House." The difference between the EOB and the West Wing was far greater than the forty or so yards that separated them.

Brzezinski couldn't watch everything, and Thurlow's White House office gave him access to every significant discussion of policy options. And unlike Brzezinski, Thurlow was a relative unknown to the Washington media, which Thurlow considered a blessing, because without a pack of reporters on his tracks, he enjoyed considerably greater freedom.

Thurlow read the executive summary of Squires's estimate. He swung his feet off his desk and brought his chair up from a dangerous back-tilt. He handed the booklet to Alan Squires.

"Barnes told me you were working on it."

"Well?" Squires asked impatiently.

Thurlow had a cherubic smile on his round, chubby face. "Hell, Alan, I like it. But," he pursed his lips, "I thought the South Korea section would be a little stronger."

Squires felt a burning in his stomach reaching up toward his throat. Thurlow had always been good with the needle. Sometimes he did it as a tactic—get the other fellow upset, off balance. Other times, Squires thought, Thurlow did it for the sheer hell of it. He breathed deeply.

"Rodgers, in the proliferation business you couldn't get much stronger unless you caught them with a bomb in their hands. Let's walk through a couple of points.

"First, there's the ROK accounting for nuclear materials in their industrial power and research programs. In those programs weapons-grade uranium and plutonium get generated. All of it is supposed to be certified and close tabs kept of it. We show," Squires pointed to the estimate, "that there's a lot missing. Too much for MUFNOL."

"Explain."

"Explain what? The losses?"

"No. The acronym—'muff nole.'"

"Material unaccounted for, normal operating loss. It's a term the International Atomic Energy Agency uses. Even with the best accounting, there's always some loss of radioactive material. But the shortfall the IAEA reports for South Korea far exceeds that."

"So they're losing the stuff."

"That's one point we make, Rodgers. Then you look at the documentation of shipments—the kind of electronics needed for the fuzing mechanism. The same components were sent from Germany to Seoul and Pretoria. All shipments were arranged by the same South Korean trading company—an outfit that normally handles only heavy industrial sales, farm implements, heavy tooling, things like that."

Thurlow was attentive, missing nothing. He absent-mindedly twisted a college class ring on his right hand.

"And we have the Blue House memo on theoretical work the ROK's are doing. A detailed report on machining high-explosive spheres—the kind you'd need to compress the radioactive stuff into a critical mass."

"Alan, we've got to have a good case. They stopped the troop business. We can argue that it's still a repressive dictatorship and that we shouldn't underwrite their attempts to build nuclear weapons. But if we're going to cut off foreign aid to Seoul, we've got to be convincing."

"Goddamnit, Rodgers, it's there—there in that NIE. You guys over here ought to be able to make a damn good case that the ROK's are on the verge of building something."

"How big?"

"That's speculative. No fusion stuff; probably low-yield tactical weapons, anywhere from one to twenty kilotons."

"What're you doing with this?" Thurlow held up the estimate. Seeing the puzzled look on Squires's face, Thurlow smiled and leaned forward conspiratorially, hunching over forward, elbows on knees, one hand in the fist of the other. "The Hill, Alan, the Hill. We'll get some of the Hill staff to ask you to come up and brief their bosses. You do it behind enough closed doors and it'll get around." Thurlow looked at his watch, signaling the end of the appointment. "I'll walk you out."

On the way to the Executive Avenue entrance, Thurlow stopped in the hallway. "Oh. Something else. Franks was by here the other day. Stuck his head in the office for a minute. Said DIA had told him that they thought Moscow was still up to something in North Korea—bringing in nukes. He didn't think it was much; it had to do with Yuri Andropov and a place called Chelyabinsk. DIA was apparently basing it on some insider source of theirs. Franks thought the source might be on the Central Committee or the KGB."

Thurlow couldn't resist the temptation to taunt Squires, whose face was suddenly ashen. "You mean Franks didn't tell you, Alan? I thought you people at least spoke to each other."

Moscow

Yuri Andropov studied the file's contents, frequently referring back to documents at the front of the file, cross-checking them with the later entries. He had been reading for over an hour, oblivious of Vasili Kiktev, who wished he'd not taken the hard chair just opposite the KGB chief. If I'd known he'd be this long at it, Kiktev thought, I'd have at least sat over by the window in a softer chair.

Andropov lit another cigarette, picked up the telephone and called out for coffee to be brought in. He went back to the file, still ignoring Kiktev. The coffee arrived along with a light dinner for two. Kiktev poured coffee for Andropov, putting the cup and saucer in the pool of light of the desk lamp. Andropov took a sip from the cup, continued reading for a few moments, then took the cup up again, pushed back from the desk, and came around to sit by Kiktev.

Andropov had a trouble frown. "Are you certain? Absolutely certain? It's Korznikov?"

"Yes, Comrade Andropov. He is the only one to have access to all files. He had to sign personally for them because of their sensitivity. Others have looked at individual files, but he's the only one to have seen all of them."

"Who knows this—that it's Korznikov?" Andropov asked, motioning toward the thick folder on his desk.

Kiktev was tired and slumped in his chair. He had worked excusively on the Korznikov report for days, hampered by Andropov's injunction that only he, Kiktev, and Gregori Romanov track down just how Roswell Franks had learned of the visit to Chelyabinsk. "Me, Comrade Andropov. And Romanov, who helped me. And now you."

"Birch?"

"No. Birch knows only that CIA has put a spy in Moscow Center. According to our Washington *rezident*, he is apparently quite frightened. But he knows nothing for certain." Kiktev leaned forward across Andropov's desk and found Alan Squires's report, which had started the investigation.

"Porsynko was that long-winded scientist. . . ."

"Yes. In Chelyabinsk." At least, Kiktev thought, the damage assessment would be made easier since the spy would be in hand. The difficult ones were defections, when you never really could find out what had been given away and you had to assume that everything the defector had was handed over to the other side. Of course, Korznikov would be done away with when he was no longer of any use. Even his death might be milked in some beneficial way.

"And so there is no other way that Birch could know that the CIA agent was specifically Korznikov?"

Kiktev was puzzled by Andropov's probing on this point. "No. Birch told us as much as he knew. If he'd known it was Korznikov, he would have told us. It was in his interest to tell us everything he knew—to hold nothing back. He would have wanted to protect himself. Once he learned of a person such as Korznikov, he would have wanted him eliminated because Birch's own safety would be in jeopardy."

"And Korznikov? Does he know of Birch?"

Another question Kiktev had considered and investigated. "No. Korznikov has no access to those files. As broad as his powers are—or were—" he amended, "he could not get into that compartment. The identities of all our foreign agents are too closely held for that.

"Moreover, Comrade Andropov, had he known of Birch, he would have instantly told the Americans, because then it would be Korznikov's life that would be in danger. Which, of course, is what happened."

With a trace of irony, Andropov nodded toward Kiktev. "Thank you for the lesson, Vasili Petrovich. Your assurance that we know what happened is most welcome." The younger man blushed, and devoted his attention to making inconsequential notes on the pad in his lap.

Yuri Andropov moved back behind his desk, lit another cigarette, then leafed through the documents. "Comrade Korznikov and his wife are accorded very special privileges. They have a large apartment, they are able to shop at the Party stores. His daughter is married to an Aeroflot pilot and is pregnant with the first grandchild. He has been treated well. Why do you suppose, Vasili Petrovich, he has done this?"

Knowing Andropov's question to be rhetorical, Kiktev merely shrugged in response.

"There is no evidence that Comrade Korznikov is in it for money or sex," Andropov mused. "And it doesn't look like he would lead the kind of life that would give them an opportunity to blackmail him." Andropov looked at Kiktev. "What would you do were you in my place, Vasili Petrovich?"

Arlington Hall Station—Arlington, Virginia

Eleanor looked around the table. Susan Forbes and John Freeman had called from 312. There had been a hitch in computer processing several photographs, and they would be delayed. The meeting had begun in the cool of the early morning, and now the Washington summer was taking over. A heavy mugginess was settling in the room. They would soon be forced to close the windows and turn on the air-conditioning, which always played havoc with her sinuses. "I don't know that we're saying anything new about all this. Moe, you start the summary."

"Two points. There's the MISER coverage of the *spetznaz* operations. We haven't worked that through the analysts, but we ought to have something within a week. And then there's the 280th Commando Brigade. The Soviets are now in the process of bringing in an entirely new *spetznaz* team from the USSR. We'll have the names about the same time we give you a dump on the MISER take. What we can say now is that there's more activity in the *spetznaz* comms than we've seen since the Warsaw Pact moved into Prague."

Andrew Cabot looked at his notes of the latest Hotspur report. "Moscow reporting brings up three things. First, it backs up the *spetznaz* activity. The personnel in the new teams alerted for movement to Korea are trained in nuclear-weapons delivery. Second, there's evidence that Andropov himself has been spending time getting briefings by nuclear-weapons design specialists." Cabot nodded to Hirsch. "And through the efforts of NSA, we know that after the initial meeting between Andropov and Porsynko, a direct, secure communications link was set up between Chelyabinsk and KGB's Moscow Center.

"The third point doesn't seem to connect with the first two, although our source seems to think so. And that's the Service A—the KGB disinformation operation—Service A's requirement to link South Africa and South Korea together."

Jack Bronowski was the first to speak. "Sam Bartlett has reservations about the Service A involvement. I got the idea he thinks it might not be related—it might be a separate operation. He could be right. We could be overreacting to— "

Moe Hirsch interrupted. "Jack, I don't want to get too far out in front of this *spetznaz* business we're still working on, but the sheer volume of comms traffic and the patterns of it just don't fit anything we have on file. I'm certain there's something in there that can tell us something when we break it out."

Eleanor tore the used pages from the pad in front of her and picked up a fresh pencil. "Requirements," she announced, beginning a new list. "First, Moe, you will get your people to concentrate on the *spetznaz* activity and on getting a list of the names of those going to Korea." She looked up at Hirsch, who was taking notes and nodding.

"Andrew, Moscow Station should follow up if they can, but I doubt that we should expect a prompt response, given the normal delays in arranging a contact." Cabot nodded his agreement.

"But," Eleanor continued, "Sam Bartlett aside, we can't overlook the matter of Service A and South Africa."

Jeremiah Scruggs, who'd said little during the morning's discussion, raised his hand. "I'll work on that, Eleanor."

Eleanor made another note.

She turned to Bronowski, who sat at her right. "Jack, can we get some photography of the areas where Moe's people reported the *spetznaz* activity?"

Bronowski said nothing, but he nodded and wrote in a small green government notebook.

Jack Bronowski remained in Eleanor's office after the morning meeting. He pushed his chair away from the table, leaned back and crossed his legs. "You know, we can get the photography, but it's not going to be easy."

"Didn't Roswell Franks promise Sam—"

"Yeah, he promised. But there's still the matter of

getting priority time on the KH-11. That'll take a lot of negotiating. But we'll do it. We'll call in a few chits around town and get it done."

Eleanor cocked her head. "I suppose I shouldn't be surprised, Jack. In a way, what we're doing now will be harder than the troop withdrawal."

Bronowski raised his eyebrows.

"What we were doing before required only that we make a good case—present evidence about the numbers of tanks and army units. Things like that. Things that could be counted. But this—what we talked about this morning— this deals with Moscow. Even if everything falls into our laps, we'll never have a clear-cut case because we'll be talking about intentions, not capabilities. It's easy to believe the North Koreans are capable of nearly anything. It's a different matter when you get to the Soviets."

Sakata, Japan

Ken Watanabe, the NSA specialist who'd first found the Algernon frequency, had rotated to the States. His replacement, Air Force Master Sergeant Herbert Rawlings, had learned Japanese, Korean, and Cantonese at the Defense Language Institute in Monterey, California.

This morning, while having his cup of coffee, Rawlings saw the amber lights come on. He took a pad of paper with him to the console along with his coffee and cigarettes.

Three quarters of an hour later, Rawlings looked at two sheets of paper covered with his neat printing. Another *spetznaz* rotation in process. Jesus, he thought with some envy, those bastards didn't have to spend much time in Korea before they went back home again. But then, he reflected, look where they had to go home to.

Moscow

The car came earlier than usual. But that was as Yuri Andropov had asked. There were always interruptions at the office, no matter what the orders. Overnight, every night, matters accumulated that had to be decided by him alone. As soon as he got to Dzerzhinsky Square, the pressure would be on to begin making those decisions. And so he'd allowed time for a long roundabout drive to the office, time to think.

Had power rested only on the state of Brezhnev's health, Yuri Andropov thought, gaining control of leadership would not be so difficult. But in spite of his obvious deterioration, Leonid Brezhnev was formidable. At last Tuesday's meeting of the Defense Council, Ogarkov, accompanied by Tolubko, Commander in Chief of the Strategic Rocket Forces, had reported on the successful testing of the new inertial guidance systems for the SS-18, and how the Mod-4 SS-18 was now capable of eliminating the American land-based Minuteman missiles, formerly the invulnerable backbone of the American nuclear arsenal—a backbone that up to now had given Washington an ultimate threat with which to thwart Moscow's strategic aims.

With the advent of the Mod-4, the Americans could no longer threaten or bully. The missile silos in the American heartland could be wiped out in a single, devastating surprise attack. A bolt from the blue. And by now the Americans' efficient technical intelligence would have told the White House of the passing of an era. There would be no more humiliating retreats of Soviet forces as in the Cuban affair; the Americans had been disarmed by their knowledge of the Mod-4.

"We have, comrades, entered a period in which the correlation of forces greatly favors us," the old man had wheezed. "In addition to the achievements of our scientists and military experts, who have lifted us from any possibility of American retaliation, we have been blessed by Providence, which has given us American leaders who are steadfast only in their devotion to indecision." There were the obligatory laughs around the table. Brezhnev had been seized by a coughing fit, and an aide rushed to wipe the spittle from his chin and give him a sip of mineral water, holding the glass to the General Secretary's lips.

The Korea operation, if successful, would virtually

assure the dominance of Brezhnev and his hangers-on. Having demonstrated that they could neutralize the American nuclear threat, they could then show that they could dismember Washington's major alliance: after Korea—NATO. Already it was being talked about among Brezhnev's followers. But NATO—particularly the Germans—might be a different kettle of fish. It would be a dangerous roll of the dice. Should NATO withstand the Kremlin's machinations, the Americans and their friends could then outdistance the creaking Soviet military machine which, like its maker, was still dangerous, but on its last legs.

There were so few he could trust. Brezhnev had shrewdly put loyalists in critical positions throughout the armed forces and even in the KGB. And he had made certain that the GRU never fell under Andropov's control.

"Stop here, Sasha."

Taken unaware after driving in silence for nearly half an hour, the driver swerved to the side of the road. The escort vehicle in the rear, similarly caught off guard, screeched its brakes and barely avoided a rear-end collision. The lead Chaika proceeded on for several hundred meters before its driver realized he was alone. Yuri Andropov got out of the car and walked to a large stone obelisk. Sasha, a compact Israeli Uzi submachine gun slung under his jacket, hurried to Andropov's side. Occupants of the two Chaikas formed a rough perimeter, keeping the occasional curious pedestrian away.

"It is a monument," Andropov told Sasha. "A monument to Moscow, the 'Hero City.'" Andropov pointed westward. "They used to call that the Mozhayskoye Highway. We marched down that highway in 1941 to fight the Germans." He stood staring down the road. "We marched to save Mother Russia. And now they've changed the name of the road. They have wiped it from existence."

"And so, Comrade General Korznikov, how does your work proceed in the Special Investigations Department?" In spite of the bright mid-morning sun outside, the heavy velvet drapes were tightly shut, casting the office in darkness. Yuri Andropov sat behind his desk, his chair pushed back so that only his hands, folded on the green blotter, were visible in the pool of light from the desk lamp.

Standing before the desk, Petr Korznikov tried in vain to read Andropov's face. He knows, Korznikov thought. Even major generals of the KGB were not casually asked to drop by the chairman's office for polite conversations. He forced himself to breathe deeply and slowly, but he couldn't control the tremblors in his chest or the growing fear.

"Sit, Comrade General. Please sit. You and I have much to talk about this morning. I find it commendable when senior officers set the example for hard work and perseverance. I'm particularly heartened by your industry in investigating my trip to Chelyabinsk and our *spetznaz* assignments to North Korea."

Arlington Hall Station—Arlington, Virginia

Moe Hirsch put his notes and slides on the podium, stepped to the window to close the curtains, then adjusted the projector. To his right were Eleanor Trowbridge, Jack Bronowski, and Jeremiah Scruggs. Opposite them were John Freeman, Susan Forbes, Andrew Cabot, and Peter Smith.

"My portion of this briefing will be classified Top Secret Penta," Hirsch solemnly announced, then switched on the projector. "This map shows the area of a recent *spetznaz* exercise." He circled the pointer around the screen. "It is the hill region of the Kazakh Soviet Socialist Republic. Familiar landmarks are the Aral Sea—here," Hirsch wiggled the pointer, "and Lake Balkash—here. Somewhat to the south, between the Aral Sea and Lake Balkash, is the small city of Arys'. The 23rd Spetznaz Regiment is garrisoned seven miles northeast of Arys'.

"Two days ago the regiment mounted an unusual exercise, one that didn't fit in with our history of the unit. A team of seven people took off from the airfield at 2045 hours local time and flew at an altitude of not more than seven hundred feet to a location some thirty miles northwest of Saryshagan. Their aircraft descended to an altitude of approximately 450 feet and the team parachuted, with the last man leaving the airplane at 2318 hours local." Hirsch turned from the map. "General Bronowski?"

"I didn't want to interrupt, Moe, but do you know what these guys had for breakfast?"

Moe Hirsch didn't respond to Bronowski's joke. "If they talked about it on the radio, General, we do." He frowned and drew himself up with an air of ruffled dignity that can be carried off to great effect by some big men.

"A second aircraft departed the Arys' vicinity at 2240 hours local. While its flight path was somewhat different, the flight profile was similar. This second aircraft dropped a single parachutist near Saryshagan at 0214 local. Apparently, the earlier mission was flown to infiltrate a reception party to set up the DZ for this sortie. Immediately thereafter, we got an initial entry report." Seeing Scruggs's puzzlement, Hirsch explained, "It's standard procedure for the *spetznaz*. A message back to home base to tell headquarters you've successfully penetrated hostile territory and you're on your way to run the rest of the mission.

"Just before dawn, the team moved four miles to the southwest. They broadcast one last message, then terminated the exercise."

Eleanor's glasses reflected the slide on the screen. "Tell us about this last message, Moe."

"They probably used a one-time code pad. We couldn't decipher it. But there wasn't any need to. It was a standard format—'nuclear detonation pending.' They use them to give headquarters one last chance to call off an operation before the team leaves a demolition device and gets the hell out of the area."

Moe Hirsch snapped off the projector. "That's it for the exercise." He reached down to the briefcase on the floor at his feet and pulled out a loose-leaf notebook. "But there's something you'll find of interest about the *spetznaz* personnel changes in North Korea." He turned several pages until he found one that caused him to purse his lips and nod. He ran a finger down the page then looked up. "The overall strengths of the *spetznaz* units haven't changed much. Oh, there're the usual fluctuations due to transfers, sickness, all that. But nothing significant. What we do find is that the composition of the *spetznaz* teams in North Korea is changing to include more ethnic Koreans of Soviet citizenship." Seeing there were no more questions, Moe Hirsch finished gathering his notes, carefully put the pointer against the podium, and moved back to his chair.

Peter Smith waved a hand. "Just a minute, Moe. I'm not sure I understand the thing about the ethnic Koreans in the *spetznaz*."

Hirsch stopped midway to his chair. "There are a significant number of Koreans who've lived for generations in Russia. They're Soviet citizens, and a number have been assigned to the *spetznaz* units with contingency missions in Asia."

Eleanor looked across the table. "Susan?"

As the younger woman got up and moved toward the projector, Eleanor noticed that she rested her hand briefly on John Freeman's shoulder. Eleanor's eyes misted, then she reproved herself for her sentimentality.

"Peter and I have been looking at the photography based on the tip-offs provided by Moe and his people." The first of the black and white satellite photographs flashed on the screen. "This is the *spetznaz* airfield near Arys'. It was taken three days before the exercise."

Andrew Cabot interrupted. "How did you know—"

"We didn't. It was dumb luck. We had gotten satellite coverage of six *spetznaz* facilities in European Russia, and this happened to be one of them." She turned back to the slide. "Hangar facilities are pretty much lacking, so the aircraft are parked along this ramp in the lower right of the picture. Note the last four." On the parking ramp, parallel to the single runway, were a handful of AN-2 biplanes, which were dwarfed by a nearby IL-76. At some distance from these were a pair of AN-12's, and beside these, four smaller airplanes."

"C-47's," injected Peter Smith.

"It's not surprising, since we gave a hundred or so to the Soviet government during World War Two," Susan Forbes added. "They've apparently kept some for special operations—just as we have some of their stuff at our own air bases.

"We were able to do some computer enhancements of this photograph and come up with the tail numbers of the last two C-47's." The next slide was of the rudder assemblies of the C-47's. An enlargement of a satellite photo had been broken down into discrete bits and reassembled by a high-speed computer in the Navy Yard. Each airplane's identifying tail number was clearly visible.

"We passed the tail numbers to Moe." She gestured toward the big man now seated at the far end of the table. "And a review of the tapes of the radio intercepts show that these two planes were used in the nuclear exercise."

"Before I move on to the next slide, take another look at the other two C-47's. The paint jobs are of interest. They've duplicated the camouflage scheme that's used by the South Korean Air Force.

"Again, using clues from the NSA intercepts, we did a photo search of the exercise area." Another slide came on the screen. "This is our nominee for the target of the *spetznaz* exercise." The flat airfield near Arys' was replaced by a photograph of the craggy hills northwest of Lake Balkash. The only man-made objects were two square buildings that the KH-11 had photographed at a slight angle.

"The analysts say this is a mock-up of a headquarters complex. The buildings are constructed of heavily reinforced concrete and surrounded by a double fence and mine field. From the size of the electric transformer field in this revetted area, they have a power capacity far in excess of anything they could put in those two buildings. So it's a safe bet that there's a lot more underground. While the—"

"How do we know it's a mock-up?" asked Jeremiah Scruggs.

"Among other things, the road leading in isn't used as much as a road to a place like that should be," Susan explained. Pointing to the areas between the two buildings, she said, "and there aren't any vehicles here at all, nor do we see any signs of habitation. The soccer field, for instance, doesn't appear to have been played on, and there are no nets in the goals at either end. And, thanks again to Moe, we know there's never been any communications activity in this area."

Eleanor turned and looked down the table to Jeremiah Scruggs. "Jeremiah, your turn on the stand."

"Normally," Jeremiah Scruggs began, "we have to sift through mountains of Soviet open source publications to identify major propaganda themes. In this case we were asked to look specifically to Soviet media to sort out what the Kremlin's been saying about South Africa." While Jeremiah Scruggs had not been told of the Hotspur report, he knew that his search had been prompted by more than idle curiosity from the seventh floor at Langley.

"We've taken the weekly 'International Review' column from *Pravda* as well as a large number of articles from *New Times*—also a weekly—and subjected them to a computerized form of content analysis. We then—" Scruggs gestured down the table. "Question?" The presentation wouldn't be easy. They never were. Most intelligence officers looked on Scruggs's Foreign Broadcast Information Service as a poor second cousin. Certainly, FBIS wasn't in the front ranks of intelligence. No nation would reveal anything of value in its government-controlled propaganda, the arguments ran, particularly the Soviet Union. And so FBIS was allowed to sit at the table with a condescension which, though slight, was nonetheless very real.

"Only two sources, Jeremiah?" asked John Freeman.

"Actually, one would be enough. You've got to remember you're not dealing with a nation that has independent journalists. They all work for the Kremlin. Every word in a *Pravda* story, where they place that story in the paper, what day they run it, and how long they cover it—they're all matters that're decided by the political leadership. *New Times* makes no pretense at being a 'government' publication. It's strictly party. It's published by the International Department of the CPSU. While it may be turgid reading, it *is* the party line, and it's what the party wants the outside world to see."

Taking the lead Freeman provided, Scruggs continued. "So our job is to look at what the party wants the outside world to believe about South Africa, to look also at the treatment of these themes over time—something we call longitudinal analysis. Now, our first chart."

Freeman bent forward, retrieved the pointer Hirsch had used, and handed it over to Scruggs.

"This shows the attention the Soviets have paid to the overall subject of South Africa. Our programmers had the computers do a count of column inches devoted to South Africa and express that as a percentage of total column inches devoted to all foreign-policy issues. Those percentages are plotted against time." Scruggs could tell from the angle of the heads around the table that he'd captured their attention.

"There are blips, of course. Here, for instance," he pointed to 1966. A sharp upward spike was clearly apparent. "B. J. Vorster was named Prime Minister. And here, in 1968, Moscow mounted a short campaign linking the assassination of Martin Luther King to American support of Pretoria and apartheid. Obviously they said nothing about their activities in Czechoslovakia in this same period.

"Aside from these, we see a relatively flat level of activity until recently. But here, just after Saigon fell, the upward trend in South African articles began. Now, the total still isn't much, especially when measured against all other issues the Soviets address, but comparatively speaking, the coverage of South Africa within the past year equals the coverage for the previous ten years combined." He turned the projector off and faced his audience. "Our methodology is, of course, subject to endless debate, and I'd be the last to say there aren't good arguments against trying to read too much from an exercise such as this. But even in the grossest of quantitative terms, this magnitude of increase is meaningful."

He raised his voice to underscore his conclusion. "Somewhere in the Kremlin, for some reason, a decision's been made that it's important to shape opinions about South Africa."

Scruggs waited a second or two. He was well-known as one of the Agency's better briefers. What wasn't known was that he'd worked at it—even to the extent of practicing before a television recorder in one of Langley's video studios. A moment before the first sign of impatience might be manifested in a cough or restless shuffling of feet, he turned the projector back on, showing the second chart.

"We see here that the increase in Moscow's coverage of South Africa has been caused by the introduction of three themes. The baseline topic—one that's been running for years—has dealt with various aspects of apartheid. Moscow has been persistent in telling the emerging nations of Africa that the West is no friend of the black.

"There are two new themes. The first is that South Africa is a rogue nation involved in a clandestine nuclear-weapons program. The kickoff in this campaign was a story in *New Times*, which ran a fabricated story by a Libyan journalist who's been on the KGB payroll for years. The Libyan reported that a secret meeting between South Africa, Israel, and Portugal was held in 1969 in Bloemfontein, in the Orange Free State. At this meeting an agreement was reached on nuclear-weapons-development cooperation."

Scruggs took a sip of water. "From there on, various Marxist and left-wing media around the world have repeatedly used the theme. The Bloemfontein meeting has become a nuclear version of the Protocols of the Elders of Zion, itself an earlier example, from czarist times, of the Russian proclivity toward forgery and disinformation. As you might suspect, Moscow's taken advantage of every opportunity to hammer this nuclear theme home, mixing falsehoods with the truth. To no one's surprise, they made extensive use of our report last year that contended Israel was in the bomb business. They then linked that with Pretoria's decision that same year to expand production of enriched uranium.

"The other new theme is much more recent than the South African nuclear program, and that is a linkage between Pretoria and Seoul. From almost nothing eight months ago, we've seen a significant increase in articles such as trade and cultural agreements between South Africa and South Korea. Again, the sheer volume isn't much. But it's new, and it wouldn't be there unless some decisions had been made to make it happen."

He hesitated. "And, of course, the Brezhnev letter to President Carter about a pending South African nuclear test seems very suspicious when viewed against the context of the Soviet media effort. It simply seems to fit too well into their campaign to be a mere coincidence."

Again Scruggs turned off the projector. "That's what we have on the questions you asked, Eleanor."

Eleanor regarded the slender man for a moment over the top of her glasses. "And what do you have, Jeremiah, on the questions I didn't ask?"

Scruggs seemed startled, then laughed. "I do have another chart or two," he admitted.

"I thought you would."

"We also sampled Moscow's statements about South Korea." Another graph flashed on the screen. "We found that Moscow started a campaign about a South Korean secret nuclear-weapons production program about the same time they began the South African operation. There are also some statistically insignificant but interesting articles in which *New Times* castigates Seoul for small-arms exports to Pretoria—strictly racist—yellow man colluding with South Africa to oppress the black—that kind of thing. They usually follow up on that theme with something laudatory about how Pyongyang is helping the black revolutionaries."

Jeremiah Scruggs took his last slide from the folder. "A closing thought: Although FBIS doesn't ordinarily cover our own output, our people looked at American media as well as CIA reporting in such regular publications as the *National Intelligence Daily* and the President's Daily Brief."

The slide flashed on the screen. The line of the graph snaked upward toward the top right corner, paralleling the slope of the Soviet graph. "This shows how our own reports on South Korea and South Africa have increased."

Jack Bronowski's hoarse voice jarred the room. "Jeremiah, you mean we've fallen into following the Soviet lead on this nuclear business?"

"That's one way of putting it, Jack. That our output—our interest—has been sparked by the Soviet interest in the topic."

"There's another way, Jeremiah?" asked Bronowski.

"Certainly," Scruggs answered. "The KGB could be manipulating us."

There was the usual snarl of commuters on the Shirley Highway, but John and Susan had driven across the Memorial Bridge and easily found a parking place. They walked eastward, toward the Washington Monument.

Susan was the first to speak, softly but with reproach. "You wish I'd kept quiet."

They walked perhaps twenty or so feet. John looked thoughtfully down the green archway of giant trees. Then, to see that no one was within earshot, he glanced around, settling finally on Susan's profile. He saw a slight bead of perspiration on her forehead. "No. No, I don't. But the evidence was pretty clear."

"It was a rush to judgment," she countered. "Everyone jumped on the bandwagon: the *spetznaz* are going to kick off a war in Korea by infiltrating nuclear-weapons teams into the South to destroy key ROK headquarters and communications facilities." She paused, looking squarely at him, then asked, "Do you believe that?"

"What else is there to believe? All the pieces are there."

"But they just don't fit, John."

"I—all of us—thought they fit pretty well."

Susan tossed her head in exasperation. "Oh, shit, John, what you and the rest of them are saying is that the Kremlin's planning a war in Korea and will start it by furnishing nuclear weapons to be used against South Korea. Do you really think they're that foolish?"

"You're saying we ought to ignore what's in front of us because it's unthinkable," Freeman retorted. "It was also unthinkable that the Japanese fleet would sail halfway across the Pacific and mount a surprise attack on Pearl Harbor." He paused, watching a line of ducklings waddle along behind their mother on their way to the pool. "We get surprised because we think the other fellow's going to act rationally. Maybe there's a group of Soviet policy makers who've looked at this for years and to whom it makes imminently good sense."

"I never said we should ignore anything, John. I didn't say that at all. As a matter of fact, I don't think we've considered some things. . . ."

"Such as?"

"Such as the obvious campaign to link the ROK's and the South Africans. And why all the effort? Why do they want us to believe that Pretoria and Seoul are putting together nuclear weapons on the sly? And that exercise. The mock-up of the target . . . we couldn't find the real one."

He thought for a moment. "It's just a generic target—a representative-type headquarters complex that wasn't intended to be an exact replica."

Susan quickly shook her head in disagreement. "I don't think so, John. It just isn't the way they do things."

"They might be changing." He shrugged. "God knows, you and Peter Smith spent enough time searching for the place. Probably not a building in South Korea you guys didn't feed through the computer."

Susan, talking to herself, whispered something unintelligible, then turned and began walking quickly toward Constitution Avenue.

"Where're you going?" John asked.

She half waved, half threw a kiss. "To catch a cab. To the Navy Yard. You go on home. Feed Bandit. I'll be along later."

Washington, D.C.

Eleanor paid the cabbie, crossed Columbia Road against the light and walked down a side street. She passed an alley at mid-block. Then, abruptly stopping in the manner of one who's forgotten something at home, she turned and walked back, watching both sides of the street. Drawing near the alley, she slowed as a battered brown Chevrolet station wagon slowly nosed out into the street, blocking the sidewalk. She opened the front door and got in.

"The motor pool is falling on hard times. But at least the air-conditioning works." Andrew Cabot wheeled the big car out into the street, retracing the route Eleanor had taken. He motioned over his shoulder to the back seat. "It's back there. Try forty-two, sixteen, thirty-seven."

She spun the combination lock and opened the stiff canvas dispatch case. The message covered two sheets of thin but very tough, almost parchmentlike paper. Eleanor recognized the paper as a KGB specialty item that would quickly dissolve in the mouth or go up in a flash with the smallest spark. It was handwritten, the letters making up the five-character groups firm and bold. Only after carefully examining the original message did she turn to the decoded text. A string of unintelligible garble was in place: Its absence would have served as a warning that the rest of the message had been written under coercion. She studied the papers intently then put them away in the dispatch case.

The couple walked the rolling lawn of Mount Vernon, away from the crowds of tourists. "You're worried, Andrew."

Cabot gathered his thoughts, trying to shape them into some kind of coherence. "Something bothers me. The handwriting's his. All the duress codes are there. Everything's technically perfect."

"Yet?"

"There's the timing. It hasn't been that long since our last contact. . . ."

"But this wasn't exactly a routine—"

"No. Obviously not. But the structure of the thing's as troubling as the timing. First he drops a bombshell: He's found a mole at Langley. But then, in the second part, he shifts subjects and talks about this Service A connection

with the South Africans. Here he's found out about someone who could get him put into the furnace feet first, and
then he goes on to business as usual. No sense of urgency
comes through. . . ."

Eleanor Trowbridge looked at her friend as they
walked along the river to the dock where George Washington had shipped the produce of his farm. "He's a professional, Andrew. And he knows you're one too. Perhaps it's
just that he feels there's no need for him to go on about the
mole, about . . ."

"About Beriozka, you mean? Birch?"

Throughout Andrew Cabot's recital, Eleanor sat at her
desk, taking notes. Her questions were rare; Cabot outlined the relevant points in the clear, terse phrases of the
experienced field man. John Freeman listened carefully,
sitting very still in a wicker chair between Andrew and
Eleanor. They had been interrupted only once, toward the
end of the day, when the secretary knocked to ask if
Eleanor needed her further. She left, and closed the outer
door after setting the internal alarm and monitoring system.

Eleanor stood, put her hands on her hips and
stretched, arching her back. She walked to the wall switch,
and turned on the lights, sat down again and looked from
Freeman to Cabot. "Andrew? How do you see it?"

Cabot pinched his lower lip reflectively between
thumb and forefinger. The lamplight showed the flat dull-
ness of his artificial eye. He dropped his hand to the arm of
the chair and looked into his palm before answering.
"Obviously, I'll get counterintelligence working on Birch.
He didn't get in place overnight. Finding him could take
months. In the meantime we have to work on the premise
that he has access to everything that goes to Franks."

"What about our friend Squires?" asked Eleanor.

"He's at the top of the list."

Eleanor nodded, looked at her notes, then back to
Cabot. She adjusted her glasses as if to be able to see his
reaction more clearly. She took a breath and asked,
"Hotspur—might they have gotten to him?"

She asked the question with reluctance, even though it was the prudent thing to do. It was the first question you always asked about an agent, no matter if you'd been his control for years. You learned in basic tradecraft, whether you were CIA, MI-6, or KGB: always ask the question. Is your agent still a trusted observer, peering through the curtains for you? Or was he now the mouthpiece for the opposition? If so, for whom was your agent now speaking? And if the message was contrived, what effect did its originator have in mind?

To ask the question was one thing. But to then seek the answer was to open a door to endless conjecture, to enter a house of mirrors.

Cabot wearily passed his hand over his face, feeling the stubble of his beard. He got up and walked slowly to the coffee urn. Eleanor and John Freeman joined him. Instead of returning to Eleanor's desk and the chairs around it, they moved to the table.

Eleanor put her mug on the table then retrieved her notes from the desk. "If they've turned Hotspur, it raises a number of other questions. Why, for example, would they expose Birch? Getting him in place is the accomplishment of a lifetime. And there's Algernon's reporting—it corroborates much of the information we've been getting from Hotspur. Does that mean they've gotten on to Algernon, too? Or are they letting Hotspur pass on a little good information in order to deceive us about something else?"

"There's MISER, Eleanor," Cabot offered. "We got *spetznaz* Korea-replacement information from satellite monitoring independently of Hotspur and Algernon. And it says pretty much the same thing. Hotspur hasn't lied to us; not yet, anyway."

Eleanor tapped a pencil lightly on the tabletop. "And Jeremiah Scruggs's analysis supports Hotspur's earlier reporting about Service A and South Africa."

Freeman interrupted. "This's triple-think. If Moscow Center's controlling Hotspur, anything we ask him for tells them where we're blind." He raised his hands in supplication and frustration. "Who're we talking to and what do we want them to believe?"

The three were silent. Eleanor sat, elbows on the chair arms, staring into the space below the tabletop. Andrew

Cabot drank the last of his coffee and remembered glumly that he'd left his car to be serviced and that the garage was now closed.

Freeman broke the silence. "We don't know he's been turned. All we have is your suspicions, Andrew." He shrugged. "Of course, that's all we may ever have."

Eleanor took her coffee mug to the sink and rinsed it. Turning, she faced the two men who were still seated. "For now, it seems we have to work under the assumption that Birch exists and has the access Hotspur tells us he has. And we must also assume that Hotspur has been doubled."

Walking with John Freeman and Andrew Cabot toward the parking lot, Eleanor took Cabot's elbow. They had stopped on the walkway, and Eleanor looked at the two men.

"I don't mean to make this more complicated than it already is, but could it be that they turned Hotspur to make certain he tells us the truth?"

Arlington Hall Station—Arlington, Virginia

Eleanor Trowbridge's office was chilled by the overnight work of the air conditioners. The curtains were already drawn, and the secretary had set the long table with writing pads and pencils at each chair. Eleanor was at her desk, editing a memorandum to Sam Bartlett. Scruggs, Cabot, and Freeman were talking together at the end of the table most distant from the projection screen.

Susan Forbes looked up to acknowledge Jack Bronowski and Moe Hirsch as they entered, then dropped her head again to her notes. I've got to settle down, she thought. It's all there—the evidence. We've gone over it endlessly. There're no other conclusions. All those years of analysis. Dredging up little bits and pieces to put together to make a somewhat larger piece that you hand over to someone else to add to *their* bits and pieces. Contributions so small that your part of the whole picture's lost. Even when you look at it, you can't find the brush stroke you added, the brush stroke that took months of painstaking work, round after round of mind-warping meetings and conferences, and bitter arguing and negotiation with other analysts about the meaning of some tiny fragment of information from a source of unknown reliability.

She'd known analysts—damn good ones—who'd spent their lives dealing with shreds and snippets; analysts who'd worked decades in cramped cubicles, never once having the satisfaction of coming up with an irrefutable finding that brought order and understanding to the puzzling and sometimes contradictory work of others. Analysts had grown old fruitlessly looking for the keystone that, once dropped in place, made everyone say, "Ah, yes, of course, that's the way it is. That's the way it must be."

She felt her heart racing. What's happening to me? Relax. Slow down. God, I shouldn't have had that coffee.

Eleanor's crisp voice cut through Susan Forbes's thoughts. ". . . asked you here this morning for a briefing by Susan Forbes. She came to me with this yesterday, and I thought we should meet as soon as possible." Eleanor motioned to Susan with her right arm outstretched, then sat down at the head of the table.

Susan took her place at the podium, looking down the length of the table toward Eleanor. They'd spent nearly three hours together yesterday, after Susan had come over from Peter Smith's office. "When we last met here, most of us came to the conclusion that we had evidence pointing toward using nuclear demolitions to destroy critical South Korean command and control facilities at the outset of an attack by the North." Moe Hirsch gave a slight nod of agreement. The others sat impassive but attentive.

Susan forced herself to pause. She saw John give a wink and smile. "We've overlooked a less obvious scenario, one that is more complex, one that could be even more dangerous and difficult to contend with."

Eleanor gave her an approving glance. "Now that you have our attention, Susan, how about the rest of it?"

"The key is the *spetznaz* training exercise near Sary-shagan. It was a rehearsal in which a C-47 with South Korean markings dropped a parachutist who was carrying a small nuclear weapon. The target for the infiltration team was this facility." The projector hummed on, showing the now-familiar satellite photograph of the buildings in the headquarters complex. "Over the years, the Soviets have always built detailed mock-ups of targets for training use. We assumed that they'd make some kind of exception because we couldn't find a similar set of buildings in South Korea."

She gave a quick glance to John, then adjusted the projector, a second satellite photograph taking its place beside the first. "We did, however, find a match for the *spetznaz* target—but it's in North Korea. It's the headquarters of the Ninth Corps of the Peoples' Army of Korea, approximately sixteen miles north of the DMZ." The photographs, although taken under differing weather conditions and at slightly different angles, showed what were obviously the same buildings and surrounding areas, including the roads, steep granite hills, and double-security fencing.

In the silence, Susan watched as those around the table made their own judgments from the photographs on the screen.

"Okay, young lady, I'll bite. Why?" asked Bronowski.

"Let me try, Susan," offered Scruggs. Eyes fixed on the photographs, Scruggs leaned forward, putting his elbows on the table, a man hugely enjoying the unfolding of a surprising story and now happy to have a part in it. "The nukes go off. Then Kim comes on television and radio to denounce the warmongers in the South. A surprise attack with nuclear weapons. Given Hiroshima and Nagasaki, the shock in Asia would be tremendous. Certainly a cause for retaliation by North Korea. The tanks roll, and a few hours later Seoul falls. The end."

"It's all too complicated," Cabot objected. "If all they want is to fabricate an excuse to go to war, why should they go to all the trouble to do an infiltration with *spetznaz*? Why not just truck in the demolition device and cook if off?"

Hirsch spoke for the first time. "Because that wouldn't spook us. The Soviets know what we can do, that we would have a complete record of communications intercepts leading up to the incident. They want to use our own collection capabilities against us. It's a massive deception. They'd make certain our initial analysis would show that it *was* an ROK operation. They'd duplicate ROK comm procedures—"

"And those C-47's that're painted to mimic the ROK Air Force planes would add to the detail, along with ethnic Korean *spetznaz* members," added Bronowski. "I wouldn't put it past those bastards to have the North Korean gunners shoot down one of the C-47's just to have some phony ROK corpses and equipment to show."

Freeman interjected, "But what about the Americans? There's the second Infantry Division, our tac air—"

An excited Jeremiah Scruggs cut him off. "Kim will say the whole thing is a Blue House provocation, that Park Chung Hee, frightened that his bribing of American congressmen and suppression of human rights would lose Washington's support, ordered this to draw the Americans into a war alongside South Korea. Kim will say that the Americans are as much victims as the North, and he's given orders for his troops to bypass U.S. forces whenever possible."

"It tells us why Service A is so intent on the disinformation campaign about Seoul's secret nuclear weapons," offered Freeman.

Scruggs frowned. "It's a good story. But as good as it is, Moscow must know it wouldn't hold up long."

"It doesn't have to," Eleanor Trowbridge responded. "They aren't concerned with fooling the general public. Their target is the White House—it has been all along. They want to create confusion, uncertainty. To paralyze Carter and the decision-making machinery. They're out to gain time. If they can get the White House to grope around for, say, twelve hours or so, the North Koreans can take Seoul. Without Seoul, South Korea would collapse. It would all be over."

Chapter 9

Fort McNair—Washington, D.C.

Sam Bartlett suggested they talk over dinner at his home at Fort McNair on Greenleaf Point, a lush, parklike enclave that shelters the National War College from the squalor and noise of southwest Washington.

It was Sunday evening, just after six. The heat of the summer's day had retreated, and a light northeast breeze was clearing the afternoon haze. Bartlett, dressed in frayed khaki slacks and a light blue polo shirt, sat in a large oak rocker on his wide front porch with a gin and tonic. He finished the drink and got up from the chair to go to the back, where he'd fire up the grill and help his wife Jan set the table.

Jack Bronowski had offered to pick Eleanor up and drive her to Fort McNair. He arrived a few minutes early. Letting him in, Eleanor pointed to the kitchen and refrigerator, then went back upstairs to gather some notes and, as an afterthought, to put on lipstick and more carefully comb her hair.

Bronowski was standing in front of the bay window, a glass of red wine in one hand, engrossed in a book he'd taken from the bookcase nearby. He was oblivious of her, his broken face softened by the fading light. Surprised, he looked up, then nodded to the book in his hands. "Dickinson. A passage I last read in England. Thirty-five years ago." He shut the book and held it out to her. "My life closed twice before its close; it yet remains to see—"

Eleanor took the book. "If Immortality unveil a third event to me," she finished.

Sam had grilled the thick steaks to perfection, the potato salad was properly spicy, and the beer ached the throat with its coldness. Andrew Cabot and Sam arranged folding deck chairs on the terrace while Jack and Eleanor helped Jan Bartlett clear the table. The sunset was reaching its finale when Jan excused herself and Sam motioned to the chairs.

"Who's first?" he asked.

"I'll start," Eleanor volunteered. She quickly explained Susan Forbes's conclusion that the Soviets would supply Kim Il-Sung with a cause for war, and Jeremiah Scruggs's analysis that the Soviets wished to implicate South Africa in some way as a nuclear accomplice. Andrew Cabot then summarized his unease about Hotspur and the implications of a Soviet agent so placed as to have access to every issue brought to the CIA Director.

"I'd like to know," Bartlett began slowly, "where Andropov is in all this. We met a number of times while I was the attaché in Moscow. This was 1968, a year after he'd taken over at the Center. He knew, of course, that I'd gone off to the Army as a boy not yet out of high school, and he mentioned that he'd left home early too. Had read Mark Twain and worked as a sailor on a Volga River tug." Bartlett watched the lights of the automobiles as they slowly drove around Hains Point across the channel. "Wanted to be a riverboat captain, and ended up as chairman of the KGB."

"Some of us contend that Andropov's running to be General Secretary after Brezhnev, but that Brezhnev has others in mind," suggested Cabot.

Bartlett puffed again on his cigar. "I don't doubt it. I never got the impression that Andropov would stay forever at Dzerzhinsky Square." He brought himself back from the years in Moscow. "But the immediate question we have is the problem Ms. Forbes left on our doorstep.

"There're things we do know. We know, for instance, that the South Africans do have a weapons program. They haven't joined forces with Israel, that we know of, but that's irrelevant here."

"Sam," Eleanor interrupted, "it seems we have some basic elements that're somehow connected. First, there's North Korea, sitting armed to the teeth, apparently waiting for the Soviets to give them a nuclear excuse to attack the South. Second, we know that there's been work done at one of the Russian nuclear-design labs. And last, there's the Soviet disinformation effort to bring in Pretoria. Can we—" Eleanor stopped and corrected herself, and pointed to Sam Bartlett and Andrew Cabot. "Can you put out a call for any information that involves any activities in those three areas? We'd then—"

Cabot finished for her. "We'd cast a net. Deeper penetration of the South African nuclear program, and any Soviet interest in it as well." He turned to Bartlett. "Sam, DIA and NSA could put a watch on the Chelyabinsk design people. . . ."

"I suppose we could," Sam Bartlett agreed. "A lot of that stuff's going on, anyway. It's largely a matter of asking the right questions of the right people and sharing the take with you folks at Arlington Hall. We can activate some of our standby people in the port-watcher programs—see if there's any unusual movement of Russians abroad, that kind of thing. I don't know that we could keep it up indefinitely, though."

Jack Bronowski shifted in his chair. "I don't think we'll have to, Sam. If Susan is right, the North's planning on a massive tank assault down the Chorwon corridor before winter sets in but after the last of the clear-sky season in autumn—just in case American tactical air power does get a piece of the action."

"What kind of window does that give us, Jack?" asked Bartlett.

"I'd say they'd want to run that kind of operation between the last of October and the middle of December at the very latest. They'd want to have their players and the nukes in place before then, say, by the last of September. It'd give them a month to work out the last details."

Cabot got up and stretched. "And that'd give us less than three months to figure out how to stop them. Good night, Eleanor, Jack. Sam, my best to Jan, and thank you for the dinner and the good company."

S E C R E T/NILDIS/EXCLUDED FROM AUTOMATIC DOWNGRADING

CITE COS/BONN STATION
    3906 DTG110937ZAUG79
TO: DDCI HQTRS (EYES ONLY)

SUBJECT: SOUTH AFRICA NUCLEAR
            PROGRAM (S)

REF: HQTRS 43078 DTG092234ZAUG79
        DDCI SPECIAL QUERY

SOURCE: (S) SMSOSAS IS A KNOWLEDGE-
        ABLE   AND   LONGSTANDING
        SOURCE WHOSE PAST REPORTING
        HAS BEEN TIMELY AND RELIABLE.
        SMSOSAS IS IN A POSITION
        WHEREIN HE CAN BE EXPECTED
        TO HAVE ACCESS TO INFORMA-
        TION IN THIS REPORT.

1. (S) SOUTH AFRICAN BUREAU OF STATE SECURITY (BOSS) HAS TAKEN AS TOP PRI-ORITY SEARCH FOR WHEREABOUTS OF JAN (NMN) ARKLUUNDS WHO HAS BEEN MISSING SINCE 23 FEBRUARY 79. CEN-TRAL REFERENCE BIO FILES SHOW ARK-LUUNDS WAS EXECUTIVE ON SOUTH AFRICAN NUCLEAR POWER COMMISSION (SANPC) AND WAS A SPECIALIST IN REAC-TOR DESIGN. BOSS SOURCES, HOWEVER, SAY THAT SANPC POSITION WAS A COVER

FOR SUBJECT'S ACTIVITIES IN THE AGENCY FOR EMERGENCY PLANNING (AEP), PRETORIA'S CLANDESTINE NUCLEAR WEAPONS PROJECT.

2. (S) BOSS ALSO CONCERNED WITH SENSITIVE INVENTORY RECORDS LATER DETERMINED TO HAVE BEEN REMOVED FROM CLASSIFIED CENTRAL REGISTRY O/A 23 FEBRUARY.

3. (S) BOSS WORKING ON ASSUMPTION THAT ARKLUUNDS'S DISAPPEARANCE WAS VOLUNTARY AND CONNECTED WITH MISSING FILES. BOSS HAS NO RPT NO INFORMATION REGARDING SUBJECT'S WHEREABOUTS.

4. (S) DIGITAL PHOTO INFO FOLLOWS: ZSC000100111001TTT0011111100101010000. . . .

RYERSON

Alan Squires made the reservation from a telephone booth in the lobby of a K Street office building, then left the building through a side exit onto Eighteenth Street. He crossed the street and hailed a cab that dropped him near an aging commercial hotel on the fringe of Washington's inner city. The withered desk clerk scarcely looked at the registration card after Squires paid cash in advance for the room.

The small lobby was a study in shabbiness. The elevator was in a small alcove. Rounding the corner, Squires could see the elevator door beginning to close. He thrust his hand into the opening and the door reopened. He was into the elevator before he realized he would not be alone.

The woman was pretty. A blonde of medium height, her face was defined by high cheekbones and a generous mouth. The man was older. Much taller than the woman, he was well-dressed and carried himself with an assurance born of years of others scrambling, even competing, to do his bidding. He was solid, no trace of a belly, and his thinning silver hair was neatly combed back with no attempt to scatter it over his baldness. They were standing close together in the corner of the elevator car, and both had been looking at each other and smiling when Squires burst in.

All three were startled. The couple moved deeper into their corner, the woman standing between Squires and her companion. Squires moved into the opposite corner and rested his back against the walls of the car. The elevator door, having been pushed back by Squires, was now taking its time to close again. Aware the couple was staring at him, Squires looked down at his shoes. He imagined he could hear their breathing, and then wondered if they could hear him. The elevator door finally closed with a grinding noise of neglected bearings.

Through the corner of his eye he saw the woman shift her feet, pointing them more toward the other man. He chanced looking up. They were ignoring him, looking now at each other. They weren't dressed like tourists. Obviously worked somewhere in the city. Coming here for nooners.

She probably has pink nipples, Squires thought. He imagined her as she would be in a few minutes, making her partner suck those nipples, and later, her with her mouth full of him. Bitch. Bitches. They'd always ignored him. He'd had his first woman comparatively late in life; a blowsy slut in Vienna who'd suddenly come on to him while he and Chebrakin had been making the late-night rounds. He'd thought later that Chebrakin had put her up to it. Paid her for it. But he'd never had a woman who'd go to a place like this just to have him. His throat grew thick. He looked over her shoulder and saw that the man was staring at him, slitted eyes glittering, smiling in triumph. Squires felt the rage well up. Bastard. Son of a bitch. His kind always got what they wanted. It wasn't as if they fought Squires and had come out the winners. That would have been different. At least the fighting itself would acknowledge that he existed, that he was someone. No. They just walked in and took. Took. As if Squires weren't there at all. A man who never was.

Alan Squires opened the door. Without speaking, Yakov Lishinsky brushed by him, strode into the center of the small room and surveyed his surroundings. The tall Russian poked his head into the bathroom, then clucked in disapproval at a locked door that apparently connected Squires's room to an adjacent one. From his attaché case Lishinsky took a small black box about the size of a cigarette packet, which he fastened to the window with a suction cup. He connected a power cord from a nearby wall outlet to the box, then turned a switch. The box made it impossible for anyone in a nearby building with a laser monitor to pick up vibrations caused by conversations inside the room. From the attaché case the KGB officer then took two other devices. One he used to search for hidden microphones, the other he would leave turned on for the duration of their meeting to detect any electronic activity inside the room from bugs he'd missed. When he was satisfied everything was working, he nodded to Squires, then crossed the room to the only chair and sat down, motioning Squires to sit on the corner of the bed.

"You used the emergency procedure." Lishinsky made it an accusation. He sat in the overstuffed chair, his arms on the rest, hands dangling off the ends, his chin slightly down into his chest.

Squires, flustered, part of his thoughts still taken up with the couple on the elevator, gasped. "Yes. Emergency. Fat bastard Thurlow—"

Lishinsky frowned. "We haven't all day, what is it? What's the emergency?"

Alan Squires gave a stumbling recital, a repetition of his written report, of the meeting with Rodgers Thurlow and of Thurlow's remark about American intelligence having penetrated the KGB. He rambled, repeating several points, but Lishinsky said nothing. The American finally wound down and looked imploringly at Lishinsky.

The Russian tilted his head to the side and slightly

arched his eyebrows. "So? You gave us a written account of this days ago."

"So?" Squires's voice cracked in sudden rage. "So? Goddamnit, is that all you can say? Jesus Christ, if they've got somebody that high up in the KGB, then they could find out about me. I want to know if you've found him. If he has access to the files . . ."

At once Lishinsky was conciliatory, soothing. "Alan. Calm yourself. I assure you, Alan, you are safe. You are valuable to us, Alan. We recognize your courage. I cannot go into details, but know, Alan, that your files are kept in such a way so that you are in no danger."

Alan Squires sat, barely listening to the Russian. They'd told him they'd take him in any time. Chebrakin had talked about the commission they held for him, a commission as a colonel in the KGB. There would be a small but comfortable apartment in Moscow, or, if he preferred, Leningrad. Substantive work in foreign-policy analysis, perhaps even with Arbatov at the USA and Canada Institute.

When Chebrakin described it, it had all seemed so worthwhile, so real. After all, Chebrakin had sought him out, listened to him, had encouraged him. Chebrakin had treated him as someone whose views were worthy of consideration. This was long before Squires had entered CIA. Long before he'd become KGB property—one of Yakov Lishinsky's assets.

"What?" asked a startled Alan Squires.

"The estimate. I asked you about its progress," repeated an impatient Lishinsky.

"Oh. Franks has signed off on it, but there's little interest in it," Squires responded listlessly.

Lishinsky persisted. "And Congress?"

"Much the same." Squires fidgeted. Sitting straight on the bed without support for his back, his feet did not touch the floor. The posture tired him, robbed him of any initiative, made him a supplicant to the Russian, who sat comfortably in the chair, fully in command. Gathering himself, Squires asked, "Why do you care so much about Korea? Why's it so goddamn important to you?"

For the first time in their meeting, Lishinsky told the truth. "I don't know, Alan. I just don't know."

Believing that he'd reassured Squires of his safety, Lishinsky encouraged the American to press forward with the estimate on South Korean nuclear production and intimated that he, Lishinsky, would see that requests for briefings would come to Alan from influential offices on Capitol Hill. With practiced efficiency, Yakov Lishinsky gathered in his electronic sentinels and left, having shaken Squires's hand and clasped him solidly on the shoulder.

Squires forced himself to sit for perhaps ten minutes after Lishinsky left. He got up, his back stiff from the bed. A wave of fatigue and sadness overwhelmed him. He thought of Chebrakin and the way out. He stood for a moment, his eyes closed. He felt trapped. It was awful here in the States. But it would be no better in Moscow or Leningrad. Taking a deep breath, he walked out into the corridor, quietly pulling the room door shut behind him. He stopped at the elevator and stood staring at the closed doors. He saw an exit sign down the corridor and turned away from the elevator. He would use the stairs instead.

Maputo, Mozambique

Arkady Porsynko had sweat through his cheap white shirt. His collar was greasy around his throat, the armpits and back clammy and sour, while the tail hung outside his trousers in the back. A large, overweight man, Porsynko never slept well on airplanes, and the trip to Maputo was one he had come to dread. He had tried desperately to shift into a comfortable position, but no matter how he twisted and turned on the seventeen-hour flight, the best he could manage was to doze fitfully for perhaps four or five minutes before waking with a cramped muscle in his back or legs. He had missed the twice-weekly Aeroflot flight from Moscow, and so had to make connections in Sofia with LAM, the Mozambique state airline. The food and service were better than Aeroflot, but it was unsettling to look up into the black faces of the flight attendants. Arkady Porsynko understood the importance of his mission, but he wished it had taken him instead to a more civilized place.

As it was, Porsynko grumbled and waved his passport impatiently under the nose of the customs guard, who, not convinced that the Russians were an improvement over the Portuguese, took his time applying the entry stamp to the visa. Sufficient time to allow Corporal Paulo Gwambe to take three high-quality photographs of the fat Russian through the one-way glass set in the wall.

Ironically, the photography operation at the airport was a wrinkle taught the Serviço Nacional de Segurança Popular—the secret police of Mozambique—by its new fraternal advisors from Moscow. Corporal Gwambe was of mixed blood, a *mestiço*, and because of this he knew promotions would be rare in SNASP. And so he had no qualms about parlaying his job into extra spending money by sending additional prints into South Africa with his cousin, who was one of thousands of itinerant laborers who left the workers' paradise of Mozambique to feed his family by working in the South African gold fields. The cousin was paid by a labor-gang recruiter in Lyndenburg, who in turn delivered the photos and a thumb-print receipt to an earnest young American in Germiston—the American being the Assistant Air Force Attaché with the U.S. Embassy in Pretoria.

Variations of the chain existed around the world, in what the Defense Intelligence Agency called Travel Watch program. Travel Watch bulletins carrying the latest surveillance requirements periodically went out from the Pentagon's National Military Intelligence Center to selected attachés in American embassies around the world.

That the Pentagon wasn't flooded with photographs of itinerant ninth-level trade secretaries was due to a small machine resembling a photocopier. Facescan, using the same technology as Eagle Eye, swallowed each photograph and broke the picture into microscopic pixels, or dots. A laser beam then swept the gathered pixels, assigning a binary number code to each nearly invisible dot, depending on whether that particular dot was black, white, or any of thirty-two shades of gray. The result was processed and stored by an IBM mainframe. This permitted analysts to retrieve the picture or, as was more often the case, run a quantitative comparison of the incoming photo code against the millions of other photo codes already in the memory banks.

Sergeant Doris Flannery was in charge of the grave-yard shift in the communications center of the Defense Intelligence Agency, a vaulted and heavily guarded complex cut into the foothills of the Blue Ridge Mountains near Front Royal, Virginia. Into the center came all messages for DIA from its activities aboard, including the Facescan cables for the Travel Watch operation. Sergeant Flannery stubbed out her cigarette. She was needed in the cable room to see to the distribution of a priority message. She got up from the high-backed command chair and looked directly at the heavy leather binder that contained the Travel Watch routing requests. Only briefly did she consider taking the binder with her.

In the cable room Doris scanned the flimsy sheet of telex paper—a TWX from the embassy in Pretoria. The long alphanumeric code at the top of the cable told her that the message was in response to a DIA Immediate Priority Request. The leather binder two floors above contained the identity of the requesting section of DIA. She thought about the trek down the hall, the wait for the elevator to get the book, and then a return trip. No need—she remembered the originator designations. Without hesitating, she dashed the five-character message-routing reference across the top. The cable would be delivered to the classified registry of the Pacific Studies Group by break of day. Instead of going back to her desk and checking the routing code as she'd intended, she dropped by the coffee shop to buy another pack of cigarettes.

At eight that same morning the registry clerk in the DIA office specializing in petroleum estimates looked at the Travel Watch cable Doris Flannery had mistakenly sent him, snorted, and fed it into the shredder, thinking that certainly the people who *really* needed the cable had gotten their copy.

PRIORITY PRIORITY PRIORITY PRIORITY
PRIORITY PRIORITY PRIORITY

T O P   S E C R E T/NILDIS/EXCLUDED
FROM AUTOMATIC DOWNGRADING

CITE COS/BONN STATION
4002 DTG191957ZAUG79
TO: DDCI HQTRS (EYES ONLY)

SUBJECT: SOUTH AFRICA NUCLEAR
PROGRAM (S)

REF: HQTRS 43078 DTG092234ZAUG79
(DDCI SPECIAL QUERY)
BONN 3906 DTG110937ZAUG79
(DDCI EYES ONLY)
HQTRS 62559 DTG132253ZAUG79
(DDCI SPECIAL QUERY)

SOURCE: (S) SMSOSAS IS A KNOWLEDGE-
ABLE AND LONGSTANDING
SOURCE WHOSE PAST REPORTING
HAS BEEN TIMELY AND RELIABLE.
SMSOSAS IS IN A POSITION
WHEREIN HE CAN BE EXPECTED
TO HAVE ACCESS TO INFORMA-
TION IN THIS REPORT.

1. (S) REPORT RECEIVED THIS DATE OF
BUREAU OF STATE SECURITY (BOSS) LO-
CATION OF REMAINS OF JAN (NMN) ARK-
LUUNDS. REF INDV FOUND BY LOCAL
CONSTABULARY IN WATER-FILLED
DRAINAGE CANAL IN MOAMBA, MOZAM-
BIQUE O/A 18AUG79. CAUSE OF DEATH
UNKNOWN DUE TO CONDITION OF RE-
MAINS. REF INDV'S MEDICAL RECORDS
REFLECT NO RPT NO PROBLEMS IN GEN-
ERAL HEALTH.

2. (TS) BOSS BELIEVES MISSING STOCK
RECORDS REPRESENT ATTEMPT BY ARK-

LUUNDS TO COVER DIVERSION OF
WEAPONS-GRADE MATERIALS. FOUR MA-
CHINED SHELLS OF URANIUM 238 ARE
UNACCOUNTED FOR IN RECENT INVEN-
TORY AS WELL AS APPROXIMATELY
FORTY-SIX RPT FORTY-SIX KILOGRAMS OF
URANIUM 235.

CHIEF OF STATION COMMENT:
3. (TS) ARKLUUNDS CASE APPEARS TO
HAVE BEEN ELEVATED TO HIGHEST LEV-
ELS SAF GOVERNMENT. BOSS CI IS WORK-
ING ON LEADS INDICATING THAT
ARKLUUNDS MAY HAVE BEEN LONG
TERM AGENT OF USSR. OUR TRADI-
TIONAL SOURCES ARE DRYING UP,
CLAIMING EITHER THEY HAVE LITTLE
ACCESS TO DISCUSSIONS OR THAT RISK
OF COMMUNICATING WITH US HAS
GREATLY INCREASED. PRETORIA IS VERY
DEEPLY WORRIED ABOUT THIS ONE,
MORE SO THAN I HAVE SEEN IN PAST FIVE
YEARS.

RYERSON

T O P S E C R E T/NILDIS/EXCLUDED
FROM AUTOMATIC DOWNGRADING

Moscow

The inmates of Lubyanka Prison—those who were in
Category II and allowed to leave their cells—had worked all
night to be ready for Yuri Andropov's early morning visit.
The guard-force boots glistened, and the gray stone and
concrete corridors were still damp from scrubbing.

The prisoner, shod in wooden clogs and dressed in a
soiled gray gown resembling a nightshirt, remained facing
the wall. Jutting from the wall was a concrete sleeping
platform on which his mattress—little more than a thin

pad—was doubled into an S roll. Folded into a small square on top of the pad was a frayed, dark green blanket. There was no toilet; a bucket was shoved in through the door twice daily, then removed five minutes later.

The officer brought a chair from the corridor into the cell, put it down opposite the sleeping platform, then stood expectantly, looking at Yuri Andropov.

Andropov motioned to the corridor. "Bring the other chair. The guard can stand." Only momentarily taken aback, the officer quickly brought in the guard's chair. Uncertain where to put it in the small cell, he arranged it just behind the prisoner who remained facing the wall. Andropov motioned to the corridor. "Leave us. Close the door."

As the door shut, Andropov sat in the chair nearest him. "Come now, Petr Aleksandrovich. Let us talk."

Petr Korznikov turned to face Andropov. Standard interrogation procedure had been followed to render Korznikov more cooperative. This called for a thorough beating after arrest, to bring home to the prisoner that his or her fate lay entirely in the hands of the State. Andropov noted with approval that Korznikov's hands and face had been spared in case he might have to make a public appearance. But the results of the treatment were nonetheless evident. Korznikiov's hair was matted and tangled. His face was that of a derelict; stubble covered a skin totally washed of color save for a greenish-gray undertone around eyes that were flat and lusterless. He had been a stocky man, but now he seemed to have collapsed from within. He moved like an arthritic as he stepped around to sit in the chair.

"An unexpected pleasure, Comrade Andropov. Do you have more messages for me to send to the Americans?"

"Perhaps later. Not now." Andropov caught a whiff of Korznikov's foul breath, a smell of spoiled meat and a rotting mouth. Korznikov had a look, a deep penetrating stare, as if he could see into the very corners of Andropov's soul.

Petr Korznikov sat quietly, determined to force Andropov to carry on the conversation. The KGB chairman had come with no clear intention other than a compelling urge to talk with Korznikov. Andropov studied the man. After a long silence he abruptly asked, "Why did you do it? Why did you work with the Americans?"

Korznikov shook his head. "I find it surprising that you have to ask. You are not a foolish man. You read. Hegel. Kant. You know the gulf between reality and the swill we feed the masses." Korznikov smiled ruefully. "I did it, Comrade Andropov, because I have seen too much. We have not brought about a revolution. We have spilled the blood of millions to create a new privileged class. A new nobility. The further we move from 1917, the worse it gets. The anti-Semitism, the discrimination against women in any meaningful positions . . . the corruption—the awful corruption. We have built a slave state in order that the members of the Politburo can have limousines and hunting preserves."

"There were other ways, Petr Aleksandrovich. One can work from within. . . ."

"You mean the factions, Comrade Andropov? Like the Caucasians who kept Stalin in power? Or the Ukrainians around Khrushchev? It only gets worse. Now it's Brezhnev's clique: Chernenko, Kirilinko—all the rest of them. They're the only ones that pathetic old man trusts. And they would have a taxidermist stuff him when he dies to keep themselves in power. They care nothing for Russia, only for their own wealth and luxury."

"They cannot last forever. . . ."

"No, Comrade Andropov, they can't. But what shall we see emerge? The long-awaited New Soviet Man? As that clown Khrushchev used to say, the shrimps will whistle first. It's not a question of getting the right clique in the Kremlin. It's the system itself. It breeds political depravity." Korznikov's eyes flashed, his mouth curled in defiance. His hands were clenched fists. "No one's accountable to the Russian people, you see. There are only those elites who are in power and those who wish to be."

Andropov responded sharply, lashing Korznikov with his contempt. "You agreed quickly enough to help us."

Andropov was startled by the sudden change in Korznikov. The man shrank, as if recoiling from the memory of his surrender. He gave a slight nod in agreement, then dropped his eyes to his lap, where one hand now picked listlessly at the dirty robe. He looked up again to meet Andropov.

"Yes. Yes I did. I did it because no one would know or care if I resisted. Except, of course, my family. They would suffer, and it would be for nothing. Perhaps had I been a younger man . . ."

Andropov went to the door and rapped to call the guard. An eye appeared at the spy hole, then the door was swung open. Vasili Kiktev waited in the corridor to escort Andropov back to his office.

Andropov turned. Korznikov was slumped in the chair, staring at his hands lying in his lap, seemingly lifeless. Andropov took a step toward Korznikov, as if to comfort him in some way. The man looked up, tears in his eyes. Andropov spun on his heel and walked quickly down the corridor, Kiktev was at his side.

Kiktev saw his own face roundly distorted in Andropov's glasses. "Vasili Petrovich," Andropov spoke in a whisper, "Korznikov. Have him shot. At once. Send me the necessary papers at your first opportunity."

Los Alamos, New Mexico

Dr. Robert Helm regarded his visitors over the top of his wire-rimmed reading glasses. The suddenness with which he'd been notified was itself curious. That the visitors were two women of whom he'd heard absolutely nothing in the nuclear community added to his curiosity. They had come out on a special-mission Air Force VIP jet to the Los Alamos Scientific Laboratory with interim access clearances from the Department of Energy, clearances that vaguely described them as special assistants to the Undersecretary of Defense.

Helm sat at a huge antique oak harvest table. He read the clearance cable again, then rustled it in a fanning motion. "Says you have some questions about the design of small nuclear devices."

Eleanor Trowbridge pulled a worn stenographer pad from the canvas shopping bag at her feet. Pursing her lips, she leafed through the pad and finally found the page she sought. "Yes. Here it is. Something man-portable. I believe they describe them that way. A yield in the range of .01 to .05 kilotons." She squinted at the page, turned it over and continued. "Total weight, to include carrying case, estimated at about eighty pounds."

Helm replied, "The design's relatively simple. Imagine a series of small uranium-235 or plutonium-239 plates arranged over the face of a ball—a sphere." He patted the spherical glass paperweight on his desk. "On top of each plate is an explosive charge—an explosive with a high detonation rate—like the plastic explosives. All these are wired together so they will go off at the same time, precisely the same time. The explosion drives the uranium or plutonium plates inward, in to the center of the ball. When the fissile material is squeezed into a sufficiently small volume, this produces a huge number of self-sustaining nuclear reactions."

Susan Forbes leaned forward. "How long does this take? From setting off the charges to the nuclear detonation?"

Helm picked up the paperweight as if to test the heft of it. "A microsecond—a millionth of a second."

Eleanor dashed notes into the stenographer's pad then looked up, moving her eyes from Helm's face to the paperweight. "Is it possible to determine the origin of one of those things? After? I mean, after it explodes?"

"By origin you mean . . ."

"I mean, who made it?"

Helm abruptly brought his hand down, slapping the table. "Well, we never had the problem before. We've always known from seismological readings where the things had gone off, and the presumption has always been that the owner of the real estate was the builder of the bomb."

Susan Forbes interrupted. "But if one went off—one of the man-portable kind—if it went off in—"

Helm flushed beneath his tan. "Goddamnit," he snapped angrily, "I've got clearances for stuff that'd end the human race." He gestured toward the pile of papers. "I'm behind several weeks in my basic correspondence and reading, and you people come in here and run me around the goddamn mulberry bush with your carefully veiled questions. Either you trust me or you don't. But stop wasting my time and give it to me straight out—what the hell do you want to know?"

Seeing Susan's mouth tighten and her eyes grow wide, Eleanor spoke up. "What we want to know, Dr. Helm, is whether we could tell the national origin of a small nuclear explosion that went off in North Korea. One which the North Koreans claim was built by Seoul with the aid of the South Africans. If the bomb were furnished by the Soviets instead, could we tell?"

Helm's anger subsided at once, cooled by the implications of the question. He got up from his chair and walked to the first French door and looked out at the desert and the mountains the Spanish conquistadores had named the Blood of Christ. "Yes," he finally responded. "The sphere I told you about—it'd be surrounded by an outer shell of normal uranium—uranium-238. We call it a tamper. That holds the critical mass together for a fraction of a microsecond, enabling a larger yield from a small amount of U-235 or plutonium. Analysis of the airborne fallout would give us an indication of origin as well as how the weapon behaves when it explodes. Things like the percentage of gamma radiation, overall temperature of the weapon-debris plasma, and neutron emission have become pretty much characteristics of record. We have a reliable profile of Soviet weapons behavior." Halm turned from the doorway and folded his arms across his chest. "No doubt. None. We'd be able to spot one of theirs with a very high degree of certainty. Immediately."

Eleanor whispered to Susan, asking her if she was ready to go. When Susan nodded, Eleanor put away her pencil, then, taken by a last question on the note pad, she looked up at Helm, who was leaning against the doorway. "The process of determining who set it off . . . How long would it take?"

Helm sought the answer on the ceiling for a moment. "Within hours. We'd know within hours."

Alexandria, Virginia

The telephone startled John Freeman out of a sound sleep. It took several seconds to realize it was indeed the telephone and another moment or two fumbling to get the receiver to his ear. He was momentarily puzzled that he was alone, until he remembered that Susan and Eleanor wouldn't be landing until morning.

"John? John Freeman?" came the voice out of the instrument. "Is this—"

Freeman swung his feet to the floor and sat up on the edge of the bed. "Who's—"

"John, it's Moe. Moe Hirsch. I've got to talk to you."

Still getting his thoughts together, Freeman shook his head then rubbed his eyes with his free hand. He looked at the digital clock—3:37 A.M. "Moe? Moe, go ahead. What is it?"

"John, I called Eleanor, couldn't reach her. I'm at my office. I can't talk to you where you are. How long will it take you to get to a secure phone?"

Freeman sighed softly. No more sleep. And it had been a late night. It never seemed to get easier. Increasingly, he'd thought more about Susan and how the two of them had to get away somewhere. Anywhere, just so long as it was away from the telephones. And away from anything to do with Korea or the Russians. To do nothing but eat, make love, and sleep. He looked at the clock, then figured driving time and security check-in requirements at Arlington Hall. "About thirty minutes, Moe. I'll call you."

It took three tries until he heard Moe's voice, made ducklike by the shifting-frequency scrambler. "John, one of our ground stations picked up a priority message out of Pyongyang for Mozambique." Even over the secure phone, Freeman noted, Hirsch did not identify the collecting station. Probably one of the South Korea sites, like Sosan, perched on a finger jutting out into the Yellow Sea. "The message evidently responded to an earlier query from a North Korean entity in Mozambique. Pyongyang has a ship in Mozambique that's down for repairs. The Soviets have gotten into the act. Pyongyang is telling its Mozambique station that an Aeroflot special flight is being laid on to bring in the parts needed."

"Our friends are going to a lot of trouble to fix a ship. Do we have a status on North Korean shipping in the area?"

"It's gotten active over the past two years. The Koreans have been exporting more artillery and small arms. Usually their ships deadhead back. There's not much Pyongyang wants from Mozambique."

"What do you show in port now?"

"One steamer: thirty thousand tons. The *Chosen Nampò*. Pulled into Maputo harbor a week ago. Off loaded some M-1976 152-millimeter guns and a half-dozen T-55 tanks. I think it's safe to say that the *Nampò* is the ship in question."

"Did they give any date for sailing?"

"No. But I shouldn't imagine the size of the repair job is such that it'll take a long time, or they'd use one of the ships they have en route now. I'd say they want the *Nampò* and its cargo out of port within the next week. Ten days at the most."

Holding the telephone to his ear with his shoulder, Freeman began flipping through the Rolodex. As if he could see Freeman, Moe Hirsch, in a plummy Charles Laughton voice, added, "Before you call for the photo boys, John, you ought to know we have a twofer. Those *spetznaz* C-47's? The ones with the South Korean markings? They're on the move. They left the airfield at Arys' last night. Our people say they're flying east."

After he'd gotten off the telephone with Hirsch, Freeman walked to the stand that held the huge Hammond atlas. The haze-muffled sky promised another sweltering day. He turned in the worn book to Mozambique and located Maputo, the national capital, a city not far from the town of Moamba, where the body of Arkluunds, the South

African nuclear specialist, had been found. As Freeman watched the day come on, he felt again the rush of emotion he'd first known in Southeast Asia—the fearful anticipation of combat.

Mildenhall Royal Air Force Base—England

When Major Phil Beach pushed the throttles forward at the end of the runway, powerful moment forces twisted the engines into perfect alignment. Minutes later the Lockheed SR-71 climbed past 100,000 feet at 2700 miles an hour. Beach's voice was laconic. "India Papa coming up in one-five minutes."

"Roger." At the Initial Point, Beach would turn the Blackbird over to the automatic pilot and the celestial navigation system, which would fly the plane on an arrow-straight course set into the computer by Michael Sternberg, the Reconnaissance Systems Officer. From his cramped compartment behind Beach, Sternberg now began the complicated sequence that activated the SCT-134 (TIMBAL) high-resolution cameras.

Although the State Department had had its way in stopping SR-71 overflights of the USSR, the spy plane had years of service ahead of it elsewhere in the world, for there were large numbers of admirers in the American and NATO intelligence communities who considered the SR-71 an espionage platform superior to the more costly and less responsive satellites. For several years the Americans had been using Mildenhall as a base for the Blackbirds to monitor events in the Mediterranean and Persian Gulf.

SR-71 Mission 79-19J had lifted off from Mildenhall at 6:47 A.M., or 0647Z, as Soviet radar operators noted aboard the sea-going trawlers that operated in the North Sea, just out of landfall of Suffolk. As 19J's location was passed to long-range H Model Bear bombers for further tracking, Russian analysts had already concluded that the Blackbird's flight path was nothing out of the ordinary.

After the run along latitude thirty-degrees north from Tripoli to Kuwait, the Mildenhall missions generally veered southward, out into the Indian Ocean over the Straits of Hormuz, then returned to England. Mission 19J's route would take it along the same general path, with a slight exception: the north-south axis of the recovery loop would be extended by about ten minutes to allow the Blackbird to avoid a squall line Air Weather Service reported moving up the English Channel.

"Three-zero seconds to India Papa." Sternberg made certain of the ultra-high frequency link between the SR-71 and the Defense Communications Satellite in a stationary orbit some 23,000 miles over the mid-Atlantic. The DCS bird would relay the digital photography from the TIMBAL cameras to the Washington ground station. Sternberg checked signal strength of the uplink to the satellite. This had to be a high priority mission. Ordinarily, DIA waited for the photography to be processed in England and sent by courier, since the satellite link-up with the SR-71 would cause delays in processing the KH-11 take from over the Soviet Union.

"India Papa in one-zero seconds, nine, eight . . ."

The final leg of Mission 19J began on the exact second planned. Michael Sternberg hummed a bar from the Petula Clark classic, "Downtown," as the banks of amber lights turned green, indicating that the cameras were beginning to photograph over eight hundred miles of the Indian Ocean coastline of southern Africa. Sternberg would have been surprised to know, as would the Soviets tracking him, that Mission 19J was flown just for this final leg. And that the final leg had been stretched ten minutes by the false weather report to produce a single photograph—that of the *Chosen Nampò* at its berth in the harbor of Maputo, Mozambique.

National Military Intelligence Center—The Pentagon

Sam Bartlett was the last to arrive at the National Military Intelligence Center. The others had taken up seats at one end of the conference table, clustered around Eleanor. On either side of her were Jack Bronowski and

Andrew Cabot, and in two chairs behind her were John Freeman and Susan Forbes.

Eleanor looks tired, Bartlett thought. She was normally a fidgeter, her boiling inquisitiveness manifesting itself in a physical restlessness. Now she sat quietly, as if her energy had been drained by curiosity satisfied. She was wearing what John Freeman had once identified as "the Dress," a white shirtwaist affair with incredibly large red and yellow flowers on it—a dress that fit the personality of its owner better than it fit her body.

As Bartlett made an apology for being late, Eleanor opened a portfolio. "Sam, we asked for this meeting because we've gotten about as far as I think we can get." Her voice was cracked but still retained an edge, a characteristic keenness. "You know our earlier hypothesis—that the Soviets would engineer a nuclear explosion or two in North Korea to give Kim Il-Sung an excuse to march south." She paused, a professor looking to see that the student had dutifully digested the summary of the last lesson, then continued, "And it is only necessary that this subterfuge retain plausibility long enough to keep the White House from immediately opposing the North Korean incursion. Given thirty or so hours without American assistance, there is every likelihood that South Korea would fall."

Bartlett nodded. "And now, Eleanor?"

She put the notes flat on the table and leaned forward, resting on her folded arms, oblivious of the others around her, concentrating only on Bartlett. "They are going to do exactly that, Sam. And we know how they intend to go about it."

Over the next hour, Eleanor talked, drinking occasionally from a glass of water. She recounted the Helm revelation that the origin of a Soviet nuclear weapon could be traced. She then detailed the Arkluunds affair; how he had been recruited by the KGB or GRU and had apparently assembled a number of small weapons in Mozambique, using nuclear materials he'd diverted from South Africa's clandestine laboratory. And, of course, there were the NSA intercepts and the mission of the *Chosen Nampò*. Sam

Bartlett felt a mounting fear as the diminutive woman before him emotionlessly laid out the facts—a fortune-teller, relentlessly laying down card after card that could only reach a prediction of disaster.

Eleanor, finished, sat back in her chair, silent, expectant, her hands before her on the table, fingers interlocked. The room was hushed except for the faint whir of the air-conditioning. Bartlett briefly closed his eyes, then opened them again, looking from face to face. They'd done their job. They had tracked the quarry and run it to earth. Now they were waiting. Watching him.

It was not a superior-subordinate relationship. Rather, it was a partnership. They'd met their side of the agreement. They expected—no, demanded—that he live up to his. Outsiders could never really understand it. No matter how high your rank, you never really exercised absolute command. Not of a first-class outfit, anyway. He'd learned that from Merrill in Burma. Whether a second lieutenant in combat or a three-star general in the Pentagon, rank was only what the law could give you—bits of metal on the collar tab. But the law couldn't give you the loyalty of those who would go out on a certain day to die because you told them to. You had to earn it, and those who might die for you demanded that you earn it time and again. It was the secret binding force of a brotherhood—the tyranny of subordinates. Fail to live up to their expectations, fail to carry out your side of the partnership, and you'd find yourself in the shit.

Bartlett pushed back from the table, walked over to the glass wall and looked out on the display screens, then turned and walked back to his chair. "If we know how they're going to do it, why don't we just make it all public? Wouldn't that put a crimp in their hose?"

"We've thought about that, Sam," answered Andrew Cabot. The short man pursed his lips, then proceeded. "What we've found is the trigger—how the Soviets intend to start a war in Korea. If we expose this one, who knows if we'll be able to find the next one in time? Do you think that having to abandon this little bit of their plan will cause them to change their overall intentions? They've built the North

Koreans up over a period of years. In so doing, Moscow's put its credibility on the line. If the Soviets back away, then Kim's likely to boot them out and jump in bed with the Chinese.

"Secondly, we believe—though it's mostly conjecture—that this Korea thing fits somehow into the struggle between Brezhnev and Andropov. It has to be Brezhnev's idea, and if it succeeds, it's the Brezhnev gang that'll be running the Kremlin after the old man goes."

Bartlett interrupted, waving his hand at Cabot. "But if the nuke plan is publicized—"

"Brezhnev will find someone to blame—possibly Andropov himself—and then look for another way to start his war in Korea," Eleanor interjected. "As long as Brezhnev maintains backing within the Politburo for the Korea venture, and as long as Franks and the White House refuse to recognize what's going on," she gestured to the notes before her with a sweep of her hand, "we face a war in Korea."

Bartlett thought, then, "We've tried the White House route. That's closed. There's a way to erode Brezhnev's support?"

"We have an idea, Sam," offered Eleanor.

"I somehow thought you would, Eleanor."

Chapter 10

Andrews Air Force Base—Maryland

In the dry Tables of Organization and Equipment, nothing distinguishes the 89th Military Airlift Wing from any of many other transport units in the U.S. Air Force. But the 89th MAW has a unique mission—the ferrying of congressional delegations (CODEL) around the world. Members of Congress call on the 89th MAW to fly them to some of the more desolate places on earth: war zones, sites of famine and plague, and occasionally to places like Gstaad during the ski season or the Riviera in the early summer. Understandably, the Gstaads and Rivieras have caught the attention of American journalists who have made "junket" an epithet of currency in American politics. Consequently, if only to preserve their own hides, successive commanders of the 89th MAW have judiciously lowered the unit's profile to such an extent that it is nearly invisible in official Washington.

And so it was that no one paid attention when a VC-137 from the 89th MAW was quickly dispatched to Nellis Air Force Base, Nevada, for "communications modifications" prior to the departure of a congressional delegation that had been scheduled at the insistence of Senator Frank Church, chairman of the Committee on Foreign Relations. The military version of the Boeing 707 didn't spend all that much time at Nellis, and on its return it was hangared under unobtrusive guard in a distant corner of the 89th MAW ramp area.

The steward gently shook Eleanor Trowbridge's elbow until he saw the sleeping woman's eyelids flutter. "Two hours out, ma'am," he whispered, leaving behind a mug of steaming coffee. The VC-137 forward cabin seats folded flat into comfortable if somewhat narrow bunks. She lay quietly for a moment, then sat up, swinging her feet to the floor. She raised the window screen an inch or so and was rewarded with a golden-red sunrise over the rim of East Africa. Her mouth was gummy and dry from the air in the pressurized cabin, and she sipped gratefully at the coffee. I ought to have drunk more water, she thought. The others were asleep; Jack Bronowski and Laurence Mitchell huddled motionless beneath blue Air Force blankets, John Freeman starting to stir.

Bud Mitchell hadn't been exactly overjoyed the week before, when Eleanor had insisted on a walk down the Mall instead of talking in his office. She'd brought the Missouri Senator up to date, detailing the *spetznaz* exercise and the evidence supporting the case for a shipment of nuclear weapons from Mozambique aboard the *Chosen Nampò*. Anticipating Mitchell, she explained the danger of attempting to stop the Russians by publicizing the affair.

"I understand that, Eleanor, but why not run an air strike against the *Nampò* after she gets under way? Or put a charge on her at the dock? Sink her in place? Why do we have to get aboard?"

"We couldn't send the regular military on a mission like that without White House approval," she replied. "And anyway, just sinking the ship isn't what we're after. We've got to destroy the weapons themselves. An air strike mightn't do that. And if we sink her at dockside, Maputo harbor's so shallow they could easily retrieve the weapons and probably even refloat the ship. With the weapons in hand, they can improvise and still go on with it.

"But if we can destroy the weapons," Eleanor continued, "we'll not only stop the operation, but put Moscow in a very bad spot. They won't just be at square one again, they'll be much worse off." She raised an index finger. "First, obviously, the weapons are gone. And they've done away with this fellow Arkluunds, who was their designer and source for uranium from South Africa.

"And then, there'll be the radioactivity—the low-order contamination. If a portion of the conventional explosive primer of a nuclear weapon goes off—they call it a single-point detonation—the uranium doesn't get squeezed into a critical mass—it gets blown out the other side of the weapon. There's no big bang and no fallout, but there is an unmistakable amount of radioactivity that would convince even our Mr. Carter."

At this, Mitchell laughed. "I suppose the nation's First Nuclear Engineer might be intrigued by something like that."

"And there's a side benefit in Africa. Samora Machel's a Marxist, but I can't imagine he'd appreciate his Russian friends irradiating his country. We'd spread word of the incident throughout the world press. It would especially hurt Moscow in the Third World," Eleanor smiled. "The new white colonialists—that sort of thing."

"You think the Mozambique government doesn't know?" Mitchell asked.

"We don't believe so. The Soviets and North Koreans have a place on the Maputo docks that's been given over to them to off-load arms shipments. They've got some barracks for dockworkers and security forces. They use their own people. No locals allowed in."

Eleanor's pace slowed. They came to a stop. "But what happens in Africa is secondary to the effect this could have within the Kremlin."

Mitchell listened without interruption as Eleanor explained the premise that the Korean affair was an episode in the struggle between Brezhnev and Andropov. When she finished, they resumed their walk and soon reached the crosswalk of Fifteenth Street.

"Isn't Andropov the greater danger of the two? If this thing succeeds, aren't we helping him?" asked Mitchell.

Eleanor nodded. Speckles of rain dotted her glasses.

"Yes. Certainly. But if we do nothing, it means a war in Korea before Thanksgiving." Eleanor shrugged, a gambler reduced to playing on the margin. "It's not really our game, you see. The real game's in Moscow. Whoever wins, we're still the intended victim. The question is a matter of timing— now or later? Brezhnev wants us now. Andropov's willing to wait."

Eleanor reached into her raincoat for a handkerchief and blew her nose. "I'm not a Soviet specialist. I've always found the Russians too dreary. But over the years, I've seen them advance. They built their bomb much sooner than we thought— thanks to their espionage. Then came their space program. We thought we were ahead, then we rested on our laurels. Tortoise and the hare all over again. What they lacked in sophisticated technology, they made up with brute force. That and determination.

"And so they've pulled even with us. Perhaps even a bit ahead. We have to be more careful. The British survived as a major power because they learned to play sides in the struggle for power on the Continent. They chose their allies so no one nation would dominate Europe. This is much the same. Our best hope is that we can weaken Brezhnev sufficiently to make him give up on the Korea operation, but leave him strong enough to stay in power and keep Andropov at bay."

They had reached the concrete walk around the base of the Washington Monument. The afternoon had gotten darker and the rain was picking up, falling now in a steady drizzle.

Bud Mitchell looked through the rainwater that was now streaming steadily off the edge of the umbrella. "Aren't there any options? Any way at all this can be stopped without . . ." His voice trailed off.

"Without?" asked Eleanor.

Mitchell waved his hand helplessly. "We aren't . . . this isn't the way something like this should be decided."

"You're right, of course, Bud," Eleanor agreed. "But do you see any alternatives?"

There was a long pause. Mitchell, grim-faced, rocked

back and forth slightly. "No . . . no, Eleanor, I don't," he admitted in frustration. "But this isn't some small infringement. This is a major excursion. We just ran Nixon out of the White House for less than this. It's not a government when Presidents—or Senators—go outside the system."

Eleanor put her hand on Mitchell's arm. "Bud. Sometimes the system comes down to people. And it's been people like Franks and Cummings who've kept the system from working."

Mitchell snapped his head around to look at her. "Who's to say? You? Me? If we do this thing this time, then what's next? Do we start taking on all the other little jobs 'the system' didn't handle to our satisfaction?"

"Bud," Eleanor protested, "It isn't like that at all. We aren't the kind of people who—"

"Who'd run amok? Maybe you and I aren't, Eleanor. I'll give us that. What about the others? There'll be knowledge of this. You and I aren't going to pull it off by ourselves. And there's the irony: If we succeed, we could make things even worse. Success comes so infrequently these days. The people who'll know of it will be tempted to try that kind of thing again . . ."

Eleanor tugged on Mitchell's arm. "Bud, you're wrestling with cosmic questions. What about the next several weeks? We know what has to be done. And we know what will happen if we don't do it." She raised her eyebrows, widening her eyes. "There's nobody else, Bud. There's only you and me. If we do it and make it come out all right, we've set a dangerous precedent. I know that. And it'll bother me to my death. But we will have stopped a war."

"I don't doubt it, Eleanor. Not at all. Nonetheless, it bothers the hell out of me. I know what it's like to fight when they hamstring you with petty restrictions and mountains of rules. And I know what it's like to cut free of all that. But still I worry about what we'd be turning loose."

Her grip was strong on his arm. "It is a bad precedent, Bud," she repeated. Her voice was firm, insistent. "But damnit, man, we have no other alternative. We need you. You could mean the difference between success or failure. But if we have to, we'll go on without you."

He finally spoke, so quietly that Eleanor missed the first words. ". . . can't take them on in Korea. Not now. Viet Nam is too recent a memory. If Kim claims he's been attacked by the South Koreans, Carter would probably futz around until it was too late. And even if he did try to respond, Congress would probably tie his hands with the War Powers Act."

In that instant he was finished with the agonizing deliberations that had absorbed him for months. The former fighter pilot turned to Eleanor, his decision made. "We need to play for time." He smiled at her, then nodded toward the car. "Let's get started."

Mitchell awoke and looked over to the empty tangle of Eleanor's blankets. Listening intently, he reflexively sorted out and analyzed the subdued sounds of the jet engines and the intermittent hisses of hydraulics and air-conditioning systems. "We have to move a few people into Mozambique in a hurry without State knowing about it," she'd explained to him, "and a congressional delegation's the only way we can do it on short notice." Mitchell had taken advantage of Frank Church's preoccupation with the SALT II Treaty ratification battle. Without his characteristic cross-examination, Frank Church had approved Mitchell's request for a plane and clearance to visit Mozambique.

Mitchell raised his window screen. Eleanor had made her case. The evidence was there. Strictly on the basis of cold logic, of realpolitik, this all made sense. Yet he wondered if he hadn't gone along simply for the excitement of it, the challenge. As they had walked on the Mall, as she'd explained what had to be done, Mitchell had felt his pulse quicken, a tingling on the backs of his hands. Something's going to be done, he thought. We are going to go somewhere and do something, run some risks.

Ninety-five minutes later, Lieutenant Colonel "Moose" Fredericks pulled the VC-137 into a sloppy bank that took the airplane half a mile off the VFR approach to Maputo International Airport. Normally Moose would have come down the centerline, but that wouldn't have gotten sufficiently close to Maputo harbor. As the CODEL aircraft lowered its landing gear and flaps, the flight engineer was busy at a hooded console in the rear of the plane. Within seconds the *Chosen Nampò* had been probed from bow to stern by an array of sophisticated optics, infrared scanners, and millimeter wave sensors that had been mounted in the VC-137 during its stay in Nevada. Tower control at Maputo wasn't particularly upset with Moose Fredericks. Compared to all too many pilots flying into Mozambique, Moose had been right on the money.

Maputo—People's Republic of Mozambique

The U.S. Ambassador to Mozambique met the delegation at Maputo International Airport. His black limousine led a small convoy of three embassy sedans of lesser majesty and a small carryall for the Air Force crew of the VC-137. Nearby, two bored and raggedly-uniformed members of the People's Police smoked and leaned against an aged Citroen, listlessly watching the Americans they would escort to the Majestica Hotel in the city.

At Cairo, the last fuel stop before Maputo, Mitchell had been radioed the details of the appointments that had finally been coordinated with the Mozambique ministries of Defense, Foreign Affairs, and Foreign Trade. After takeoff, Eleanor suggested a meeting in the large aft compartment.

Jack Bronowski and Laurence Mitchell sat to one side of a large navigator table that extended from the side of the airplane toward the aisle. John Freeman slid into a seat opposite the older men. Behind him, near the banks of communications equipment and clandestine surveillance systems, Eleanor worked a code into the electronic lock of a small safe.

Taking the seat beside Freeman, Eleanor handed out three slim manila folders and opened her own. "We have two schedules. One for Bud and me and another for you two." She looked from Bronowski to Freeman.

Mitchell pulled a pair of reading glasses from a leather case and marched down his schedule with a pencil, ticking off each entry with a small checkmark in the margin. Finished, he studied the schedule for Bronowski and Freeman, then looked up at Eleanor. "What's 'isolation'?" he asked.

"It's when we move to a safe house," offered Bronowski. "We can't work in the hotel—our rooms will be bugged."

"Andrew Cabot arranged for the Maputo Chief of Station to set up a place," explained Eleanor. "There'll also be some specialists who came in across the border a few days ago. They'll meet up with Jack and John at the safe house. There'll be more information available about the *Nampò* and the security situation in the harbor vicinity. Most of the second day will be spent in the detailed planning."

Laurence Mitchell pointed to the paper with his pencil. "And the thing itself?" He fumbled for a word.

"You mean, when we blow the nukes?" asked Freeman. "We do that the evening of the second day—while the two of you are having dinner with their president."

At one end of the room a chalkboard and three easels faced six folding metal chairs. Packets of freeze-dried meals, containers of water, and a large coffee thermos covered a table behind the metal chairs. Various-sized wood crates, some with Cyrillic markings, served as a screen for a chemical toilet in the far corner.

Carl Mopley stood before the chalkboard. The deputy chief of CIA's Maputo Station, he was rail-thin and afflicted with a slight stutter, a deferential man of halting, birdlike motions and a large Adam's apple. Mopely had intended to make a comfortable if unexciting career in the Agency as a logistics specialist. And so, he'd spent two years as Maputo Station's supply officer. But with Roswell Franks's decimation of the DDO, Mopely found himself pressed into the unfamiliar and sometimes frightening world of operations.

Mopely had set up the isolation area from which the *Chosen Nampò* mission would be run. And long before CODEL Mitchell had come into being, it had been Mopely who directed the surveillance of the harbor area and the North Korean freighter. It was late morning of the second day of Mitchell's stay, and the thin man had spent three hours going over the geography of the docks, using SR-71 photographs and the readouts from the secret sensors aboard the VC-137.

"Getting inside," repeated John Freeman. "How do we go about it?"

"You d-drive in. The Koreans guard the g-gate." Mopely pointed behind him toward the chalkboard showing the layout of the North Korean dock compound. "The Russians moved a s-small contingent into the compound se-seven months ago. But they l-left the gate security to the Koreans. You will d-drive," he pointed to John Freeman, "and G-General Bronowski will ride as passenger beside you. B-Both of you will be dressed in Soviet enlisted work uniforms. We've d-documented you as a senior sergeant, General." He turned to Joseph Chun and Frank Kim. "You f-fellows will be in the rear of the truck in one of the c-crates."

"If there aren't very many Russians," Jack Bronowski asked, "don't we run the risk of the guards getting curious?"

Nervously clutching one hand in the other, Mopely's mouth opened in a small O and his watery blue eyes widened as he formed a reply. "The Russ-Russians don't mingle with t-the K-K-Koreans at all," he exploded. He closed his eyes momentarily, took a slow, deep breath, and willed himself to relax. "It'll b-be near the end of the guards' shift, and . . ." He hesitated, looking over to Chun and Kim.

"And, General," Frank Kim finished, "you round-eyes all look pretty much alike."

Mopely gave a small smile to the stocky Korean, a reward for blunting John Freeman's hostility.

Joseph Chun, who, with Frank Kim, had arrived in

Maputo three days before the congressional delegation, turned in his chair to face Freeman and Bronowski. "There are three groups of people in the compound: the Koreans who are permanently residents of the place, the small group of Russians who stick pretty much to their own little enclave, and the Korean crew of the *Nampò*, who live on the ship. They all have their own very different jobs. There's no overlap. Carl, here," he motioned with his hand to Mopely, who now was sweating profusely, dark circles staining the underarms of his sport shirt, "has taken advantage of that. We work in the gaps between those groups. You guys handle the Koreans; Frank and I deal with the Russians."

No one spoke as Bronowski got up and walked over to pour himself a cup of tepid water. Drinking thirstily, the stocky general refilled his cup and brought it back to his chair. Still standing, he pointed to the easel that supported a plan of the *Chosen Nampò*. "You said the weapons are on board, in that compartment in the lower hold."

Warily, Mopely looked at the easel, then jerked his head in agreement.

"How confident are you?"

"Very co-confident. V-very."

Freeman, unconvinced, interrupted. "What are your sources?"

For the first time Mopely stood absolutely still, transfixed by Freeman's challenge. "They're very good sources."

"That's not good enough," Freeman snapped back. "What, specifically, are those sources? How do you know those weapons are in that particular compartment?"

Bronowski, who had remained standing, put a hand on Freeman's shoulder. "John, you know—"

"Fuck it, Jack. We're the ones going in. It's going to be our asses. At least we . . ."

Frank Kim watched the interplay between the three men. Joseph Chun carefully whetted the thick blade of a Buck folding knife on a small stone. He ran the blade lightly over his thumb and was rewarded with a thin line of dark blood.

"At least you ought t-to know how well I've d-done my

j-j-job," Mopely offered in seeming capitulation. Pulling up an empty chair, he sat facing the four, looking directly into Freeman's eyes. He explained how swimmers had attached hydrophonic microphones to the hull of the *Chosen Nampò*, microphones that picked up conversations inside the ship, and how Tokyo Station had gotten the drawings of the *Nampò* from the Japanese shipyard that had built it twenty years before. Finally, Mopely outlined the cooperation with NSA, which had intercepted the transmissions of the hand-held radios of the *spetznaz* security element when the four nuclear weapons were moved from Soviet custody into the ship.

What Carl Mopely did not reveal was that his primary source was none of the above. Rather, it was a tenuous human chain. Mopely's predecessor had recruited an intelligence officer in SNASP who, in turn, developed a relationship with a North Korean who worked in the compound, supervisor of the arms shipments from Pyongyang. It had been the Mozambican who had reported on the Soviet *spetznaz* guards standing twenty-four-hour watch on the locked compartment in the lower hold. That this report was buttressed by the intercepts and listening devices would not have kept John Freeman from picking apart Mopely's assessment. Too, Mopely was concerned that if any Americans were taken prisoner, the rather brutal but efficient interrogation techniques of the North Koreans and Russians would result in the complete loss of some rather hard-won agents. Not that Carl Mopely—or any other intelligence officer, for that matter—had excessive qualms about burning a source; it was just that the game had to be worth the candle. And as far as Carl Mopely was concerned, reassuring a bastard like this fellow Freeman didn't justify risking hard-to-replace assets.

The rest of the morning and early afternoon were spent poring over every detail of the plan Mopely had presented. Adjustments were made based on the expected composition and times of shift changes of the Russian guards on the ship. Frank Kim instructed Bronowski and Freeman on the small charges that would be strapped to each nuclear weapon and how the small pencil-like detonators would be triggered by a high-frequency transmitter once they were safely off the ship. Carl Mopely pushed a small handcart into the center of the chairs and removed a heavy canvas cover to show a small drumlike container.

"This," he explained, "is a mock-up of the nuclear weapons on the *N-Nampò*." He looked directly at Freeman. "It was m-made up by our technical people from the d-design notes Arkluunds left in his f-files." To head off Freeman's next question, he quickly added, "We got the notes through our l-liaison with Boss." Mopely opened the access hatch. He pointed first to a knob and then to a switch. "The time d-delay is set with this knob, then the whole thing is started on the c-countdown by flipping th-this."

After a lunch of reconstituted shrimp and noodles, John Freeman stretched out on one of the air mattresses among the jumble of supplies made available for that evening's mission. Jack Bronowski came over and sat on the floor, his back against a wooden box. "Thinking?" he asked Freeman.

Freeman was on his back, both hands under his head as he looked at the ceiling. "When I realized we'd actually do this, I remembered how it'd been in Viet Nam. It came back to me, the incredible clarity of everything. Colors, smell, touch—everything seemed so sharp. There were times, Jack, when I felt invulnerable. I had that feeling again, coming here on the plane. But now I remember, too, that in Viet Nam I was afraid of dying. Like bad memories, I suppose I suppressed that part of it."

Freeman shifted one hand out from under his head to look at his watch and sat up, attempting to shake off his fear. "Shit, Jack, it's natural, I guess. Been away from this kind of thing too long. The way this's been thrown together isn't reassuring either. Mopely's plan depends on those people down at the docks not knowing each other. Are we any better off?" He nodded his head toward Kim and Chun, who were uncrating a container of Kalashnikov assault rifles. "Who are *our* Koreans? Franks fired them from the

Agency and Bartlett's picked them up on a contract. DIA told us they were shit-hot, but talk's cheap. And the planning for this thing's been done by Mopely, who isn't going to risk his ass with us."

Bronowski dropped his chin to his chest and closed his eyes. "Johnny, pat hands aren't dealt very often."

Just after dark the flimsy side slats gave way on an aged diesel truck, with the result that three quarters of a ton of tomatoes and squash spilled across the street that a block later ran past the American warehouse. The driver, a low-level agent of Carl Mopely, stood helplessly while a member of the People's Police tried to figure out how the roadway could be cleared and how to reroute the traffic that was backing up behind the accident. Given an all-clear by Mopely's lookouts, Freeman drove the small Moskva truck out of the warehouse onto the now-deserted street. He'd spent half an hour familiarizing himself with the Russian army vehicle inside the large building, checking fuel and oil levels, trying the various switches, getting the feel of its handling by backing and turning small circles.

An hour before leaving, they had stripped, putting their clothing, watches, and personal belongings in heavy plastic bags. Mopely would have the bags waiting in yet another safe house after the operation. Bronowski and Freeman dressed in mottled-green camouflaged *spetznaz* combat uniforms, while Frank Kim and Joseph Chun put on the dark blue cotton work coveralls worn by the North Korean stevedores. Mopely had given them Japanese digital watches and "pocket trash": matches, a stub of a locally made pencil, a clipping from *Notícias*—Maputo's daily newspaper, packets of Russian and Portuguese cigarettes, and small wads of crumpled low denomination paper money.

Freeman and Bronowski would leave the docks in the Moskva, clearing the gate guards before setting off the demolition charges. "You should b-be in and out within forty-five m-minutes," Mopely told them, "an hour at th-the m-most. It's another fifteen minutes to the s-safe house. That'll give us an hour and forty-five minutes to get you back on the p-p-plane." He looked at his watch. "Takeoff's s-scheduled for 2300 hours."

"There's the Caltex tank farm." Bronowski pointed to the silver petroleum storage tanks ahead on the right. All four had memorized the primary and alternate routes into and out of the dock area and had quizzed each other on the smallest details. "Another kilometer and we take a right on the harbor road."

The Moskva coughed and sputtered, threatening to die. Freeman downshifted, revving the engine while the clutch was in. The engine caught and ran smoothly. "Water in the gas," he muttered to Bronowski. His hands were suddenly greasy with sweat, and his pulse pounded in his throat.

He looked in the rearview mirror. He saw no one. Yet Mopely had said an escort would be trailing behind for security and backup until the Moskva got to the gate. The shifting wind brought with it the damp, fetid air of the harbor: Metallic tendrils of salt threaded through with hints of the rotten egg of sulfurous tidal flats.

Bronowski motioned toward the windshield. "Here it is." The harbor road, newly paved, stretched off to the right. Not more than a mile away, lights of the ships at anchor made a sparkling necklace against the black of the night.

Freeman was suddenly short of breath. He couldn't inhale deeply enough to rid himself of the feeling of being smothered.

"Here's to us, Johnny." Bronowski held a Stechkin automatic in his right hand. With his left he pulled the slide back and released it, letting the forward motion slam a cartridge into the receiver. Both Kalashnikovs were propped butt first on the floor of the cab, their barrels resting on the edge of the seat. If they were surprised in the truck, they'd have no room to swing the rifles into use. Bronowski put the pistol on the floor between his seat and the door, so that he could quickly have it in hand.

As Mopely had predicted, the gate was open. "They've gotten lazy," Mopely explained, "but the guards can swing it shut in a second or two." Freeman eased the truck to a stop in the center of a pool of blinding blue-white light cast by floodlamps on tall poles. He could make out two figures standing near the guardhouse, which itself was nearly invisible in the dark shadows outside the perimeter of light.

One guard moved toward the truck while the other stayed in the darkness. Probably covering us, Freeman thought. From the corner of his eye Freeman saw Bronowski's hand drop toward the pistol.

The guard asked for identification in broken Russian. He wore a rumpled grease-stained uniform of dark brown cotton and low black boots of cheap leather which were beyond benefiting from polish. He thrust his left hand toward Freeman, palm up, making impatient gestures, bringing his joined fingers back and forth toward his palm. His right hand rested on a canvas holster at his waist. Nodding, Freeman pulled from his breast pocket a sheaf of papers folded into quarters and handed them out the window, holding them close to the truck to force the guard to take another step forward, making him a better target for Bronowski.

Holding the papers to catch the overhead light, the guard leafed to the last page, to the signatures and the rubber-stamped round red seal with the inevitable star and hammer and sickle in the middle. Looking up, he motioned toward the shadows, barked an order in Korean, then pointed to the rear of the truck. He continued his examination of the forged papers.

A loud shout snapped the guard's eyes up from the paper, first to Freeman and then toward the back of the truck. Freeman depressed the clutch and prepared to slip the truck into reverse. At the same time Bronowski shifted slightly forward, dropping his left shoulder as he began to bring his pistol up. Freeman tightened his shoulder blades against the expected burst of automatic fire as Chun and Kim were shot in the packing crates.

The guard at the window reached out of Freeman's sight and came back with a *Playboy* magazine which he thrust through the window. Freeman had last seen the magazine in isolation on top of one of the wooden boxes.

Somehow in the loading process it had been put on the truck. Miss July's blue eyes and seductive smile peeked at Freeman over the Korean's cracked and grease-begrimed thumbnail. Freeman could smell the odor of sour pickled cabbage on the guard's breath.

Suddenly Bronowski rapped out a stream of Korean. Startled, the guard made a sound of inquiry to which Bronowski responded, while at the same time pumping his clenched fist.

The Korean's flat face broke into a smile showing a mouth of broken and missing teeth as he repeated Bronowski's gesture with the hand that held the magazine. He then laughed derisively, tossed the magazine into the cab and waved Freeman on through.

Freeman slipped the Moskva into gear, gathering speed past the gate. "Care to tell me what that was all about?"

Bronowski stuffed the magazine under his seat. "Told him you hadn't been here long enough for the locals to start looking good and you had to have something to jerk off to."

They parked the truck between two buildings Mopely had said were not in use. While Bronowski kept lookout, Freeman prised open the two wooden crates in which Kim and Chun had been hidden. The two Koreans silently stretched out cramped muscles, then methodically checked the foam-padded equipment that had ridden with them. First came the silenced nine-millimeter Berettas and the extra clips of ammunition, then the demolitions and the subminiature two-way UHF radios resembling hearing aids, which would link each member of the team as well as provide communications with Mopely at the safe house.

The passageway formed by the two abandoned buildings pointed to the harbor seawalls. To the right, at a distance of about one hundred yards, was the *Chosen Nampò*; to the left, and much closer, was the compound power station with its transformers and standby generators. The night was silent, save for the sound of a distant donkey engine pushing a late shipment somewhere in the Mozambican portion of the harbor. Although the barracks of the Russians and North Koreans were lighted, only an occasional shadow on the curtained windows suggested life within.

Once at the fence surrounding the power station, Freeman looked back to the black bulk of the two buildings that sheltered the Moskva. Kim and Chun were there, somewhere, invisible in the shadows, keeping watch through the starlight scopes that turned the darkness into day. Freeman turned and he and Bronowski began to work with their wire cutters.

Twenty minutes later they had nearly finished. Bronowski had put the plastic charges on the transformer-yard main junction boxes and then on the nearest four transformers. Around the remaining six transformers the stocky general had wrapped several turns of primacord, an explosive that resembled nothing more deadly than clothes-line but which was unsurpassed for its cutting capability. Freeman, meanwhile, laid out the parallel blasting circuit. Into each puttylike plastic charge he stuck two electric blasting caps, small aluminum tubes with a solidified nitroglycerin droplet that would be set off by an electric current through a wire whose bare ends stuck from the open end of the tube. Freeman had tested each cap for circuit continuity in the warehouse, but he did so again, nodding in satisfaction as the galvanometer needle gave him a full-scale deflection. He connected the blasting caps to the free ends of two pairs of wires, then crouch-walked to Bronowski, playing out wire behind him from a compact reel.

He nudged Bronowski and pointed to the hole in the fence.

Freeman relaxed. After the transformer yard, the buildings and the truck seemed a safe haven. He made a last check of the electrical circuits with the galvanometer. Again the needle swung all the way to the right. He twisted each wire pair together until the time came to connect the small blasting generators. He turned and nodded to Kim and Chun, then pointed to the *Chosen Nampò*.

Frank Kim slipped his arm through a coil of electrical cable while Joseph Chun picked up a large metal toolbox. Both carried large flashlights. Before he left the shelter of the darkened alley, Kim stopped momentarily to squeeze Bronowski's elbow.

While Freeman and Bronowski had been setting up the demolitions, Kim had swung his starlight scope across the *Chosen Nampò*. Although he'd seen no one on deck, he felt as if he and Chun were under hostile scrutiny and that any moment they would be gunned down as they walked to the freighter. He knew they could only succeed by bluff, but Kim's every instinct screamed in protest. Instead of seeking the dark, they carried lights; rather than silence, here they were, chattering away as if their only care was missing dinner—repairmen on an off-hours call, complaining loudly about their foreman's obvious contempt for proletarian egalitarianism.

A short burly crewman stopped them at the top of the aft gangway. He was unarmed, and obviously unimpressed with the burdens of the harbor repairmen, landsmen who didn't know what hard work was really like. Frowning in concentration, he consulted a list on a clipboard. The man asked their names again, and Frank Kim sensed his growing irritation as he flipped back through the pages of the list.

"Our foreman is Park Tae Jong. Perhaps his name is there."

The crewman quickly found Park, whose presence on the list was enough to vouch for Kim and Chun. He put the clipboard aside. "Where are you going?"

Kim consulted a cheap notebook he took from his coverall pocket, thumbed through several pages, then smiled. "Deck D. Our Russian friends demand a new cable for—"

"All right," the crewman interrupted. "Go on." He jerked his thumb over his shoulder to the passageway leading to the decks below. His captain had told all crew that Deck D belonged to the Russian contingent that would be sailing with them back to Wonsan. The Russians, it seemed, would keep to themselves, and the *Nampò* crew would stay out of their way. Naturally, this raised curiosity and conjecture among the Koreans, but if you wanted to remain a seaman, you'd better keep your nose out of business that didn't concern you. And the *Nampò*'s skipper had made it very clear that Deck D didn't concern him or his crew.

The *Nampò* surprised Frank Kim. Because of its age and the nature of its service, he'd expected the usual signs of disrepair and slovenliness that generally accompanied small freighters working ports in the Third World. But the decks were clean, painting had been attended to, and lines and cables were neatly coiled. What little brightwork there was had recently been polished, and the smell wasn't at all bad.

According to Mopely, the nuclear weapons were in a compartment midway down the Deck D corridor toward the bow of the ship. Two guards would be on duty at all times, Mopely had told them, with compartments on either side of the weapons set aside for bunking down their reliefs once the *Nampò* put out to sea. Tonight the relief guards would stay on shore in their barracks. The bow end of Deck D opened up on the forward cargo hold, which was serviced by a huge hatch that permitted the *Nampò* to carry tanks, armored cars, and artillery pieces to Pyongyang's fraternal allies and cash customers around the world.

Kim and Chun stood outside a watertight compartment door. On the other side was the Deck D passageway, 118 feet long. Forty-seven feet down the corridor was the compartment with the nukes, and outside it, two guards. At least that's the picture Mopely had given them. They would go through the door, still posing as repairmen. Take out the two guards, then put the demolitions on the nukes. No more than fifteen minutes, twenty at most. If a diversion were needed, Freeman would blow the junction box and the transformers.

Kim looked at his watch. They left Bronowski and Freeman nine minutes ago. Reaching under the collar of his coveralls, he found the small headset, which he twisted into his ear. He pressed a rubber-encased button on the transceiver in his pocket and immediately heard a rushing noise. He pressed the transmit button three times in succession, three times cutting into the rushing sound. He listened. Two quick and one long interruption came in response: Freeman's acknowledgment. Now the point of no return.

Once through the door in front of them, they would be in the corridor with the Russian guard. There could be no turning back.

Kim nodded to Chun, who lifted the heavy steel lever, opened the door and stepped out into the passageway. Kim followed closely behind. Over Chun's shoulder the narrow passageway stretched into the darkness of the cargo hold. Ahead, to the left, was the compartment with the weapons. The door to an adjacent compartment stood open. The guards were nowhere in sight. Suddenly, a Russian charged through the open compartment doorway, mouth open, only partially awake, both hands occupied, struggling with the buckle to his pistol belt.

They've been screwing off, Frank thought. Sacking out on a dull duty shift. The other guard had to be in the same compartment. Chun waved nonchalantly with his free hand, then pointed to his toolbox and the corridor lighting cables. The Russian, eyes wide, began to pull his pistol from its holster.

He's not buying Chun's act, Kim realized.

But before Kim could move, Chun had dropped his toolkit and fired twice with his silenced Beretta, both shots hitting the Russian full in the chest, slamming him backward into the red mist of blood from the exit wound. As Chun moved to the compartment where the nuclear weapons were stored, Kim ducked into the compartment from which the Russian had appeared. He brushed through the doorway; a shot crashed into the bulkhead, inches from him. He fired low and to the right of the muzzle flash. He heard a gasping breath which dissolved into a gurgle, then the sound of a heavy body falling. He gave Chun a low recognition whistle. Receiving a response, he flicked on a high-intensity penlight. He'd caught the Russian just above the left eye. An AK-47 lay on the deck near the bunk beside the Russian's boots and tunic. Chun whistled again. Kim picked up the assault rifle and went out into the passageway.

"I'm havin' trouble with this fucking door," Chun whispered. He was feverishly working on the heavy lock with a set of carbon-steel picks.

Grunting to show that he'd heard, Kim opened Chun's toolkit, and under the false bottom found the small demolition charges and the radio-controlled detonators. While Chun continued to work on the lock, Kim peeled away a section of plastic explosive and softened it by kneading it in his hands. When it had reached a degree of pliability, he pushed Chun away from the lock and slapped the plastic around it, then jammed one of the detonators into the doughy mass. He turned the cap of the detonator then pulled the pin that would cause the pencil-like device to explode after a three-second delay. He and Chun, in a tangle of arms and legs, moved down the corridor toward the cargo hold. The plastic charge went off, rolling shock waves down the narrow corridor.

Before the explosion reverberations had completely subsided, Kim and Chun heard the sound of heavy boots descending the metal stairway. The far doorway slammed open and bullets sprayed down the corridor. Frank Kim flipped the AK-47 onto automatic and fired a burst shattering the nearest two overhead lights. The two Koreans retreated toward the cargo hold, Kim in the rear, now firing single shots down the darkened corridor.

As Kim struggled to change magazines in the AK-47, he heard a rattling metal noise. When the flash grenade exploded, the corridor was filled with an intense white light that nearly blinded Kim and Chun. Two *spetznaz* marksmen sprang from the doorway and fired. Chun saw Kim stagger back, spurting a fountain of blood from a head wound. He caught Kim before he fell and dragged him toward the deep darkness of the cargo hold.

"Try to make contact," Bronowski whispered when the firing started aboard the *Chosen Nampò*.

Freeman called into the throat mike of the UHF, listened, called again, then shook his head.

The two men lay in the alleyway, watching the Korean freighter from the shadows. At the first shot, Bronowski had crawled so that his shoulder touched Freeman's. Neither said anything until the muffled sound of Kim's attempt to blow in the compartment door reached them. At this, Bronowski squeezed Freeman's shoulder. "Johnny, they're in the shit now."

It had never been intended that the four would leave the compound together. After setting the charges, Kim and Chun were to go overboard, swim to a jetty outside the security area, and make their way to the harbor road to rendezvous with Freeman and Bronowski.

Freeman twisted to face Bronowski. "Ready?" Even before Bronowski could finish nodding his assent, Freeman cranked the handle of the first blasting machine. The second reserve circuit he prepared wasn't needed. A ripping blast of light and sound shook the ground and sent a compression wave that squeezed the breath from their lungs. The transformer yard erupted in sputtering cascades of sparks and flame. Heavy fragments of transformer ceramics and structural steel made deep moaning sounds as they rushed and tumbled through the air. The powerhouse was demolished. A Korean worker staggered, then ran on, unaware for several seconds that a sliver of metal had slit open his belly and his guts were spilling onto the ground.

Freeman picked up his AK-47 and ran to the truck with Bronowski beside him. A hand-cranked siren was working up in pitch, and from the darkness came sounds of confused shouting.

Throwing himself into the truck, Freeman gave his rifle to Bronowski, then unholstered his pistol and put it on the seat between his legs. Bronowski flicked his AK-47 to full automatic as Freeman started the truck and ground it into gear.

A small emergency generator nearby coughed and sputtered into life. The Moskva had no sooner pulled from the alley when Bronowski hit Freeman's shoulder. "Look." His voice cracked with excitement. Off to their right in the dim lighting, three Caucasians were sprinting toward the *Chosen Nampò*. "*Spetznaz*."

Freeman quickly turned the wheel and accelerated. The tight cluster of Russians was now framed in the windshield only ten yards away, still unaware of the dark truck bearing down on them. Jerking the wheel to the left,

Freeman brought the truck parallel to the three men. One Russian opened his mouth in surprise just as Bronowski fired short bursts, playing the Kalashnikov back and forth over the running men.

Freeman again turned, this time pointing the truck toward the gate and switching on the headlights. "Get them?"

"Two," Bronowski grunted, reloading the Kalashnikov, "maybe all three."

Increasingly heavy shooting was now breaking out behind them, started by Bronowski's killing of the Russians. In the dark, the confusion between the Koreans, Russians, and, later, the Mozambican troops would continue for almost an hour, with small pitched battles breaking out throughout the harbor area, frustrating attempts to determine exactly what had happened.

The gate was closed. "Where're the guards?" Bronowski asked.

As if in response, a flashlight probed the cab. "Don't stop," shouted Bronowski. "Get this bastard out of here." He hunched over his AK-47 and fired toward the guard. The flashlight fell to the ground, spinning in the darkness. Another Korean leaped into the glare of the headlights and fired shot after shot from a large automatic which he held in a two-handed combat grip. The cab and windshield were hit twice with heavy sledgehammer blows. A sliver of glass opened a deep cut in Freeman's forehead. Immediately his right eye filled with blood.

The Moskva crushed the Korean into the gate. The hinges gave way and the truck was soon on the harbor road. Freeman gently spun the steering wheel right, then left, and shook the guard's body from the hood. Within seconds headlights glared from around a curve. Two truckloads of Mozambican soldiers passed, reinforcements to the chaos that was now reigning on the docks around the *Chosen Nampò*. The road ahead was deserted. Freeman slowed to a stop to wrap a rag around his forehead. He found his hands were trembling so badly that he could hardly tie a knot.

"Johnny," came Bronowski's voice, drained, rasping, "I

took one." He pointed to his chest. "Here. It hurts, Johnny. Christ, it hurts."

Samora Moises Machel, President of Mozambique and leader of the Marxist Frente de Libertaçao de Mozambique, held the silver spoon at arm's length, examining it in the light. Finding it to his satisfaction, he stirred his tea. "What do you think of our country, Senator Mitchell?"

Laurence Mitchell hesitated. "It's difficult to say much after only a day and a half."

"You have impressions." Machel made it a statement. "You certainly must have impressions."

Eleanor Trowbridge, seated to Machel's left, looked across the table at Mitchell. He's distracted, she thought. She stole a fleeting glance at her watch. They should be on board the *Chosen Nampò*. She hid her trembling hands in her lap. The worst of it was sitting here, at this grotesque dinner. She'd offered to stay on radio watch with that Mopely fellow, but Bud had insisted she be here. "We all can't be in on the fun," Mitchell told her.

"Mozambique is a nation of potential," Mitchell began. Noticing Machel arch his eyebrows, Mitchell continued, "But it escapes me how you believe a Marxist economy and government can develop that potential." The Missouri Senator pushed his plate away, folded his hands on the table and awaited Machel's response.

Before the Mozambican could reply, a uniformed aide entered the small dining room and whispered in his ear. Machel excused himself, leaving Mitchell and Eleanor with the Minister of Defense, who spoke only broken English. The two Americans looked at each other, then smiled self-consciously at the minister, who had finished his dessert and motioned to Eleanor. Nonplussed, she smiled even more broadly and feverishly searched her memory for a few remnants of Portuguese. Mitchell leaned forward to whisper: "I think, Eleanor, he wants your ice cream."

Samora Machel returned, followed by a large uniformed man whose pockmarked skin was a deep black, with purplish highlights. "Gentlemen, General dos Santos, my

Minister of Public Security. It seems there is a disturbance." Machel motioned to the general to explain further.

"It seems there are . . ." He hesitated, looking for a
word. "Difficulties. Difficulties at the harbor. I am afraid
they may interfere with your departure."

Mitchell forced himself to remain inscrutable, a man
mulling over information of no great importance to him.
"Difficulties?"

General dos Santos's mouth operated silently, opening
and closing before attempting to continue. The white man
in front of him had the same demanding posture, the same
arrogance of demeanor as the cursed Portuguese. They
were always so superior, so condescending. But the Russians were no different, in spite of their high-flung Marxist
rhetoric about equality. Even now they were demanding
that he delay the American departure until the mess in the
harbor could be evaluated. "A temporary thing . . ."

Eleanor stood. She had seen Machel start when dos
Santos mentioned their departure. Dos Santos had pulled a
rabbit out of the hat on his boss. Whatever they'd talked
about outside the dining room, it had not involved inter-
fering with an American congressional delegation. She
addressed dos Santos. "Is it political? A coup, perhaps?"

Machel's eyes widened. "Of course not," he snapped,
angered by the impertinence—that an American, and a
woman at that, would ask such a question. He turned a
withering glare on the heavily perspiring and obviously
unhappy dos Santos. The fool turned to jelly around
whites—Americans, Portuguese, Russians, it made no difference. Machel knew of dos Santos's indiscretions while in
Moscow, of the pictures the KGB had taken of him.
Mozambique's Minister of Public Security in the embrace
of a white male prostitute. Now, here this fool was, doing
the Russians' bidding at the expense of making Machel out
to be an incompetent. "It is nothing more than some
dockside thievery," snarled Machel.

Mitchell followed Eleanor's lead, adopting an expression of concern. "Of course, if there is danger to the
delegation," he paused, "if there is significant danger to

American citizens, I think we ought to let the embassy know. . . ."

Machel made a deprecating gesture. "While General dos Santos sees the possibility of some delay in your flight, I think he will agree with me that the probability is slight."

The big man retreated. "Yes. Of course." He drew himself up thrusting out his chest. "A disturbance. A nuisance, really . . ."

"And, General, a matter your police can no doubt handle with a minimum of fuss," finished Mitchell.

The second safe house was little more than a tumbledown cowshed off a dirt track on the one road to the airport. Freeman parked the Moskva to the side of the shed alongside a van bearing diplomatic license plates. Carl Mopely came from around a corner of the shed, zipping up his pants, carelessly shining his flashlight in Freeman's eyes. Instantly out of the truck, Freeman ran to Mopely.

"You fucking son of a bitch." Freeman clenched Mopely's coat at the lapels, lifted him up on tiptoe and slapped him, striking him on the ear with his cupped palm and then snapping his head with a vicious backhand. "You screwed this up from the beginning."

Mopely struggled, holding his hands up to ward off Freeman's hand. "You're late . . ."

"You goddamn asshole. Kim and Chun are dead, Jack's dying, and you snivel about the inconvenience." Freeman's lips curled in contempt. He pulled his pistol and jammed the barrel into Mopely's nose. Their breathing was harsh, ragged. Mopely's nose began to trickle blood. Freeman thumbed the hammer back with a metallic double click, cocking the automatic. His knuckles whitened as he took up the slack on the trigger. "You've got one job left, you scumbag." He pushed the barrel harder against Mopely's nose. "You get us on that goddamn airplane. If we don't make it, then you don't either."

Moscow

Yuri Andropov had run his fingers through his unruly hair and thrown on a worn flannel robe over his pajamas before opening the door. "Come in, Vasili Petrovich. We will talk in the kitchen."

It was Kiktev's first visit to Andropov's apartment. Elsewhere in the huge building Leonid Brezhnev maintained a residence, though far grander than the small place chosen by Andropov.

Andropov drew two glasses of scalding water from an antique samovar and set them on saucers on a painted table. "Sit, Vasili Petrovich." He motioned to a straight wood chair. Kiktev took in the kitchen as Andropov carefully measured out a pungent black tea. Most striking were the books. Books everywhere. On shelves, in stacks on the floor, even on the windowsill. In the middle of the table was a carving of Don Quixote. Andropov took a chair facing Kiktev across a corner of the table. He reached into his robe and came up with a package of American cigarettes and a box of matches, which he put on the table between them.

"I would not disturb you at home, comrade—"

"Unless you had something that couldn't wait until morning," Andropov finished, smiling. "Relax, Vasili Petrovich, relax."

"It is the GRU operation. The one in Mozambique." Kiktev paused as Andropov lit a cigarette. "There has been an action on the freighter that will bring the weapons to Korea."

"Serious?"

"It happened less than an hour ago. We have only fragmentary information. It seems that two Orientals made their way onto the Korean ship. They killed two *spetznaz* guards and exploded a charge to open the door to the storage room where the weapons were kept." Andropov listened quietly, making no sign of concern. "They did not get in. They were apparently surprised by a new guard relief coming on duty."

"The Orientals?"

"One dead. His body was found in the cargo bay. The other apparently got away. Perhaps he jumped overboard and swam for it."

"I don't suppose there was any identification?"

Kiktev shook his head and took a sip of his tea. "No. Nothing. Absolutely nothing."

Andropov sat back in his chair and stubbed his cigarette out in the saucer for his tea. "No doubt our American friends. I suppose they will mark this day with a black stone." He exhaled a cloud of smoke. "I had thought they'd show more professional competency." He shook his head. "And the Korean ship, Comrade Kiktev?"

Kiktev looked at his watch. "They're getting under way. They should be out of the harbor within the hour."

Before the Mozambican police escorted the U.S. Ambassador, Laurence Mitchell, and Eleanor Trowbridge to the airport, Carl Mopely had arrived in the embassy van carrying the congressional delegation's luggage. At the same time, Moose Fredericks started the engines of the Boeing jet. John Freeman, his slashed forehead covered by a knit cap, waited for Mopely's all-clear rap on the van siding then eased an unconscious Jack Bronowski into a fireman's carry, up the mobile steps and into the plane.

Fifteen minutes later Laurence Mitchell stood talking in whispers to Freeman in the aft compartment. The two men swayed as the airplane taxied along the ramp. A few feet away Eleanor knelt with the delegation doctor, a Navy surgeon, as he finished dressing an unconscious Bronowski's wound. Mitchell knew it would be best if they could get the general to the American hospital at Rhein-Main Air Force Base in Frankfurt, Germany. But that was out of the question, so he told Moose Fredericks to plot a course for Pretoria, a flight of about forty-five minutes. When the plane swiveled onto the end of the runway, Fredericks immediately pushed the four throttles forward. As the big plane rumbled down the rough runway, Eleanor took the

only place beside Bronowski. Mitchell and Freeman took
seats in the forward cabin.

With the change in wind directions, the VC-137 took
off in a path over the harbor. From their windows, Mitchell
and Freeman saw no unusual activity along the docks.
Shortly, however, the flight engineer told them that the
airplane's millimeter-wave side-looking radar had detected
the movement of the *Chosen Nampò* as it slipped away from
its berth.

Freeman doodled listlessly on a slip of paper as
Mitchell loosened his tie. Between them was the sour taste
of defeat. There would be no stories of triumph to be
treasured, to be endlessly embellished in future tellings to
close friends.

Mitchell pointed to Freeman's head. "You ought to
take care of that." Freeman's face was puffy beneath the
dirty gauze bandage and he kept dabbing at a rivulet of
blood that persisted in running down his right cheek. The
spetznaz uniform was soiled and torn and reeked of sweat
and burned gunpowder.

Freeman touched a blood-encrusted rag to his face.
"It's nothing. The doc'll see to it after . . ." He pointed to
the rear compartment, where the surgeon was working on
Bronowski.

"How do you feel?" asked Mitchell.

"Feel?" His voice held the sharp edge of his anger. "I
feel like shit. Absolute, goddamn shit." His hands, nicked
and dirt-stained from the action in Maputo harbor, were
clenched into fists.

"We've failed. Jack's back there with a bullet in him.
Kim and Chun are probably dead, and we're still left with
the Korea mess."

The VC-137 clawed for altitude, its four Pratt and
Whitney engines screaming, a roar punctuated by the
metallic chunking sounds of the landing gear being raised
and locked into place.

The noise from the engines faded. From above, the
reading lamp cast a narrow beam down over Freeman's
head, the shadows from the bulky bandage sinking his eyes
into pools of darkness.

"We've still got Korea on our hands," Freeman repeated.

Mitchell unbuckled his seat belt, then leaned toward Freeman and took the younger man's wrist. "They were long odds, but the attempt had to be made."

Freeman's voice was bitter. "Yes, the attempt had to be made. And the odds were made all the worse by Franks and the White House."

"It's not over yet, John."

Freeman looked steadily at Mitchell. "My part in it is."

Mitchell shook his head in disagreement. "There're other things you can do, John. And other places to do them from."

The Navy surgeon bent over Jack Bronowski, then turned to Eleanor Trowbridge. "He's conscious."

She loosened her seat belt and knelt beside Bronowski's bunk. A respirator was feeding him oxygen while intravenous solutions dripped from bottles suspended overhead. Bronowski's complexion was a jaundiced yellow-white. His eyes had taken on the rheumy film of the aged, and his breathing was shallow and fitful.

"Sorry to be a wet blanket, Eleanor."

She took Bronowski's hand. The skin was cool and dry. His hand lay in hers without strength. Bronowski labored to take a deep breath of oxygen. "Kim and Chun. did they . . ."

He can read it on my face, she thought. "They weren't at the pickup point. But they're tough, they've made it out before." As she spoke to reassure him, she felt a deepening depression over the failed operation.

Bronowski's hand surged with strength. "Ah, what the hell, at least we tried." He squeezed her hand again and smiled. "It doesn't hurt anymore, Eleanor."

She leaned forward and kissed him.

Freeman watched without expression as Eleanor walked up the darkened aisle from the aft compartment to stand behind Bud Mitchell. She touched Mitchell's shoulder. "We needn't stop in Pretoria. Jack's dead."

Longitude 36°E
Latitude 29°S
(The Indian Ocean)
2:45 A.M., September 22, 1979

The metal plates in the floor amplified the throb of the engines, making the pain in his head all the more excruciating. The right side of his face was encrusted with dried blood. Slowly, gently, he probed the gashed scalp where the bullet had grazed his skull. The bleeding had stopped and a mushy but hardening clot was forming over his ear. He opened his eyes to a darkness relieved only by a dim and distant light somewhere out of his line of sight. Frank Kim lay beneath an armored personnel carrier which had hidden him from the cursory search of the Russians after they'd killed Joseph Chun.

Kim reached up, grabbing the heavy chain that anchored the armored vehicle to the deck. Wincing at the effort, he pulled himself to a sitting position. The *Chosen Nampò* was sweltering, and his thirst was overpowering. He looked at his watch. He had been unconscious more than four hours. The rocking motion told him the ship was at sea, and judging from the vibrations of the engines, they were making maximum speed. They had to be at least sixty miles off the coast.

The earplug receiver of the UHF radio dangled at his neck. He listened. Nothing. He felt for his shoulder holster, for the Beretta and its silencer. He took the pistol, freed the clip, and counted the stubby nine-millimeter parabellum cartridges. Carefully, quietly, he moved the operating slide back and forth, satisfying himself that the gun was probably in working order. Reholstering the pistol, he slipped his belt around, bringing to his side the canvas kit bag that had been digging into the small of his back. He did an inventory in the dark, his fingers moving over each item. Tool kit, two pencil detonators, a quarter-pound block of C-4 plastic explosive, an extra clip for the Beretta, a roll of tape, and a coil of insulated wire. He zipped the pouch shut then twisted around to bring his back against the steel track of the personnel carrier. He stared into the darkness and willed himself to think.

Surrender was out of the question. They'd torture him, then kill him. He massaged the back of his neck. He could probably get off the ship. Free up a raft or even a life vest and go over the side. That could be done. It was a reasonable thing to do, especially after all the fuck-ups. Why risk your ass in an operation you had to hide from the very people you wanted to save? Save from their own stupidity. Chun was dead. Bronowski and Freeman were probably dead too. It wouldn't help to add another.

Kim lay down, rolled over, and crawled out from under the personnel carrier.

It took nearly fifteen minutes to explore the hold. Kim circled the light from the D Deck corridor, taking care to stay in the protecting darkness. He found a ladder mounted on a bulkhead four feet from the D Deck corridor entrance. Above, through an open hatch, he could see the sky, a heaven full of stars. Once up the ladder, he would be on deck. He looked at his watch again. Topside would be deserted, and the ship would probably be running with minimum lights. He swung onto the ladder, then, five rungs up, hesitated. He looked upward to the open hatch and the stars, shrugged, then descended.

They hadn't told Joe and him that this was connected to the tap they'd put on the North Korean land line. But it had to be. He looked toward the corridor. They'd come too far, gotten too close, not to finish the job.

A battery lantern lit the corridor. The guard sat on a small wooden crate, his head back against the wall of the passageway. From the dark shadows of the cargo bay, Kim lay motionless, watching for several minutes. There were no sounds save for the engine noise and the metal-to-metal grating of the ship working on itself in the rolling seas.

The Russian suddenly slipped off his box and crumpled on the deck, a finger-sized hole in his left temple. Frank Kim, the Beretta still in hand, moved quickly, quietly down the corridor. They hadn't repaired the lock to the door he'd blown hours before. He pushed the door open, then pulled the dead Russian into the compartment. Then he turned to the metal rack supporting the nuclear weapons—four grey metal cylinders, each eighteen inches in diameter and forty inches long.

He stepped into the corridor and moved the lantern so it cast a shadow over the open door of the compartment. Returning, he opened the small tool kit and, with a combination tool, unfastened six slotted screw fasteners on the access plate of the nearest weapon. In the dim light he saw the switches and dials, a close approximation of the mock-up Mopely had had for them in isolation.

"Georgi? Georgi?"

Kim started at the voice from the corridor. Picking up the Beretta, he flopped on his belly, crawled quickly to the door, and peered around the doorway from the deck. A short stocky man stood about twenty feet away, holding a tray of food in both hands. Kim brought the pistol up and fired, aiming for the man's chest. The hasty shot was wild, and even with the silencer, the sound of the slug crashing into the metal walls caused the Russian to drop the tray and run, ducking off the corridor before Kim could fire again.

Kim scrambled to his feet and looked at the open access plate on the weapon, then made a move toward the pencil timer. As he did so, there came a sound of shouting as someone opened up with a submachine gun, spraying bullets down the corridor.

"Shit." Kim kicked aside the body of the dead guard in order to slam shut the compartment door, then wedged the guard's Kalashnikov rifle between the door and the compartment wall. Outside in the corridor came the sounds of more shouting and finally a blow on the door. The Kalashnikov was securely jammed. For a moment there was silence, then the compartment door shuddered under heavy crashing blows.

Kim looked at the gray cylinder lying waist high in the rack before him. What was it they'd told Joe and him in training at Los Alamos? Something that Oppenheimer, the nuclear scientist, had said on seeing the first atomic bomb explode at the Trinity test site.

He set the timer to one second. The door gave way; automatic weapons fire came through the opening as two heavy fragmentation grenades rolled across the floor. His body was rocked as two 7.62 millimeter slugs found their target.

Kim remembered the quote. "If the radiance of a thousand suns were to burst forth at once in the sky, that would be like the splendor of the Mighty One."

He threw the switch to fire.

Epilogue

The Washington Post—October 27, 1979

TWO FLASHES NEAR SOUTH AFRICA: JUST WHAT HAPPENED THAT NIGHT?
by Don Oberdorfer
and Thomas O'Toole

High U.S. officials expressed uncertainty and some puzzlement yesterday about the cause of a mysterious event near South Africa five weeks ago today that registered on a nuclear detection satellite as an atomic explosion. . . .

The sighting by a U.S. Vela satellite about 60,000 miles in space was of two bright flashes, or pulses, in a sequence and timing characteristic of an atomic explosion.

According to Sen. John Glenn (D-Ohio), the former astronaut who is chairman of a Senate subcommittee on nuclear weapons proliferation, Vela satellites have picked up signs of atomic explosions in the atmosphere 41 times since having been sent into space in 1963, and each of those 41 was later confirmed to be an atomic weapons test.

The immediate suspect, and still the most likely in some official minds, was South Africa, the only nation in the area believed capable of a nuclear explosion. However, there had been no hint of an imminent South African blast, and there was no announcement by that country that it had tested a nuclear device.

Moscow

Yuri Andropov tapped the closed file before him on his desk. His face was drawn and he stubbed out a cigarette he'd only just lighted. "It makes a damning case."

"Yes, Comrade Andropov. He put together a meticulous record: that you did not report the tap on the commando line, thus permitting the Americans to gain information about the *spetznaz* involvement in Korea; that you used the traitor Korznikov to warn CIA that we had penetrated its highest levels."

The man continued. "There are other embellishments. He wrote that he suspected you knew of Korznikov's connection with the Americans months before Birch exposed him.

"Conjectures—unfounded accusations with little but circumstantial evidence. But nonetheless, that"—he pointed to the fire—"that would have been enough for Leonid Brezhnev to blame you for his failure in Korea."

Andropov felt a chill pass over him. He motioned to the red-striped folder. "And Vasili Kiktev kept this to himself? He shared it with no one?"

Gregori Romanov smiled and turned to leave. "With no one except me, Yuri Vladimirovich."

Andropov's parting question stopped Romanov at the door. The younger man's smile broadened. "Vacation? No. Not this year. Lydia wants to go home. So we are going home. To Stavropol."

Press Release
Office of Senator Laurence Mitchell
Embargo until 12:00 noon, February 15, 1980

Senator Laurence Mitchell today appointed Mr. John Freeman to the professional staff of the Committee on Foreign Relations. . . . Mr. Freeman, a retired military officer, is married to the former Susan Styles Forbes of Windham Hill, Maine.

Press Release
The Foundation for International Relations
For immediate distribution

Quentin Barnes, Executive Director of the Foundation for International Relations, announced that Mr. Alan Squires will be joining the foundation as Director of Strategic Studies. Mr. Squires comes to the foundation from a senior position on the staff of the Director of Central Intelligence.

THRILLERS

Gripping suspense . . . explosive action . . . dynamic characters
. . . international settings . . . these are the elements that make for
great thrillers. Books guaranteed to keep you riveted to your seat.

Robert Ludlum:

☐ 28179	TREVAYNE	$5.95
☐ 27800	THE ICARUS AGENDA	$5.95
☐ 26256	THE AQUITAINE PROGRESSION	$5.95
☐ 26011	THE BOURNE IDENTITY	$5.95
☐ 26094	THE CHANCELLOR MANUSCRIPT	$5.95
☐ 26019	THE HOLCROFT COVENANT	$5.95
☐ 25899	THE MATARESE CIRCLE	$5.95
☐ 26430	THE OSTERMAN WEEKEND	$5.95
☐ 25270	THE PARSIFAL MOSAIC	$5.95
☐ 27109	THE ROAD TO GANDOLFO	$5.95
☐ 27146	THE SCARLATTI INHERITANCE	$5.95
☐ 26322	THE BOURNE SUPREMACY	$5.95

Frederick Forsyth:

☐ 05361	THE NEGOTIATOR	$19.95
☐ 25113	THE FOURTH PROTOCOL	$4.95
☐ 27673	NO COMEBACKS	$4.95
☐ 26630	DAY OF THE JACKAL	$4.95
☐ 26490	THE DEVIL'S ALTERNATIVE	$4.95
☐ 26846	THE DOGS OF WAR	$4.95
☐ 27198	THE ODESSA FILE	$4.95

Prices and availability subject to change without notice.

Buy them at your local bookstore or use this page to order.

- -

Bantam Books, Dept. TH, 414 East Golf Road, Des Plaines, IL 60016

Please send me the books I have checked above. I am enclosing $_____
(please add $2.00 to cover postage and handling). Send check or money order
—no cash or C.O.D.s please.

Mr/Ms _____

Address _____

City/State _____ Zip _____

TH—9/89

Please allow four to six weeks for delivery.

John le Carré

"John le Carré belongs in the select company of the best spy and detective writers. In all of his books, le Carré shows how endowed he is with the art of storytelling."

(The Times—London)

☐ 26757 LITTLE DRUMMER GIRL $4.95

☐ 26487 SMILEY'S PEOPLE $4.95

☐ 23693 LOOKING-GLASS WAR $4.50

☐ 26623 CALL FOR THE DEAD $3.95

☐ 27437 THE HONOURABLE SCHOOLBOY $4.95

☐ 26443 A MURDER OF QUALITY $3.95

☐ 27995 THE NAIVE AND SENTIMENTAL LOVER $4.95

☐ 26442 THE SPY WHO CAME IN FROM THE COLD $4.50

☐ 26778 TINKER, TAILOR, SOLDIER, SPY $4.95

<u>Prices and availability subject to change without notice.</u>